THE OFFICER
FROM SPECIAL BRANCH

The Officer from Special Branch

HAYDEN

TOM LILLEY

DOUBLEDAY & COMPANY, INC.
Garden City, New York   *1971*

All of the characters in this book
are fictitious, and any resemblance
to actual persons, living or dead,
is purely coincidental.

Library of Congress Catalog Card Number 79–131091
Copyright © 1970 by Thomas Lilley
All Rights Reserved
Printed in the United States of America

FOR:

Takahide Okubo
Kwan Yui Ming
Abdul Rahman bin Ahmad

Foreword

The Cominform decision that "the time was ripe for revolution," and that the Communist Parties throughout South East Asia should "resort to armed struggle in Wars of Liberation," was conveyed to delegates from South East Asia at the Asia Youth Conference in Calcutta in February 1948.

In the months which followed, revolution came to the State of Hyderabad in India, to Burma, the Philippines, Indonesia, and Malaya. In Malaya, the revolution was officially labelled "the Emergency" and it is in Malaya and at the height of "the Emergency," that this novel is set. But the story itself is entirely fictional, and no character therein is based on that of a living person. Nor for that matter, is it in any way suggested that any of the methods used for the "elimination" of Communist terrorists which are outlined, were ever adopted, or even considered for adoption, by the appropriate authorities in Malaya at that time.

However, as it is necessary to refer to people who perform specific functions—commissioners of police, heads of special branches and so on—to obviate the possibility of such persons being identified with real people I have used the expedient of creating an imaginary Malayan State—Kepayan.

T.L.

THE OFFICER
FROM SPECIAL BRANCH

1

Ralph Carter drove out of the gates of the Training School, paused for a break in the Saturday lunchtime traffic, turned left and stopped at the lights. He had opened the sliding roof and all the windows in an attempt to cool the car down; when he had parked some four hours before, it had been raining and he had had to leave the roof and windows shut, but for the last two hours it had been subjected to the burning rays of the tropical sun, and the inside was like an oven, the steering wheel almost too hot to touch. As he waited he acknowledged the gesture of recognition from a uniformed colleague in a car coming from the opposite direction, thankful that as a member of the Special Branch he could wear plain clothes, without the heavy cap, laden with silver braid, of an Assistant Superintendent of Police. He held no deep feelings on the subject of uniforms, but they had a restricting effect on one's activities and, given the choice, he preferred not to have to wear one. The lights changed and he drove on; away from the center of the federal capital, towards the trunk road which would lead him to his destination—Sintra, the capital of the Malayan state of Kepayan.

As he drove, he considered the new job: he was glad he had been posted to Sintra, he knew and liked the head of the Special Branch there—Charles Halroyd, whom he had met at a conference the previous year—and in any case, Sintra was generally regarded as being a "good" post, in the sense that Sintra was a fairly large town offering diverse social activity, the mess was considered to be the best in Malaya, and the Chief Police Officer was regarded as being "not really a bad old bastard when you get to know him." Carter also considered the circumstances that had lead to his appointment. He was a replacement. Only two weeks previously, Wainwright, the man he was to replace, had been shot while talking to the manager of a rubber estate, outside the door of the manager's office: shot dead at a range of 180 yards by Communist leader Nathan, who, after firing the shot had nonchalantly waved his rifle and walked, just walked, back through the rubber trees towards the jungle from which he had presumably emerged. Nathan, Carter reflected, would have to pay for that. It crossed his mind that while it was a mistake to kill a police officer, and an even bigger mistake to kill a Special Branch officer, to display contempt in the killing was to tempt fate to the screaming point.

As Carter turned on to the trunk road, he became tense and alert. He was driving along a road which, for the last year at least, had seen an average of four ambushes each week. Ambushes which ranged from the single terrorist behind a rubber tree, taking potshots with a rifle at anything which moved on the road, to a complete Communist company of 120 men firing automatic weapons from well prepared positions in the banks above the road as mines exploded along it. Carter drove fast, because he was tense and because he wanted to reach Sintra before dark, and had a long drive in front of him. He would have admitted, however, that speed did not lessen the possibility of ambush. It was possible to drive fast only on those sections of the road which were straight, across the paddy fields, for example, or by the tin mines, and through some of the rubber estates, but, and especially where the road ran through the jungle, there were hairpin bends and sharp inclines: natural sites for ambush, with sometimes, in a ditch at the side of the road, the burnt out skeleton of a bus or car to prove it. Negotiating such places, he scanned the jungle on either side and, successfully past, he sat back with relief, always surprised to find that, unconsciously, he had been leaning forward, hunched over the steering wheel, peering.

To be ambushed in a civilian car was a very unpleasant, and usually final, experience. People had sometimes survived, swerving from one side of the road to the other through a storm of bullets and miraculously emerging unscathed, but usually the car came to a halt off the road, and its passengers were shot as they ran or staggered from it and tried to seek cover. The bodies of Europeans were invariably mutilated; their penises severed—and sometimes left in their mouths—and their buttocks slashed with parangs. Where there was not hate in it—and usually there was—such barbarity was Communist policy, aimed at the myth of an innate European superiority.

From behind the sand-bagged emplacements around rubber-

12

planters' bungalows, or around sub-power stations, occasional Malay constables idly watched Carter's progress. Drawn from a population of some 2½ million, there were 80,000 of them employed as static guards at vital installations and the homes of those the Communists sought to kill. A stocky, handsome brown-skinned people, with an innate dignity and refinement, yet capable of sudden and extreme violence. Muslims, for whom Communism held little or no appeal.

Perhaps other eyes watched Carter. Possibly a courier, bearing the Party's latest directive from one jungle camp to another, waited in the thick grass at the side of the road for the car to pass, before making a dash across the open road, to resume his journey through the jungle on the other side. Possibly also, a group of terrorists in ambush positions kept silent vigil; waiting patiently for a particular vehicle, a private car carrying "an Imperialist running-dog"—a Chinese detective whose death had been ordered—or a lorry which had to be destroyed to impress upon the owner that "subscriptions" to the Party were to be paid on time. There were some 10,000 Communist terrorists throughout Malaya; drawn almost exclusively from Malaya's two-million Chinese population, they operated from jungle camps which were sometimes big enough to accommodate 200 men. But ninety per cent of Malaya is jungle. Even in a country no larger than England, such camps were usually found only by chance, and when found, invariably empty.

Carter was in Kepayan State now, with three-quarters of his journey behind him; he didn't relax, but was conscious that the odds against his being ambushed were lengthening all the time. When he reached the village of Korek he slowed down to negotiate the inevitable road block at its entrance, nodded to the Malay special constable on duty, drove through the open gates, stopped at the solitary petrol pump 150 yards farther on, where he told the attendant to fill the tank, and stood looking at the village. Resembling a dozen other Chinese villages through which he had passed that afternoon, Korek was a shanty town consisting of twenty single-storey wooden shops, facing each other in two rows of ten on either side of the road. Two or three of these shops had corrugated iron roofs, but mostly they were of attap; each shop was open to the street for its full width.

Carter knew that behind the two rows would be an interminable maze of outbuildings, storerooms, chicken-runs and latrines. No bedrooms or dining rooms; the shops themselves fulfilled such functions. He hazarded a guess that the village housed 2,000 souls. It was enclosed by a high, square-meshed wire fence at the top of which strands of barbed-wire ran between "V" shaped supports. The fence formed an oblong around the village and was never less than 150–200 yards from the nearest building; the area between being heavily cultivated with vegetables of the quick-growing variety. In the corners of the oblong made by the fence, mid-way along each side of it, and at the gates, were wooden towers from which Malay Special Constables kept constant watch. During the hours of curfew and darkness, the fence was lit and the gates shut. The purpose of the fence and the guards had been described—not inaccurately—as "to keep the wolves from the sheep, the sheep from the wolves, and to make life difficult for the wolves in sheep's clothing." The only two legal exits from the village were the main gates, and their use involved inspection and possible search by the Malay Constables, for it was forbidden to take out of the village food, medical, or any other kind of supplies likely to be of use to the Communist terrorists. The effect of this strictly enforced regulation was to ensure that villagers who wanted to give supplies to the Communists couldn't readily do it, while the others—frightened of reprisals if they refused the demands made by the Communists—had a welcome excuse for not doing so. The members of the second group far outnumbered the first, having, in place of an interest in either Communism or Democracy, only the sincere but forlorn hope that they could be simply ignored by the devotees of either cause.

The petrol pump was at one end of the two rows of shops and Carter was looking down the short street. There was something odd about Korek, but it was a moment or two before he realised what it was. It was the lack of noise. The Chinese like noise—or else they are unaware of it. If a Chinese has a radio he automatically switches it to maximum volume and carries on with whatever he was doing, even including studying, yet Korek was quiet, and strangely peaceful, with hardly anyone about. Apathy, he decided; an apathy born of the barbed-wire fence, and the sentries, and the heat. He was sure that the old man at the Mah-Mee stall a few yards away hadn't even bothered to glance in his direction since he'd entered the village.

14

Carter paid for the petrol and got back into his car. He looked at his watch and calculated that he would arrive in Sintra well before dark, so that there was no reason to hurry . . . or to stay. He drove off along the almost deserted street, but after a few yards he stopped. He had caught sight of the three Chinese characters which read "cold beer." An excellent reason to stay. The sign was outside what was clearly the most prosperous shop in the village: for in addition to its corrugated iron roof it also boasted a neon sign, "Wa Fung's." Carter parked his car on the other side of the road in the shade of a tree and walked across.

The inside was dominated by a large glass-fronted wall refrigerator which took up most of the rear partition against which it was set, and in the various illuminated compartments of which could be seen bottles and cans, meat and fish and vegetables. In front of the refrigerator, crowded together on the tiny floor, were seven or eight round marble-topped iron tables, at one of which, set against a side wall, two aged men played Chinese checkers. There was no one else in the shop, but as Carter sat at a table one of the old men, without lifting his eyes from the game, called "Ah Wah," and a moment later a fat Chinese wearing only a vest and cotton shorts appeared from a curtained doorway. Acknowledging Carter's order, he took a can of beer from the refrigerator, opened it, placed it together with an empty glass in front of Carter, and disappeared through the curtained doorway.

Carter filled the glass from the tin, carefully, holding it at an angle so as not to get too much froth. He was facing the street, but hadn't seen the strained face of the young Chinese who had looked in as he walked past the shop while Carter was pouring his beer. A moment later when the young Chinese reappeared, Carter saw him for the first time, for one fleeting second, as he stopped on the verandah four yards away, turned, and as one might toss a bunch of keys to a friend, tossed a hand-grenade on to Carter's table. Carter pushed the table over a fraction of a second after the grenade hit its surface, simultaneously flinging himself sideways to the wooden floor. But in the cramped space he fell across a chair, and, as it splintered under him, across the iron supports of a table. His chest three inches from the floor, he was trying to squirm off the supports and flatten himself to the ground when the grenade exploded.

15

After the explosion Carter was aware first of the silence and then of the smell of explosive. Only then did he feel the pain which stretched down the whole left side of his body—a pain which came in waves. He gave himself to the waves: his mind a darkness across which shafts of light advanced and receded in time with the waves, seeking each other in the darkness and finally meeting in one great surge of brightness.

Ah Chan, the Mah-Mee seller, prepared to tell the story for the fifth time; he could tell a good story, and his customers had come to hear him tell it. He had seen it all: from the moment the European had driven into the village, to the moment when the van with the red crosses on a white background had borne him out. He cast his eyes over his audience sitting and standing around his stall, each one with a bowl of Mah-Mee, who were waiting expectantly, giving him their whole attention. He cleared his throat, "I do not know if the European will live or die," he paused and spat before continuing, "nor do I care. But if he lives it will not be for long. He came out of the womb unlucky, that one. Bad luck will always be following him."

Ah Chan stopped, took what looked like a piece of straw from the breast pocket of his shirt, placed one end of it in his mouth, lit it with a piece of wood from the fire beneath the cauldron, and puffed smoke at his audience. They waited patiently.

Assured of their interest, Ah Chan continued, "When he got out of his car he stood just there"—pointing to a spot a few yards away—"and seeing him, I said to myself, 'this one is not long for this world.' I know the signs! Bad luck will follow him as faithfully as . . ." Ah Chan paused, looking round for something, then pointed at a mangy dog basking in the sun nearby, "as faithfully as that useless overfed animal follows me. It had to be in this village that he stopped for petrol. Not the last: nor yet the next. This one. And he stood by his car waiting for petrol, not just looking at the signs above the shops, as most Europeans do, but reading them."

Ah Chan paused and looked from face to face. The first time he had said this they had grinned at such an absurdity. Until the petrol pump attendant said that the European had spoken to him in Cantonese, and Ah Wah confirmed that the European had indeed ordered his beer in Cantonese. But this time nobody grinned.

16

Ah Chan then went on to repeat his description of the European. "He was tall; perhaps 5 foot 10 inches, with that banana-coloured hair that some Europeans have. Medium build, large hands and feet, and with the coarse features of the European. He was aged"—Ah Chan paused—"perhaps 18, perhaps 35. Who can tell the age of a European? And do not all of them with those round bulging eyes and high noses look alike?"

The European had got into his car and driven off, but, after driving only a few yards, he had stopped outside Wa Fung's bar.

"And what made him stop?" Ah Chan demanded rhetorically. "He stopped because he read the sign made from twisted glass which lights and reads, 'Wa Fung's.' And the other painted one which reads, 'cold beer.' And do we not all know that next to women, Europeans love beer most? So he stopped and walked across the road and went inside."

Then Ah Chan related how he had noticed "a person" loitering about near Wa Fung's bar; and how, just after the bang and the cloud of dust, that person had run past him and disappeared he knew not where.

For all his seventy-three years, Ah Chan was not unaware of the dangers of a good memory: and he emphasised the fact that although he had glimpsed the person, he had not seen him clearly, and could not remember whether he was young or old, short or tall, thin or fat, Chinese or Malay, or even whether he was male or female. Having made this quite plain—to the accompaniment of understanding nods from his audience—Ah Chan went on to relate how, just after the arrival of the Malay special constables, he had walked up the street behind them and peered into Wa Fung's, and had seen the European stretched out on the floor, silent in a pool of blood. And how the Loh brothers still sat at their usual table, the checker board in front of them: the younger with his head on his chest as if he had fallen asleep, the elder, head half-turned towards the center of the room, eyes still open, his face wearing a look of surprise; his left hand on the board and his fingers clasping a checker as he made the last move in the game that out-lasted the players.

Ah Chan did not need to describe the arrival of the British soldiers, and their search of the village: for this was known to all. But as became his age and his nature, he felt he should conclude with a hint of impending doom, "I heard a Malay constable say that the European was a high-ranking police officer. I hope this is not so. For the government will take no note that two of our people also died."

2

The Chief Police Officer for Kepayan State flicked the ash from his cigarette. "I see from his personal file, Charles, that he went to quite a good school, was something of an athlete and had a good war record. Bomber Command, I seem to remember. He had his 26th birthday only a week or so ago."

Charles Halroyd winced; the remark was typically Claude Davidson, so irrelevant and such an illumination of his standard of values: standards destined to die with the Claude Davidsons of this world. Ignoring his thoughts, he replied, "He'd just completed a Chinese course, sir, and more recently, the Special Branch Projects course."

"Hmm," Davidson murmured, "I'm not at all sure that I quite approve of Chinese-speakers. Eccentric, you know. But projects, Charles, what on earth are those?"

"Well, sir, the Projects Section is a new Special Branch section which will confine itself to finding ways and means of eliminating Communist leaders. Carter was to have set it up here, and I hope still will."

"Do you think, Charles, that the attempt on Carter's life was planned, or was it purely fortuitous?"

On the other side of the Chief Police Officer's desk Halroyd sighed heavily. "It was just incredibly bad luck, sir. Carter stopped for petrol and decided to have a beer: there happened to be a Communist killer-squad in the village and one of them saw his chance and took it. Mind you, he's lucky to be alive at all, I understand they're *still* taking bits of metal out of him."

"Did the search reveal anything?"

"Nothing sir, I never expected it would. But the twenty-two hour curfew might."

"Twenty-two hour curfew, Charles?" Davidson was clearly hor-

19

rified as he asked, "Are you seriously telling me that you are proposing a twenty-two hour curfew for Korek village?"

"I am indeed sir. During your absence I canvassed the other members of the State War Executive Committee and they are all in agreement that a twenty-two hour curfew is justifiable. It started this morning—a day late in my opinion."

"Why not make it a twenty-four hour curfew, Charles? It would be more humane: go some way towards winning the hearts and minds of the people."

Halroyd felt the anger rising in him, but he replied equably enough as he said, "The villagers have to buy food, sir, and they also have to feed their animals. They will be allowed out of their homes from seven to eight in the morning, and from five to six in the afternoon. They will not, of course, be permitted to leave the village."

"I don't like it, Charles," Davidson retorted. "These repressive measures make enemies, and we become more of a police state each day."

"We have two choices, sir. A Communist state indefinitely, or a police state temporarily."

Halroyd's voice had an edge to it. He had not liked Davidson's crack about "repressive measures," nor his sarcastic use of the overworked phrase about "winning the hearts and minds of the people." If, he thought savagely, Davidson had no fucking idea whatsoever how to cope with an emergency situation, then the least he could do was keep his stupid trap shut and let those who could cope, get on with it. But he took the edge off his voice. "May I point out sir, that there can hardly have been a single Chinese adult in Korek who was unaware of the presence of terrorists there; you know how they live: cheek by jowl and all that. If there had been one, just one anti-Communist adult in that village, he could have tipped us off by dropping an anonymous letter to the police P.O. box. But far from doing that, they didn't even hear the bang when the grenade went off. Even the people in the shops on either side didn't hear it. And as for anyone actually seeing anything . . . They deserve to be punished for their lack of co-operation, sir, and confining them to their homes for a week or so is not exactly terribly repressive. But I have a more important reason than just punishment."

20

"Oh?" Davidson managed to convey "You don't say," with the word.

"Yes sir," Halroyd continued equably. "Tomorrow, I propose sending all our interrogation teams to Korek for the period of the curfew. They will interview every person in the village for precisely four minutes each; whether they give us information or not. This will mean that every adult will at least have the opportunity to give information to the police without anyone else's knowledge, so they need have no fear of Communist reprisals. There's the further point, sir, that the twenty-two hour curfew one way and another will hit a lot of people where it hurts most—in their pockets. Shopkeepers and farmers and so on; these people are going to have a strong incentive to co-operate so that the curfew is lifted."

"Simple blackmail in fact, Charles." Davidson stubbed out his cigarette with an angry gesture.

Halroyd smiled and stood up. "Not really sir. Let us say an effective counter to Communist terror tactics; giving the villagers an unusual opportunity of helping the police, in confidence, and without fear of Communist reprisal."

They didn't like each other. The gulf between their respective attitudes of mind was far wider than the difference between their ages. At fifty, Davidson was a product of the public school system, the heyday of Empire and thirty years privilege; by instinct, training and example, he had learned what was right, what was wrong. But at thirty-five, Halroyd was the product of a decade of war: in Africa and Europe, Palestine, and now Malaya. A decade in which he had learned that power was for using, the words "right" and "wrong" meaningless, and the only criterion success.

Davidson knew that even in war—indeed especially in war—there was a natural code of conduct which applied to all men: men of all races, colours and creeds: the common bond of the fighting man.

Halroyd knew that men fighting for survival knew nothing of such codes, had no time nor reason to learn.

Davidson knew that if men were to remain men, even in war, there must be room for chivalry, compassion, humanity.

Halroyd knew that such qualities were weaknesses this enemy would seek to exploit, and that in war men cease being men.

21

There was no common ground between them: they didn't speak the same language.

Back in his office, Halroyd stood in front of the window lost in thought. A big man, six feet tall and heavily built without being fat, his thick-framed spectacles made him look more like a bank manager than the head of a Special Branch unit—despite the thin two-inch horizontal scar above his right eyebrow. Genial and good natured he was nevertheless completely ruthless in obtaining the objectives he had set himself, and thoroughly unscrupulous in his methods. He was thinking about his interrogation exercise at Korek. He expected little in the way of information from the people of the village; the Government couldn't protect them, so why should they risk their lives to assist the Government? But a document found in a dead Communist terrorist's haversack revealed that the Min Yuen—The Communist Liberation Army's supply organisation—had recruited a total of forty-two persons in Korek. Prolonged and cautious investigation had revealed the identity of five of these forty-two, but Halroyd had ordered that none of the five was to be arrested, and that they be left at liberty pending a time when the knowledge that they were members of the Min Yuen might be exploited. That time had now come.

Halroyd proposed that during the course of the following day's four-minute interrogations, the first of the five known Min Yuen members to arrive for interrogation be questioned not for four minutes, but for five hours. At the end of this period, detectives would arrest the remaining four. The first man would then be released, the impression being given that the other four were arrested on his information. Halroyd calculated that the other thirty-seven Min Yuen members, thinking that their names were now known to the police, and that their arrest was only a matter of time, would try to break out of the village the same night—and would then run into one of the Gurkha ambushes provided for such an eventuality. Certainly, there would be at least two illegal ways out of the village, probably tunnels under the fence; if the police tracking dogs could locate these shortly after dusk, the Gurkhas' task would be simplified, and they could set up their ambushes near the tunnel exits.

It did not disturb Halroyd that by giving the impression that the man released had informed on the four arrested, he was sentencing him to death. If he was a Min Yuen member, the others were bound to settle their accounts with him before they tried to escape from the village. It would disturb Halroyd only if he wasn't killed. This would mean that neither he nor the four arrested were in fact Min Yuen members and the arrests did not demand Communist vengeance. In turn this would mean that one of his detectives had given him incorrect information, possibly deliberately. Halroyd would then have the problem of ascertaining whether the detective was being used as a channel of mis-information by the Communists, or whether the detective was working for them. And if so, why? Political sympathy? A family hostage? Life insurance? It could mean a lot of work.

Halroyd grinned at the thought of Davidson's reaction had he told him his full intentions regarding Korek village. Righteous indignation, he speculated, possibly resulting in flat orders forbidding him to risk any lives, suspected Communist or otherwise.

In this, Halroyd would have been wrong. Davidson knew that Halroyd had not given him a complete outline of his intentions regarding Korek and also that had he been fully informed it would not have pleased him. But while intimating disapproval he would never have forbidden it. The truth was that he didn't want to know, especially about plans which hinged on psychological reaction. Davidson couldn't make the necessary mental effort to grasp the subtle psychology which seemed to govern every move, and the ceaseless intrigue and constant distrust wearied and repelled him. Yet he was too honest a man not to have a feeling of inadequacy: he hated his job now and longed for retirement, but he could not keep his two sons at university on his pension and his retirement awaited their graduation.

3

In a private ward in Sintra General Hospital, nursing sister Nancy
Chong took Carter's temperature. It was 104°. She stood, examining his face closely; he was, she decided, very sexy looking, and she
loved fair hair. For some reason or other, European hair was much
softer, silkier, than Asian hair. Although she had attended a party
at the police officers' Mess and knew most European police officers
at least by sight she had never seen him before. He must be a
new arrival, in which case he'd certainly had a hot reception. She
entered the figures on the chart and sat down on the chair at the
bedside: she had to call Doctor Kowalski immediately, if there was
any marked change in the patient's temperature or pulse. She
hoped her patient would not die because she wanted to know him. He
had certainly been near death. The metal splinter at the base of his
skull need only have gone a shade deeper. She tried to understand
the words of his delirium, but they were almost meaningless.
Several times he had said quite clearly, "Gentlemen, there are no
holds barred. Every facet of human nature can be turned to your
advantage; love as much as hate, charity as much as greed, loyalty
as much as . . ." His voice had always trailed off at that point,
leaving her puzzling over the source of that fragment of memory. It
could only be from a lecture, she had concluded; but what a strange
thing to say in a lecture.

The background to the patient's next remarks was clear enough.
Talking slowly and in a dispassionate tone he began, "Turning on.
Bomb doors open. Bombs selected and fused. Left, left. Steady,
steady, steady, bombs gone." Then he tried to sit up in bed as in a
voice tight with fear he cried, "Fighter, fighter ten o'clock . . ."
She leaned over him and tried to soothe him, talking to him as if he
were a child. She wiped the perspiration from his face, until he seemed
calmer, and finally lay quiet.

Two days later, and for the first time in five days, Carter opened

24

his eyes. The light hurt. But it hurt less if he opened them only very slightly. The first thing that he saw was a Chinese nurse, sitting reading in a chair beside the bed. He examined her for a minute or two.

"You're nice."

Nancy Chong looked up, startled, then smiling stood and said, "You're awake! I'll get doctor," before disappearing through the door.

Doctor Stanislaus Kowalski was a big man with a large head, big ears and a big nose, and he was the doctor in charge of Sintra General Hospital and the surgeon who had removed the metal splinters from Carter's body. As he came into Carter's room he said, "You are all right now, yes?"

Carter half-opened his eyes, but closed them again before saying, "Are you the doctor?"

"I am Doctor Kowalski. Stanislaus Kowalski."

Carter didn't reply for a moment, but then he asked in an over-casual voice, "Am I still in one piece, doctor?"

"You are all right. Perfectly all right. Small scars are all you are having. I am telling you, in a few days you will be up and about, and the day after tomorrow you can have visitors."

From the point of view of acquiring information, hospital beds are vantage points—visitors bring news and views as well as gifts. But Halroyd was the exception. He came not to impart information but to seek it, so that after perfunctory enquiries about Carter's progress he went straight to the point.

Had Carter seen the person who had thrown the grenade? Carter had, but only for a moment. A male Chinese aged about 19, height 5' 2"–5' 3", thin, wearing a white shirt and brown trousers. Not a particularly useful description.

Would Carter recognise him again? Carter doubted it, but he might. At that, Halroyd opened his brief case and took out a large envelope, saying "Have a look at these." The envelope contained individual photographs of twelve dead and six living bodies. Carter examined each one carefully, keeping them in order and turning them face downward in a neat pile on the sheet beside him. With one photo he gave an expression of disgust, holding it up to Halroyd he said, "Bullets didn't cause that little lot, that's for sure."

25

Halroyd glanced at the photo, said, "It was done in the barber's shop. That's the barber's chair. They thought he'd informed on them; they cut his tongue out as well."

"Charming," Carter murmured as he examined the rest of the photos. Finally he selected one of the six who were still alive and remarked, "It could have been this one, sir. But I'd never swear to it. Who are they anyway?"

Halroyd wrote something on the back of the photo before replying, "They're from Korek. They ran into a Gurkha ambush a couple of nights ago, just after they crawled out from a tunnel under the fence: got caught between the Gurkhas and the fence," he held up the photos, "this was the result. Unfortunately they represent only about half the total number in the village, but nevertheless the only real success we've had in months."

Halroyd put the photos back in his brief case and stood up, saying, "Your secretary, Elizabeth McLeod, will be here shortly. She's built rather along the lines of a barrage balloon, but she's efficient and cheerful; you'll like her. I asked her to bring along the personal files of all the members of your staff: after you've read them, you might like to have them along for interviews. If you're not happy about any of them, let me know and I'll arrange the necessary transfers."

At the door Halroyd turned and said, "I've great hopes of the Projects Section, and from a staff point of view, the dice has been heavily loaded in its favour."

By the time he was discharged from hospital, some ten days later, Carter had formed a fairly accurate assessment of the emergency situation in Kepayan State. It was bad and getting worse. "Incidents" were running at the rate of five or six each day. These involved Communist attacks on vital points: power stations, telephone exchanges; isolated police stations, planters' bungalows, tin-mine dredges, ambushes on the roads, the occasional derailment of trains. They also involved straightforward terrorism, grenades in crowded places such as cinemas and markets, but above all they indicated what had become almost ritual killings of Chinese "traitors" in the form of executions carried out with breath-taking cruelty. As Chinese tend to live in large family units, the executions invariably included the whole of the "traitor's" family from his grandmother to his youngest son. One could be a "traitor" by having a brother who

26

was in the police, or by being the nephew of a businessman who had neglected to pay his monthly "subscription" to the Malayan Communist Party.

The Sintra police officers' mess consisted of a large two-storey house and twelve adjacent bungalows set on a hill in the residential area some three miles from the center of town. The house had been built for a Chinese millionaire who had sold it to the police at the end of the war. The bungalows, each with bedroom, bathroom, and lounge, were built along a loop road that curved in front of the main building, which itself contained accommodation for a further twelve officers, and which housed on its ground floor a large dining room and an equally large lounge containing a bar. A chain-link fence, patrolled by armed guards, ran round the edge of the grounds. The mess usually housed about twenty officers, bachelors, and, occasionally, one or two married men whose wives had elected not to join them in Malaya.

On the afternoon of his discharge from hospital, Carter sat in the shade on the verandah outside his bungalow admiring the view over Sintra. Doctor Kowalski had forbidden him to leave the mess grounds "for at least two weeks," and he was not looking forward to two weeks confined to reading the files that his secretary brought every morning, and playing cards every—and sometimes, as it would turn out, all—night. He wondered if it would be possible for Nancy Chong to visit him in the quiet of the afternoon when nobody was about, to "dress his wounds," even though this was no longer necessary. He thought of his last few nights in hospital, and the prolonged good-night kisses as he lay in his bed; and of one in particular which had wandered slowly across his neck and over his chest and down his body. And how, finally, he had gripped her hair and tried to draw her head away; but she had resisted and his grip had slowly relaxed. And how she had continued even after the climax was past, forcing him to clutch and pull her hair with both hands until, eventually, she released him. Her complete lack of embarrassment: so that it was he who said, "I'm sorry. I couldn't help that." As if it was his fault, not hers. It was tragic, he thought, that within a matter of only forty-eight hours, she was leaving to attend a medical course in the U.K.

He found himself thinking about his job. He was more than

27

satisfied with his staff, especially with Elizabeth, his secretary, who was Scottish, thirtyish, and as efficient and cheerful as Halroyd had forecast. But it was his Asian staff of seven—excluding the two Chinese translators—who most impressed him. This was his "field" staff: a Chief Inspector, two Inspectors, a Sergeant Major and three sergeants. One Indian, one Malay and five Chinese, all of whom had personal reasons for hating the guts of the Communists in Malaya.

Sergeant Major Lim's younger brother, who appeared to have no bad enemies, had owned and run a small garage and his whole time and effort were devoted to building up his business. One night while working late he had received a visit from a Communist killer-squad. Given enough time, such squads frequently showed much ingenuity in their methods of execution. That night they excelled themselves. Who would have thought of using the air pressure pump as an instrument of death? Sergeant Major Lim's younger brother's crime was—of course—that he was Sergeant Major Lim's younger brother.

The Malay, Sergeant "Jimmy" Abdul Rahman, while coming out of a coffee-shop one afternoon, happened to notice that the man standing at the side of the second step below him was wearing a leather gauntlet on his right hand. As Jimmy deliberately stopped to light a cigarette, he watched the man transfer an electric light bulb from his left hand to the gauntlet on his right, so Jimmy turned and shot him, without removing his pistol from its shoulder holster. An electric light bulb rammed in the face is extremely unpleasant, especially when it's filled with acid.

The Indian Inspector, Chivapathy, had not been in his house when the grenade had been tossed through the window. His wife had. Although she had not been hurt, she had lost their first child through a miscarriage.

Every member of Carter's staff had had similar experiences, for, as members of the police force, and especially as members of the Special Branch, they had identified themselves with the Imperialists, and had therefore to be punished. The Communists used cruelty as an instrument of policy. Not the least of their motives was the knowledge that a comrade who has been associated with an atrocity is committed: unlikely either to surrender or to permit himself to be captured alive, to say nothing of the

28

fact that he has in any case been taught that all comrades captured by the Imperialists are tortured as a matter of routine. In addition, a guerrilla army, if it is to survive, must ensure that the civilian population does not act against it. It can do this in two ways; by so winning the respect and admiration of the civilian population that civilians will not willingly assist the government in any matter adversely affecting the guerrillas, or alternatively, by instilling such fear into the civilian population that they dare not do so. The second way is quicker: but it engenders hate. And those who are prepared to act against the Communists are those who have cause to hate; and who are prepared to risk and lose their lives in giving expression to that hate. Halroyd had selected Carter's staff with care and deliberation, seeking to concentrate the hate; seeking also to ensure that there was little chance of any Communist penetration of the Projects—or as he sometimes preferred to think of it—the Revenge Section. Even Carter, Halroyd had recently thought, had a motive for revenge.

Carter was relieved when Doctor Kowalski pronounced him fit, and capable of work—and play. His neck and side were still sore but had almost healed, and he was bored to distraction reading the intelligence reports, assessments, summaries, and translations of captured documents which Elizabeth brought him every morning and collected every afternoon.

This morning after Doctor Kowalski's reprieve Carter identified himself to one of the guards at the gate outside Police H.Q., drove into the courtyard, and parked his car. Police H.Q. had a forbidding aspect. A long two-storeyed white concrete building with sand-bagged emplacements at vantage points and wire mesh over the windows as a protection against hand-grenades. The Special Branch offices were on the top floor, but Carter had to telephone Elizabeth to establish his bona fides before the guard admitted him. As they walked along the long corridor to his new offices Carter read the signs above the doors on either side; signs which—to the initiated—announced the function of those within. "Comag," the section which dealt only with Communist aggression, kept details of all incidents, strategy and policy. "Comprop," a section which studied Communist propaganda and advised on counter-propaganda. "Compen," the section which dealt with attempts to penetrate Trades Unions, Political Parties, schools, and indeed, all organisations.

"Comorg," which kept details of the administrative and organisational structure of the Communist Liberation Army's Kepayan Regiment, and its supply organisation, the Min Yuen. Elizabeth explained that Special Branch had only half of the top floor. The other half was occupied by Combined Services staff, with offices for wireless staff, an Operations Room, and an Operations Conference Room. Carter discovered that the Projects Section consisted of four offices, one for the two Chinese translators—Mr. Peng, in his middle thirties, and Mr. Ong who was about twenty-five—one for O.C. Projects, one for his secretary, and the fourth, used as a staff common room, for the detectives.

Carter had only been in his office for a matter of two minutes when the buzzer on his desk sounded and Halroyd's voice said, "Carter?"

He flicked the switch, "Sir."

"Welcome aboard. You're just in time for the monthly conference, pop along to my office and I'll take you along."

The Special Branch monthly conference was held in the Operations Conference Room, a large, windowless and air-conditioned place, with strip lighting and every square inch of wall space covered by maps, charts and diagrams. It had a rostrum at one end, and was in almost constant use for briefings, lectures and meetings. On this occasion, some fifteen Special Branch officers—every Special Branch officer above the rank of Chief Inspector in Kepayan—sitting at a long table, stood up as Halroyd entered the room accompanied by Carter. After introducing him, Halroyd dealt at once with the agenda, which described the intelligence information acquired during the course of the last month. There was not a great deal of it; the Chinese population was far too terrified to supply the Security Forces with information. A small occupied Communist camp had been discovered by a British army patrol: the Communists had fled, leaving two dead comrades. A British soldier also died. A number of documents, probably valueless, were found in the camp and these were being translated. A certain number of second-hand reports had come from uniformed police sources; there were a number of anonymous letters, but little else.

The other items on the agenda related to police/military cooperation, codes, and Communist propaganda; these were dealt with speedily, matters with which those present were overly familiar. It was a dull and tedious meeting until the item on the agenda dealing with "other business." A certain amount of argument began about whether a captured Communist terrorist who was co-operating with the Special Branch should be correctly classified as C.E.P. (Captured Enemy Personnel), in which case he would be charged, sent to court and no doubt hanged, or whether, because he was providing useful information he should be incorrectly classified as S.E.P. (Surrendered Enemy Personnel), in which case he would simply be detained. Halroyd brought this argument to a conclusion with the comment, "I thought I had already made my attitude on this matter clear; while I'm Head S.B., we will not bring charges against captured terrorists. It achieves nothing! Even if they give us no information whatsoever, there is always the possibility that one day they might, and in any case it's better to leave the Communists in doubt as to whether or not our captures are co-operating. It makes them nervous."

Towards the end of the meeting Halroyd asked Carter if he had anything to suggest. Carter spoke for several minutes. Then there was a moment's silence, and someone said, "Now why the bloody hell didn't anyone think of that before!" Carter had said that during the course of the previous few weeks he had spent a considerable amount of time reading translations of Communist documents. He pointed out that, "For reasons which are in accordance with thought-control techniques with which you are all familiar, the Politburo of the Malayan Communist Party had issued a directive requiring all comrades to keep and maintain a regular diary." He continued by saying that one of the side effects of this directive was that more diaries than any other kind of Communist document had fallen into the hands of the Special Branch. Because of their very volume there had been a tendency to ignore them. Consequently, they had rarely been translated and either not read at all, or merely been scanned; "Yet," Carter maintained, "from those diaries I have read, I could pinpoint two Communist camps on the map to within a distance of three-quarters of a mile." He declared that a more careful study of diaries would enable the police and army jungle squads to focus their attention on those particular localities in which Communist camps were known to exist, rather than continuing to have such squads hack their way through the jungle in the hope of stumbling across one.

31

As an example of how the position of a camp might be arrived at by the study of a diary, Carter explained that he had been reading one maintained by Ho Bping, a nurse attached to the 3rd Company of the Kepayan Regiment. The diary covered a period of nine months, during the first seven of which she was stationed at Camp 4. "At one point she makes the following comment, 'I like Camp 4 the best. I was on sentry duty last night and watched the sun sink behind Mount Tajam. It was a beautiful sight, etc., etc.'

"So clearly, to start with, gentlemen," Carter had observed, "Camp 4 is east of Mount Tajam. Elsewhere she writes that, 'a comrade from the Min Yuen warned us that when the wind was in the east our bugle could be heard in the Lok Wah squatter-area.' So Camp 4 is west of the Lok Wah squatter-area. Again, she comments, 'The Imperialists are very active; I counted twenty-four army lorries on the trunk road today, and beyond them in the bay I could see two small warships on patrol.' That puts Camp 4 west of the main road. She goes on to write, 'from the third sentry post I could see Ventnor bridge.' A long way, gentlemen. And she could see Ventnor bridge only if she was looking down, and not across, the valley. A fact which, with the others, reduces the position of Camp 4 to within one map square. She supplies further clues which I cannot remember off-hand, but I think the point is made?"

It was, for the decision was taken that, as a matter of high priority, captured diaries should be studied with a view to the collation of all clues that might lead to the location of Communist camps.

"Any more ideas, Carter?" Halroyd asked.

"I have one other, sir, relating to the current policy of destroying Communist camps when they are found empty. I think that it would be smarter to leave them intact with a view to their future exploitation. Why destroy them? They only build others which we then have to try to locate."

"What do you mean by 'future exploitation'?" someone asked, "Should we booby trap them?"

"No," Carter replied, "I mean that we should mine them with a view to their complete destruction if they are ever re-occupied."

"Yes, but if we do that we've got to have a squad there permanently waiting for them to re-occupy it, in order to press the button," one man objected, adding, "and how long do we keep the

32

squad there? A week? A month? Six? It's not a practical proposition: they might never re-occupy it!"

"I was thinking more along the lines of persuading, or more accurately, tricking them into re-occupying," Carter replied, "I confess I haven't worked it out fully, but for all that, I would like—certainly any large camps—to be preserved, when they're found empty."

Halroyd looked thoughtful. He sensed the germ of a project. If a Communist company could, actually, be tricked into re-occupying a mined camp; they could kill more in one minute. . . . He told the meeting that he would give instructions that Security Force patrols discovering vacant Communist camps were to leave them intact.

"—And remove all traces of their visit," Carter interrupted.

"Exactly," Halroyd agreed.

Later, Halroyd decided to place the "X" squad—some fifteen surrendered terrorists who had shown themselves more than willing to act against their former comrades—under the control of O.C. Projects. If Carter's in charge of them, he'll dream up ways of using them, he mused.

4

As O.C. Projects, Carter's main targets were the president and the six members of the Malayan Communist Party's Kepayan State Committee, the men who also commanded the Kepayan Regiment of the Communist Liberation Army.

Much had been recorded concerning these seven men, but it described their pre-emergency public lives and activities, rather than their private lives and backgrounds. Without exception, each had held important positions in the Trades Union movement, and in the political parties that had proliferated in Malaya at the end of the war. They had organised strikes, staged demonstrations, rallies and marches; created Councils For Joint Action; blackmailed the weak, suborned the reluctant, and, where necessary, destroyed the recalcitrant: they had in fact, used all possible "peaceful" means to achieve the end which, they believed, would one day justify the means used. Until the day, when, on Cominform instructions, they restored to violent means—armed revolution. The seven Special Branch files told Carter all this, but they omitted details of background, intelligence and of the motives which had led them into Communism. And it was this type of personal information that Carter sought. If you are planning the death of a man, it is imperative for you to learn everything possible about him: not to know that he is colour-blind or left-handed might make all the difference between success and failure.

Carter had lectured his staff on the importance of discovering everything about a target: "Where he was born and when. Who his neighbours had been. What school he went to. Was he clever? Lazy? Popular? Respected? Where did he work? How did he get the job? Who were his workmates, schoolmates and playmates? Did he go to church? Did he frequent brothels? Does he smoke? How much? What brand?" He was surprised to learn how much of this type of information was already known to individual members of his staff. Sintra was a small place. Men of the same age group had gone to the same school, joined the same badminton club, or even attended the same church. Sergeant Major Lim, for example, had volunteered the information that a friend of his, an instructor at the police Training School, had sat next to State Committee member Khan Hock Loi—known as "Tommy" Loi—at school, and that this friend had told him that Tommy had been a popular boxer there, was highly intelligent, and had won a scholarship to a school in Singapore, before going to Cambridge just before the outbreak of war. Carter sent both Sergeant Major Lim and his friend to Singapore to examine the school files, and to find out as much as possible about the younger Tommy Loi. They returned with photostat copies of school records, and with sundry photos of Tommy Loi in boxing trunks being awarded trophies. One of these photos was of particular interest: it showed Tommy Loi receiving a trophy from a Mr. David Cresswell, no doubt the D. Cresswell whose name appeared in the records as having paid for extra tuition in maths for the boy. Questioned about this, a teacher who had known Tommy Loi, replied, "Oh, yes. Lieutenant Colonel Cresswell took a great interest in him at one time; even paying his fees to university in England."

"Lieutenant Colonel Cresswell is still in Singapore, sir," Sergeant Major Lim had remarked brightly, "a very rich man, sir. A barrister. Of course, Tommy Loi's parents couldn't have paid his university fees: they own that coffee-shop just down the road from here, at least, his mother does; his father died years ago. You know the one, sir, Khan Hock Lum's coffee-shop: it's only a small place, no more than a hundred yards after turning right at the main gate."

Carter did know it; but he hadn't known that Tommy Loi's mother ran it.

Sergeant Major Lim had been given another job in Singapore. In addition to his enquiries regarding Tommy Loi Carter had handed him a letter of introduction to a friend in the Singapore Special Branch, asking him to help in finding an agent "for a very dangerous job, which, if successful, will do the Communists a lot of harm, and will pay off handsomely in reward money."

The sergeant major had been successful. "I have just the man, sir. Thirty-five years old, tough and intelligent. Religious sir, and very anti-Communist. I will guarantee his reliability. Just one week's notice sir, and he can be here."

Carter had replied, "Make that twenty-four hours' notice, sergeant major, and I'll accept your agent."

"That's very short notice sir; it may not be possible . . ."

"That's how it will have to be sergeant major: the Communists are not likely to give us a lot of notice, and in any case Singapore is only a short flight from here."

Sergeant Major Lim had thought for a moment before replying, "He'll probably agree sir, he's very anti-Communist. If he can of course."

Reward money, Carter had thought, could be quite an incentive. The president and six members of the Kepayan State Committee were together worth three million two hundred thousand dollars, dead or alive: $450,000 for each member, and $500,000 for the president. A lot of money in any language. Even a lowly comrade was worth $5,000.

When Carter walked past Elizabeth into his office one afternoon, he noticed that for the second time that day she was too absorbed in her reading to notice him, so he stopped and asked, "What are you so concentrated on, Elizabeth?"

Elizabeth looked up, startled, then blushed as she replied, "It's a translation, Mr. Carter, the diary of a Communist nurse."

"Not Comrade nurse Ho Bping, surely?" Carter asked with interest.

"Yes, I think it is," Elizabeth replied, clearly embarrassed.

"Really," Carter said, "I'm already acquainted with Miss Ho Bping. I'll just have a quick glance through it," adding as he picked it up. "There seems an awful lot of it, doesn't there."

In his office, Carter was quick to discover that this was not Ho Bping's official diary; certainly not of the type that she submitted each week for examination by her Company Commander, especially as he was Khan Hock Loi, alias Tommy Loi, and he figured so extensively in it. This was a private and personal diary: one kept in defiance of Communist rules and regulations. It told of Ho Bping's unrequited love for Tommy Loi. "When he spoke to me today my heart leapt," Carter read, "when it's my turn to do the cooking, I always try to give him the choicest pieces. I go to sleep

36

thinking of you, Loi. I dream of you, Loi. Why, oh why won't you smile at me. Once. Just once." Page after page was like this, but Ho Bping occasionally gave full rein to her imagination in detailed and vivid accounts of how she eventually succeeded in seducing Tommy Loi. More honestly, she occasionally referred to the uses to which she put certain items of jungle produce while thinking of Loi. ("I had to. I had to.") But she revealed the secret of what was after all a mundane situation, in her references to Ah Bpo. "But he seems more interested in Ah Bpo than in me," she wrote, "he takes Ah Bpo with him on every patrol, and I once saw them kissing, though they didn't know I was watching."

Tommy Loi, Carter concluded, prefers Comrade nurse Ah Bpo, to Comrade nurse Ho Bping. He glanced at the cover of the translation and saw that it had been made by Mr. Ong. He pressed one of the buttons on his desk.

Ong came into Carter's office and accepted the invitation to sit down.

Carter held up the translation. "How long did it take you to translate this, Mr. Ong?"

Ong peered at it through thick lenses before replying, "About ten days, sir."

"And is it all about Comrade nurse Ho Bping's unrequited love for Tommy Loi?"

"Yes sir."

"And is there nothing in it which deals with anything of security interest?"

Looking thoroughly unhappy, Mr. Ong replied, "No sir."

Carter pursed his lips before saying, "I know it's compulsive reading, Mr. Ong, and indeed it has to be read to see if it contains anything of security interest, but there are far more important documents awaiting translation than this."

Mr. Ong looked so abject that Carter was constrained to add, and in a somewhat lighter tone, "All you need have said about this diary, Mr. Ong, was that Comrade Ho Bping at great length outlines her love for Comrade Tommy Loi; Tommy Loi, however, is more attracted to Comrade Ah Bpo, who is no doubt a much nicer popsie anyway. That's all, Mr. Ong. I don't want to know about the bananas."

"Yes sir," Mr. Ong replied, adding with some hesitation, "Er, Ah Bpo, sir. He's not a popsie, he's a he. And Bpo is a man's name."

Carter sat back in his chair and looked hard at Mr. Ong before saying, unnecessarily, "Are you sure?"

"Oh yes, sir. In fact there's a file on Ah Bpo, sir. Shall I get it?"

As Carter gazed in the next few minutes at the photographs on the inside covers of the file, it crossed his mind that the Shanghainese must surely be among the most handsome people in the world: with features as clearly defined as if they had been carved in granite, yet refined, delicate; and with eyes of proud dignity which hinted of knowledge and compassion. Ah Bpo was certainly good-looking, Carter thought. The file told him that he was twenty-five years old; at twenty-three he had taken a leading part in an unlawful assembly, and had therefore spent two weeks in prison: a member of the Party, he went into the jungle just before the outbreak of the Emergency. Educated at St. Mary's secondary school, Sintra, he had reached senior Cambridge standard and spoke fluent English. Five feet nine inches in height, and with broad shoulders, he looked a formidable opponent, proud even in the police photographs.

A few months after his arrival in Sintra, Carter's dossiers on the president and members of the Kepayan State Committee were virtually complete. With the exception of the activities of Lee Chin and Tommy Loi while they were in England, he knew everything, or very nearly everything, there was to know about all of them, information being acquired from every conceivable source; from the records of the Registrar of Births and Deaths to the recollections of the most recently surrendered comrade. It remained only to decide whose deaths from among them would have the most adverse effects on the Malayan Communist Party—a decision which would have to be reached in consultation with the heads of each Special Branch section, and in which, Carter thought gloomily, each section was likely to reveal a vested interest, seeking a high priority for the death of the target who was causing *his* particular section the most trouble. For the purpose of agreeing final priorities, Halroyd convened a meeting of his section heads in the Conference Room— a meeting which he had thought would perhaps take three-quarters of an hour, but which took three and a half.

Halroyd opened the proceedings by reading out the list of

38

priorities prepared by Carter. It began with the name of Emmanuel Nathan, the twenty-eight-year-old Indian Commander of the 4th Company, and concluded with the name of Lo Heng, the forty-five-year-old President of the State Committee. This was received first with silence and then with protest.

"Why," someone demanded, "should Lo Heng, who was not only President of the Kepayan State Committee and the Regimental Commander of the Kepayan Regiment, but also the State representative on the Central Executive Committee of the Malayan Communist Party, be given such an absurdly low priority? His death would be an immense propaganda victory."

"Because," Carter replied, "Lo Heng is a coward and a drunk, and a bloody bad Regimental Commander. He drinks at least one bottle of Benedictine a day and is rarely sober: he's got himself holed-up in the deep jungle with a whole platoon of bodyguards and he never comes out. He's almost inaccessible even to his company commanders, and he does little or nothing to co-ordinate their activities. We should let him live," Carter asserted. "If we kill him he might be replaced by someone efficient. As for propaganda victories, they don't win wars."

It crossed Halroyd's mind that Carter was not exactly over-burdened with tact. He suggested that Carter go through his list, stating in each case his reasons for the priorities he had allotted, before the matter was opened for general discussion.

Carter explained that he had given Emmanuel Nathan the top priority because he was an Indian, and his existence lent credence to the Malayan Communist Party's claim that it was multi-racial, rather than what it in fact was—ninety-five per cent Chinese. Additionally, Nathan had become something of a legend among the younger Indian rubber-tappers on the estates: he projected a good image of the Party and there was a danger that he might win Indian recruits. He was also a good organiser, the attacks for which he had been responsible and which he had himself led, had been carefully planned and skilfully executed. He was, Carter concluded, "Efficient, flamboyant, courageous and highly dangerous."

He then went on to explain why his next choice had been the fifty-two-year-old Party theoretician, Cambridge graduate, and one-time lawyer Lee Chin. "He's a thoroughly dedicated and utterly sincere Communist who devotes every minute of his time to the Party.

A skilful propagandist, he writes the Party's weekly newspaper almost in its entirety: yet some of his articles are good enough to be reproduced in the International Communist press. Despite his age, and the fact that he's a diabetic, he travels long distances through the jungle to visit camps, make speeches and stimulate morale. His loss would be a severe blow to the Party.

"I put Khan Hock Loi alias Tommy Loi down as No. 3," Carter went on, "because of his efficiency and popularity. As you know, he is the Company Commander of No. 3 Company; but it might possibly have escaped your notice that the Communists enjoy more popularity among the Chinese squatters in No. 3 Company's operational area, than anywhere else. Time and again, interrogations of captured or surrendered terrorists have indicated that from a Communist point of view, the squatters in No. 3 Company's operational area are, quote, 'completely reliable.' This is because Tommy Loi has been at pains to impress on his men that in all their dealings with the civilian population, and particularly the squatters, they are to seek to win their respect and affection. Significantly, a document recovered when one of No. 3 Company's camps was discovered by Hussars, turned out to be a letter from Lo Heng demanding to know why Loi hadn't reached his allotted monthly financial target. The reason was simply that Tommy Loi refuses to collect subscriptions from the Chinese squatters; he collects from the workers on the estates, and from all traders, shopkeepers and so on, but not the squatters. Once again we have a man who projects a good image of the Party.

"Betty Wong, in fourth place on my list, is also someone who helps to project a good image of the Party. A trained nurse, apart from being a dedicated Communist, she gives lectures on hygiene to the squatters' wives, and delivers their children. The remaining three," Carter went on, "William Lai, the commander of No. 2 Company, Lim Tsing Wa, the boss of the killer-squads, and Lo Heng, the president, are clearly people who do the Party harm. William Lai is just a bandit chief who goes in for loot and rape, while Lim Tsing Wa's executions are carried out with such ingenuity and savagery that he's clearly a sadist. William Lai and Lim Tsing Wa are feared and hated by everybody—including their own men in several cases. Quite a high proportion of those who have surrendered were serving under them at the time of their surrender.

I think little is to be achieved by eliminating any of the last three on the list, each in his own way is doing the Party harm, which after all, is what we are trying to do ourselves. I'm not of course suggesting that should the opportunity arise we should refrain from killing any of them, I am simply saying that in my opinion we should devote our limited resources towards eliminating those whom the Party can least afford to lose."

Discussion lasted for two hours, but finally left Carter's original list unchanged. Lim Tsing Wa's name had proved the most controversial, not everybody subscribing to Carter's view that, "It is precisely because he *is* such a nasty bastard, that we should make no effort to eliminate him."

5

Lieutenant Hamilton stank and he knew it. It embarrassed him, but there was not much he could do about it as he sat in the Conference Room smoking a cigarette and answering Carter's questions. He had just returned from a seven day patrol in the jungle with a platoon of Gurkhas, a patrol in which he had discovered a large camp—empty. Behind him, sitting listening, were his brigadier, his colonel, his company commander, and Halroyd, so that despite the air-conditioning, Lieutenant Hamilton continued to sweat as he replied to Carter's questions, looking at him with eyes that almost pleaded not to be asked a question he couldn't answer.

Carter was like a caged tiger. Eyes glued to the floor, he paced up and down in front of the lieutenant as he shot his questions. Once, he paused in front of him long enough to say, "You must forgive me, Lieutenant, for asking what must appear to you to be rather point-less questions, but your answers might enable us to identify the camp. The Communists number their camps, and if we can discover the number of the camp you found yesterday, then we might, we just might, be able to trick them into re-occupying it."

The lieutenant nodded his understanding: at twenty-two he was a natural for an army recruiting poster.

"You say there were eight huts each capable of accommodating fifteen men?" Carter continued.

"Yes sir. In twos beneath the trees on each side of the parade ground; two to each side."

"What other buildings were there?"

"The hut containing the stores, the kitchen, which was little more than an attap roof on four supports, but which had a brick stove; next to it a partly attap-walled hut bigger than any of the others, which I took to be a lecture cum dining room. And, about fifty or sixty yards away, a much smaller hut which could offer accommodation only for a couple of men."

42

Lieutenant Hamilton smiled apologetically as he went on, "I couldn't make out quite what it was for; in fact we only discovered it at the last moment: very nearly missed it altogether."

"Probably the hospital," Carter replied, "a big camp like that is bound to have one. But tell me, did you see where they dumped their rubbish?"

"Yes sir. It was quite some way from the camp buildings, eighty yards perhaps, on the edge of a small cliff."

"What exactly was the rubbish?"

"Well, empty tins mostly, sir."

"You didn't examine it?"

"One of my men did; he climbed down and held things up for me to see. Quaker Oats, corned beef, mutton curry, coffee, sugar, stuff like that, cartons and tins."

"Nothing else?" Carter persevered.

"I don't think so, sir."

"No bottles?"

"Oh yes! There were. There was quite a little heap of them. Benedictine bottles, mostly."

Behind him Halroyd laughed and slapped the side of his chair, so the lieutenant turned and said, "Is that important, sir?"

"Well, lots of Benedictine bottles," Halroyd explained, "means that at some time or other, Lo Heng, our No. 1 Communist, was living in that camp. The Chinese drink rather more Benedictine than one might imagine, as they regard it as having medicinal properties, but Lo Heng drinks over a bottle a day, I'm told. Presumably he lived in this camp before he got really scared; he's known to have moved to a more secure camp some months ago."

The lieutenant turned back to Carter, who asked, "Can you think of any reason at all why the Communists should discover that the camp had been visited?"

"No sir. I don't think I can."

"No cigarette butts?"

"No sir."

"No doors left open which had previously been shut?"

"No sir."

Addressing Halroyd, Carter said, "I think that that's about all sir. Judging by its position, size, estimated age, and the fact that Lo

Heng has apparently lived in it, it can only be Camp 4. According to a Communist diary, Lo Heng left Camp 4 six or seven months ago, for Camp 12."

Within the course of the next few hours, plans which had awaited the discovery of a vacated Communist camp were put into effect. Flight Lieutenant Harper, a communications expert, arrived, complaining of the short notice which had dragged him from his comfortable flat in Singapore, and would shortly be sending him trekking through the jungle. He and the explosives expert—a Major Faulkner—spent much of their time with Carter, discussing what had been christened—as all Operations must have names—Operation Buttercup, the mining of Camp 4.

The same night, Sergeant Major Lim introduced his agent, one Yip Thau Meng, to Carter, who was much impressed with him. A tough thirty-five-year-old Hakka Chinese, he looked, Carter thought, the perfect choice for the job—and with perhaps the purest motive: "The Communists killed his brother, sir; it is a debt for payment in blood only."

Chief Inspector Ramanath was an acknowledged expert on hand-writing and ballistics, not only because his book, *Finger, Thumb and Palm Prints,* had become a standard work and was compulsory reading in a dozen police-forces, but also because of the excellence of his speech on ballistics at a recent Interpol Conference of Scientific Officers. In a Colonial Police Force not over-hasty in the promotion of Asians to gazetted rank, he had steadfastly refused promotion, being content to remain where he was, doing what he enjoyed doing and knew best, rather than to try to hold down the dull administrative job which promotion would inevitably entail.

He had been peering through a microscope when the O.C., C.I.D., had phoned.

"Yes, Mr. Vardon?"

"Mr. Ramanath, Mr. Carter of Special Branch has just rung asking if you could be free for a few minutes, sometime this morning: apparently he wants your opinion on some hand-writing."

Ramanath had said "Certainly," and was now sitting beside Carter in the semi-darkness of a small room in the Special Branch offices, looking from one to the other of the pictures projected on the two screens in front of him.

The picture on the left read:

12th May.

Comrade Coy Commander Nathan,
    4th Coy,
        Kepayan Regt.
Comrade,
    Expect strong Imperialist drive, your operational area, next few days. Your Coy to transfer to Camp 7 immediately.

Lo Heng.
Regt. Commander.

The picture on the right was exactly the same, except for the date, which was the ninth of September—the previous day. And the camp number, which read 4 instead of 7.

Carter said, "All I want you to tell me, Mr. Ramanath, is if these letters were written by the same man."

"Would you make the picture on the left sharper, please?" Ramanath asked. On the projectors, Chief Inspector Lau complied. "Would you adjust them both now, to the size of the whole screen." Ramanath turned to Carter and said, "This is only being one of the many ways to detect a forgery Mr. Carter. I am also needing to make a microscopic examination. With this simple blow-up on the screens, it is not possible to see the differences in shape between many things, the dots on the 'i's' and 'j's' for example, or the full stops. But of course these letters were not being written by the same man; the downstrokes on the two fours in the pictures on the right are not at the same angle as each other, nor are they at quite the same angle as the fours in the picture on the left. The letter on the right is the forgery, Mr. Carter, but a very good one. Very good indeed. So much care he has taken. May I see the envelopes now, Mr. Carter?"

"We have only one envelope, Mr. Ramanath," Carter replied, "and that is genuine."

Back in his office Carter buzzed for Mr. Ong. When he arrived Carter asked, "How old did you say this relative of yours is? The one that did the letter?"

"My maternal grandfather," Ong replied, "an old man. He is

seventy-seven now and his sight is failing, but I hope the letter was satisfactory."

"It was, Mr. Ong. Your grandfather has earned his $500. But what did you say his job was?"

"He was an engraver, sir, but his hobby is writing Chinese characters on pin-heads."

"On pin-heads?"

"Yes, sir. He's quite famous for it: it requires large magnifying glasses. An old Chinese art, sir, but unfortunately dying out; the modern generation is not interested."

Carter looked at Mr. Ong bemusedly, before saying, "No they wouldn't be would they?" Then added in a different tone, "You are sure he really is secure, Mr. Ong? He's not going to sit in a coffee-shop boasting how he earned $500 by forging Communist letters for the Special Branch?"

"Oh no sir!" Mr. Ong was quite hurt as he continued, "He thinks he was doing a small job for a wealthy friend of mine, and in any case, as I already told you, sir, he cannot read English."

When Carter walked into the Conference Room just before eight p.m., it was packed. He took his seat at one end of the row and casually surveyed the fifty-odd persons in the room. Army officers predominated, but there was a fair sprinkling of police officers, and even two R.A.F. and two R.N. officers. All chatting, laughing and smoking. It was, thought Carter, an unusual scene; British, Gurkhas and Malays; one or two turbanned Sikhs, two Chinese; sitting together awaiting instructions which would lead most of them and thousands of others into the jungle for at least four days and possibly considerably more.

Punctually at 8 p.m., Davidson, accompanied by an Army brigadier and Halroyd, walked down the center aisle to the front of the room. Davidson stood on the rostrum and the brigadier and Halroyd sat in the front row near Carter.

Davidson's opening address was brief and to the point. He had just returned from Federal Police H.Q.; he understood that a large Communist terrorist camp had been discovered during his absence, and that this fact was to be exploited; he himself was not yet au fait with all the details, and he would therefore make way for those who were. Glancing at the brigadier he said, "Brigadier," stepped down from the rostrum and sat next to Halroyd in the front row.

It occurred to Halroyd that he most disliked Davidson when he was in the spotlight. He knew Davidson to be a bloody old fool; yet in public he gave an entirely different impression. Crisp and incisive, dignified and bemedalled, he gave the impression that he exercised a quiet but effective control over the Emergency situation in Kepayan: whereas, thought Halroyd, as far as the Emergency was concerned, it simply hadn't registered with Davidson, and so far from controlling it, he didn't even know what it was all about. It irked Halroyd that Davidson could cloak his incompetence in such bright garments.

The brigadier, a dapper, almost slight little man, took his place on the rostrum and outlined the plan for the operation in broad terms with the aid of a wooden pointer and the map at the back of the rostrum. A Gurkha patrol had located a vacant Communist camp in central Kepayan—he pointed to a red star on the map. That patrol was now on its way back to the camp, but accompanied this time by telecom and explosive experts. It would mine the camp and bivouac in the jungle nearby. It should have completed its allocated task by three o'clock the following afternoon.

Thirty miles north of the camp, in the jungle somewhere in the vicinity of this large squatter-area here—again the pointer on the map—there was known to be another camp, housing elements of the 4th Company of the Kepayan Regiment, under the command of a character called "Killer Nathan." The object of the exercise was to saturate that area so heavily with police and troops, that the 4th Company would think it too hot to stay, and might make their way to the vacant camp. The head of the Special Branch would be talking more about that in a moment, but whether or not the 4th Company did go to the mined camp, there was every reason to suppose that, in view of the heavy concentration of police and troops we were putting into what was a comparatively restricted area, contacts with the enemy would be made. He concluded by emphasising the importance of units keeping within their allotted areas, rigidly adhering to their prescribed routes and timetables, and maintaining their wireless schedules. He handed over to Halroyd.

Halroyd was good at briefings. Big and genial, he displayed enthusiasm and exuded confidence. He stepped up to the rostrum as

47

if he couldn't get there quickly enough to impart his information. Yet once arrived, he stood for a moment as if collecting his thoughts; one hand in a trouser pocket of his civilian suit, the knuckles of the other resting on the rostrum table, before beginning. "This is not gentlemen, an operation which was planned today, or even yesterday. It is in fact an operation which was planned months ago, and which needed only the discovery of an empty Communist camp, before being put into effect. An empty Communist camp has now been found. A large camp. And by this time tomorrow night it should be mined; awaiting the moment when the deflection of a switch will blow it to bits." Halroyd paused, and in a slightly lower tone which lent his words more emphasis added, "and those in it.

"By this time tomorrow night also," Halroyd continued, "three torch-battery size radio transmitters will have been installed in the camp: installed in such a way that they will start transmitting only when the camp is occupied. One, for example, will be installed in the kitchen chimney, and will be triggered-off by the heat of the fire if anyone starts cooking: another one will be triggered-off by the opening of the store-room door, and the third by the weight of a body on sleeping boards. We should therefore, not only know when the camp is re-occupied—without running the risk of sending people to keep it under constant observation—but we shall know also if it is re-occupied during the hours of darkness, when watching it would not in any case be a practical proposition.

"By this time tomorrow night also, gentlemen, in a pro-Communist squatter-area some thirty miles north of the mined camp, an apparently wounded Communist terrorist will have sought sanctuary, and, when given it, will have requested that the letter he is carrying be conveyed to the Communist camp which we know to be in that area, and which we know to be occupied by Killer Nathan's Company, i.e., No. 4 Company. The letter is an instruction to Nathan from Regimental Commander Lo Heng to move his Company to Camp 4—the camp which has been mined. We do not know where Nathan's present camp is, and neither perhaps, do the Chinese squatters, but we do know that the squatters—whom as I have already said are pro-Communist—have been told by the Communists that if they wish to get in touch with them urgently, then they must light a fire by night, and by day must place a triangular sheet on the roof of a hut facing the jungle. So, gentlemen, let us hope that some time tomorrow night a fire brews up in that squatter-area, and that the letter is safely delivered to Nathan."

Had Halroyd looked at Carter he might have noticed him glowering. Their attitudes towards briefings were in sharp contrast. Halroyd considered that officers taking part in an operation should be told as much about the Special Branch side of that operation as was "consistent with security," while Carter considered they should be told "only as much as they need know to carry out their function." There was something to be said for both attitudes. Halroyd thought that the dangers of a security leak were more than counterbalanced by the fact that if every officer knew the whole plan and intention of an operation, no officer could unwittingly commit an action at variance with that plan or intention; and in any case, in the event of unforeseen circumstances—and there were always unforeseen circumstances—he might still, knowing the whole plan, be able to use his initiative and contribute towards its success. Carter agreed with all that, but he could not see the need for a completely detailed briefing down to the last crossed "t" and dotted "i." He also thought that it positively invited a security leak. There were more than fifty officers in the room: were they all thoroughly reliable? Wouldn't they sit in half a dozen different officers' messes talking about the operation? And wasn't there a Communist directive urging civilian comrades to try and obtain employment in Naval, Military and R.A.F. establishments? And in particular officers' and sergeants' messes? Why tempt fate? was Carter's attitude. Why not simply say "An attempt will be made to trick Nathan into transferring his Company to Camp 4." And leave it at that: but for Christ's sake don't explain *how* the attempt is to be made.

When Halroyd asked if there were any questions, he was subjected to a barrage. Not having been involved in the detailed planning, he continually found himself looking to Carter for confirmation. Finally, he looked at Carter and grinning, said, "As designer and engineer of this particular project, you're better qualified to answer these nuts and bolts questions than I am, so you'd better come up here and take your share of the punishment."

Carter took his place on the rostrum resignedly, standing directly behind the table but leaning forward slightly with finger and thumb tips on the table partly supporting his weight. It crossed his mind that Halroyd's comment about his being the "designer and engineer of this particular project," was unfortunate, because it told his audience that he was—to some extent at least—responsible for the fact that they would have to spend the next few days in the jungle, on what most of them probably considered would prove to be yet another wild goose chase. He anticipated a severe cross-examination. His first question was from a major in the center of the room who stood up and said, "The Head Special Branch spoke of a 'small arms fight' which would precede the arrival of your wounded agent in the squatter-area. I'm afraid I'm not altogether with that, sir."

"Sir." The Army, Carter thought, could be very polite at times; the major was at least ten years Carter's senior, and was wearing an M.C. and bar.

"The object of the apparent 'small arms fight,'" Carter replied, "is to give the Chinese squatters in the area the impression that the Security Forces are chasing someone: it will start about three-quarters of a mile from the squatter-area, and will get nearer and nearer to it. It will be laid on by a police jungle squad under the command of Sergeant Morgan, and will cease just short of the squatter-area after dark at 1835 hours. At about 1845 hours, our agent, wounded and in Communist uniform, will totter into the squatter-area, hammer on a door and collapse."

"Won't that be a bit difficult for him, sir?" queried a lieutenant, "in the pitch dark, in an area he doesn't know."

"I can't imagine why you should assume he doesn't know the area, lieutenant," Carter replied, "and in any case, it is not pitch dark, the moon doesn't set till one a.m. But," Carter glanced at his watch, "he should by now have completed the dummy run laid on for this evening. He will know which door to collapse against, but in that squatter-area any door would do, they are all pro-Communist: it used to be within the operational area of Tommy Loi, the present Commander of No. 3 Company; he's a great one for winning people to the Cause."

"Would you mind going over the bit about the letter again?" a lieutenant-colonel asked. "Who's supposed to have written it, and to whom?"

"It is supposed to have been written to Emmanuel Nathan, the O.C. No. 4 Company, by his boss, Lo Heng, the president of the Malayan Communist Party's Kepayan State Committee and also Regimental Commander of the Communist Liberation Army's Kepayan Regiment. It is in fact, almost a facsimile of a letter found on the dead body of a Communist courier some months ago; a letter which was not of course delivered. We have altered the date and the camp number, and now propose that it be delivered. The envelope will be heavily blood-stained; a fact which will tend towards obviating the possibility of its being regarded as being other than genuine."

In the momentary silence which followed this answer, Carter registered Davidson's open mouth, and Halroyd's sardonic grin.

"What guarantee is there that Lo Heng, or whatever his name is, the president anyway, won't actually be in Nathan's camp when the letter's delivered? If he's in the camp, then he and everybody else will know that he didn't write it." A flight lieutenant.

Carter was irritated by this question. "There is no guarantee whatsoever flight lieutenant," he replied tartly. "I can no more guarantee that the man who was supposed to have written the letter won't actually be in the camp when it's delivered than I can guarantee that our agent won't be struck by lightning or bitten by a snake." Carter paused, "But,"—he almost spat the word—"Lo Heng is lazy, and he's a drunk; nevertheless, in this State he's the Communist boss: if he wants to talk to Nathan he sends for him, he doesn't walk twenty or thirty miles through the jungle to do it." Carter took the edge off his voice as he concluded, "We don't deal in guarantees flight lieutenant, we deal only in what might be called a balance of probabilities."

At the back of the room a white-faced second lieutenant stood up suddenly and said, "But if the president is in Nathan's camp, then your agent will be executed; he'll be shot!" His voice held a note of remonstrance and incredulity. He was very young.

Carter sighed audibly before replying, "He will certainly be executed, but he will be very lucky if he is simply shot, lieutenant, very lucky indeed." Carter broke the following silence by asking, "No more questions gentlemen?"

"I'm afraid I have, sir!"—a heavily moustachioed colonel in the front row—"If these Communist fellows look after their own, and I've every reason to believe they do," he paused and looked round challengingly as if defying anyone to contradict him, "then they're going to collect your agent, put him in a bloody litter and cart him off to Camp 4; where the poor bastard is going to get himself blown up!"

When the laughter had subsided Carter said, "I hope they do cart him off to Camp 4 sir. It is precisely what we want them to do, and is in fact one of the reasons why the Navy and R.A.F. are represented here tonight. The butt of our agent's carbine will contain a transmitter, a transmitter similar to those to be installed in Camp 4 tomorrow; when he makes contact with armed Communist terrorists he will switch his transmitter on and R.A.F. and Naval direction-finders will track his journey through the jungle to, I hope, Camp 4."

"But he's still going to get blown up when he gets there, isn't he?" the colonel insisted.

"He might be, sir," Carter replied, "but he shouldn't be. Camp 4, like every other large Communist camp, has a small hospital, and he should be put in that. Instructions have been given that the hospital in Camp 4 is not to be mined."

"But they may not put him in the hospital," the colonel asserted, "they might put him in one of the main barracks where they can keep an eye on him if he is sick."

"They might well, sir; they might well," agreed Carter, "but," —again the emphasis—"he has been instructed to groan like hell all the way from the squatter-area to Camp 4. People don't want to have to listen to a wounded man groaning all night, so it's highly likely that they'll use the hospital for the purpose for which it was built, and put him in it."

Somehow or other Carter knew that the colonel was going to reply, it seemed it was expected of him. He was not surprised when the colonel lent forward slightly, each hand on an arm rest of his chair as he said quietly and evenly, "You know, if your agent gets out of this little lot alive, I think I'd like the chance to shake his hand."

"I hope I'll be able to arrange that, sir," Carter replied soberly.

"What happens if they take his carbine from him?" a Malay lieutenant asked suddenly, "after all he's badly wounded isn't he? He won't be able to switch it on then, will he?"

"His carbine, lieutenant," Carter replied, "will be covered in gore, and if the two Chinese officers present will forgive the observation, Chinese have an even greater aversion to handling gory carbines than Europeans. In any case, our agent has been instructed to squeal like a scalded cat if anyone tries to take it from him. In this way he will earn respect, not giving up his weapon though wounded, etc., etc.; beyond this again there is always a tendency to humour a wounded man and let him have his own way."

"You said your agent would be wounded sir?" A very intense lieutenant asked.

"I did indeed," Carter replied. "He will be dripping blood from a bullet-hole through the thigh."

"But who's going to wound him?" The lieutenant's voice held a tremor.

"Not me, lieutenant," Carter answered. "It will be done under full medical supervision. The impression will be given that a bullet has passed completely through his thigh, but in actual fact it will merely be an incision at each side. It is necessary that it look messy."

"But any doctor who does that, will be contravening his Hippocratic oath." There was no tremor now, only indignation.

Someone hissed, "Sit down, you clot." And someone else, "Don't you know there's a fucking war on?"

The embarrassed silence which followed these whispers held no sympathy for the lieutenant; it was neither the time nor the place for a discussion on medical ethics, and there were murmurs of agreement when Carter, in a level tone replied, "Save your cries of protest, lieutenant, for what the Communists will do to our agent, should they discover he is our agent." He paused before adding, "We ourselves will use a local anaesthetic."

Carter cast an appealing look at the brigadier: surely this had gone on far too long, but a captain asked, "Why does your agent have to be wounded at all?"

"Because as a Communist courier he would have been told the way to the camp currently occupied by Nathan's Company, or, perhaps more accurately, he would have been told who among the squatters he should contact, and where to find him: matters which we ourselves do not know, and cannot therefore tell him. In any case, unwounded, he would be subjected to all sorts of questions, such as, 'How long did it take you to get here from Lo Heng's camp?' Questions which it would be dangerous for him to attempt to answer. No. Better that he be wounded: people cannot, or don't, ask many questions of a man in pain." Carter sounded quite certain about it.

"Yes Inspector?" Carter asked. One of the two Chinese police officers had raised his hand.

"Sir, if your plan is successful, and the Communist camp is destroyed, your agent will be the only person in it left alive. But he will be in Communist terrorist uniform, so how will the Gurkhas know he is not a terrorist? He might get shot by the Gurkhas as they go in."

"If he is alive," Carter replied, "he will be in the camp hospital, and has been told to stay in it. The platoon which mines the camp will of course be the first people to visit it after the explosion. One of my staff is with that platoon, and the agent is known to him."

Carter was relieved to see the brigadier getting to his feet, and he stepped thankfully from the rostrum and took his seat in the front row. The brigadier had little to say beyond wishing everybody success. The briefing was over.

6

In the afternoon following the briefing, Carter sat with Halroyd on the Operations Room verandah waiting to hear if Camp 4 had been successfully mined. The last message from Lieutenant Hamilton had said that his platoon had reconnoitred the camp, that it appeared to be deserted, that they were going to make sure that it was in fact empty. If so, they were going to begin to install transmitters and plant explosives. The message had come twenty minutes ago. A further message was expected at any moment.

"Eerie," was the word that Carter used to described the Operations Room. As big as a large chapel, it was in a permanent state of semi-darkness, such light as there was being provided by the illuminated frosted-glass of the "Table," and one of the walls. There were also one or two spotlights, but these provided only enough light for an anonymous hand to write a message on a pad, or for unseen eyes to read it; neither the spotlights nor the reflected light from the Table and the wall provided enough light to identify the shadowy figures who hovered around the Table. The Table itself—perhaps slightly larger than four full-sized billiards tables—depicted on its surface a vast map of Kepayan State. On it multi-coloured symbols—circles, squares, triangles and stars—told of the progress of the operation, of the progress of "units," more particularly perhaps, of the progress of men: men from London and Glasgow, from Katmandu and Kuala Lumpur, who hacked their way through swamp and jungle for reasons most of them never thought about, or would even comprehend, if they did. Some 4,000 of them.

At one end of the Table, on a chair set some three feet higher than its surface, sat the Table "Supervisor," his presence revealed only by the hand in the spotlight on the small table beside him, a hand which held a signal paper as his voice intoned over the loudspeaker system, "X-Ray to 792381." A wooden rake moved one of the symbols an inch or more, a shadowy figure raised a phosphorescent finger, and another voice, this time the voice of the Table Verifier, who was similarly seated to the Table Supervisor but at the other end of the Table, said, "X-Ray at 792381." All signals relating to positions were double-checked in this way.

The illuminated wall was a huge timetable which gave the code names of each unit, its last position, and the time at which it was in that position. If the numbers were in red, it meant that that particular unit was behind schedule; green figures meant it was on time. An excess of red figures meant anything from bad luck to bad planning. Shadows climbed step-ladders to keep the timetable up to the minute. A few feet above the Table, but set back from it so that all parts of the Table were visible, a wide verandah ran round the side of the other walls. In the center of the long side of this verandah, facing the timetable, sat the Duty Officer, and, beside him, the Special Branch Duty Officer. In common with the Table Supervisor, the Duty Officer had a small table for reading and writing signals and also a microphone. But the Table Supervisor simply recorded events, whereas the Duty Officer was responsible for making decisions, giving orders or seeking explanations.

"Zebra Abel to explain delay." The Duty Officer.

"Contact being made with Zebra Abel." Table Supervisor.

And then a few minutes later, "Zebra Abel reports delay caused by unmapped swamp; requests permission to detour 400 yards South of planned route for distance one mile."

The Duty Officer looks at the Table, then leans forward to his mike, "Permission granted to Zebra Abel to detour 400 yards South of planned route for distance one mile. George Fox to be advised of Zebra Abel's new route."

The messages were almost continuous.

As Carter and Halroyd waited on the verandah, an area on the Table some two inches square lit up suddenly, so that it became a focus of attention as the Voice intoned, "Ulu Tiram power station under attack by estimated two enemy platoons. Requests immediate assistance." A red star moved into the square.

As the Voice continued, Halroyd turned towards Carter and murmured, "I hope they're not Nathan's boys, otherwise they might not be back in camp tonight when the letter's delivered."

"It's not 4 coy's operational area, sir," Carter whispered, "it's Tommy Loi's, No. 3 coy."

56

"Yes, of course it is," Halroyd replied, "he's far too busy altogether, that bugger."

Halroyd also spoke in a whisper; one always spoke in a whisper in the Operations Room; there was rarely any sound except the Voice. The Table staff wore slippers, and their rakes made no sound as they moved the symbols on the Table.

Carter sat up with a start as the Voice announced, "Abel Baker reports successful completion of Operation Buttercup. Now bivouacked at 791782."

A small blue cone propelled by a rake moved across the Table near a black square marked "A.B." and stopped on a large red star indicating Camp 4. The blue cone denoted the transmitters now installed in the camp. Should they begin transmitting a switch on the side of the cone would be depressed, and it would emit a blue glow. Carter and Halroyd stood up simultaneously. They could go now. Camp 4 was again empty, and mined.

Outside the Operations Room, Halroyd looked at his watch and said, "Aren't you running it a bit fine?"

Carter looked at his watch, "Not really, sir. Everything's laid on. All I've got to do is change."

Three hours later, Carter sat in the darkness in the back of a police armoured personnel carrier parked below the rubber trees on an Estate road half a mile away from the squatter-area. Despite the fact that the heavy steel door had been flung back wide, the heat was stifling. The mosquitoes tormented him, apparently immune to the repellent with which he had doused his hands, ankles, face and neck; in any case, the repellent was itself irritating. Sitting opposite him, three feet away but unseen in the darkness, was Sergeant Major Lim's agent, Yip Thau Meng. Beside him, softly humming an unrecognisable tune, sat Dr. Kowalski, his enormous head making the faintest of silhouettes against the dark blue square which was the open door. They sat, waiting, only half-listening to the approach of Sergeant Morgan's "fire-fight."

Carter recalled his careful approach to Dr. Kowalski. "How, Stan, would one so wound a man as to make a messy and impressive wound yet do him the minimum of harm? A bullet wound, I mean."

"You are shooting him across the cheeks of the arse, yes?"

"No, Stan. That would cause complications."

"Well then, you are shooting him in the thigh; but not to hit the big vein here," demonstrating with a huge forefinger and thumb on Carter's thigh, "yes?"

"He doesn't need actually to be shot, Stan. Couldn't incisions be made on either side of the thigh to give the impression that a bullet had gone right through?"

"Of course. But if anyone is treating the wound and pushing a probe through it to clean it, as is necessary, then they are finding out it is not a true hole, yes?"

"That would not happen, Stan."

They had sat in silence for a while. Smoking. In Stan's office in the General Hospital. Then the doctor had said, "You are wanting me to do this for you, yes?"

"Yes, Stan, I am."

"Some plan against the Communists?"

"A plan against the Communists."

"Of course I am doing it for you!" Stan had exploded. "There is a focking Red Army major in my house in Krakow! And I am not forgetting Warsaw."

Stan's mood had changed at that juncture. He had become more temperate as he asked, "But no one is knowing that I have helped you? They have long arms these Communists, and my mother still lives in Krakow. In one of our gardener's cottages. Yet she is luckier than most people of her class."

"No one will know, Stan, except the person on whom the operation is performed; but he is not from Sintra and doesn't know you."

"Then bring him to me at any time, Ralph; any time at all."

"I cannot bring him here, Stan; it would be most insecure: there are always people here, even at night. The operation would have to be carried out in the back of a police lorry."

"While it's moving?"

"Of course not! It will be parked in a rubber estate."

A thoughtful silence. Then, "All right, I will do it. But for this you are inviting me to one of your Chinese dinners I am hearing about."

Sergeant Morgan's phoney fire-fight was getting nearer. Carter grinned in the darkness as he thought of the briefing in his office that morning.

"It's right up my alley, sir. Dead center and right up. It warms me heart, sir. It's what I joined for. Any chance of it being a permanent job, like? Pity! My men to fire blanks only. Very sensible I'd say. Very sensible indeed. And me to fire live rounds in the direction of the squatter-area. But supposing I hit some bastard, sir?"

Carter had replied to the effect that that would be most unlikely; but that if anyone were hit, it would be their bad luck, and would in any case lend authenticity to the project.

"I like it, sir; I like it. Lend authenticity to the project. Very good, sir."

"Incidentally," Carter had warned, "keep your heads down, because our agent will be firing live bullets back at you."

The look of horror on Morgan's face, and then, "Here, half a moment, sir. A joke's a joke, but fuck a pantomime! What does he want to go firing at us for? We're *his* muckers for Christ's sake. We're on his side! Remember?"

"He'll only fire a few rounds," Carter had replied, "just to warm up the barrel of his carbine in case somebody touches it. He won't try to hit anybody. Another thing, if your boys know they are being fired at with live rounds, they'll take the whole thing more seriously, advance from tree to tree through the rubber, instead of giggling around like a bunch of merry-making fauns."

"Too bloody right they will! And they won't be the only ones, neither."

Carter looked at his watch and said, "It's time, George." Earlier he had explained, "In the presence of the agent, Stan, I shall call you 'George,' so that if he is ever interrogated he will only be able to tell them that the doctor's name was George." Carter stood up and closed the heavy steel door as quietly as he could, then lit the pressure lamp. Stan opened a black leather bag and laid out cotton-wool, two small bottles of a colourless fluid, a hypodermic and several surgical instruments on the seat by the lamp. Yip sat, looking up enquiringly. In answer to Carter's nod, he stood up, took a clasp knife from a pocket, opened it and commenced hacking away at the left leg of his long khaki trousers. "I am a footballer, sir. If it makes no difference, I wish it to be the left leg." Carter recalled. The trouser leg fell to the floor.

"Sit here," Stan whispered, motioning towards the seat. He opened one of the bottles and soaked some cotton-wool, then wiped Yip's naked left thigh carefully. They watched him fill the hypodermic from the other bottle, then place a thumb and forefinger on the fleshy part of Yip's thigh; heard him say, "This won't hurt. It's only a local anaesthetic, but it will be very sore when it wears off in about half an hour's time." They watched the fluid disappear into Yip's thigh.

"We must wait two or three minutes for it to 'take,'" Stan said.

Carter looked at his watch and told himself he should have thought of that. Fortunately, Sergeant Morgan was already late, and by the sound of his fire-fight, still a couple of hundred yards away.

After two minutes, Stan picked up a pointed surgical instrument and pricked Yip's thigh. "Did you feel that?" he asked.

Yip shook his head.

Stan soaked more cotton-wool and carefully wiped two places on the underside of Yip's thigh. As he put the cotton-wool down and reached for a surgical instrument, Carter put a forefinger under Yip's chin, raising his head. In answer to his enquiring look, Carter said, "What the eye doesn't see. . . ."

In less than a minute Stan straightened up, "It is finished."

Yip looked down, saw the blood running down his leg from the two incisions, said, "Ai yah," very softly. Then Carter handed him a khaki haversack, watched him as he opened it, took out a British-type field-dressing and unwrapped it. Yip started to tie the field-dressing round his thigh. As he was doing it so badly Stan made as if to help him.

Carter held up a restraining hand, "No S . . . George, he must do it himself. It must not look as if anyone else tied it."

Finally it was tied.

Carter said, "Wipe your hand in the blood."

Yip wiped his hand in the blood on his calf.

"Undo the top two buttons of your tunic."

Yip did so, leaving smears of blood on the tunic.

"Take the letter from the haversack and put it into your tunic."

Yip did so.

"Now do up the buttons."

When this was done Carter said, "Put more blood on your hand, close the haversack and then put it on."

Carter helped him with it, then, when he turned round, handed him the khaki cap, with, at its front, the red star. Yip put it on. Grinned.

Sergeant Morgan was nearer now; fifty yards perhaps. Carter extinguished the pressure lamp and pushed open the door. Behind him in the darkness he heard Stan say, "You are very brave, yes?" He sensed they were shaking hands.

"On your way, Yip." Carter's voice.

Yip clambered out. Stood for a moment on the metal step outside, facing Carter, their faces a few inches apart. A moment of uncertainty. All at once it flooded in upon Carter. It was his plan. This man's life depended on his plan. His foresight. What had he forgotten? Sergeant Major Lim's voice came back to him, "The Communists killed his brother, sir. It is a debt for payment in blood only." And, "He is the sportsmaster, sir. A footballer. Very religious he is, sir; a Roman Catholic."

Carter gripped the shoulder in front of him, "The road is straight behind you. Let your eyes get accustomed to the darkness for a minute. Walk, don't run. After a hundred yards or so, fire your carbine. Don't forget, the safety-catch controls the transmitter, it is very stiff! Turn it to the 'on' position only when you want to transmit, when you've met up with armed Communists. The safety-catch is now in the 'off' position and the carbine will fire. Take it, but don't touch the trigger, not yet anyway."

Holding the carbine vertically, Carter held it towards him in the semi-darkness: their hands touched, both holding the barrel. "Have you got it?"

"Yes."

"Go with God!" Carter almost added, "Brasso,"—his code name. Carter had given him the name.

Carter watched as he jumped down from the back of the lorry; saw him fall, get up, sling his carbine over his shoulder, hold his left knee with his left hand and stomp away into the darkness.

Sergeant Morgan's fight still raged noisily.

Two minutes, and then, tat tat tat, tat tat tat; very near. A different sound from the ones made by Sergeant Morgan's squad.

Shorter, sharper. In Carter's mind it conjured up a picture of a Dachshund being pursued by wolves.

Carter closed the steel door. He felt weak. "Go with God." "Wolves," he thought, "I'm losing my grip."

He lit the pressure lamp, carried it to the wireless behind the driver's cabin and hung it from the roof, then he picked up the microphone, switched the wireless on, and spoke. "Hotchkiss to Hereford, how do you read? Over."

The reply was immediate, "Hereford to Hotchkiss, am receiving you strength five. Over."

"Receiving you strength five also. Brasso delivered as planned."

"Understand Brasso delivered as planned."

"That is correct. Over and out."

As he switched the wireless off, Carter visualised a small red cone propelled by a rake moving across the Table, as the Voice intoned, "Brasso delivered as planned."

He found himself wondering why he'd called him "Brasso." As he offered Stan a cigarette, Carter asked, "Will he be all right, Stan? With that wound, I mean."

"Of course he'll be all right." Stan sounded irritable.

"He fell when he jumped down."

"Well his leg is still numb, yes."

"There seemed an awful lot of blood, Stan."

"Stop worrying. I am telling you he is all right. In three weeks he will not even be finding where I am making the incisions. Did you see the size of his thigh? He is tough: built like a bull. He will be all right."

They sat in silence, smoking for a minute or two, then Stan said, "And now?"

"We wait. In a few minutes time two police armoured personnel carriers will come down the main road. We shall see them, or at least, the driver will. The second one will stop, back into this road, turn and go back: we will start up, drive out and follow it back to Sintra. In this way, those who are interested in the movements of police lorries will see two go out and two come back."

"But the number plates?" Stan queried.

"Are the same," Carter replied.

"And the first lorry?"

"Continues south to Kampong Puteh."

62

A pause, then, "You think of everything my friend."

"I would like to really think so Stan. Believe me I would."

Back in his bungalow, Carter picked up the house 'phone, "Any calls for me?"

"None Tuan."

"Tell cookie I won't be in for dinner please."

"Tuan."

Carter didn't feel hungry. He had a bath and half an hour later walked on to the Operations Room verandah.

Halroyd was there. "No snags?"

"None."

Carter looked at the Table. As he had guessed, Brasso had been allotted a little red cone, as opposed to the blue cone allotted to the transmitters in Camp 4. He looked at his watch; 8:36 p.m. At any moment a yellow star would move across the Table as the Voice intoned, "Fire reported in squatter-area at . . ."

They'd had plenty of time to light it, Carter thought, Brasso must have arrived in the squatter-area over an hour ago. He began to get worried. He moved away from the small group standing near the Duty Officer, to one of the two short sides of the verandah. For a while he stood looking down at the Table, hands on the back of one of the seats that stood in a single row behind the verandah rail, but then he began pacing up and down the carpeted floor behind the row of seats. Fifteen paces; each way.

At 9:30 p.m. the only other people on the verandah were the Duty Officer, and, sitting next to him, the Special Branch Duty Officer. Everyone else had gone. It wasn't interesting any more. The fire hadn't been lit. Something had gone wrong. The plan hadn't jelled. Carter's agony of mind was scarcely bearable: Oh Brasso, he thought, Christ, what will they do to him? What are they doing to him? Why in the name of God hadn't he thought to give him a suicide pill? He could have got one easily enough.

It was 10 o'clock. There were long periods of silence now. Four thousand men bivouacked in the jungle; no need to report their positions again, not until after dawn, after they had moved. One didn't travel at night in the jungle: not unless one were a Communist terrorist; and then, only when one had to.

63

10:15. The Voice remained silent. There weren't even any Communist attacks.

10:45. Fifteen paces. Up and Down. Up and Down. And then, "R.A.F. and Naval direction-finders report transmitter Brasso in operation at 782135."

Both hands on the back of the seat in front of him, Carter gazed at the Table in stupefaction. In the squatter-area, where there should have been a yellow star, Brasso's cone glowed with a little red light! No fire. But Brasso was in contact. He'd met up with the Communists. Carter walked to the end of the row of seats; sank into the first. Utter relief. Bewilderment. There were Communists in the squatter-area when Brasso arrived? No! In that case he would have started transmitting hours ago. The squatters knew the Communists would be visiting the squatter-area that night? Perhaps Betty Wong was giving one of her lectures on hygiene? Possibly, but unlikely. The Communists didn't indicate their future movements. A squatter went to the Communist camp and reported Brasso's arrival? Could be, but the Communists didn't usually let squatters know where their camp was.

A hand on his shoulder, he leant back, looking up. The brigadier. Carter stood up.

"Brasso seems to have turned up trumps, Ralph."

"Ralph." How did he know his name was Ralph? "It looks like it, sir."

"I wouldn't like to be in his position. He's got plenty of courage, I must say. What prompts such a man to stick his neck out as far as he's doing? It can't be money surely, even though there's an awful lot involved."

"It's not, sir, it's revenge. A debt payable in blood, was how it was put to me."

"I see."

They stood, looking at the Table. A square on the Table lit up and a red star moved into it as the Voice intoned, "Manager's bungalow, Lockwood Estate under heavy attack." Another square lit up. Another red star moved across the Table. Train derailed. Yet another. A police post under attack.

They had been expecting this: almost all the mobile Security Forces were concentrated in the North. All these attacks were in the South. The Communists sought to relieve the pressure on them in the North by making the Security Forces send reinforcements to the South. More and more squares lit up as the attacks continued. By dawn one police post had been destroyed with the loss of eight police constables, but the other places attacked had held.

Not all the messages had told of Communist attacks; at 11:14 p.m. the Voice had said, "R.A.F. report transmitter Brasso moving slowly Eastwards." And again at 00:25 hours, "R.A.F. report Brasso now stationary at 782491." Brasso was in the jungle now, and almost certainly in a camp.

Ah Ling, Carter's orderly, woke him at 13:30 hours: half an hour later he was sitting in the Operations Room verandah, looking down at the Table. It was his turn as Special Branch Duty Officer. Next to him, as Duty Officer, sat the heavily moustachioed colonel who'd shown such an interest in Brasso at the briefing. They sat in the semi-darkness listening to the Voice droning out its messages, and watching the symbols inching their way across the Table. Brasso's cone glowed dull red. He was still transmitting. Since 05:50 hours, he had moved eight miles through the jungle—towards the South, in the general direction of Camp 4, and on two occasions had been less than a mile from Security Force patrols.

Carter was mesmerised by the little red light. What message did it convey? The position of Brasso's carbine? Was Brasso with it? The slow rate of progress—at least for terrorists—seemed to indicate that Brasso was being carried in a litter. By four men? Alone? Or with a party of ten, or fifty, or a hundred? Perhaps he would never know.

"Peter Abel to 782409." The Voice.

The colonel turned towards Carter, "You know those buggers are on an almost converging course with Brasso's lot." He was uneasy.

The last thing that anyone wanted at this stage was a clash between a Security Force patrol and Brasso's party: in a litter, Brasso might even be captured, and therefore never reach Camp 4—which was presumably where he was going—and the success of the whole operation would be jeopardised. But the area was alive with Security Force patrols, and Brasso's intended route was not, of course, known, so little could be done to ensure that Security Force patrols avoided

Brasso's position; even if they were told to remain stationary, Brasso might still run into them.

In answer to the colonel's remark, Carter said, "Peter Abel's map-reading, sir, he could be a couple of miles away from the position he's given."

"I'm not so sure," was the colonel's reply, "they're Hussars, and they've done a lot of jungle-bashing."

"R.A.F. reports one of Central Transmitters in operation." The Voice.

The blue light at Camp 4 on the Table glowed dully.

"Blast! Who the hell are they? Can't be Nathan's lot, it'll take him another three days to get there." Central's transmission was not welcome to the colonel.

"Lieutenant Hamilton will have to send a recce patrol back to the camp to find out sir," Carter remarked, "and the R.A.F. communications officer will have to go with it. Maybe the wind has blown the store-room door open, in which case he'll have to set it all up again. It could of course, be a whole Communist Company returning after one of last night's attacks, or it could be a Communist courier making himself a cup of tea before pressing on with his journey. Or a python perhaps, curling up on the bed boards, or even monkeys for that matter: someone will have to go and find out."

The colonel lent forward to the mike on the verandah rail, and the Voice announced, "Abel Baker to be advised that one of Central's transmitters is in operation. Recce patrol to ascertain cause. Patrol to include Flight Lieutenant Harper to rectify possible accidental transmission. Contact with any enemy to be avoided if possible."

There was no point in risking the whole operation just to kill two or even a dozen Communist terrorists who might happen to be in the camp. Some were bound to escape, and give warning that the Security Forces were in possession of the camp.

A square on the Table, some ten miles North of Brasso's position, lit up while the colonel was speaking; when he had finished, he sat back in his chair and listened as the Voice—this time the Table Supervisor's voice—announced, "Dog Item in contact with party approximately thirty terrorists at 794021. Three enemy dead. Two of ours wounded, one seriously. Fluid battle continues."

The colonel leant forward to his mike, "R.A.F. Helicopter Flight to be alerted for removal of two wounded, North Kepayan area."

Behind them, a voice murmured, "Things seem to be hotting up somewhat." Carter turned his head. The brigadier. "Now who would they be, Ralph?"

"It's William Lai's operational area, sir. One of his platoons, I'd say."

"You talk of him as if you knew him personally." The brigadier seemed amused.

"I think I do, in a way. I certainly know a lot about him."

"Know thy enemy, eh, Ralph?"

"Exactly, sir."

"What sort of a man is he? Dedicated Communist? Idealist? Or does he simply hate white men? So many people do these days." The brigadier was genuinely interested.

"None of those sir, he's just a thug, with perhaps slightly more than average intelligence."

"And that's all?"

"Well yes, it is sir," Carter seemed surprised that the brigadier thought that there might be anything more worth knowing about William Lai, but he went on, "I think it was Lenin, sir, who said that you can't make revolution without getting your hands dirty; but the trouble is that revolutions attract those whose hands are already dirty, and gives them full scope for dirtying them even further. William Lai would be in any movement that was against the established order of things, anytime, anywhere; especially if that movement was disposed towards violence. In Russia, he'd have been in the vanguard of the revolution and then boss of O.G.P.U.; in Germany he'd have been at Nuremberg and then in the S.S."

"And in England?" the brigadier pursued.

"Mosley's lot I should think, with a protection racket in Soho as his main source . . ."

He stopped as the Voice said, "Dog Item reports terrorists have broken off engagement. Five enemy dead; one of ours dead, four of ours wounded and one missing. Will emerge from jungle as planned approximately 17:30 hours and will prepare clearing for evacuation of dead and wounded."

"One of ours missing," the brigadier murmured questioningly.

The colonel leant forward to his mike. "Dog Item to make every effort to locate missing fusilier. One platoon only to go forward to prepare helicopter clearing."

There were no brightly lit squares on the Table now: Dog Item was no longer in contact with the enemy. Brasso's red light glowed, and, three feet away, Central's blue light remained lit.

"Peter Abel to 783129." The Voice at its most bland.

"Jesus!" the colonel exclaimed, "How the hell did that happen! They should have missed by at least three-quarters of a mile."

Peter Abel was so close to Brasso, that its symbol—a flat green square marked P.A.—was pushed slightly under Brasso's cone. If Peter Abel had given his position accurately, they were within yards of each other. They stared at the Table in fascination, waiting for the square to light up as the Voice announced, "Peter Abel in contact with enemy force. . . ." Then the colonel leaned forward towards his mike, but from behind him the brigadier put forward a restraining hand. The colonel half turned. "We must tell them sir. Nathan's whole Company might be there. We must warn them that there are an unknown number of Communist terrorists in their near vicinity and they'd better watch out." The colonel was alarmed.

"Ralph?" The brigadier turned to Carter.

"With respect to the colonel sir, I'd prefer that they didn't watch out. If Nathan's there with his whole Company he won't want to announce that he is there. He'll try to avoid an engagement. He's no fool. If he shows us where he is he's inviting us to put more troops into that area to find him."

"But they might just run into each other," the colonel expostulated.

"They might, sir; but British troops in the jungle are not exactly light-footed, the Communists will know they're there before they know the Communists are," Carter replied.

"All the more reason to tell them then," the colonel snapped.

"Not if the Communists want to avoid an engagement, sir," Carter replied, but his voice lacked conviction.

The Voice interrupted them, "R.A.F. report Brasso now stationary at 783129."

The colonel put one hand on his microphone, "Shall I tell them now, sir?"

"No, David. Don't!" The brigadier spoke clearly, firmly. A bead of sweat detached itself from the grey hair and threaded its way down his cheek. He brushed it away.

They stared at the dull red light. If that square lit up more brightly it might mean the deaths of British soldiers. Ambushed. Outnumbered. It was four o'clock in the afternoon; they'd probably been on the move since six. It had rained during the night and they probably hadn't had much sleep: they could hardly be at a peak of alertness. But they could be brought to it easily enough. Just by a few words in the mike. Brasso had stopped, so the Communists knew they were there. The assumption was that the Communists wanted to avoid an engagement. To alert the British troops would be to deny the Communists precise knowledge of their movements; the troops would proceed with stealth and caution; the Communists might not hear them, might not be able to get out of their way. But not to alert them might be to sentence some of them to death. The assumption was . . .

Ten minutes passed and then, some three feet from Brasso's red light, a square lit up as the Voice announced, "Dog Item reports six further terrorists killed at 794022 in an engagement resulting in the recovery of Fusilier Stone, who had been badly skinned and may not recover. No other casualties. Now going forward with casualties to landing zone." On the verandah they exchanged glances. Carter shook his head. He didn't understand either.

The brigadier nodded towards the mike and the colonel leant forward; the Voice demanded full details of Fusilier Stone.

A moment's pause, and again the Voice, "R.A.F. reports Brasso now moving slowly East."

Away from Peter Abel.

The colonel pursed his lips. They hadn't met. At least, not yet.

The Voice. "Fusilier Stone was captured during the first skirmish by an enemy party of four men and two women. They gagged him, tied his arms behind his back and led him to a small clearing some three-quarters of a mile away where they stripped him naked and hung him by his heels from the branch of a tree. The two women then commenced to skin him from the ankles. The gag was removed after a few minutes, as they apparently wanted to hear him scream. Attracted by his screams, Oboe Easy platoon surrounded the clearing and in the short fire-fight which followed the six enemy were killed. The skin from Fusilier Stone's legs and thighs was hanging over his chest when he was found: he is still conscious but our medical attendant says he has only a fifty-fifty chance of survival."

One of the Table staff said, "Jesus Christ!" the first words Carter had ever heard any of them utter; then there was a shocked silence. No one even moved.

A minute passed, then the Voice announced, "R.A.F. report cessation of transmissions from transmitters Central."

The colonel turned to the brigadier, "That could mean that Hamilton's blown it up, sir."

"I sincerely hope not," the brigadier replied.

They didn't want to talk about Stone.

In the next hour, the Voice spoke of dead and wounded and helicopter clearings: routine stuff. It also reported the fact that Brasso had moved due East for half a mile, due South for a mile, then due West for half a mile. There was not much doubt as to who was avoiding whom.

One further signal before Carter's relief arrived. Abel Baker reported that one of the transmitters in Camp 4 had been triggered by the heat from the sun on the kitchen chimney. (The chimney had been made from kerosene tins, but as Flight Lieutenant Harper subsequently explained, he had not expected the sun to heat it up to the 135 degrees Fahrenheit necessary to set off the transmitter.) The transmitter in question had now been transferred to the kitchen door and would be triggered off if it were opened.

"That bloody blue job should have thought of that in the first place, the twit," the colonel said savagely.

As Carter walked out of the Operations Room, the Voice echoed and re-echoed in his mind, "In the short fire-fight which followed, the six enemy were killed." None wounded. None captured. The clearing was small, small enough for them to surround it. They had said so. Presumably, Fusilier Stone, under similar circumstances, had surrendered. But the six Communist terrorists hadn't. They had all been killed. One knew why. But one didn't know how. What had the British soldiers been moved to do in that small jungle clearing? How long exactly, had it taken for the six Communist terrorists to be . . . killed?

70

7

It was 3:55 a.m. The Operations Room verandah was packed; the single row of seats at the verandah rail was full, and behind it, standing two and three deep, were the officers who had taken part in the operation. Only a few hours before, many of them had still been in the jungle, and by rights should now be in bed, but as one of them put it, they wanted to be "in at the kill." The "kill" would take place in five minutes time. At four o'clock. There would be nothing to see; they just felt that they had to be there when the command was given.

There were few symbols standing on the Table: static defence posts were marked on its surface and therefore didn't need symbols. Symbols were for units which moved, and most of the men who commanded such units were on the verandah. No squares stood out from the Table glowing more brightly; no Communist attacks. Perhaps the Communists were in bed. It was certainly to be hoped that they were—in Camp 4 at any rate. Lots of them. Camp 4 was marked by a large red star on the surface of the Table. On it, side by side, stood two cones, one glowing with a red, the other with a blue light. It had taken the red four days to reach the blue. They had met twelve hours ago when the Voice announced, "Transmitter Brasso now stationary at Camp 4." But long before this, as the red had neared the blue, and drawn farther and farther away from the heavy concentration of troops in North Kepayan, the brigadier had ordered more and more units to return to base. In the jungle, most of them had met only the heat and the sweat, the hills and the swamps, the leeches and mosquitoes; the fatigue. But they had had to enter it, if for no other reason than by their very presence to lend credence to the letter ordering Nathan to transfer his Company to Camp 4 because of a "strong Imperialist drive."

Halroyd stood with the brigadier behind the Duty Officer's chair. He was jubilant. The whole plan had worked like a charm; not only had Nathan's Company moved to Camp 4, but they had spent each night of the journey in a different camp. Camps whose existence hadn't even been suspected but whose positions—thanks to Brasso's transmitter, and the R.A.F. and Naval direction-finders—were now known to within twenty yards. Even Carter had agreed that the positions in which Brasso had spent the night were, "Almost certainly Communist camps; even if only small staging posts." And Carter's caution, his downright pessimism, his insistence on interpreting everything in the worst possible light, had now become almost legendary: one could almost clinch an argument by simply saying, "Well Carter agrees with me." He had said about the camps along the route, "Brasso stopped shortly after 16:00 hours today sir, yet there were still two hours of daylight in which he could have travelled. Presumably he's at today's destination—a camp." And again, "Brasso didn't stop today until 18:45 hours; so the last half hour of the journey was spent in darkness: not a thing that one would willingly do with a wounded man in a litter. Presumably they pressed on to reach today's destination—another camp."

Halroyd was glad that so many of the Army officers were present; it was a good thing for Special Branch/Army relations: glad also, that they had been given a blow by blow account of the Special Branch side of the operation at the briefing. A little respect and admiration never did Special Branch any harm. All these chaps had been present at the briefing; and the fact that they were prepared to lose a night's sleep betrayed a genuine interest. Even that conscript, the medical student who had bleated about Hippocratic oaths was present. Halroyd looked at his watch; two minutes to go. He recalled the meeting with Carter and the brigadier in his office the previous day, and Carter replying to the brigadier's question, "I would suggest that four o'clock, four a.m., is the time to press the button, sir. You see, they do rather curious things. Despite the fact that they have been travelling all day, they might still sit around the parade ground wringing out their consciences until half past three. 'At the time,'" Carter had mimicked, "'I thought the Party decision to delay the strike was wrong. But I can see now that it was presumptuous of me to question Party decisions. I have neither the knowledge nor the wisdom of the Party. But I have blotted out my shameful thoughts with the firm resolution of unquestioning obedience,' that sort of thing, sir," Carter had continued. "On the other hand, if they've got a job on the following day, they're likely to be up and about by 4:30 a.m.; I'd settle for four o'clock, myself."

So four o'clock it was. But how many Communist terrorists were in the camp? The transmitters in the camp had started transmitting when Brasso was still ten miles away from it—presumably a forward party; no need to limit their speed to that of the litter. Even Carter had agreed to a minimum of one platoon—thirty men. But it could be the whole Company, ninety, a hundred perhaps.

The moustachioed colonel, sitting in the Duty Officer's chair, turned to the brigadier, "It's almost time, sir, shall I give the word?"

The brigadier nodded.

The colonel leant forward to his mike, "Abel Baker to detonate mines."

Silence. To each his own imagination.

The verandah door opened and someone said in a loud whisper, "It went off all right. I was on the roof, I saw the flash."

Then the Voice; "Abel Baker reports loud flash from direction of Camp 4." Chuckles of amusement, and comments; "a loud flash!"

The Voice again; "R.A.F. reports cessation of transmitters at Camp 4."

A roar of laughter; comments: "I'll bet!" "Surprise, surprise."

In the semi-darkness, Halroyd heard a mild commotion coming from one end of the verandah, heard someone say, "What's the hurry?" and someone else, "Steady on old chap." Someone pushing through the crowd: maybe the medical student on his way to have a good puke, he hoped. But in the light from the Duty Officer's spotlight, Halroyd saw it was Carter, a Carter who had somewhat unceremoniously pushed past the brigadier and was now talking to the Duty Officer. He saw the strain on Carter's face, sensed the urgency of his whisper; heard the Duty Officer say, "Yes of course," before leaning forward to the mike.

"R.A.F. to check cessation of transmissions from Camp 4. Transmitter Brasso should still be functioning."

So that was it.

Carter stood, half-turned, looking down at the Table; his left arm on the verandah rail, his right hand gripping the arm of the Duty Officer's chair; in the light from the Duty Officer's spotlight the microphone cast a shadow on his face, but the shadow did not hide the anxiety and foreboding.

They waited; in the taut silence no one whispered or moved. They scarcely breathed. They had all been at the briefing: they all understood. A minute perhaps? Two? Then the Voice, "R.A.F. confirm cessation of all transmitters. Repeat, all transmitters." An audible sigh, then the Voice again; but a different Voice, a Voice which spoke in a choked whisper and which betrayed grief and rage, incredulity and despair, "God, it can't be true. It can't!"

At the verandah rail Carter straightened up and turned, unaware that he had whispered aloud at all, and even less that his whisper had been picked up by the Duty Officer's mike just a few inches from his face. They stood aside for him as he walked through them, walked as if in a trance, along the verandah to the door at the end.

It was nearly six, light enough for them to make their way to the camp. Lieutenant Hamilton nodded to his number two; in the jungle around him his men made ready to leave. Hamilton picked up his pack and put it on, then bent and shook Harper. Flight Lieutenant Harper opened his eyes and grunted. "Huh?"

"This is it. We're on our way!"

"Thank Christ for that," Harper replied wearily, struggling to his feet. The last five days had been torture to him; he ached in every limb; yearned for a cup of tea, a hot bath, and sleep. He ran his hand over the stubble on his chin: the shave could wait, sleep was more important.

Major Faulkner joined them and remarked, "I wonder how many we've got."

They knew they'd got a lot; they were only three hundred yards from the camp, and in the night they had heard men singing: lots of men, and for a long time. The Special Branch sergeant major had said they were singing in Mandarin, and that the songs told of the glory of revolution. "How secure they must feel," Hamilton had commented, when they first realised that the sounds were the voices of men singing. He had wondered at the time whether he should report it, but his orders were to use the radio only when absolutely necessary. Several of his men filed past him and he took up his position in the file with the Special Branch sergeant major, Lieutenant Harper, and Major Faulkner immediately behind him.

As they neared the camp, the column of men halted and Hamilton went forward; the leading scout beckoned him and pointed: the trunk of a human body lay suspended in a bush. The scout pointed upwards and Hamilton looked up to see another body, sixty feet above them in the branches of a tree. The scout beckoned him forward again and he followed; through the bushes he could see an open space: the parade ground, and on it, among the dead bodies and the debris from the huts, something that moved, a man, dragging himself inch by inch on his elbows. He was dragging himself away from Hamilton's position, and Hamilton could see the cloth on the stump of each leg showing scarlet.

As Hamilton looked, he found it difficult to recall what the camp had once been: it wasn't that it no longer existed, so much as the fact that such little debris as remained seemed insufficient evidence that it ever had existed. No doors, no large pieces of roof, no thick bamboo supports—but of course the explosives had been inserted in the supports—and anyway, the whole camp had been built of bamboo and attap. The main evidence of the existence of the vanished camp was the bodies. These were everywhere. There were several on the parade ground, but mostly they were in the trees; trees which had been stripped of their foliage, some of them even of their branches and of bark. He had intended to reconnoitre the camp and come in from two sides, but there was nothing left to reconnoitre, they might just as well walk straight in and straight across. While he gazed in silence through the foliage, someone pulled at his sleeve; the Special Branch sergeant major.

"Yes sergeant major?"

"My brother, sir."

Hamilton looked blank, said, "I beg your pardon."

"My brother, sir; Thau Meng. The agent who led them here. He is in the camp hospital sir; we must find him."

"Your brother! Yes. Yes we must." Hamilton looked at Lim strangely. No one had told him this.

"The hospital, sir, where is the hospital?"

"I know where it is, sergeant major, stay with me."

Hamilton turned and raised an arm in signal to his men; they followed him on to the parade ground and spread right and left at its edges. One of them retched violently. Hamilton hissed something at him in Gurkhali, but the sound had been heard. One of the bodies on the parade ground raised its head and looked at them, then leapt to its feet screaming and came at them stark naked, arms out-stretched, fingers splayed as if to claw them. A Gurkha soldier stepped forward, the butt of his rifle raised. The screaming ceased.

A warning shout; they fell flat as a sub-machine gun fired a short burst. Only the Gurkha who'd fired remained standing; he walked over to the body with the scarlet stumps and kicked the pistol from the now lifeless hand.

Hamilton gave some orders, and as the men moved forward to make sure all the bodies were dead he turned to Lim and said, "I think it must be over there, sergeant major."

They skirted the edge of the parade ground, and followed a narrow path through the bushes. Suddenly Hamilton stopped dead. Squatting immobile in the center of the path, wearing Communist uniform and with a rifle across his knees, was a sixteen-year-old boy, his sightless eyes gazing fixedly in front of him. He made no move as they walked round him, perhaps he was also deaf.

The attap roof of the little hut had gone, but the sides were intact: the door was partly open. Hamilton approached with caution, intending to peer through a crack in one of the sides, but Sergeant Major Lim pushed past him and through the door.

A man lay on his back on the bamboo slats that were the bed; a sack of rice was lying on his chest. A sack of rice from the store-room that used to be fifty yards away. Brasso, alias Yip Thau Meng. Real name Lim Thau Meng; Sergeant Major Lim's elder brother. As Sergeant Major Lim laid a hand on his forehead, Brasso opened his eyes and smiled. He whispered, "I knew you would come, Ah Tsai."* The sergeant major made as if to lift the sack of rice, but his brother whispered, "Don't," then half opened his eyes and asked in a hoarse whisper, "Did many die?"

"All. They all died. Many." The sergeant major's voice was savage.

Brasso closed his eyes and shook his head slightly as he whispered, "No, not all; not the Indian. He sat with me all night . . . Wiped my face, brushed away mosquitoes . . . I'm glad he did not die." He spoke jerkingly, with difficulty.

"Please do not try to speak, Ah Meng," the sergeant major pleaded. "The lieutenant has gone for the medical attendant, he will be back in a moment."

* Younger brother.

76

But when Hamilton returned, Brasso was dead.

They lifted the sack of rice; saw the carbine that had been forced into the chest. The broken ribs. The blood.

Hamilton didn't notice that when the medical attendant removed the carbine, he checked the safety catch; pushed it to the "on" position: trained soldiers, accustomed to handling arms, check the safety catch of a weapon automatically, almost unconsciously.

Hamilton walked back along the path to the parade ground. Already the flies swarmed. He checked his watch; 06:25, they'd been in the camp seven minutes. He took off his haversack and knelt with it on the ground in front of him; he undid the straps and lifted the flap. They looked at him from the photograph fixed to the inside of the flap: his mother and father. In the garden in Surrey. Sanity. Love. He looked up, over the parade ground, at the trees around it. His parents weren't simply eight thousand miles away, they were on another planet, in another universe. As his wireless operator came towards him gesturing at his watch, he took a signal pad from his pack and began writing.

The verandah again; crowded in the semi-darkness. The brigadier in the Duty Officer's chair. An air of expectancy, of excitement, in no way lessened by the baffling announcement some minutes before, "R.A.F. report transmitter Brasso in operation at Camp 4," 06:30 hours. Below them, a signal paper in the Table Supervisor's spotlight as the Voice begins, "Abel Baker reports complete success. At least sixty bodies counted so far, but accurate count not yet possible as many bodies in disintegrated state, and many hanging in trees. All camp buildings totally destroyed except camp hospital, which is still standing but without its roof. Brasso was inside and was still alive when his brother reached him, but he has since died, a sack of rice from the storeroom having landed on his chest as a result of the explosion. We had to shoot one man as we came in, as although he had lost the lower part of both legs, he aimed a pistol at us. We captured one other man who ran at us screaming: he has been identified by Sergeant Major Lim as the Commander of No. 2 platoon of No. 4 Company: he has clearly lost his reason. We have one other captured, a sixteen-year-old boy who was apparently blinded by the explosion, and who must have been on sentry duty when it occurred. A helicopter will be able to land on the parade ground when we have cleared it in about one hour from now. Will report further details soonest."

A moment's awed silence, then a buzz of conversation. "Sixty! At least sixty! Pity about the agent though."

The brigadier, who had been speaking to Halroyd, nodded agreement then lent forward to the mike, "Abel Baker to be informed Colonel Warburton will arrive Camp 4 by helicopter, eight o'clock; will be accompanied by Special Branch team of four. A search is to be made for the body of an Indian. All bodies to be made ready for photography where possible, and all documents, arms and ammunition to be collected. Brasso's transmitter to be switched off."

In the course of the next few minutes the verandah almost cleared, leaving the brigadier still talking to Halroyd and the Special Branch Duty Officer, two or three others, and Carter, sitting alone at one end of the verandah. The party was over. Carter felt exhausted, drained of all vitality; yet his mind still operated at high pitch. A fucking sack of rice! It could have landed anywhere. A foot to the left, a foot to the right. But no! It had to land on the only place forbidden to it. As if it had a mind of its own. Or as if acting in accordance with some awful law of retribution. And why hadn't Lim told him that Brasso was his elder brother? Why not say, "This is my brother Lim Thau Meng?" Why disguise the fact? It wouldn't have made any difference. Perhaps he thought that Carter would say, "You've already lost one brother Lim; I won't let you risk another."

Carter felt too tired to move. The operation had been successful; "At least sixty bodies counted so far." A glorious success. He supposed he should feel elated, but he didn't feel anything. Nothing. He wondered vaguely how he would have felt if the operation had been a total failure. He gazed dully down at the Table; the blue and red cones had gone and in their place a square marked "A.B." rested on the red star that had been Camp 4.

The Voice, "Abel Baker reports no Indian among the 84, repeat 84, bodies counted so far, but Sergeant Major Lim said his brother's last words included the remark, quote 'I am glad the Indian did not die. He sat with me all night, wiped my face and brushed the mosquitoes away.' Unquote. The helicopter clearing will be completed in half an hour from now."

Carter sat bolt upright. Brasso dies, Nathan lives. A yard to the right or left and that sack of rice might have got Nathan, but it didn't of course. Nathan; saved by an act of charity. Ministering to a wounded comrade who was neither wounded nor a comrade, but a bitter enemy who made groaning noises. And what was the Company Commander doing ministering to the wounded? All night. "What a complex character!" Carter thought. An ex-dresser from a hospital in Port Dickson. A notorious womaniser. A skilled tactician and a marksman. He'd shot Wainwright at 180 yards. "Killer" Nathan. "Sharpshooter" Nathan. Suddenly Carter stood up and walked swiftly towards the brigadier, still sitting in the Duty Officer's chair: a new thought had crossed his mind; Nathan was still alive, and he was near Camp 4. As Carter came within the circle of light by the Duty Officer's chair, something in his face made the brigadier ask, "What is it, Ralph?"

It was a question that was never answered, for at that precise moment the Voice announced, "Abel Baker reports Lieutenant Hamilton shot dead by sniper: Flight Lieutenant Harper wounded. Four-man patrol in hot pursuit."

Carter turned and stood, looking down at the Table; but he didn't see it, he saw only Hamilton's face, the eyes almost pleading not to be asked a question he couldn't answer: and his voice, "There were several Benedictine bottles. Is that important, sir?"

A hand on his wrist; Carter turned and saw it was the brigadier. He read the pain in the eyes and said the one word, "Nathan."

"They'll get him Ralph. They'll get him. Those Gurkhas will track him for a month. They'll come back with his head. They don't like their officers being shot, and they particularly won't like Hamilton being shot." The brigadier paused and added in a quieter tone, "He was very popular, you know."

So swiftly does the present become the past. "He is" becomes "he was." Carter didn't share the brigadier's view that the four-man Gurkha patrol would get Nathan; Nathan was a jungle craftsman and was on his own ground. But Carter was absent from the Operations Room that afternoon, when the Voice confirmed his misgivings, announcing that the four-man patrol had returned as a three-man patrol, carrying a dead comrade. But it made no difference, Carter had left the Operations Room determined that if the Gurkhas didn't get Nathan, somewhere somehow, he would.

8

It was curious, Carter thought, how the Chinese had acquired the reputation of being impassive; he had seen them run the whole gamut of human emotion, not once but a hundred times. As Sergeant Major Lim wiped his eyes with his handkerchief, Carter leant across his desk and offered him a cigarette. He lit it for him and glanced at his watch. Half past ten! He could scarcely believe it; he looked at his watch again to check that the second hand was still moving. It was. Just six and one half hours after four o'clock in the morning.

Lim put his handkerchief away and said, "I'm sorry, sir, but it was so . . . so unfair. No other sacks of rice had been blown so far: they were all near where the store had been. I looked. Just that one sack, sir. Everything went according to plan except that one sack of rice!"

"And Hamilton," Carter interposed softly.

"Yes sir. So sudden it was. He was standing on the parade ground looking at some photographs from a Communist pack, then there was a sharp crack, and then another, and he was on the ground. So was Flight Lieutenant Harper. And the boy, sir, the one that was blinded. It is not two months since he was playing football on the padang. I saw him myself."

Carter let him talk; it seemed to be doing him good. Lim was somewhat calmer now, more weary than angry. Still in jungle green, and with a five day growth of beard. He was near the end of his tether. It must, thought Carter, have been a harrowing experience. And Lim's chubby body didn't exactly lend itself to jungle treks, nor to helicopter rides for that matter. Carter knew that Lim had accompanied his brother's body back in the first helicopter lift. When Lim paused in his speech, Carter said, "By the way, Lim, both the brigadier and the commissioner have asked me to ask you if they can attend your brother's funeral."

80

Lim looked horrified as he replied, "Oh no, sir. That's not possible. Not at all! I am having my brother's body flown to Singapore for a very quiet burial." He paused before adding, "My brother has two young children, sir; I want them to live."

Carter had told them this would be the answer.

"And for the same reason, Lim, no medals?"

Lim shook his head.

Halroyd wasted no time in coming to the point. As Carter sat down he said, "We know, Ralph, that a Communist directive exists which instructs civilian comrades to endeavour to obtain employment at military camps, and particularly in Officers' and Sergeants' messes. On the premise that this directive has been obeyed, it follows that if the Communists do not know that you were largely responsible for the success of this morning's operation, they bloody well soon will."

It crossed Carter's mind that if Halroyd hadn't insisted on such a detailed briefing there would have been no reason to suppose that the Communists would have held him any more responsible than anyone else, but he listened attentively. Halroyd went on. "Your social activities must be severely curtailed. You must not make appointments or accept invitations. You must not reserve seats at the cinema, or anywhere else for that matter. In short, you must do nothing which might indicate your future movements." Halroyd paused, "Those friends of yours on Chadwick Estate, the planters?"

"The Erringtons," Carter supplied.

"Yes; you've been seeing too much of them. Cut down heavily on your visits; it's a long drive and a dangerous road, and having got there, you've got to come back. I'm giving you as a police driver and bodyguard a detective named Chan On Yan."

"My orderly can drive, sir," Carter remarked.

"No doubt. But he can't shoot, and Chan On Yan's a marksman. Anyway, you've now got Chan On Yan as driver and bodyguard, and you will go nowhere without him. But this does not mean that you are to sit in the back of your car reading a newspaper, or reading anything else for that matter. And if the car has to stop suddenly, for any reason whatsoever—someone stepping out from behind a parked vehicle, a car coming out of a side-turning, for example—then you must be screamingly alert." Carter nodded glumly. "And another thing," Halroyd continued, "you will not wait at one o'clock in the morning at the junction of Claremont and Davis streets for a Malay waitress called Aminah to emerge from the Jubilee restaurant. . . ."

Not by a flicker of an eyelash did Carter reveal his astonishment that Halroyd should have known this, but even before his astonishment subsided it crossed his mind that there was no reason why Aminah shouldn't be one of Halroyd's agents.

"Chan On Yan can collect her and deliver her at your bungalow as necessary," Halroyd added drily.

For a long moment they sat looking impassively at each other across Halroyd's desk. Carter was thinking, "he forces me to tempt fate by giving unnecessarily detailed briefings, and then blandly tells me that the killer-squads have put the finger on me and I'd better watch it."

Halroyd knew what Carter was thinking, but he regarded killer-squad interest in a police officer measure of that officer's efficiency. One of the bitter fruits of success, in fact. Halroyd broke the silence by asking, "What do you have in mind for the four camps that Brasso's transmitter turned up for us?"

"They could be simply staging posts," Carter observed.

"Even so."

"The 'X' squad should have no difficulty in finding them. We know their positions to within fifty yards, I suggest they set about it right away. When one of the camps is re-occupied they simply nip out of the jungle and tip us off."

"Another mining job?"

"I don't think that's the sort of thing one gets away with twice, sir. But we could consider it in the light of what turns up. The important thing is to locate the camps without the Communists knowing that we have done so."

"Isn't it a bit risky letting the 'X' squad operate on its own, Ralph?"

"How do you mean, sir?"

"Well as one-time comrades, they're not exactly trustworthy."

"They might not be trustworthy but they've sense enough to know that as defectors their chances of rejoining the flock are nil."

"I wasn't thinking of their trying to rejoin the flock. I was thinking that as a group of a dozen armed men, they might be tempted to turn their hand to robbery or rape or something."

"It's possible, sir, but as they're wearing Communist uniforms I don't think it would matter all that much if they did; they'd simply be making more enemies for the Communists. I'm rather more concerned that they might run into a Security Force patrol. As the Communists don't carry wirelesses, our 'X' squad can't. So once they're back in the jungle they're out of touch—and control."

"How long do you propose they should stay in the jungle, Ralph?"

"Three or four weeks perhaps, less if they find one of the camps is re-occupied."

"They don't need to stay that long just to cover the ground covered by Brasso, surely?"

"No, sir, but if all the camps or staging posts are empty, they must stick around until one of them is re-occupied."

"I see."

"But there's one other thing, sir. We know that near some Communist camps, they have their supply dumps; the location of these dumps is known only to senior ranking terrorists, and even they don't know where *all* the dumps are. I'm hoping that when the 'X' squad has located an empty camp, they might also, during the course of a search of the jungle in the vicinity of that camp, locate a dump."

"That's a long shot, Ralph. A very long shot indeed."

"Not all that long, sir. After all, the 'X' squad is made up of ex-terrorists; they should be able to spot likely sites for such dumps. I gathered from a Communist diary that caves are normally used for this purpose."

"And if you find a dump, what then?"

"Well, sir, it depends what's in it; but arms and ammunition can be doctored so that they're lethal to the persons who use them. A rifle barrel, for example, can be put in a vice and bent so slightly that it isn't even noticeable, but it'll blow up in the face of anyone who tries to fire it. Hand-grenade detonators can be replaced with instantaneous fuses. Bren, point four-five and sten ammo can be fixed so that, say every tenth bullet explodes in the breach."

"And who does all this doctoring?"

"The Army. I've already sounded out one of their armament experts, I've been thinking about this for weeks."

"And he's agreed?"

"Of course. He's got a stock of doctored ammo under preparation."

"Well don't let him build up too big a stock; in my view the chances of finding a Communist dump are pretty slim."

As Carter stood up, Halroyd said, "Don't go, Ralph. There's something else."

Carter sat down again, registering the faint note of admonition in Halroyd's voice.

"I was quite astonished Ralph, over the depth of feeling you showed this morning over Brasso, especially as you hardly knew him. Admittedly, when one of one's better agents gets chopped it's regrettable, but in this business, there's no room for grief. One simply cannot afford to let oneself become emotionally involved. I'm surprised that it should be necessary for me to have to point this out."

Halroyd sighed wearily; his voice had held reproof, but it vanished as he added, "I don't know who said it, but it's true for all that, 'to count your own casualties shows a defeatist attitude of mind.' Try and cultivate a clinical detachment, Ralph; when you're planning an operation, pretend you're a surgeon."

Carter stood up.

"And while you're at it, Ralph, dream up an operation involving the castration of Nathan."

Nathan's death or capture, thought Halroyd, was long overdue.

They were naked. Carter lay on his back on the bed, his head in her lap. Nancy Chong sat sideways across the bed, her back supported by the pillow she had propped against the wall.

Carter was smoking a cigarette. Occasionally he tapped it against the ashtray on the floor. He did this without moving his body or turning his head. He didn't want to move: he was content to lie there for ever. Nancy was tying knots in his hair. They had not spoken much. Once she had said, "You didn't turn the shower off properly, I can hear it dripping." But Carter had replied, "I didn't have the strength."

That had been half an hour ago, and the shower was still dripping.

"Were you surprised?" Nancy asked suddenly, breaking a long silence.

84

Carter raised his eyelids and looked at her, "About what?" he asked.

"About me being a virgin."

Carter answered thoughtfully, "Yes, I was."

"Why so surprised? I know lots of virgins much older than me."

"You remember that night in hospital before you left for England?"

Nancy laughed, "Of course." But she blushed at the memory.

"You committed a most unvirginlike act, Nancy."

"I had never done anything like that before, Ralph, really I hadn't." It suddenly became important to her that he should know this.

"Then why did you do it then?" Carter said, looking up at her again.

She shrugged, and her voice sounded perplexed as she replied, "I don't know."

She really didn't know: she was being perfectly honest. She had often wondered why she had done it. It had been a sudden compulsion, and it frightened her. Though she had hidden it from him at the time, she had nevertheless felt deeply ashamed.

"You realise that it was a very serious offence against the Penal Code?" he asked in a severe tone of voice.

"You're joking."

"I most certainly am not," he replied, shaking his head in her lap. "You rendered yourself liable to a maximum sentence of seven years rigorous imprisonment." As Nancy didn't reply, he went on, "It's much more serious than causing death by a rash or negligent act, you know. You can only get a maximum of two years for that."

"Then why didn't you arrest me?"

"I should have done. It was failing in my duty not to have taken cognisance of the offence. It's been on my conscience ever since."

"But you collaborated!"

"Nonsense! I was wounded. Remember? Too weak to resist."

"That was afterwards."

They lapsed into silence for a few minutes, then Nancy noticed a smile on Carter's face and said, "What are you smiling at?"

"Thoughts. Fifteen sixty-five and all that."

"Fifteen sixty-five?"

"Yes. That was the year in which Suleiman the Magnificent launched an attack against the Christian Knights at Malta."

"Really," Nancy replied bemusedly.

"Oh yes. The Holy Fathers rallied the Faithful by telling them that if they died in battle against the Infidel, they would promptly go to a heaven wondrous beyond all the telling of it. On the Muslim side, the Mullahs rallied the Faithful by telling them—in rather more detail—that if they died in battle against the Infidel, they would promptly go to a heaven in which the 'crisis of love,' which was the way they put it, would last for a thousand years. I was just thinking that after about the first five minutes of the thousand years things would start happening: the enamel would start dropping off your teeth, your pubic hair would turn white, your toenails would start revolving. . . ."

"But did they actually believe this heaven business?" Nancy interrupted.

"Of course they did. They died for it didn't they?"

"But both sides couldn't be right. . . ."

"It's not a question of being right Nancy, it's a question of Faith. 'Tis a wondrous thing. Gives one great strength. In the furtherance of the teachings of gentle Jesus meek and mild it gave the Jesuits sufficient strength to overcome the misgivings they might have felt about pouring boiling lead into the apertures of the bodies of heretics. And in earnest fulfilment of the teachings of Karl Marx it gave Joe Stalin fortitude enough to dismiss the deliberate starvation of millions of peasants as a statistic."

"Did Stalin do that?" she asked unbelievingly.

"He did just that. And according to his interpretation of Marxist philosophy he was quite right. Peasants are Capitalists without any capital, like all those people who fill in football coupons and buy lottery tickets."

"How can you be sure that Stalin really did starve those peasants?" Nancy asked. She was on the point of adding, "it might simply be Imperialist Propaganda," but she checked herself as a sudden thought assailed her. She had been on the point of doing the very thing that Lim Tsing Wa had most strongly warned her against. His exact words had been, "Don't take part in any kind of political discussion, comrade. Pretend you're not interested in, and

86

don't understand, politics. Your assignment is to get information: nothing else matters!"

She respected and feared Lim Tsing Wa. Four years before, at high school, he had recruited her into the Party. He had been 22 then, the same age as she was now. He had been her English teacher, and the main organiser of the network of Communist cells throughout the school, but she had never realised how important he was until after the outbreak of the Emergency, when she had seen his picture on the "wanted" posters: $450,000 reward. Dead or alive. For State Committee Member Lim Tsing Wa, boss of the Communist killer-squads in Kepayan. After the outbreak of the Emergency, she had gone into the Nurses' Training College, and lost touch with the Party. Until a year ago when, on the short walk from the hospital to the Nurses' Hostel, Lim Tsing Wa had smiled at her from inside a parked car and said quietly, "Can I give you a lift, comrade?"

He had courage. The dark glasses and the moustache did not do all that much to conceal his identity in broad daylight. She had got into the car and he had driven her to Bukit Merah, where they had left the car and walked along a jungle path to a clearing on the cliff overlooking the sea. It was a very secluded place, and she had half-wondered if he wanted to make love to her; she had hoped he wouldn't as he didn't attract her in that way, yet she stood in such awe of him that she doubted if she could have refused him. She need not have worried; there was only one love in Lim Tsing Wa's life—the Party.

"What would you do for the Party, comrade?" he had asked her.

"Anything, comrade. You know that," she had replied.

He looked out to sea and he told her that he had recently lost the services of a useful comrade—a policewoman telephonist who had been transferred elsewhere. "We need someone in a similar position comrade, and we have selected you."

"Me!" she exclaimed. "What can I do?"

"Yes. You, comrade. You are young, beautiful, you speak English, and you are a nurse. We have noticed that police officers— and particularly European police officers—are attracted to members of the nursing profession. Or perhaps it is that the nature of their work brings them into frequent contact with nurses. It does not matter either way, all you need do is make friends with one."

"But I don't know any."

"But you sometimes see them in hospital, and perhaps you will have one as a patient."

"Perhaps."

"Well, smile at him—and leave the rest to him."

"But even if I do become friendly with one, he won't tell me anything secret," she had remonstrated.

"They all drink, comrade," he had explained patiently, "all you need do is listen. We particularly want to know their future plans, and the future movements of individuals. When you learn something interesting, ring this number and ask for Dr. Lum."

He had written a number in his pocket book, torn out the page and handed it to her, saying, "Don't be surprised if you get a different voice each time, and always speak in a roundabout way as if you are a friend of the doctor."

She had read the number on the piece of paper before putting it in her handbag. Sintra 72109. Then she had listened carefully as he had explained some elementary rules of security. "Don't use the telephone in the hospital: it has its own exchange, the operator might be listening. Memorise that number and burn—don't just tear up—that piece of paper," and so on. She had listened to his advice all the way back to the hospital.

He had not oversimplified her task. Two days later she had smiled at the European police officer waiting outside Dr. Kowalski's surgery. He had returned the smile and had engaged her in conversation. Would she go with him to the cinema? She would and did. Would she like to go to a cocktail party at the Police Officers' Mess? She would. She had stood with him in the Mess eating silly little mouthfuls of food brought round on huge silver trays by a constant stream of waiters. She had noted the disapproval with which the European mems greeted her presence, and the sly winks given to her escort by some of his colleagues. She had particularly noted her escort's answers when one of these colleagues asked him, "Can you be a good chap and stand in for me at morning prayers tomorrow?" "I really can't Bob. I've got to be at Ayer Biru Estate at ten for a natter with the manager."

She had excused herself early from the party and rung Dr. Lum.

"Mr. White would be visiting the manager of Ayer Biru Estate at ten tomorrow; perhaps the doctor could find time to pop over and see him? He'd try? Good!"

It was Nathan who had kept the appointment for Dr. Lum.

She hadn't attended Wainwright's funeral. She'd been too ill. Constant migraine, sleeplessness and a high temperature had kept her in bed for a week. Lim Tsing Wa had omitted to tell her the use to which her information would be put.

Carter stopped talking and looked up at her. Miles away. She hadn't listened to a word. He turned his head very slowly until his lips met her thigh. Gently, he put his teeth to the smooth flesh.

"You bit me!"

"I'm hungry. And you weren't listening."

"You're horrible. And you talk too much."

She lifted his head, bent forward and kissed his lips, then twisted her body until she lay facing him.

Later, in her room in the Nurses' Hostel, she looked at herself in the mirror. She didn't look any different she decided. But she felt different!

She had a curious feeling of elation and excitement, and a wonderment that it had happened as it had. That it had happened at all. She had returned from England just four days previously and had hardly set foot outside the Hostel, spending most of her time unpacking, making curtains and altering the cushion covers. Yesterday afternoon, Dr. Kowalski had telephoned and invited her to a cocktail party at his house the same evening.

"But doctor, I'm not unpacked yet, and I haven't got a dress that's . . ."

"You are coming! Of course you are, yes?" he had boomed.

"All right doctor, thank you, I'll come."

It had been very dull; a staff party mainly, with very few people who were not in the Medical Department among those present. Matron sat looking as if she was mentally recording each drink drunk by each nurse—not that Nancy wanted to drink: she didn't like alcoholic drinks, they gave her headaches, but it was easier to accept a gin and orange from Dr. Kowalski than to try to persuade him that she would be happier with just the orange. It had been very dull—until a man's voice whispered in her ear in Chinese, "As beautiful as ever," and she had turned and found herself looking into the blue eyes of Carter.

"I didn't know you could speak Chinese," she exclaimed.

"I only know one sentence. It's 'you're as beautiful as ever,' and to make conversation I have to keep repeating it, over and over again like a gramophone record with the needle stuck."

He had again spoken in Cantonese.

She was confused. She felt so strongly drawn to him that she couldn't think, finally she was able to say, "Are you fully recovered now?"

"Are you fully recovered now, Ralph?" he corrected, adding "Yes, Nancy, I am. Thanks to your angelic ministrations."

She had blushed redly at that: but he hadn't meant what she had thought he had meant.

After the party he had offered her a lift home and she had accepted. He had a Chinese chauffeur, she noted. It seemed odd to her that he had a chauffeur and yet such an old car. An uncomfortable car too, with no covers on the inside of the doors, so that you could see all the works. They had sat in the back of the car, and with one hand round her shoulders he had said, "My bungalow lies on the most direct route from Dr. Kowalski's house to the Nurses' Hostel, and I've just remembered I left the fridge door open, so we must stop on the way and close it. Mustn't we?"

"I don't believe you," she had said, snuggling up to him.

She had been hoping he would say something like that. He had been so good, so very gentle. So anxious for her.

She lifted her hair and looked at her ears in the mirror. She closed her eyes and felt the lobe of each ear caressed between his lips: first the right, then the left. Heard and felt his quick breath. She opened her eyes and traced the course of the top of his tongue along each eyebrow.

She stood up and switched off the light, then she opened the curtains in front of the french windows and looked out into the moonlight. The moon never shone so brightly in England, she thought, nor did it look so big. It was directly overhead and cast no shadows. The bougainvillaeas showed bottle-green above the whiteness of the lawn. The flat top of the low sandstone wall was a phosphorescent grey; beyond it was the blackness of the valley, beyond the valley, the mountains, purple and silver.

90

Something moved above the sandstone wall. She caught her breath until it flew above one of the bougainvillaeas, and she saw it was a flying fox.

Suddenly the name Lim Tsing Wa came crowding in upon her, filling every crevice of her mind: and with the memory, chill fear. She drew the curtains.

She would have nothing to do with him, she told herself. Nothing. She could not stop the men fighting, but she was a nurse, this was her vocation; her function was to save lives, not cause deaths.

The directive read: "In order to prevent a recurrence of the tragic loss of life caused by the criminal and treacherous act of mining carried out at Camp 4 by the Imperialists and their running-dogs, no major camp is to be left unguarded at any time.

"A minimum of two comrades shall be detailed to keep guard at such camps in the absence of their comrades. Additionally, comrades transferring from one camp to another are to make a careful examination and search to ensure that the camp into which they are moving has not been mined before its re-occupation. In future, camps are to be of a less permanent nature, and more temporary camps are to be built.

"This directive is to come into effect immediately, and is to be obeyed."

It was signed "Lo Heng. Comrade President of the Kepayan State Committee of the Malayan Communist Party," and was for distribution down to Platoon level.

Carter minuted it "for info" to Head S.B., and tossed it into his "out" tray. The buzzer on his desk sounded and he flicked a switch.

"Sergeant Major Lim to see you, sir." Elizabeth's voice.

"Send him in, Elizabeth."

Lim came in grinning. "The 'X' squad is returning, sir."

"Any joy?"

"Oh yes, sir. Two of the camps are staging posts only, sir, but the others have been identified as Camps 2 and 9."

"How big?"

91

"Accommodation for fifty men sir, in each." Lim's grin broadened.

"Occupied?"

"Camp 2 had two sentries guarding it, sir. But no one else. Camp 9 also had only two sentries in it until yesterday afternoon when about forty or fifty terrorists moved in."

"But no Communist dumps?"

"Afraid not, sir."

"Right, Lim. When they get back I want to see them. We've got to move fast now; they'll have to go back early tomorrow morning."

Two hours later, Carter sat in the Operations Conference Room listening to the brigadier. The only people present were the officers of the two Gurkha Companies involved in the operation.

The plan was quite simple: one Gurkha Company would attack Camp 9; Communist survivors would retreat away from the direction of the attack—in the direction of Camp 2. Ambushes would be arranged to discourage them from retreating in any other direction. While this was being done, the other Gurkha Company would account for the sentries at Camp 2. These sentries were to be captured, rendered unconscious by injections, and then left lying around apparently dead drunk. Carter had provided a jar of rice wine for the necessary stage-setting. When the survivors from Camp 9 arrived at Camp 2, they would be ambushed by the second Gurkha Company.

"It is important, gentlemen," the brigadier was saying, "that the path along which the Communist terrorist scouts enter Camp 2 be discovered. You must impress upon your men that they must let the scouts enter, and if necessary, leave Camp 2 unharmed. Make sure that they understand that all Communist terrorists on the move employ scouts, and that there's no point in letting twenty or thirty terrorists get away, just for the sake of killing a couple of scouts. It is the main body we're after; you must find out the track used by the scouts and lay your ambush accordingly. Any questions?"

"To what extent are we to trust these 'X' squad fellows, sir, our guides?" someone asked.

The brigadier looked enquiringly at Carter, so Carter said, "They are trustworthy to the extent that they are committed to us, and if the terrorists ever caught up with them they would be in for a very unpleasant time. But strange things can happen; it is possible that a member of the 'X' squad might be got at; he might be obliged to co-operate in order, for example, to save the lives of his parents, who might be in terrorist hands. But we watch for that sort of thing, and as far as we know it hasn't happened yet. Nevertheless it is a possibility, and if an 'X' squad guide looks as if he's leading you into a narrow defile or a tricky bit of swamp, I would strongly recommend the use of scouts. 'X' squad members must be regarded with suspicion but treated as if they were completely reliable; the suspicion must be completely concealed if their full co-operation is to be achieved."

The Conference Room again, thirty-six hours later. A meeting of Special Branch section heads with Halroyd in the chair.

"The object of this meeting," he began, "is to discuss a Project aimed at the elimination of Emmanuel Nathan. It is called Project Chameleon. Ralph will outline it for you and it will then be open for critical discussion. Go ahead, Ralph."

"We know of only four persons who might lead us to Emmanuel Nathan," Carter began. "Of these, three are women, while the fourth is his elder brother Daniel, a teacher in the Basle Mission Primary School. The women are all rubber-tappers who have borne him children, but there is nothing to indicate that he has any particular fondness for any one of them, nor for that matter, that he is even aware that they have each borne him a child: none of them is likely to be of any use for our purposes, and we are not even sure that he still visits any of them. So, gentlemen, the object of this Project is to acquire control over Daniel.

"At thirty, Daniel is just two years older than his brother, but he could scarcely be less like him; whereas Emmanuel is flamboyant, tough, good-looking and popular, Daniel is quiet and cautious—a rather unhappy, ugly little man whom nobody likes. I have garnered the impression that he feels he has been treated unjustly, in that his merit has not earned for him the promotion he feels it deserves. In only one respect does he compare with his younger brother; he has a mistress, one Khatijah, an Indonesian whore at Kampong Glam whom he visits regularly every week. He has five young children, but his wife is a quarrelsome acidulous bitch with whom he has incessant quarrels—usually over Khatijah,

93

according to gossip among the neighbours. As a schoolteacher, he earns one hundred and seventy-five dollars a month." Carter paused and looked slowly around the table from one face to another before he went on, "We must act on the assumption that somehow or other Daniel is in touch with—or can get in touch with—his younger brother. There are grounds for believing that the two brothers are very close: at school, Emmanuel was in frequent fights protecting the unpopular Daniel, who, though older, was very small for his age, and prior to the outbreak of the Emergency, they were inseparable. Now in order to gain control over Daniel," Carter was speaking more slowly now, choosing his words carefully, "we must send him an anonymous $1,000 note regularly on the first of each month. We will send it to him for such a long period of time that he will come to rely on it. Then he will start spending it: a bigger house, a car, servants and so on. We will in fact be taking him out of his present income bracket and putting him in one higher up the scale. When he has become thoroughly accustomed to his new found standard of living, we will switch off the $1,000 a month and intimate to him that for a little co-operation we are prepared to continue payment. And that is Project Chameleon."

Carter scanned the faces at the table. Only one was expressionless—Halroyd's. The rest showed incredulity, bewilderment, or a total lack of comprehension.

"Well gentlemen?" Halroyd enquired.

"I think perhaps I'm stupid, sir," someone remarked, "I just don't get it. We give Daniel an anonymous $1,000 per month in the hope that he'll spend it, become accustomed to what it can buy, and come to rely on it: then when we think that he is relying on it, we stop giving it to him. But supposing he doesn't spend it! Supposing he just hangs on to it, puts it into the Post Office Savings Bank, or hides it in a mattress for that matter. What then?"

"We lose $1,000 per month," Carter replied blandly.

"And that's all right?"

"Yes of course it's all right," Carter replied with irritation, "it's a sprat to catch a mackerel. It should not be forgotten that there's $450,000 on Emmanuel Nathan's head."

"If Daniel doesn't spend his $1,000 a month, for how long are we to continue to provide it?" someone asked.

"I think from 18–24 months would not be an unreasonable

94

period of time," Carter replied mildly. As this was greeted with derision he went on, "Look, gentlemen. $1,000 is more money than Daniel's ever had in his whole life." Carter banged his fist on the table, "He'll be under a compulsion to spend it!"

"But when we put the screws on him, he simply reverts to his present standard of living and is no worse off," someone objected.

Carter raised his eyes to the ceiling before replying; he was beginning to lose his patience. "In the first place," he remarked icily, "we will not put the screws on him until we know that it's impossible for him to revert to his present standard of living, and in the second place there's nothing simple about a reversion in one's standard of living. It hurts like hell. In fact, if he commits himself, puts the kids in a more expensive school or buys a new house, for example, a reversion to his present standard of living will be out of the question. And to take a lesser example, how do you think his wife will react to the loss of the servant that the extra $1,000 has been able to provide?"

"That brings up another point," someone put in, "how does he explain his new found wealth to his wife?"

"In this part of the world, he doesn't have to," Carter said, "as long as the money's coming in she's unlikely to complain, but there are such things as inheritances and lottery tickets if explanations are unavoidable."

"He might guess where it's coming from," someone remarked.

Carter shot him a withering look and snapped, "How the bloody hell can he? But," he went on more equably, "it'll certainly baffle him. He'll spend months running through all the possibilities, from anonymous inheritances to secret admirers; but not for one moment will he see the Special Branch as his benefactor. He'll learn *that* only when he's on the hook."

There was a long silence, then, "Why $1,000—why not $500 or $1,500?"

"$1,000," Carter explained, "is the lowest impressive figure." Carter was beginning to get worried: he was getting no support.

"How is this $1,000 to be paid?"

"The first will be in an envelope handed to him by a youth in the street; the rest will be in envelopes slipped into the post box at the school gates," Carter replied. "The envelopes will be distinctive, but we cannot risk his opening the first in the presence of others in the teachers' Common Room."

In the silence which greeted his answer to the last question, Carter sensed they had reached the moment of truth: the next few questions would decide whether or not he received any support at all.

Someone said, "I would go along with this except for just one thing. However tight the screws may become I cannot see Daniel co-operating in a plan aimed at the death of his younger brother— a brother with whom, as we have already been told, he is very close. We know for a fact that Emmanuel Nathan has accounted for Wainwright, Lieutenant Hamilton and a Gurkha so if we capture him we'll have to charge him with murder, and . . ."

"Daniel will simply be asked to co-operate in arranging his brother's surrender," Carter began, "but . . ."

"Emmanuel Nathan will never surrender. He can't . . ."

"His capture would be treated as a surrender," Carter went on doggedly, "and in any case, what we know and what we can prove in court are totally different things . . ."

"An Estate Manager actually *saw* him shoot Wainwright . . ."

"At a distance of 180 yards!" Carter snapped. "A European recognising an Indian at a distance of 180 yards. That's all the evidence there is; and there are no other witnesses prepared to come forward. Without corroborative evidence no court is going to convict Emmanuel Nathan of Wainwright's murder on a single solitary identification made at 180 yards. The facts are that even if we wanted to charge Nathan with murder, we simply haven't got a case, unless of course, we capture him in possession of arms. And that's bloody unlikely! But even if we did capture him in possession of arms, we still wouldn't charge him. It's," Carter glanced at Halroyd— "against, at any rate, local policy, to put captured terrorists in court anyway. We're trying to encourage, not discourage, surrenders: and no terrorist is going to surrender if he thinks he's going to be on the receiving end of a murder charge. But apart from all that, if we do capture him, we can sell the idea that he has surrendered and is co-operating. He is a member of the State Committee. He must know plenty. If the Communists think he's co-operating with us, they'll have to evacuate every camp he knows about; and every civilian comrade outside the jungle and known to Nathan will go in constant fear of arrest. Nathan is more use to us alive than

96

dead; so if we capture him, as far as we're concerned, he's sur-rendered. And as far as his brother Daniel is concerned, he's helping us to arrange that surrender."

There was a long silence. Then Halroyd said, "Well, gentlemen?"

"The Project has my support," someone said firmly.

"And mine," someone else added.

But no others. Nevertheless Halroyd was relieved. The best plans are often those which at first sight seem the most absurd, but he had told himself that if Carter achieved the support of just one colleague, then he would give the go-ahead for Project Chameleon. A buzzer sounded, and a red light glowed above the door. Someone had something of sufficient importance to interrupt a conference. An army orderly with a signal.

He came in, saluted, and handed the signal to Halroyd: "Im-mediate and operational, sir," he explained. He saluted and left.

Halroyd read the signal and said, "The attack on Camp 9 has been successful; seventeen Communist terrorists have been killed and four captured. A similar number are believed to have escaped and have withdrawn in a northwesterly direction: probable destina-tion, Camp 2—whose sentries have already been dealt with. A Com-munist dump containing arms, ammunition and supplies has also been found; instructions are awaited as to its disposal." Halroyd looked at Carter, "That last sentence should please you, Ralph," adding as he stood up, "We will go ahead with Chameleon, gentle-men; we've little to lose and a lot to gain."

The conference was over.

9

The attack on Camp 9 had actually taken place when the comrades were at morning parade, and it was surprising that so many of them had got away. But the Gurkhas could not completely surround the camp for fear of shooting their own men, and in any case, surrounding a camp in the jungle is rarely a practical proposition. After the attack, two Gurkhas had followed the tracks of a lone Communist, and these had led them to a cave about half a mile from the camp. A smoke grenade had brought out the man they had been tracking and the cave turned out to be a Communist dump. In accordance with Halroyd's signalled instructions the contents of the cave had been photographed and catalogued. Halroyd and Carter were now going through the final list:

3 Bren guns. 12 Lee Enfield rifles. 8 sten-guns. 6 Thompson sub-machine guns. 18 shotguns. 49 hand-grenades (17 Japanese type). 126 hand-grenade detonators. Approximately 12,000 .303, 10,000 9mm, and 7,000 rounds .45. 1,000 shotgun cartridges. Sundry medical stores—including one gross phials insulin—22 two-gallon cans of kerosene and 87 two-gallon cans of rice.

With the photographs available, it would be possible to replace these stores exactly as they had been found.

"I hope the terrorist who was captured in the dump is being kept apart from the others who were captured, sir," Carter commented. "We must spirit him as far away as possible. We don't want the opposition to learn we've located one of their dumps."

"I can guarantee his silence," Halroyd replied.

"Oh?"

"The Gurkhas who found him did a deft kukri job. The colonel's quite annoyed about it."

"I see."

98

"I think we should doctor all the Brens: I don't like them having Brens," Halroyd remarked.

"We mustn't overdo it, sir. If we doctor too much of the stuff it will all become suspect and they may cease to use it altogether. I think one-third is reasonable."

"I'll settle for two-fifths," Halroyd replied, "and have a very cautious word with Dr. Kowalski regarding the insulin."

"The general idea being that he gives himself a shot in the arm and wraps up?"

"Not at all! The general idea being that he gives himself a shot in the arm and lives, but the mixture's not as strong as it should be, and he becomes a sick man."

"But why not simply give him a shot that'll kill him?" Carter asked.

"Dead, he's replaced; alive, but intermittently sick, he's an encumbrance. He's an important man and has got to be looked after. Whoever's looking after him can't be shooting British soldiers at the same time, can they?"

"True enough," Carter replied, but not liking it.

Halroyd referred to the list and said, "The kerosene?"

"As you know, they use pressure lamps in their camps: we must find out the minimum mixture of petrol and kerosene which will cause a pressure lamp to explode. When they do explode, they go off like grenades—and with the same effect."

"Very subtle of you," Halroyd observed. "I'll get someone on to that right away, and I'll tell the Army to bring out ten tins, in addition," he added, "to all the rice."

"All the rice, sir?" Carter said perplexed, "surely you're not going to doctor that as well?"

"I most certainly am," Halroyd replied firmly, "and, Ralph, the fact that I have done so is not a subject for discussion. I suspect that certain of our senior officers would choke with indignation were they to know. They prefer that the comrades should live, so that they can capture British soldiers in honourable combat—and then, of course, skin them."

"What exactly do you propose to put into the rice, sir?" Carter asked after a moment's silence.

"Bamboo hairs," Halroyd replied curtly, "have you ever heard of them?"

Carter shook his head.

"Well, since our last discussion on the subject of Communist dumps, I've been doing a bit of research, just in case we ever found one, and I came up with bamboo hairs. They grow on bamboo trees and they're like little fish hooks, but almost invisible to the naked eye; once imbibed, they become imbedded in the walls of the stomach and set up an inflammation. The symptoms are almost indistinguishable from those of consumption, except that death usually occurs after from 6–9 months. . . ."

Carter looked faintly shocked and this irritated Halroyd. He leaned across his desk and said in a sarcastic tone of voice, "I would prefer, Ralph, that the Communists made determined and sustained attacks on some of our strong points, so that we could shoot them in the guts in accordance with the provisions of the Geneva Convention; but as they flatly refuse to co-operate in this matter, I have absolutely no choice but to destroy their guts by other methods."

"You look tired, honey," Nancy said, caressing his head in her lap.

Carter laughed, "I was on the point of saying that making love is a tiring business, but I suppose it would be more accurate to say that making love induces a comfortable fatigue."

"But you're not yourself tonight; you're not relaxed, your mind is on other things."

He turned his head and kissed her thigh before answering, "I suppose I need the leave for which I am now long overdue."

"When are you going?"

"In a few more weeks."

"Miss me?"

He took her hand and kissed it, but didn't answer.

She enjoyed such moments more than all others, because she felt he had a real need of her, a need that far transcended his sexual needs.

In this, she was right. But if Carter had been asked about it, he might have said that Nancy's naïvety and gaiety, and her preoccupation with trivia, provided a welcome relief from the bizarre world of cruelty and intrigue that had become his life. Or perhaps in one of his more bitter moods, he might have said

100

she was his main link with sanity—a constant reminder that not everyone in the world was engaged in vicious plots to "eliminate" enemies, nor did they walk in constant fear of death.

But as the weeks passed, even Carter would have had to admit to himself that these explanations did not account for the fact that she was never far from his thoughts. Did not account for the sudden stir of his heart or the dryness of his mouth when he heard her voice on the telephone. Least of all did they account for the fact that whereas, only a few weeks before, he had been aching to go on leave, he now didn't want to go at all and had even postponed it.

They spent all the time they possibly could together. Usually in Carter's bungalow. They rarely went anywhere else. Occasionally, but only very occasionally, they went to the cinema, Carter ensuring that they arrived after the lights had been lowered. Nancy had resented this, suspecting that Carter was ashamed of being seen with her. Carter could not explain that in addition to fears for his own safety, he had also to carry the burden of fear for hers. If she were with him, an attempt on his life would involve her. But he had sensed her resentment, and had taken her to the Sintra Club one Dance Night, thereby displaying not only a casual indifference to certain unwritten Club rules, but also —at least to the discerning eyes of disapproving mems—the fact that he was very much in love.

Carter knew that she had been radiantly happy all that evening, but frequent attendance at Club Dance Nights was simply not on. Most nights were spent like this one in his bungalow, making love, or content merely to be with each other. When they made love, they did so without thought for themselves, each seeking only the delight and pleasure of the other. Thus they achieved moments of mutual ecstasy denied to the selfish and the inhibited.

Carter reached for his watch on the bedside table. "We must get dressed, honey, it's getting late."

He got up from the bed, put on a dressing-gown and went into the lounge. He poured brandy into a glass and went to the fridge for some soda. "I've got to send for Ah Ling," he called, "I'm out of soda."

He didn't want her wandering around in the nude when Ah Ling arrived.

Nancy stuck her head round the bedroom door and said, "He doesn't like me!"

"Who doesn't?"

"Ah Ling."

"Of course he does. He thinks you're gorgeous."

"He never talks to me when he drives me home. On Yan always does."

Carter never drove her back to the Nurses' Hostel, it would have been far too regular a journey. She was brought and taken home either by Chan On Yan or Ah Ling.

She was quite right about Ah Ling, Carter thought. Ah Ling not only didn't like her, but could scarcely hide the fact. Vaguely he wondered why.

When Ah Ling arrived in answer to the servants' bell he was carrying two bottles of soda-water; he prided himself on knowing what was wanted before he was asked.

Carter was fond of Ah Ling; short, bandy-legged and quite remarkably ugly, he displayed a devotion to Carter which Carter sometimes found embarrassing. Ah Ling grinned as he caught sight of Carter's glass; he opened one of the bottles of soda, poured some into the glass, added two lumps of ice, put the other bottle into the fridge and said, "Will that be all, Tuan?"

"Tell On Yan to bring the car round, Ah Ling."

"Yes, Tuan."

Carter watched him pad bandily out—all five-foot-one of him. Two years before, when Carter had begun learning Chinese and was inflicting it on every Chinese he encountered, he had engaged Ah Ling in conversation outside a cinema, discovered he was Cantonese and unemployed, and had recruited him as his orderly. Subsequently, as is the way of it in the Far East, Ah Ling had produced a "younger-brother" who became an orderly for one of Carter's colleagues. Asked by Carter why he permitted his younger brother to dominate him to the extent he did, Ah Ling had explained wryly, "I am not my father's eldest son, Tuan; my younger brother is my father's eldest son: I am only my father's bought-for-money kind of son." His step-father, having no children of his own, had bought him—and then had children of his own.

Carter had sent him to the Police Training School to train as a

102

driver and he had passed the driving course with flying colours. His "younger-brother" could not drive a car.

When he heard the car outside, Carter called, "On Yan's here."

She came out of the bedroom and kissed him goodnight.

"Till tomorrow, darling."

"Till tomorrow, honey."

She said, "Goodbye," and ran up the hostel steps. Under the light outside the door she turned and waved as On Yan drove off. Her footsteps rang along the parquet floor of the corridor. Outside the door of her room she hummed to herself, fumbling in her handbag for the key. She let herself in, closed the door and switched on the light. Behind her a voice said, "You have done well, comrade."

She almost screamed as she turned round.

Lim Tsing Wa smiled at her. Impeccably dressed in a dark blue suit he looked not what he was, but what he had once been—a schoolteacher.

"I am sorry if I startled you," he said softly.

"How . . . did you get . . . in? Why did you come?"

He gestured towards the curtains in front of the french windows. They had not been drawn when she left.

"But why did you come?"

"To talk to you of course . . . comrade." A slight emphasis on the last word.

"But you mustn't come here. You must go. Men aren't allowed in the hostel; especially at night. Matron's very strict . . . I'll lose my job. . . ." She was near to hysteria.

He took hold of her arm and led her to the chair in front of the dressing table.

"Calm yourself. Nobody saw me come and nobody will see me go." His voice was quiet and held a note of mild reproof.

She sat slumped in the chair, gazing at the floor. Suddenly she looked up at him, "Please go," she pleaded.

Lim was beginning to feel annoyed; to get in had been difficult and risky. This was not the sort of reception he had anticipated, nor was it one he was prepared to tolerate. Something was wrong. His alertness sharpened. With him, as with Carter, mistrust was a mental reflex. "You forget yourself, comrade."

She looked down at the floor as she whispered, "I'm sorry, but you frightened me."

"That's better," he replied. His attitude changed immediately as he sat on the edge of the bed facing her and said confidingly in urgent tones, "I have not much time. You have done well, comrade, the police officer with whom you have become so friendly is of the highest importance; many of our comrades lie dead because of his cunning. But why have you not 'phoned Doctor Lum?"

She shook her head vaguely. "I had nothing to tell him."

"You could have told him you were back, and were in touch with Doctor White!"

"Doctor White." The code name he had given her for a European police officer. Any European police officer.

As she didn't answer he leant forward and shook her knee, "Well, why didn't you?"

"But you didn't tell me you would actually kill that police officer, Wainwright."

He hit her across the mouth with the back of his hand. His voice quivered with rage: "Are you out of your mind, comrade! Who are you to question the ways of the Party? You have one function and one only—to obey!"

He watched her with angry contempt. She sobbed quietly into her handkerchief. She had shown promise: it was he who had recruited her into the Party; but she had erred in his judgement, she lacked the fibre of the true revolutionary. She came of bourgeois stock: her father was a chemist. Too soft and weak for the Party. Before the beginning of the armed struggle, and at more than one State Committee meeting, he had argued that the recruitment targets among the High School students were too high. "Their parents can afford to pay their school fees," he had said, "their social backgrounds are against them. We are sacrificing quality for quantity, comrades; we need to recruit from among the peasants." Lim Tsing's father was a padi-planter; there had been no school fees to pay for Lim. Lim had won scholarships. Had this snivelling creature in front of him shown any faith in the Party at all, she would be in the jungle; not in this over-furnished room, with its soft bed, its carpet and its flowery curtains. But she could still be used.

When she raised her eyes, he said, "Comrade, your orders remain the same. You will 'phone Doctor Lum and tell him of Doctor White's movements."

"But . . . but he never goes anywhere," she replied dejectedly.

"You went dancing with him at the Sintra Club!" he snapped.

This information had reached him too late to be acted upon. It had come via one of the Club stewards; but it had been the first intimation to reach him that she was back from England, and, more importantly, was apparently on close terms with the very man he most desperately wanted to kill. He mentioned it now, just to discourage her from lying, and to show her that the Party had many eyes and ears. Many.

She was horrified. They were watching her, and by watching her they were also watching Ralph. "But we only went once," she said in a tiny voice.

"But comrade, you must have known where he was going to take you that night." Lim's voice had a sharp edge to it.

"I didn't, truly I didn't," she pleaded, twisting her handkerchief.

"And your dress, comrade, did you wear an ordinary dress to the dance?"

"No. No." She shook her head. "I wore the dress he bought me," she gulped, "but I keep it in his room. He told me to keep some clothes in his room in case we accepted an invitation to go anywhere at short notice."

So it was like that! And one of *his* recruits. And not just with a European, but a European Special Branch officer. *The* European Special Branch officer. Carter. No doubt he found her an improvement on the Malay waitress. Lim recalled how very nearly he had succeeded in exploiting *that* situation. And perhaps Carter had discarded the waitress in favour of the snivelling slut in front of him. The irony of it. And now she was the only way he could get at Carter, and his failure to kill Carter had earned criticism. Perhaps she had become infatuated with Carter. Such things happen. Perhaps a little persuasion would be necessary for her to do her duty. He hoped it would: persuasion appealed to him.

"The Party has many ways to exact obedience, comrade," he remarked blandly.

"But what can I do?" she asked, her voice still a whisper.

"Your duty, comrade."

"He never tells me where he's going," she assured him with

urgent shakes of her head. "And," seeking about for any excuse, "he won't be here much longer."

"Why not?"

She was appalled at her mistake. She had told him something about Ralph. But it was too late now. "Because . . . because he's going on leave. To England."

"When?"

"I don't know . . . in a few weeks time."

Lim Tsing Wa leant forward, his face very close to hers, "Listen, comrade, you will find out when he is going on leave and how he is going. If by train, by what train and to where; if by plane, by what flight, and if by ship, which ship and when. And then you will 'phone Doctor Lum. Do you understand, comrade?"

She nodded numbly.

He stood up, walked to the light switch and switched it off. In the sudden darkness she heard his voice, "I will keep in touch with you, comrade."

She heard a curtain being drawn, saw the faint blur of his shadow against one of the french windows; heard the click as he opened it. Then he was gone.

Dazed, she sat in the dark for a long time, until gradually she became aware of the loud chirp of the cicadas and the croak of the frogs. He had left the window open. She got up and closed it, stood looking out into the darkness. She wondered if he was still there; if so, he was just another shadow among many. His would be a small shadow. He was a small, almost frail, little man.

She drew the curtains and turned on the light, then stretched herself on the bed and wept. After several minutes she sat up, dried her eyes and gazed dully at the 'phone beside the bed. She must tell Ralph. He would help her out of this nightmare. Would tell her what to do. She reached for the 'phone.

But how could she tell Ralph? What could she say? I helped them kill Wainwright and now they want me to help them kill you. But I love you and I don't want to help them. Oh yes, Ralph, I was in a Communist cell; but I was only eighteen and I only joined because my school friends joined.

But Ralph hated the Communists. He had once said something about the Communists being the only people left who had faith and a cause, and how everyone else was forced to keep his powder dry. He often said things she didn't understand.

How could he be expected to understand that the cell meetings, the demonstrations and prohibited newspapers had all been . . . well, fun, really. How could they have led to this?

"Her duty."

To help kill people? A nurse? She had not wanted Wainwright killed. She hadn't thought about it. But she would not help them kill anyone again. And especially not Ralph. They could kill her if they liked.

She stood up and switched off the light, then walked to the curtains and drew them. It was getting light; the purple shadows were becoming grey. She could no longer hear the cicadas and only occasionally a frog. The creatures of night were fleeing at the approach of day. Suddenly they were gone. The birds began song, singly at first, then in twos and threes. She almost laughed aloud as a black and white cat, fur staring, ran across the lawn and jumped into one of the bougainvillaeas. Matron's bull terrier, "Crafty," was in hot pursuit but admitted a grudging defeat as it circled the tree. She opened the french windows, crossed the tiled verandah and walked slowly across the lawn.

Carter pressed the switch on his desk in answer to the buzz; "Yes, Elizabeth?"

"Chief Inspector Lau to see you, sir."

"Send him in, Elizabeth."

Carter considered Chief Inspector Lau to be the most efficient member of his staff; thirty-five years old, he never smiled and rarely spoke. "Still," thought Carter, "when one has three wives and three different families to put up with, one couldn't have a great deal to smile about." It was whispered that Chief Inspector Lau held high office in the Wah Kee secret society, and while this could never be proved it was almost certainly true. His position and rank in the police—notable though they were—did not account for the speed and efficiency with which his mildest requests were gratified: and not all the attempts on his life were considered attributable to the Communists. The Ang Bin Huoy—the other big Chinese secret society—fought a relentless battle with the Wah Kee for control of the criminal world. Tall, gaunt and expressionless, he answered Carter's gesture

107

towards the chair on the other side of the desk by sitting down, folding his arms and waiting to be invited to speak.

"I've bad news for you, C.I.," Carter's eyes twinkled, "you've been demoted. From number one, to number two."

This was a reference to the fact that whereas all killer-squad priority lists had hitherto always started with "The People's Enemy Lau Yui Ming," the most recent list to be acquired had started with "The People's Enemy Carter."

"I must congratulate you, sir, on your promotion." Lau's face was absolutely deadpan, his voice toneless.

Carter looked at him speculatively: one never knew with Lau whether he was being bitingly sarcastic or utterly sincere. It was certainly a waste of time to try to draw a grin from him.

"Well, C.I., what can I do for you?"

"I have a friend sir, who has a friend who lives in the Kong Lee squatter-area." When Chief Inspector Lau spoke he moved only his lips; he made no gesture, didn't move his facial muscles and conveyed no message with his eyes. He was very successful with interrogations. Prisoners found him unnerving. Carter could well understand why as Lau continued, "This friend of my friend is a young man, and he is getting married soon. The woman Wong often visits the Kong Lee squatter-area: she gives lectures and delivers babies. When the young man's new wife is pregnant, she can show much fear of childbirth. Perhaps the woman Wong can be persuaded to deliver her child also. A Special Branch party can also be present at the happy event."

For a brief moment, Carter looked at him, then deciding that the words "happy event" were unconscious humour, swung his chair round to look at a map on the wall behind him.

"The Kong Lee squatters are due to be resettled in a few months time, C.I."

"They do not have to be, sir, it can be postponed."

This was true. A word from Halroyd and the Resettlement Committee would simply postpone it, they had far more squatters to resettle than they could cope with anyway. In fact, thought Carter, the Resettlement Committee could be asked to concentrate on the squatter-areas on either side of the Kong Lee. This would mean that Betty Wong would have fewer squatters to whom she

108

could lecture, fewer babies to deliver. More chance of delivering the baby that mattered.

Carter looked at Lau impassively, wondering at his motives. So far, the message had been, "A junior member of the Wah Kee is getting married." Perhaps the Wah Kee had told him to get married—just to get Betty Wong. Lau hated the Communists—one can have only hatred for those who make repeated attempts on one's life. Perhaps also a senior member of the Wah Kee had a rubber estate near the Kong Lee and the squatters worked on it part-time, and he didn't want to lose their labour. Perhaps the Wah Kee was running profitable illicit stills in the Kong Lee. No. The Communists wouldn't permit that. Perhaps, perhaps, perhaps. Perhaps Chief Inspector Lau simply wanted to kill Betty Wong. She was a worthy prize, regardless of Lau's other motives—if any.

"The newly-weds will need cool nerves, C.I."

"The wife need not know, sir, and the thought of the $450,000 reward money will be a source of great strength to the husband."

"And fertility also, C.I." Matching Lau's cynicism.

"He has already proved it, sir."

"What, with his future wife?"

"No sir. With an Indian girl."

"Whom he doesn't want to marry?"

"Oh no, sir, she is Indian, and in any case she doesn't live in the Kong Lee squatter-area."

Halroyd was reading the reports from his various sections. He was in high good humour. There was no doubt about it at all; the tide was turning, the statistics proved it. The Communists, though not actually losing, were beginning to stop winning. Surrenders were a trickle—but a steady trickle: attacks on Security Force positions were becoming fewer and were not being carried out with their usual vigour. Except in one area. The area allotted to the 3rd Company of the Kepayan Regiment. The Company under the command of Khan Hock Loi. "Tommy Loi," Halroyd mused, "has become more important than Nathan." After all, Nathan had lost his whole Company: he now had only an independent platoon, two members of which had already surrendered, having—so they said—no confidence in the leadership of an Indian.

It was a pity about Camp 2, he thought. Everything had gone

perfectly, the attack on Camp 9 had accounted for about half a platoon, and the sentries at Camp 2 had actually been caught having breakfast; they hadn't even seen the Gurkhas until the kukris had been at their throats. Then they had been given injections and had been left slumped on a bench by the parade ground; a couple of tin mugs in their hands and a jar of rice wine within handy reach. But though the Gurkhas had waited four days the survivors from Camp 9 hadn't shown up. This had left Halroyd with the problem of what to do with the two sentries. If they had simply been captured and taken away, any Communists who showed up at Camp 9 later would have thought they had surrendered and would not have used the Camp again. Halroyd had solved the problem by instructing the "X" squad to arrange things so that it looked as if the two sentries had shot each other in a drunken brawl. He recalled with irritation Carter's subsequent indignation.

"Did the Army agree to this?" Carter had asked.

"No. It was carried out by the 'X' squad after the Army had gone."

"But those sentries might have co-operated."

"They were more use dead than alive, Ralph. They were captured armed and in uniform, and were therefore legally liable to to be hanged anyway, even if they wouldn't have been. The most important thing was that the Communists didn't find out that we knew about Camp 2."

"With respect, sir," Carter's voice had been icy, "you put me in charge of the 'X' squad and then give it direct orders without my knowledge. . . ."

"Let's face it, Ralph. If I'd asked you you wouldn't have agreed."

"I wouldn't and I don't now, sir, and for the additional reason that with two rotting corpses in the Camp, the Chinese Communists will regard the place as being unlucky or haunted or both, and will never use it again anyway."

And that had been that.

But for all that, Halroyd thought, it was quite extraordinary how some people felt about killing enemies in cold blood. One could trick them into a mined camp and blow them all up, one could doctor their weapons so that they blew themselves up, but to kill a couple of them for a clear tactical advantage turned people purple

110

with righteous indignation. Curious how so many people just couldn't understand that to have qualms about killing prisoners might be to deny oneself a tactical advantage, which, if properly exploited, might result in, say, the elimination of a whole Communist platoon. A Communist platoon, which if not so eliminated, might at some time or other put paid to a couple of dozen British soldiers. British soldiers who—but for one's qualms—would not have died.

"In the final analysis," Halroyd concluded, "qualms cost lives."

Still, Carter had been quite right about the sentries; the Chinese *were* notoriously superstitious, he should have thought of that himself.

He deflected one of the switches on his desk, heard Carter's acknowledgement and said, "Pop in in a minute, Ralph."

As Carter sat down on the other side of his desk, Halroyd said, "Any developments as a result of Daniel Nathan's receipt of his first payment?"

"No, sir," Carter replied, "but I don't expect any; not yet anyway. Payment was made as planned and now we simply make our payments regularly and sit back and await developments."

"What is your guess—your private and personal guess, that is—as to how long we are going to have to sit, Ralph?"

Carter shrugged. "For what it's worth, fifteen months. But it could be more."

"But if it hasn't worked by the end of two years, we quit?"

"It depends entirely upon what he does, sir. We might even make a discovery that would justify continued payments for another six months."

"Such as?"

"Well suppose that as of right now he's got debts we just don't know about, say, debts amounting to $6,000; wouldn't that justify a six months extension? All we'd be doing for the first six months is paying his debts."

They sat looking at each other for a moment, then Halroyd said, "Thirty long patient months."

Carter nodded. He said equably, "That's right."

"And thirty thousand dollars!"

"Yes, but we can always reduce the reward on his brother's head, sir, devalue him. Bring it down to $400,000."

Halroyd frowned at Carter's facetiousness. "Well at least it's a plan, and I even think it's going to work—although I hope to God it doesn't take thirty months. But we've nothing at all for our three other major targets."

"There's Lee Chin's insulin, sir," Carter pointed out. "That should fix him eventually: I can't imagine it's for anyone else. None of our surrenders have any knowledge of anyone else using insulin, or so they say."

"True enough," Halroyd agreed, stroking his chin thoughtfully.

"And C.I. Lau has come up with a jolly little plan for the elimination of Comrade State Committee member Betty Wong."

After Carter explained the details, Halroyd remarked, "I can't believe that there's nothing in that for Lau."

"Neither can I, sir. A large cut of the reward money perhaps? It's anybody's guess. But the important thing is to get Betty Wong."

"It's Tommy Loi I want to see chopped. We've had no surrenders from his Company at all. Not one!" Halroyd put in, adding, "It's a pity it wasn't his Company and not Nathan's that clicked for that Camp 4 deal."

Carter looked thoughtful as he replied, "We certainly don't seem to have much on him: popular at school, highly intelligent, and a boxer—an unusual combination. Educated at Sintra, Singapore, and then Cambridge. Spent the war years in the U.K., returned immediately afterwards with all the right Communist connections and promptly became a journalist for some Communist rag. Founded the journalists' union, and within fifteen months rocketed to General Secretary of the Trades Unions and Political Party's Council of Joint Action. In short, sir, he went to England as an innocent apolitical schoolboy intent only on his studies, and returned as a trained and dedicated Communist."

Halroyd sat back in his chair, his hands behind his head, and said, "Strange isn't it? Britain makes its worst enemies in Britain."

They looked at each other. They both knew the reason. Then Halroyd asked, "Have you been on to London about him?"

"Of course, sir. But they weren't very helpful, I'm afraid. Apparently he only spent a year or so at Cambridge, then he went to live in London. His last known address disappeared in the blitz."

"That's useful," Halroyd remarked gloomily.

112

"But I'll check on all that when I'm on leave, sir."

"No reason given as to why he left Cambridge?"

"None at all."

They sat in thoughtful silence for a few moments, then Carter went on, "The only other lead is the Lieutenant Colonel Cresswell connection. I think I'll go and see him on my way through Singapore."

"You'll find the connection could scarcely have been closer," Halroyd remarked drily, and as Carter looked blank added, "Tommy Loi's queer. He was a close associate of Cresswell's. Cresswell paid his university fees in and no doubt his passage money to the U.K. Work that one out."

"But Cresswell was in Intelligence during the war. . . ."

"The double lives which queers are forced to lead endows them with a special aptitude for intelligence work, Ralph," Halroyd put in placidly.

"But he's on neither S.B. nor C.I.D. records as such. . . ."

"Being queer, and not being on either S.B. or C.I.D. records as such, shows that in Intelligence he had found his rightful metier," Halroyd explained patiently.

"But . . ."

"No buts, Ralph." Halroyd took his hands from the back of his head, put his elbows on his desk, and sat with his hands supporting his head as he went on in the voice of one whose patience has been tried to the limit, "Would you mind, Ralph, just assuming that he *is* queer, and then taking it from there."

Carter looked put out, but said, "If you insist, sir."

"I do insist."

"The only other lead on Tommy Loi," Carter observed, deflecting the conversation, "is that his mother has been in receipt of two bunches of roses."

"And what's that supposed to signify?" Halroyd asked irritably.

"I don't know, sir. But on each occasion the roses were delivered by the Keng Wah Nurseries, with nothing to indicate who had sent them."

"This comes from Sergeant Major Lim's contact in the coffee-shop?"

Carter nodded.

"Maybe she gets them from her sister on her birthday." Clearly Halroyd didn't think much of roses as "leads."

"It's not her birthday, sir; at least not according to the records of the Registrar of Births and Deaths. And in any case, the roses didn't arrive on the same day each year, but on dates some two or three weeks apart; if they'd come from a sister there would have been a card with them saying so, wouldn't there?"

"So?" Halroyd's voice indicated a marked lack of interest.

"So I think they came from Tommy Loi, sir. The Keng Wah Nurseries are slap bang in the center of Loi's operational area. I'm convinced they came from him. On neither occasion were they accompanied by anything other than a printed card bearing the name 'Keng Wah Nurseries,' and," he added significantly, "on each occasion his mother displayed emotion on their receipt."

"How," Halroyd asked sarcastically, "does one display emotion when one receives a bunch of roses?"

"I don't know. I suppose one clutches them to one's bosom and gazes soulfully at the ceiling. Anyway, that's how his agent put it to Sergeant Major Lim."

Halroyd looked at Carter for a long moment before saying, "And that's all?"

"It is for the moment, sir."

"Well, Ralph, when bunches of roses achieve a *real* significance, perhaps you'll come and tell me about it."

There were times, Halroyd thought as he watched the door close, when Carter let his imagination run away with him. Even if the roses were from Tommy Loi it didn't mean anything. A permanent watch couldn't be kept on the Keng Wah Nurseries, and even if it could it didn't follow that Tommy Loi ordered his bloody roses personally.

114

10

Carter sat in the back of his car as it wound through downtown Sintra on his way back to the office after lunch. Chan On Yan never used the same route twice running and always sought to avoid the main roads—where taxis, buses, trishaws and even bullock-carts were everywhere—but avoidance of all the main roads was not possible. They were crawling along a main road when Chan said, "There is a man, Tuan, a young man, behind us on a bicycle."

"Yes?"

"I am not sure, but I think he has followed us round three sides of a block. A Chinese, Tuan, who wears a white shirt and black trousers."

"Then take the first right and the first left, On Yan."

"Tuan."

They had discussed this many times. The danger was at the traffic lights. They had to stop.

Carter slid forward deeper into his seat. The backs of both the front and rear seats were ¼-inch steel plate; it was tough on the springs of the car, but a wise precaution nevertheless. He took his Colt from its shoulder holster and fully cocked it. Then he adjusted the small side window—which was not a window but a mirror—to see if he could see "the young man" in its reflection, but was unable to see him from the off side of the car.

He saw that the first set of traffic lights would be green, and swore softly. He didn't want his would-be assassin to give up the chase—if there were an assassin and it were a chase. But as they approached the next lights the green changed to amber. There was a van and two civilian cars in front of the queue. If he didn't . . . Chan's eyes were glued to the driving mirror; "He is still with us, Tuan," he said quietly as he adjusted the driving mirror to keep the young man in focus.

115

Carter slipped the catch on the door at his side, heard Chan do the same, and say, "Now!"

Through the window at his side Carter watched the young man come into his line of vision, saw him stop diagonally four feet away, and take something from his shirt. As Carter kicked the door open it caught the rear wheel of the bicycle and the young man swivelled round. Carter saw the twisted mouth, read the fear and the hate, clearly saw the pin being pulled from the grenade. He fired at the half-open shirt not two feet away, felt a moment's surprise at the way the young man rose in the air as the bullets tore into him before he fell backwards from the bicycle and his dead hands dropped. As Carter ducked round the front of the car he thought he heard the grenade give a metallic clunk. He dived into a shop doorway and then he heard it explode—not a terribly loud noise, more of a crack than a bang. He turned on one elbow to gaze in sheer disbelief as a heavy lorry, its driver dead or unconscious, casually ran through a queue at a bus stop, tore away a pillar in an arcade and buried itself in a shop window beyond. Slowly, almost reluctantly, the façade of the three-storey building collapsed.

Trembling, Carter pulled himself to his feet; for a moment he stood gazing at the billowing cloud of dust, half expecting it to burst into flame, as perhaps the gas from a broken main found a lighted joss-stick which only a moment before had stood before some private shrine: then, bawling at Chan to ring the hospital, he ran towards the cloud of dust.

Davidson burst into Halroyd's office. "A terrible business, Charles. Terrible! Already twelve dead, mostly women and children. And there could be another half-dozen under the rubble." Davidson paused, "Carter will have to go, Charles, he really will."

Halroyd had stood up at Davidson's entrance: now they faced each other across the desk. Men in positions of power. Men whose decisions governed many lives and affected many more.

"May I suggest a tot of brandy, sir?" Halroyd asked politely, adding, "This has been a most upsetting business."

"Er, yes. Thank you, Charles."

Davidson was surprised. Halroyd was rarely so comradely.

As Halroyd went to a cupboard and took out a bottle of brandy and two glasses, he was planning his tactics. Davidson, he thought,

116

was at his most dangerous. As long as everything was going along reasonably smoothly, he was content not to interfere with those who were doing the work. But like all weak men, let something go wrong, and he tore in with an insane compulsion to exert his authority. He'd take up a stance on some absolutely vital issue and then nothing on God's earth, least of all common sense, would move him from it. Some issue like Carter's transfer—at a time when Carter's services were bloody nearly indispensable.

As Halroyd handed Davidson a glass of brandy he remarked mildly, "It wasn't exactly Carter's fault, sir."

"I know that," Davidson replied irritably, "but if Carter wasn't here it would never have happened."

"Someone has to be at the top of a killer-squad death list, sir."

"Yes, but it's never been a European officer before."

This was true enough. In Halroyd's eyes it reflected only credit on Carter. Nevertheless it was not the time to make the point, so he contented himself with saying, "It could have been worse, sir."

"I don't see how," Davidson snapped.

"It could have been a petrol tanker, sir," Halroyd pointed out blandly.

"It's bad enough as it is. Where is Carter anyway?"

"In his bungalow, sir. He showed up here covered in blood and dust and looking a bit wild-eyed. . . ."

"I thought he wasn't hurt," Davidson interjected.

"He wasn't, sir. It wasn't his blood. I gather he went a bit spare at the scene, trying to lift half-ton blocks of masonry off dead bodies with his bare hands, and so on. He's in a state of shock, I'd say; not so much because of the attempt on his life as because of what it led to. I told him to have a hot drink, a hot bath, and go to bed."

"Best thing he could do," Davidson agreed, "but I think he'll have to go, Charles. And not because of this hand-grenade business either," he added darkly.

"Oh?"

"Well this woman of his, this nurse. The Matron's been on to me about Carter leading one of her girls astray, and my wife's been saying, 'Claude, it's serious. If one or other isn't transferred they'll get married. I just know they will. You must *do* something.'" Davidson half-mimicked his wife's voice.

Halroyd could have laughed out loud as Davidson revealed what

117

Halroyd thought was his main reason for wanting Carter transferred, but he remarked, "I don't think it's all that serious, sir. Carter's human after all, it's not surprising that he should seek solace in a spot of female company; and she's rather a nice dish, if I may say so, sir. Few Chinese are quite so full-breasted."

"Oh I know all that, Charles," Davidson agreed in his man-of-the-world voice. "A chap's got to sow his wild oats. We've all done it. It's all right as long as it doesn't get serious. Marriage and all that. It would ruin his career."

Davidson didn't mean that marriage would ruin Carter's career: he meant that marriage to an Asian would ruin Carter's career. And it would. Because the Davidsons of this world, and particularly the Mrs. Davidsons would make sure it did.

"Why doesn't the Matron get her transferred?" Halroyd enquired.

"She's tried, but Dr. Kowalski flatly refused to consider it. You know Stan! He said something about Carter needing this nurse, that he was too introspective and too much of a loner for his own good."

"Really," Halroyd remarked in surprise, "did Stan say that?"

"So Matron tells me."

"I don't think he's right. He's certainly not the hail-fellow-well-met type. I'd say he chooses his friends rather than accepts them; he's very friendly with Harry Vardon. . . ."

"Yes. But most of his friends are Asian, Chinese and Malays and whatnot. He's an odd bird. It's almost as if," Davidson paused, "as if he preferred their company to ours, Charles."

To Davidson, this was totally incomprehensible.

"I've wondered about that myself, sir. But have you noticed that all his Asian friends are about his own age, are all well educated, wealthy or of Malay royal blood? They're interesting people in their own right, and a man like Carter would naturally enjoy their company."

"Even so."

"Well he hasn't been mixing with them for quite a considerable time now, sir. He almost never goes out, and when his beloved's on night-duty he plays Russian poker in the Mess. . . ."

"Yes, that's another thing!" Davidson snorted. "I'll have to clamp down on that. They play for high stakes. That bloody idiot Arthur Collings lost a month's salary to Carter last week."

118

Halroyd laughed. "There's a lot of skill in Russian poker, sir. And if Carter can hold his own in a Chinese school, Collings would be easy meat; but as far as Carter's concerned, sir," Halroyd continued, more serious, "he's going on leave in a few weeks. I'll bring it forward if you wish; but I'm not altogether sure that it would be wise to pack him off straight away. It might possibly give the impression that we'd been panicked into it: couldn't protect your own officers and so on."

Davidson looked thoughtful for a moment. "Yes of course. I hadn't realised that he was due for leave so soon."

"Well he is, sir," Halroyd assured him. "And that will solve the other problem too. Absence makes the heart grow fonder, you know —of the boy next door."

Davidson stood up. Relieved. There wasn't any problem any more.

"But tell him to use a bit more discretion, Charles. Not to take her to Dance Nights and so forth. Oh, and I'll double the guard on the Mess."

"And I'll make sure he doesn't leave it, sir."

Bad news travels fast. Carter had been sitting in his bungalow no more than half an hour when the door opened, and Nancy—still in her nurses' uniform—stood for a moment looking at him; but even as he made to stand, she had her arms round him, her head in his lap.

"Oh Ralph, Ralph, Ralph."

"Nancy, please! I'm all right. It's all over now. All over."

As she knelt in front of him, sobbing, he caressed her hair. She raised her head and he felt tears in his own eyes as he read the depth of grief on her face, saw her tears. "You must go, Ralph. You must, must. Go!" She let her head drop into his lap before continuing, "They will kill you, Ralph. I know they will kill you. I know!"

She raised her head again and looked at him as she said between sobs, "Go, Ralph. Please, please, please, for my sake, please go!" Again she buried her head in his lap.

He placed his hands under her hair and caressed the back of her neck as she continued to cry.

People, Carter thought miserably, were always telling him to go. Only an hour or so before, the young Chinese mother who had

119

torn herself away from the group of wailing women, her broken child in her arms . . . "It is you, you whites, who have brought this evil upon us. Why don't you go?" she had spat.

It was the first time his knowledge of Chinese had been a burden. The eyes of the little Tamil girl: huge, round and unblinking; watching him uncomprehendingly as he tightened the tourniquet above her knee. There had been nothing below the knee. But she hadn't even whimpered. He should have pinned a note to the tourniquet stating the exact time it had been tied. But he had no pen. He had used the pen to make the tourniquet. It had been a nice pen: Nancy had given it to him. But wouldn't it have been kinder to let the little girl die? Think of all the things that would be denied her. If she lived, of course.

Nancy had stopped sobbing. He moved his hands to the front of her neck and raised her head with the palms of his hands; "No more, darling. It tears me to pieces when you cry."

She looked up at him through her tears.

"You must get back to the hospital, darling. I'm sure they need you." He ran a finger along one of her eyebrows as he added, "Duty first, darling."

She tried to smile, but it was too difficult.

"How did you come? By taxi?"

She nodded.

"Is it still here?"

She found her voice and gulped, "I suppose so."

He smiled down at her. God, how he loved her. "Such extravagance; every tear costs you five cents."

He put his hands under her arms and lifted her gently to her feet as he stood up. They clung to each other for a long minute; then stood hands joined, looking into each other's eyes.

"You smell of brandy," she said wanly.

"And," he smiled, "you, darling, taste of salt."

Halroyd had said, "Nobody is to know when you are going on leave, and you will do nothing at all which might indicate that you *are* going on leave. You will not make a point of ensuring that all your bills are paid. You will not send your heavy clothing to the dry-cleaners, or have inoculations to bring your Health Card up to date. You will not make any bookings, hotels, air-passages or any-

120

thing else. *I'll* make those arrangements. The only thing you will do, is be fully packed and ready to leave at a moment's notice two weeks from today."

Carter had replied, "But I'm not due to go for another month."

"You will be fully packed and ready to go at a moment's notice in precisely two weeks from today."

That had been nearly three weeks ago.

As Carter sat down in the chair in front of Halroyd's desk, Halroyd handed him an envelope. "Your new passport."

Carter opened the envelope and took it out. It was not a new passport. It was at least three years old. The passport of a man who did a lot of travelling. Carter's photograph was on page three. Page two told him he was an insurance investigator, and page one told him his name was Claude Masters.

Carter expressed disgust. "Claude! What happened to him anyway?"

"Air crash, I believe," Halroyd replied, adding as he handed Carter a sheet of paper, "Practise your new signature a couple of dozen times, then sign page two. That page is always stuck in, we left the space for your signature blank, of course." Halroyd watched Carter practising his "new signature." He said, "You should never scrawl a signature, make it clearly legible, scrawls are easier to forge."

Carter signed the blank space at the bottom of page two, then turned the pages of the passport. Looking across at Halroyd he said, "But I've never been in Djakarta; if some zealous immigration officer starts questioning me about Djakarta, it's my lot!"

Halroyd sighed heavily, "How many zealous immigration officers *have* been in Djakarta!" Handing Carter another envelope he said, "Your health card and air tickets; they're open from Bangkok onwards, you can make your own bookings from there."

Carter opened the envelope and examined the air ticket closely, read the name "Claude Masters" said, "Christ. I'm booked on a plane leaving Singapore tonight!"

"That's right. I said nobody was to know when you were leaving. That included you."

"But I wanted to see Cresswell in Singapore."

"Well see him on your way back. By the way, get all the jabs you need in Bangkok—all the ones you are supposed to have had anyway. If you show up at London Airport with Yellow Fever, having been inoculated against it three weeks previously, you'll start a hell of a panic. There's an armoured car waiting for you: hop into it, collect your gear from the Mess, and press on to Singapore."

"In an armoured car!" Carter almost wailed, "all the way to Singapore?"

Halroyd stood up and extended his hand, "Have a good leave, Ralph." As Carter opened the door, Halroyd said, "You needn't go back to your office."

"But . . ." Carter began.

"But what?"

"Er, nothing, sir."

Carter had been on the point of saying that he was halfway through a letter he was dictating to Elizabeth, but he supposed it didn't matter all that much anyway.

On the way to the Mess he wished that Halroyd wouldn't carry things quite so far. "A false passport, for Christ's sake!" The Communists weren't all *that* efficient! Or were they? He found himself wondering about it. "They have long arms these Communists."

Back in his bungalow he scribbled a note to Nancy:

Darling Nancy,
    Sorry honey. I've gone on leave. I didn't tell you because I didn't know myself till ten minutes ago.
    Perhaps it's better this way. No time for tears. I'll write you often.
    I love you darling, so much, so very, very, much.
                                                    Ralph.

He gave the envelope to Ah Ling to give to her.

Carter's departure had given her courage. He was safe. Coming back from the post office one evening Lim Tsing Wa fell into step beside her.

"Well, comrade?"

She had steeled herself for this, she was frightened, but she was also defiant. "He's gone!" she snapped, with a toss of her head.

"I know, comrade," he rasped, "but you did not tell us when he was going."

122

She stopped walking and rounded on him. Speaking loudly and sharply she said, "Because I did not know!"

As she fumbled in her handbag he looked round anxiously: the very last thing he wanted was anything in the nature of a scene; anything which might attract attention, there in the street.

As she produced Carter's letter from her handbag, she said angrily, "And another thing. He didn't even know himself. So there." She held out the sheet of paper. "Go on, read it for yourself; then perhaps, you'll believe me."

He read it by the light of a nearby street lamp and handed it back without comment.

She snatched it from him, "Now leave me alone . . . comrade." She spat the last word over her shoulder as she turned and walked away.

He watched her go in anger and astonishment. Surely she was old enough to remember the fate of the women who had consorted with the Japanese? Tied to lamp posts and snipped to death with scissors. There was always a day of reckoning. Did she imagine that she herself would be immune from such retribution? "I love you darling, so much, so very, very, much." He almost choked with disgust. How was it possible for a well-educated *Chinese* girl to sink so low. Did his smell not sicken her? Did not the touch of his hairy skin make her gorge rise? And her insolence: her contemptuous disregard for his orders. She would pay for both.

123

11

"There's an Assistant Superintendent of Police, a Mr. Carter, to see you, sir."

Galvin welcomed the interruption; he had very few visitors, very little to distract him from the job which had held his attention for thirty-five years. College Records.

"Send him in, Miss Wallace, send him in. Don't keep him waiting. Oh, and Miss Wallace . . ." he called as she closed his office door.

She put her head round the door with just the faintest hint of weariness and said, "Yes, Mr. Galvin?"

"Bring in the file on the Chinese boy. You know the one, Chan Kan or something; some name like that. A 1939 entrant."

She returned a moment later with Carter. Galvin was surprised to see that Carter was so young, he had expected someone twice his age. They shook hands.

"Sit down, Mr. Carter. Sit down. I got your letter. It's the second enquiry we've had about the Chinese student in less than a year. Security people, I believe; he must be important. . . . Oh, thank you, Miss Wallace . . ." as she gave him the file.

Carter waited until she had gone before saying, "He *is* important, Mr. Galvin. He's a very senior officer in a Communist guerrilla army." Carter believed in arousing interest when making enquiries.

Galvin's eyes were almost as round as his mouth. "That does surprise. It really does surprise me! I'd never have thought it. Never!"

"Now why does it surprise you, Mr. Galvin?" Carter was anxious to get him talking: people rarely know the value of what they know, one simply has to listen.

"Well I remember him you know; he was such a quiet inoffensive little chap. . . ."

Carter left an hour later. He was not a great deal wiser. The file had shown that Khan Hock Loi had arrived at Cambridge in

124

September 1939, and had left in October 1940. A week after his departure he had written asking that his ration book be forwarded to him c/o Mr. Albert Brown, 48 Slade Terrace, Bermondsey. This had been done, but there was no answer to the covering letter seeking the reasons for his abrupt departure. The next letter had been from Command H.Q., Delhi. A Captain Cresswell seeking news of Mr. Khan Hock Loi, in statu pupillari. The reply referred to Khan Hock Loi's abrupt departure from college, and quoted his forwarding address. In his next letter—from New Guinea—Major Cresswell, M.C., stated he was deeply concerned about the welfare of Khan Hock Loi, that he had had no replies to his letters addressed to 48 Slade Terrace, and that he would be most grateful if he could be advised should any information come to hand. There were several such letters from Cresswell, and one could follow the course of the war in the Far East from the addresses on them—right up to the last one, Lieutenant Colonel D. Cresswell, D.S.O., M.C., Imperial Hotel, Tokyo.

Although he had not learned a great deal that he didn't already know, Carter didn't consider the visit a waste of time. He had done some useful spadework. Galvin would let him have photostat copies of "Every letter, Mr. Carter, every letter." And another specimen of Tommy Loi's hand-writing and style was always welcome. Galvin had also promised to find out the reason for Tommy Loi's abrupt departure from college. Carter had pointed out that someone must know, "His gyp, for example, or even one of the gardeners; such people are often a mine of information." Carter smiled at the memory of Galvin's conspiratorial enthusiasm; "Will it be all right if I mention that he is now a very senior officer in a Communist guerrilla army?" Galvin almost certainly would find out, Carter thought; he hoped he would, it must have been something important: a man with Tommy Loi's intelligence wouldn't throw away a university education without a very good reason.

The same afternoon Carter was in Lee Chin's old college listening to Miss Crisp. They stood facing each other on either side of a counter in a large office. It was late in the afternoon and apart from themselves the office was deserted. "Perhaps," thought Carter, "that was why she hasn't invited me into her private office."

In this, Carter was quite right. Miss Crisp frequently told her girls that one must not only conduct oneself with propriety, but one must never give cause for the slightest suspicion that one could possibly be acting otherwise. She'd been telling her girls this for thirty years.

As she adjusted her spectacles firmly on her nose she said, "I'm awfully sorry, Assistant Superintendent, but such records as we still have concerning Lee Chin are purely academic; they simply show that he took a first class honours in the Modern Languages Tripos in 1923 and that's all."

She really was sorry: it was one's duty to assist the police to the best of one's ability. "When I got your letter, Assistant Superintendent, I hunted high and low through the old administrative files—but to no avail. They simply do not go back so far. It was," she explained apologetically, "rather a long time ago. But when you mentioned on the 'phone at lunchtime that he was now a very important Communist, I went straight to the library and went through all the college magazines from 1919 to 1923: and no more than half an hour ago, Assistant Superintendent, I discovered this!" With a triumphant flourish she produced an old college magazine from beneath the counter. "And here, Assistant Superintendent, he is!"

She thrust the open magazine under Carter's nose. Carter found himself looking at a photograph. The Socialist Club Committee 1921–22: their names listed underneath. Third from the right in the front row, staring woodenly at the camera—Lee Chin.

"And, Assistant Superintendent, the man sitting next to him, on his left, was until very recently one of His Majesty's Ministers. Mr. Arnold Whitely. Now surely he can tell you all there is to know about Mr. Lee Chin!"

Carter thanked her effusively.

Ex-Ministers are more accessible than Ministers. Carter had had no difficulty in obtaining an interview with Mr. Arnold Whitely. On the telephone, Carter had explained his mission to Whitely's secretary. There had been a minute's delay and then she had asked, "Would four o'clock this afternoon suit you, Mr. Carter?"

It had.

A glass of brandy soda in his hand, Carter was listening intently to Whitely as they sat in a bar in the House of Commons. In his mid-fifties, short, stout and balding, Whitely had about him

126

the suave self-assurance of the successful politician. He spoke slowly and carefully—looking at Carter's face almost anxiously from time to time, as if it were important to him that he should be clearly understood—as he recalled the distant past.

"Of course, we were young then, younger even than you are now. Idealistic. We could not foresee that the very struggle for power to put our ideals into effect would inevitably erode the ideals themselves: nor would we have conceded that the cloth of idealism has to be trimmed before it can become the cloak of responsibility—even less that idealism is a luxury that power itself cannot always afford." Whitely gave a wry smile. "We were all Communists! We weren't by any means all members of the Party, but we were wholly sympathetic towards the Communist Movement. To us, it represented organised humanity trying to get up off its knees! Communism held a magnetic attraction for us. It inspired us. It gave us hope. It was such a glorious *idea!*"

He stopped speaking as he took out a solid gold cigarette case and held it out to Carter; Carter took a cigarette, waited for Whitely to take one, and lit both. Whitely puffed smoke towards the ceiling and said, "My word, how they have corrupted it! Who could ever have foreseen that the Sermon on the Mount would pave the way for the Spanish Inquisition?

"Lee Chin was simply one of us. Highly intelligent, reserved, except"—Whitely emphasised the word—"except when making a speech. He was so articulate and could speak with such concise clarity, that I've never forgotten him. In fact I'll freely admit that my first, well, public speeches at any rate, were modelled on his; even to using his exact words on occasion."

"Was he popular, sir?" Carter put in.

"Not exactly popular," Whitely replied thoughtfully, "he was too reserved; but I'd say he was highly respected. Oh, and he was extremely sensitive," he added emphatically.

"You seem quite definite about that, sir."

"Well I am. After you rang this morning, I was thinking about him, and I recalled one particular committee meeting of the Socialist Club. It was in my final year and I was chairman. As I recall it, we were making the arrangements for the Club's Annual Dance night—which hall to hire, how many tickets to print, what band to have, that sort of thing—when someone happened to ask Lee Chin who he was taking to the dance. He looked a bit taken aback for a moment, and then said shyly that he'd been thinking of asking Miss Wall—one of the committee members," Whitely explained. "She was there at the meeting. Well she'd been doodling on a piece of paper, not paying much attention to what was going on, but when she heard her name mentioned she looked up and said, 'I'm not going to the dance with a Chink.' Lee, of course, got up and walked out."

"Did he come back?" Carter asked.

"Not to that meeting, but he came to subsequent ones. Of course, she hadn't meant to say it. It was simply a spoken thought. One of those thoughts which by-pass the censors of the mind and emerge as speech. It happens to all of us occasionally. But that only made it worse."

"Did she apologise?"

"Well yes. But I seem to recall her telling me that Lee had gravely thanked her for such a revealing insight into the British mind."

Carter raised his eyes to the ceiling for a moment, then asked, "What happened after that?"

"Well I think it left its mark on him; I seem to remember that he became even more reserved, but I wouldn't be altogether sure about that as I left shortly afterwards." Whitely paused, stubbed out his cigarette in the ashtray on the table and said, "And that, Mr. Carter, is all I can tell you about Lee Chin. Now you tell me about the Emergency in Malaya."

Fate decreed that Carter should walk into Bermondsey East Police Station at precisely the same moment as Police Constable Colin Brown came on duty. They arrived at the Charge Room door together. P.C. Brown opened the door and stood aside for Carter to pass. Carter said, "Thanks," walked in and stood in front of the Charge Room sergeant on the other side of the counter.

He produced his Warrant Card and said, "I'm trying to trace a character called Albert Brown whose last known address was 48 Slade Terrace. But I understand that Slade Terrace went up in the blitz. I was wondering if you happened to know anything about him; it would save me the trouble of ploughing through voters' lists and whatnot."

Behind Carter, P.C. Brown said, "You're talking about my Uncle Bert, sir."

Carter turned and Brown added, "What's he been up to now, writing threatening letters to Archbishops?"

"It's not him I'm after," Carter replied, "It's a Chinese who lived with him during the war. . . ."

"Now you're talking about my Uncle Tom."

"Your Uncle Tom?" Carter was amused.

"That's right sir. At least I always called him Uncle. I was only a kid at the time, eleven or twelve I suppose, I saw a lot of him. I went along every day to collect the daily papers. He used to put the street numbers on, and I delivered them. Earned myself six bob a week. He was a nice bloke was Uncle Tom. Everybody liked him."

"He was living in your uncle's house?" Carter asked.

"That's right sir."

"But how did he earn his living?"

"He was a sorting clerk in the post office I believe. But Uncle Bert'll be able to tell you all about that," he paused and added, "if he wants to, that is."

"Is he likely not to want to?" Carter enquired.

"Just as likely as not," was the answer. "He's a touchy old devil. Argumentative. Always expressing opinions that people don't want to hear."

"Such as?"

"Well I heard him myself one night, in the local. Talking about the Working Class being its own worst enemy. 'They're all giving short change,' he said, 'and they're giving it to each other. It's not a welfare state any more, it's a warfare state. Civil bloody war.' That's the sort of thing he says sir, all the time."

"I thought he was a Communist." Carter remarked.

"Well he was. Can't say that he is now though." P.C. Brown looked as his watch and continued, "Now's the time to catch him. Before the pubs open. Mansfield House, Flat number twenty-two. They're new council flats. Just a few moments walk away."

A moment after Carter had pressed the bell on the door of Flat twenty-two it was opened by a short, almost bald little man in his sixties. Medium built, shirt sleeves rolled up, braces. As he looked

Carter up and down his head was tilted on one side aggressively. He kept a thumb in the top of his trousers and one hand on the side of the door as he said, "Well, what can I do for you?" He didn't take the cigarette from his mouth as he spoke.

"I'm looking for a Mr. Albert Brown. . . ."

"You're talking to him."

"Well," Carter produced his Warrant Card and held it out saying, "I'm an Assistant Superintendent of Police from Malaya, and I'm making enquiries about a one-time acquaintance of yours, a Chinese called Khan Hock Loi."

"Are you now!"

Brown took the card, examined it carefully, suspiciously. Looked at Carter's face; compared it with the photograph in the Warrant Card.

Carter took it back from him, said, "It's genuine. I made it myself."

Brown asked, "What's with Tommy Loi?"

"He's a very senior officer in the Communist guerrilla army in Malaya and I'm trying to save his life."

A long pause. Then, "You reckon?"

"Yes. I'm trying to arrange his surrender and," Carter shrugged, "it's therefore necessary for me to know all that there is to know about him." He paused and added, "I think perhaps you know more about him than most."

Brown took the cigarette from his mouth and said, "Yes, I suppose I would, wouldn't I." The head took a further tilt, the eyes still hostile.

And now, Carter thought, he's going to say, "Well fuck off!" But Brown pushed his head forward and said, "But if he doesn't want to surrender, then you'll have to kill him, won't you?"

"That's right," Carter agreed, face deadpan. He added placidly, "Tommy Loi's very good at causing the deaths of British soldiers."

Brown nodded, slowly, thoughtfully, "Yes, I can believe that. He'd be good at whatever he turned his hand to, would young Tommy." Brown visibly lost some of his hostility; stood looking at Carter appraisingly, running his tongue backwards and forwards behind his lower teeth; seemed to reach a decision, "Well then, we'll have a little chat about him, shall we?"

When they walked into the living-room Brown bawled in the

direction of the kitchen, "Ethel! We been raided by the police. Bloke here says he's Assistant Superintendent, but he don't look old enough to me. Wants to talk about Tommy."

A jolly little fat woman with grey hair and glasses emerged from the kitchen, drying her hands on a tea cloth. She was about Brown's age, Carter guessed. "Pleased to meet you, Mr. . . . ?"

"Carter."

"You'll have to excuse him Mr. Carter." She shook her head, "he's never learned to control his tongue; it's nearly seen the death of him more'n once."

With that she disappeared into the kitchen, mumbling apologies.

Brown nodded to an armchair beside the fire. Carter sat down and watched him as he sat in the other armchair. Brown was looking at the ceiling, nodding to himself occasionally. Carter waited for him to speak. A minute perhaps; then Brown said, "So little Tommy Loi's selling his life for the Party?"

Carter nodded.

"Well he ain't the first, and I don't reckon he'll be the last; not by a long chalk, neither."

Brown leant down and picked up a poker from the grate. He poked crevices in a large piece of coal; watched the flames climb the crevices, said, "Me and Ethel gave our whole lives to the Party. Every penny we could scrape together; every minute we could spare. Worked for it, lived for it, loved it." He looked up from the fire to Carter's face as he went on, "You see—and a bloke with your background might find this difficult to understand —we *was* the Party, Ethel and me. And thousands like us. Dedicated, we was. We had fire in our bellies, and we was . . ." He stopped, searching for words. "We was the *spirit* of the Party!" He addressed the fire again, "I nearly said we was its soul." He paused for a long moment, then in a thoroughly dispirited tone went on, "Coming to think of it, we was its soul. Then somehow or other the Party lost its way like. So it lost us and all! I suppose what happened was it started off by being *ours,* and ended up by being *theirs*. But maybe it was theirs all the time, and we was just kidding ourselves. For thirty bleeding years! . . ."

He sat looking at the fire in silence for a minute or two: an old man—who had given his life to the Party. Then he shook off his depression, "Well to get back to Tommy Loi. I was on the stations at the time and I'd been allotted Waterloo. A passenger boat had come in from the East, and I was waiting to see what the train brought in in the way of young hopefuls. . . ."

"I'm sorry, Mr. Brown," Carter put in, "but I'm not with you."

Brown gave him an expression of contempt, "An Assistant Superintendent and you don't know that! Well I'll have to spell it out for you then, won't I? Lots of students come from all over the world to London. Black, white, yellow and brown; the lot. Don't they?"

Carter nodded.

"They gets out of the train in the biggest and busiest station they've ever seen in all their bleeding lives, and they're hopelessly lost. They don't know no one: they don't know what to do, where to go, nor how to get there, do they?"

Carter shook his head in agreement.

"Well then, that's where the Party steps in. There's members of the Party who steps in and gives them a helping hand. No one else does, do they? So the only people what helps them are members of the Party. And there ain't no colour bar in the Party, neither," Brown added significantly. "So two things has happened; the Party has made contact with a young hopeful, and the young hopeful is grateful to one of its members. And another thing, that Party member is very likely the only Britisher that the young hopeful knows, isn't he?"

Carter closed his eyes, pursed his lips and nodded agreement.

"So now you know what I was doing at Waterloo, don't you? Very successful it was, and no doubt still is. It happens at all the big ports and all the big railway stations; and the airports too, now, I suppose. Very successful indeed."

Brown accepted the cigarette that Carter offered him, lit it and went on, "Well then, there I am at Waterloo, and I sees this young Chinese kid standing there with a bloody great suitcase on either side of him and looking around like a scared rabbit. Plain as the nose on your face what had happened. Whoever was going to meet him hadn't showed up. Well I lets him wait a bit like, then I goes up to him and says 'Anything I can do for you, son; you look a bit lost like, to me?'—or something like that.

132

" 'Oh no, sir,' he says, 'someone is coming to meet me.'

" 'Who's the someone?' I says.

" 'Someone from Cambridge; they said so in the letter,' he says.

" 'Well they're a bit late ain't they,' I says, 'and you won't get a train to Cambridge tonight. And in any case, you've got to go to another station if you're going to Cambridge.'

"Well he looked really scared at that, so I says 'What are you going to do if the bloke from Cambridge don't show up?'

" 'Oh, he'll come; it says so in the letter. I've got it here, look.' And he fumbles in a pocket and produces the letter. So I reads it and right enough it says that Mr. So and so is to meet him at Waterloo and put him on the train for Cambridge. So I hands him back his letter and says, 'How long have you been waiting now?'

" 'Hour and a half,' he says. 'Right,' I says, 'I'll go and have a beer, and if he don't show up by the time I come back you can come and spend the night with me and the missus. And tomorrow morning I'll put you on your train to Cambridge. You can't stand here all night, can you?'

"Well after I'd had my beer, I comes back and sure enough he's still there, so I picked up one of his bags, and off we go. It was as simple as that. If I've done it once I've done it a thousand times, one way or another. We had a constant stream of them. Of course, we was in Slade Terrace in those days, but it ain't there any more."

Brown spoke to the fire again, "The German bombers did more slum clearance in six months than any government had done in fifty bleeding years."

He leant forward and poked at the fire; became lost in his thoughts.

"So you took him home that night?" Carter said, breaking a silence that had become too long.

Brown looked up at him, "Yes, that's what I said. Ethel gives him a cup of cocoa and I shows him up to the spare room. In the morning, Ethel takes him up a cuppa and finds him reading a copy of the 'Worker' which just happens to be lying around." Brown paused, "I'll tell you about the 'Worker'; it's never thrown away you know, not by a member of the Party at any rate.

It's always left on a seat in a bus or train for someone else to read." Brown turned and tapped Carter's knee as he said, "The Party, sonny, doesn't miss a trick."

"I've already found that out," Carter replied, "but what happened after that?"

"Nothing for a long time. I'd put him on the train for Cambridge like I'd said, and a few days later we got a 'thank you' letter, and at Christmas we got a Christmas card, and that was that. For about a year at any rate. Of course, in the meantime the blitz had started. Well I was in the Posts, see; many's the time I went to deliver a letter and there wasn't no door to push it through. No house neither, come to that. Well this afternoon I comes home and sees Tommy Loi's cases outside the front door. I recognises them, see, because I carried them once. Well I knew what had happened. When he arrived old Mrs. Barrett had heard his knock at our door, and had taken him into her house, see, to wait until I come home. Being as how there wasn't nobody in ours because Ethel was a clippie and was at work."

Brown stopped again, went off at another tangent, "First steady job she'd ever been able to get," he said reminiscently. "Funny, isn't it. How the Capitalist system has to have a war before it can give full employment. Now where was I?" Looking round at Carter.

"Tommy Loi was in Mrs. Barrett's," Carter prompted.

"That's right. So I calls round, knocks, and when Mrs. 'B' opens the door I says, 'You got a visitor for me, Mrs. "B"?' And she says, 'Yes I have Bert. Must be one of your young hopefuls, I suppose, but he don't look like he's got much hope in him.'

" 'How come?' I says.

" 'Well I can't hardly get a word out of him; he just sits there,' she says.

"Well Tommy hears my voice and comes out, and I says, 'Hallo Tommy boy, you come to see your Uncle Bert?'

" 'Yes I have,' he says. 'I've got no money and nowhere to go, Mr. Brown.'

"He always called me 'Mister,'" Brown explained, "such a polite little bloke he were. So I says to him, 'Well you need your Uncle Bert then,' I says, 'he knows all about not having any money, believe you me. Come on in.'

134

"So of course he follows me in and I leaves his bags in the hall. 'Sit down,' I says, 'and I'll just make a cuppa.' But he just looks at me and says in a funny sort of voice as if he was forcing himself to speak. 'Before I can come into your house, Mr. Brown; there's something you should know about me.'

"So I thinks to myself, hallo, hallo, hallo, he's on the run—not that that would have made a hap'orth of difference to me, even if he had been," he assured Carter, "just the opposite in fact. So I says, 'Out with it Tommy; I'm dying for me cuppa.'

"So he looks at me like I'm a bleeding ghost and he whispers, 'I'm an homosexual.' Just like that he said it.

"'You what?' I says.

"'I'm homosexual,' he whispers again.

"So I looks him up and down and says, 'Well go on.' And he looks a bit blank like and says, 'There's nothing more to go on about, Mr. Brown.'

"'You mean that's all you have to tell me,' I says; and he whispers, 'Yes, Mr. Brown.'

"So I looks him up and down, 'Don't you never go frightening me like that again,' I says. 'Gave me quite a turn. I thought you was going to tell me something important; like you was on the run. Got caught pinching Winston's cigars; or joined the bleeding blackshirts. And you kept me from my cuppa and all.'" Brown paused, sat back in his armchair before continuing, "And you know what, the tears started streaming down his face and he sat down at the kitchen table, put his head on his arms and cried like he was fit to die. Well I'm not much good at the woman stuff, but I just has to put an arm round his shoulder. He looked so bleeding miserable; what with the tears streaming from his funny little eyes and all."

Carter closed his eyes for a moment: Nancy's head in his lap, "You must go, Ralph."

"So I give him more than a cuppa: I give him a good tot from a bottle of brandy that Ethel always keeps in the house for emergencies. He told me later it was the first strong drink he'd had in his life." Brown gave his attention to the fire once more, and went on, "Of course, we got the story out of him. He'd been in bed the previous night with some mate of his when a mob of others comes in and catches them at it. They paints

135

targets on them. Red, white and blue. Tommy at the back like, and the other bloke at the front." Brown paused, said, "That's what they done," and lapsed into silence.

Carter handed him a cigarette, lit it for him, and waited for him to go on. Brown took several thoughtful puffs. "So he spends the night trying to clean himself; collects all his traps together and catches the first train to London. Gets a taxi and tries to get a room. But the landladies don't want to know him, see, because he's the wrong colour, so after trying half a dozen places and getting the bird in each like, he comes to number forty-eight, because it's the only place he knows. Well, as if that wasn't enough, when he gets there, the taxi bloke overcharges him a couple of quid. 'That'll be four pound fifteen,' he says. 'But the meter only says two fifteen,' Tommy says. 'The bags is one pound each,' the taxi bloke says. So Tommy gives it to him. How would he know any different?"

Ethel came in, a glass of beer in each hand.

"What do you think you're on?" Brown asked indignantly, "my old age pension doesn't run to buying drinks for the law."

She handed a glass to each of them, then stood with her hands on her hips looking down at her husband. "You earned your old age pension, I must say," she said scornfully, "caused more strikes than you could wave a stick at, you did."

"Well you helped me," Brown replied hotly.

"Didn't have much choice, did I?" she replied with spirit. "And if I hadn't joined the Party, I'd never have seen you from one week's end to the other."

With that she turned and disappeared into the kitchen.

"You've got to know how to handle them," Brown confided with a tap on Carter's knee. "Down the hatch."

"Cheers."

Brown licked his lips appreciatively, "There's nothing like it. Now where was I? Tommy had come home, hadn't he."

Carter nodded, noting the significance of the phrase.

"Well of course I got on to him and Ethel did the same: 'Go back to Cambridge,' we said. 'Don't be stupid! Get yourself educated so you can fight them with their own weapons. It's you that'll suffer if you just quit! It's you what'll lose a university education!' We pleaded, argued, swore and bullied him for days on end. But he had a hard streak in him had Tommy. Once his mind was made up, then that was it. And he had too much pride to go back; he felt too humiliated like. So in the end we just had to accept it, because there was nothing we could do about it. It were a wicked bloody shame though. Wicked. So I gets him a job in the Posts as a sorter." Brown flicked ash into the grate and said, "Oh, I forgot to tell you, didn't I? I had to get a quart of turps to help him clean himself. I stood him in a bath in the kitchen cleaning him down. In the middle of a bleeding air raid and all. Poor little sod! And his clothes! Half of them had to be slung out. Ruined with paint. And clothes weren't so easily come by, especially not during the war, neither.

"He had a little Indian rug, you know; I'd slung it in the dustbin because it had had about half a pint of wet paint spilled on it, and I thought it was finished, but Tommy spent hours in the back yard cleaning it down with turps. Came up all right in the end. He said as how some English friend of his had given it to him in Singapore, and it was the only thing he valued. We've still got it. Come and have a look at it."

Carter followed him into a small bedroom and they stood looking at the "Indian rug" beside the bed. It was about four feet by three. "It's not Indian, Mr. Brown," Carter said, "it's Persian." Going down on one knee, Carter picked up a corner of the carpet and counted the stitches in one inch, nodded appreciatively and stood up. "These things are made by the nimble fingers of little children, Mr. Brown; adult fingers are too clumsy for such work," he explained. "And here," pointing with the toe of his shoe at the corner of the pattern in the carpet, "is what you might call the deliberate mistake. To make it perfect would be to offend Allah. It's probably worth about thirty pounds I'd say; I'd give you twenty for it without any hesitation whatsoever. It's a miniature Bokhara Princess."

Brown looked at him in surprise, "Would you now?"

"Yes I certainly would. It might be worth much more, but it can't be worth any less."

"And you'd give us twenty nicker for it?"

"Yes. If you want to sell it, that is."

Brown went to the bedroom door, called "Ethel," and came

137

back. They stood looking at the rug for a moment, then Ethel arrived, still drying her hands.

"What is it?" she asked.

"He wants to give us twenty nicker for Tommy's rug," Brown explained.

They exchanged a long thoughtful glance, then Ethel said, "I'm not sure as how we ought to part with it, Bert."

Bert said nothing, and the three of them stood looking at the carpet, till Ethel said, "Have you any special reason for wanting it, Mr. Carter?"

"Not really," Carter replied, "but when I saw it just now, I suddenly realised that I knew who'd given it to him. A man I shall be visiting in Singapore when I return in a few weeks time. I thought that perhaps I might give—or rather, sell—it back to him."

"A doctor, wasn't it?" Ethel asked.

"A barrister," Carter corrected.

"That's right, so it were. A nice looking chap a bit older than you. Tommy showed me his photo. Of course, he'll be older now, won't he?"

She looked at her husband and said gently, "We could do with the twenty Bert." But her voice sounded doubtful as she went on, "And it looks a bit out of place here, really."

Brown stretched out a hand to Carter, "Yours it is then, for twenty nicker."

They shook hands on it.

Later, in the local, Carter sat with Ethel and Bert at a glass-topped table; the "Indian rug" in a brown paper cylinder propped against his chair. They were still talking about Tommy Loi. "Of course I introduced him to the Party," Brown said in answer to Carter's question, "that's why I met him in the first place, come to that. He took to it like a duck takes to water, did Tommy. Lapped it up! Within six months he could tell you all there was to know about Marx-Leninism; the political crimes of Trotsky, and the reasons for Stalin's policy of not assisting Mao Tse Tung. I even found myself asking him questions, and if some joker in here got you tied up with some knotty political problem you went to Tommy for the answer. He was that clever, was Tommy.

And it didn't take the Party very long to start treating him special like. He was ordered not to have any obvious connection with the Party. Not to attend Party meetings. Not to deliver any more of the 'Workers.' Not even to join in any of the 'front' organisations. Nothing to do with the Party whatsoever! There'd be weeks when we hardly saw him. Weren't there Ethel? Of course, I'd of known what was going on even if he hadn't told me: they'd put him in one of the Eastern cells see. I had to go up to his room one day and happened to see what he was reading. 'Jungle survival for R.A.F. aircrew,' 'restricted' what a laugh! And things like, 'The mechanism and maintenance of the Mk I Bren gun.'"

Brown paused, said, "Judging from what he's up to now, the Party gave him the right kind of training, eh?" He emptied half a glass of brown ale before going on, "And he could use his mitts too, could young Tommy, when he had to. R.A.F. bloke in here was rude to him one night: twice the size of Tommy he was, but he found himself sitting on his arse wondering what had hit him. Tommy was that quick you didn't even see him move. He got himself a cheer. Everybody liked him, he was that polite. There was," he paused, looking for the right word, "there was a sort of softness about him, a sort of gentleness, somehow."

12

As the Malay porter closed the door of Carter's hotel room in Singapore, Carter found himself looking at the 'phone on the bedside table. All he had to do was pick it up and say, "Get me long distance," there would be a short delay, then a voice would say, "Number please," and he would answer, "Sintra 222." "I'll put you through." Another delay, and then another voice, "Sintra hospital," and Carter would say, "Put me through to the sister in charge of ward three." And then he would hear her voice. He looked at his watch, 2:30, she'd be just back from lunch. He knew her routine: her letters told him everything. Every day. He smiled; sometimes twice a day.

The temptation to ring her was almost irresistible. But there were such things as telephone operators. One in Sintra exchange and one in the hospital. He did not need Dr. Stanislaus to tell him that the Party had long arms. If he rang Nancy, the Party might arrange a reception for him on the road back from Sintra Airport.

But there was a call he could make, must make. He picked up the telephone directory and ran his finger down the C's. D. R. Cresswell. Lt. Col. D.S.O., M.C.

A female voice answered his call, "Lieutenant-Colonel Cresswell's office."

"May I speak to Lieutenant-Colonel Cresswell please?"

"May I have your name sir?"

"Carter. I'm an Assistant Superintendent of Police."

"I'm afraid Mr. Cresswell's in court, sir. May I take a message?"

"Yes. Ask him to ring me back. I'm at the Ritz. Telephone number 53217: extension 417."

"Can you state the nature of your business, sir?"

"Have you written that number down? Extension 417."

"Yes sir. . . ." Impatiently.

"Just tell him I want to talk to him about a man called Khan Hock Loi."

"Khan Hock Loi?"

"That's right."

Carter put the 'phone down. It was important that Cresswell knew the extension number. If Cresswell simply rang the Ritz Hotel and asked for Carter, they would tell him that no one of that name was in the hotel. Carter had booked in as Claude Masters. Had to, as they always asked for your passport. But Cresswell might ask to see his Warrant Card later on—which was in the name Carter. Claude Masters wouldn't have had a Police Warrant Card.

The 'phone woke him shortly after five.

"Mr. Carter?"

"Speaking."

"I understand that you are an Assistant Superintendent of Police and that you want to speak to me about someone called Khan Hock Loi?" The voice was terse and not at all friendly: in fact it contained a distinct note of annoyance.

"That is so." Remembering that Cresswell was an Unofficial Member of the Legislative Council, Carter added, "sir."

"Well I cannot for one moment imagine Mr. Carter, what the subject matter of our discussion could be. I hardly knew, and I can scarcely recall, Khan Hock Loi. And I certainly haven't seen him since I had the burden of presenting him with some kind of trophy at a school Sports Day long before the war, if my memory serves me. That is all I can recall of Loi, Mr. Carter."

"I see."

"So, Mr. Carter, no good purpose would be served by discussing Khan Hock Loi with me."

"The purpose, sir, might possibly be called one of life and death—Khan Hock Loi's."

A long pause.

"I'm afraid you'll have to be rather more forthcoming, Mr. Carter. I'm a very busy man and I have rather more important things to do than talk to junior police officers about people of whom I know nothing."

"You are aware of what he is now, sir?"

141

"I could hardly be otherwise, Mr. Carter. His face peers from every hoarding. It is precisely for that reason that I remember him at all. One does not, you know, remember the faces of all those to whom one might have presented trophies over a decade ago."

"Well, sir, in that case you will appreciate why it is impossible for me to be forthcoming over the telephone."

A very long pause.

"All right. Can you come to my house at seven, tonight?"

"I can."

"The address is, 'The Cedars.' Vernon's Way. Have you got that?"

"I have."

Abruptly, Cresswell rang off.

As Carter put the 'phone down, he recalled Halroyd's voice: "Their connection could scarcely have been closer." No doubt. But it was not one which Lieutenant-Colonel Cresswell, D.S.O., M.C. was anxious to discuss with a "junior police officer."

In the taxi, Carter ran through what he knew about Cresswell. A bachelor, forty-two years of age; one of the best known barristers in South East Asia. An Unofficial Member of Legislative Council. Legal Adviser to the Federation of Industry. Member of the Standing Finance and sundry other committees. A Malay scholar. A big wheel. Carter thought of Cresswell's tone of voice on the telephone and found himself wondering how he had ever thought—the circumstances being as they were—that he could secure Cresswell's co-operation.

"The Cedars" stood in its own grounds surrounded by a high stone wall. As the taxi drove through the gates and along the wide curved drive, Carter caught sight of the huge garden, the rockeries and lawn, the badminton court, and finally, silver in the moonlight, the swimming pool. Cresswell, Carter thought, must be stinking rich! The taxi drew up behind an Austin Princess parked under the porch and Carter saw Cresswell standing at the top of the stone steps that formed part of the imposing entrance to the house. Carter recognised him instantly from a photograph in which he was depicted presenting a trophy to one Khan Hock Loi.

Cresswell did not come down the steps as Carter paid off

142

the taxi, collected his brief case and the brown paper cylinder. As he walked up the steps Carter had plenty of time to assess Cresswell; medium build, five foot ten, full head of black hair greying at the temples, sharp featured—distinguished: wearing now a black tie and a white sharkskin jacket on which a dozen miniature medals glinted, his dress, expression and attitude combining to make it abundantly clear that Carter could hardly have come at a more inopportune moment.

Unsmilingly Cresswell extended a hand. "Mr. Carter?"

"Yes."

They shook hands briefly. Cresswell gestured towards the Austin Princess—in which a Malay chauffeur was sitting waiting—looked at his wrist watch and said, "I can give you barely five minutes I'm afraid. I have to be at Government House in less than twenty."

With that he turned and walked inside. Carter followed him across the hall to a door on the other side. As Cresswell opened the door a 'phone rang inside the room and he went to answer it. Carter followed him in, put his things on the floor against the wall just inside the door, closed the door and stood admiring what was evidently the lounge. It was worthy of admiration; a room furnished by someone of taste and refinement, someone who knew how to live and had the wealth to indulge his tastes. Everything in it oozed wealth; from the lighted showcase with its collection of jade pieces to the Persian carpets on the floor. From a Japanese garden in a small alcove, one could hear the tinkle of water. The furniture was upholstered in leather; unusual in the tropics, but eminently reasonable in an air-conditioned room such as this.

Cresswell put the 'phone down and walked swiftly across the room to where Carter was standing.

"Well, Mr. Carter?" he asked impatiently.

"As I told you on the 'phone sir, I wanted to see you about the student Khan Hock Loi—whom you knew at one time. It's my job to find out all that can be discovered about him."

"I've no doubt it is, Mr. Carter," Cresswell replied curtly, "but as I told *you* on the telephone, I hardly knew him and know nothing about him. And but for your dramatic references to life and death, that would have been the end of it."

143

"So if I asked you, Mr. Cresswell, whether or not the student Khan Hock Loi had been intelligent, you simply wouldn't know?"

Cresswell gave a gesture of exasperation. "Mr. Carter, you do understand English I presume? Just exactly how many times do you have to be told that I can tell you nothing about him? Nothing. Nothing at all. I must confess I find your persistence both tedious and presumptuous, and," looking at his wrist watch, "I shall certainly consider mentioning it to your Inspector General, whom I shall no doubt be seeing at Government House in something less than ten minutes."

Carter turned, picked up his brief case, opened it, took out some papers and handed them to Cresswell saying, "I would have thought, sir, that these letters could only have been written by someone who was *deeply* concerned about the student Khan Hock Loi, and who therefore knew more about him than most."

Galvin had been as good as his word: "Every letter, Mr. Carter, photostat copies of every letter."

Cresswell flicked through the photostats with studied boredom; not by the flicker of an eyelash did he betray the fact that he'd been caught out in a lie. Handing the photostats back to Carter he said quietly and evenly, "I do not seem to have made myself clear Mr. Carter, when I said I did not know Khan Hock Loi. I trust I make myself clear now, when I say, I am a barrister, I do not want to answer your questions, I am not obliged to answer your questions, so will you please go."

Carter flushed with anger as he put the photostats back into his brief case and fastened it: the anger showed in his voice also. "Khan Hock Loi is an important Communist. When you see the Inspector General tonight, tell him you knew Khan Hock Loi and that you knew him well. And tell him that it's in the public interest that you disclose to me all that you know about Khan Hock Loi. But tell the Inspector General also, that you don't think it would be in yours!"

Cresswell flushed, took the two paces to the door and opened it with an angry gesture. As he did so he caught sight of the brown cylindrical parcel in the corner and said, "And take that with you, whatever it is."

Carter picked it up, snapped, "It used to be yours!"

144

"Mine?" The question was drawn from Cresswell's lips despite himself.

As if in answer, Carter tore savagely at the brown paper, dropped the carpet at Cresswell's feet and unrolled it with a sharp jab from the toe of a shoe. He gaped in astonishment when he looked from the carpet to Cresswell and saw that his face had gone white and was twisted in anguish. He watched as Cresswell's head went back until his neck was fully extended, as he stood, eyes closed, swaying slightly.

Carter took his arm and asked in alarm, "Are you all right?" Then closed the door and led him towards the nearest armchair. But Cresswell shook him off, stood for a moment, walked to the cocktail cabinet, poured brandy and gulped it down.

Carter stood in the center of the room looking at Cresswell's back. A minute passed, then in a calm, thoroughly controlled voice, Cresswell said over a shoulder, "I have not displayed my usual hospitality this evening, Mr. Carter, it is most unlike me. May I now offer you a drink?"

"But you're on your way to G.H."

"I was. But I'm not now."

"Well in that case I'll have a brandy soda."

Carter watched him pour it out, pick up the ice tongs, turn and say, "One lump or two?"

"Two please."

Cresswell brought the drink across to him, "And now let us sit down."

Carter sat in an armchair, but Cresswell walked over to the door, picked up the carpet, brought it back and laid it across the top of a sofa, before sitting down half-facing both the carpet and Carter. All Cresswell's hostility was gone: he just looked weary and unhappy.

Carter recalled Halroyd's voice, "Would you mind, Ralph, just assuming he *is* queer, and then taking it from there." But there was nothing about Cresswell to indicate his sexual leanings—except perhaps, his age and his bachelorhood. But then Halroyd was a bachelor, not a great deal younger than Cresswell . . . Carter pictured Halroyd's secretary coming out of his bedroom one evening when Carter had arrived somewhat unexpectedly.

Self-consciously, Cresswell offered Carter a cigarette: he seemed apologetic, anxious to make amends for his earlier behaviour. They sat smoking in silence for a minute or two, then with an effort Cresswell said, "After the reception I gave you tonight, I deserve to be told to go to hell, but"—his voice becoming an earnest whisper— "I would dearly love to know how that carpet came into your possession."

Like a good witness in court, Carter told him the story. Speaking slowly and dispassionately, choosing his words carefully. Speaking only of what he had himself seen or heard, anxious only to be accurate and to omit nothing important; factually, careful neither to embellish nor understate.

Cresswell listened, immobile, eyes half closed, his elbow on the side of his armchair and his hand supporting his head, until Carter gave Brown's account of Tommy Loi's last night at Cambridge. Then he sat up, hands gripping the arm rests on either side of him, and said in a savage whisper, "The callous swine!" And because Carter had stopped speaking, "Go on, go on."

Carter spoke for several minutes; recounting the story of Tommy Loi's life in Britain. His job, his popularity, the fight in the pub, the type of training the Party had given him. How, despite the fact that the area had been cordoned off because of delayed-action bombs, he had gone back into the ruins of 48 Slade Terrace for his books and papers, and had emerged with Brown's overcoat and the Persian carpet as well. Everything. Until the day he had taken ship for Singapore and had given the carpet to the Browns—"My most treasured possession, comrades. I give it to you as a memento and in gratitude for all you have done for me, but above all, I give it to you for introducing me to the Party, and thus giving my life a meaning and purpose."

Remembering that Cresswell was a Malay scholar, Carter concluded his story after the fashion of the old Malay storyteller; "Demikian-lah ada-nya, And that was the way of it." It seemed appropriate somehow, with its overtones of the workings of fate, and its conclusiveness.

They sat looking at the Persian carpet on the back of the sofa for a long time, then Cresswell said, "The Browns. Are they in straightened circumstances?"

"They are pensioners; not starving, nor are they exactly un-

146

comfortable: because they have had it tough, they are content enough. But there is little in their lives beyond the telly and the pub."

"They were kind to Tommy," Cresswell remarked.

"They were indeed. In fact I think he took the place of the son they never had. They were certainly reluctant to part with that."

Carter nodded towards the Persian carpet. "Can I buy it from you?" Cresswell asked anxiously, adding, "It is worth about seventy pounds."

Carter smiled, "Really? I bought it for twenty."

"That's almost exactly what I paid for it when I bought it; but it's worth seventy pounds now."

"You can have it for twenty-one pounds. Excess baggage," Carter explained.

Cresswell looked at him curiously, said, "Why?"

"What do you mean, 'why?'"

"Well isn't that er, rather unpolicemanlike? To throw away a perfectly legal and thoroughly justifiable forty-nine pounds profit."

Carter shrugged, "I don't know. I suppose if I were a good Special Branch officer I'd say, 'You can have it by all means, Mr. Cresswell, for seventy pounds; providing you tell me all that you know about Khan Hock Loi.' As it is, I don't want it myself and even less could I make a profit on it. And so far from expecting you to enlighten me regarding your connection with Tommy Loi, I now realise I was a bloody fool ever to have even considered it—under the circumstances"—he added lamely.

Cresswell shot him a somewhat quizzical look but took out a pocket book, "What is Brown's address?" Carter gave it to him and he wrote it down; as he put the pocket book away he said, "But you know, Carter, I really don't know how anything I might be able to tell you about the Khan Hock Loi I knew over a decade ago, could possibly be of the slightest value today."

"Look, let me just give you a couple of examples, sir," Carter was solemn. "Supposing I knew nothing about him whatsoever, and you told me just two things, (a) that he'd got guts, and (b) that he had an elderly aunt living in Sintra whom he worshipped. Knowing this, if she were to die I would ensure that the mourners at her funeral included several members of my staff, because he might, he just might, take the grave risk of showing up. Not knowing anything about his affection for his aunt I would have no reason for taking such an action, thereby missing what might have been a glorious opportunity of taking him alive.

"Alternatively," Carter went on, "you might casually mention that he showed a keen interest in, say, Etruscan pottery if you like, a fact which would indicate that he had probably been living in the Communist camp that was hurriedly abandoned yesterday—a camp in which there were two or three books on the subject. Under certain circumstances, that information could be vital."

Carter looked apologetically at Cresswell as he said, "I'm afraid sir, that this is simply one of those deals in which you'll just have to tell me all you know about him—always providing you want to, of course. If you don't want to, I shall quite understand."

"You spoke of 'a glorious opportunity of taking him alive.' Am I to understand that you would prefer to take him alive rather than to kill him?"

"Indeed you are." Carter spoke at some length in his explanation as to why a live Communist—and particularly a live Communist State Committee Member—was so much more valuable than a dead one.

Cresswell was genuinely interested. "I would have thought that if the police captured a Communist terrorist armed, or simply in Communist uniform, they would, first, be only too pleased to institute proceedings against him, and, second, it would have been legally incumbent upon them so to do."

"What it is legally incumbent upon one to do, and what one actually does, sir, are matters which are often at variance."

For the first time that evening, Cresswell smiled, said, "Very succinctly put." He stood up, collected Carter's glass, took it over to the cocktail cabinet, refilled it and brought it back.

Carter thanked him.

Cresswell stood over Carter. "Who would know what I tell you?"

"No one."

"It would not be committed to writing?"

"It would be committed only to memory. My memory."

"But you would have to keep your superior informed . . ."

"Would I?" Carter raised his head and looked at Cresswell as he added, "In any case, my immediate superior has already formed his own opinions as to your connections with Khan Hock Loi. He is neither surprised nor interested, nor is he a man who bruits his

148

opinions abroad." Carter lowered his head and addressed the small Persian carpet, "Neither am I; I am interested only in so far as it might be of use to me to effect Tommy Loi's surrender or capture. Beyond that, I have not been here tonight. I do not know you. We have never met. And," looking up again at Cresswell, "if you met me you wouldn't know me either."

Cresswell paced up and down in front of Carter for several minutes, without speaking; suddenly he stopped, faced Carter and said, "Without wishing to imply any criticism of the Special Branch, Carter, I must confess to a certain surprise that *you* were selected to . . . shall we say, interrogate me. There are several police officers, some of them quite senior, who share certain of my shortcomings and with whom I could have been frank without embarrassment; I would suggest that you mention this to your 'immediate superior,' as you call him, with a view to a rather more, er, psychologically suitable choice of interrogator should similar situations arise in the future." Having said which, he resumed his pacing.

His voice had been bland, but Carter got the message: I have friends in the Police who share my tastes: powerful friends. Carter didn't doubt it. Nor all that it would imply for a "junior police officer" rash enough to betray Cresswell's confidences. Aloud, he said, "A police officer is supposed to be able to interrogate anybody, sir, but I can well appreciate that there are occasions when a higher standard of discretion is called for than is normally the case."

Cresswell said, "Good," stopped his pacing, sat down in the armchair next to Carter's and began in a conversational—almost casual—tone, "I loved Tommy Loi. In fact I would say I still love him. I certainly owe him the happiest years of my life. I first met him . . ."

After speaking for perhaps ten or fifteen minutes, Cresswell lifted his glass to Carter, said "Demikian-lah ada-nya," and drained it.

That had been the way of it. He had told Carter nothing that Carter couldn't have guessed for himself. There was no reason why a "boy meets boy" story should differ greatly from a "boy meets girl" story. Except that boy doesn't usually meet girl on the rostrum of a crowded school hall when presenting her with the school bantam-weight boxing trophy.

"When you got back to Singapore just before the outbreak of the Emergency sir, did you see anything of him?"

"No. I didn't. I think he was probably already in the jungle, no doubt making the necessary preparations for 'Der Tag.'"

"And he's made no attempt to get in touch with you? No letters or telephone calls?"

"None at all. None."

"Do you happen to have any photographs of him?"

"Lots."

Cresswell stood up, went to a cabinet, returned with two leather-bound albums and handed them to Carter saying, "Take your time. I'll get some more drinks."

Carter turned the pages slowly, examining each photograph carefully. Tommy Loi looked at him from every page. There were very few photographs that included Cresswell—or anyone else for that matter.

Cresswell put his glass on the side-table at his elbow. Carter said, "He seems to have been mad keen on swimming."

"How very odd that you should say that," Cresswell remarked with amusement. "It was the one thing that he *couldn't* do. He did a lot of sunbathing, and he loved zooming about in my launch, but he simply couldn't learn to swim. He seemed to have a fear of the water that no amount of expert tuition would ever overcome."

Carter was halfway through the second album before he came across the first photograph of a woman. A big handsome middle-aged Chinese woman, nicely dressed. Beside her, holding her arm, Tommy Loi. Presumably his mother. But it was the bunch of roses she cradled in her left arm that most aroused Carter's interest.

Carter looked up at Cresswell and with one finger on the photograph said, "The woman?"

Cresswell leant over Carter's shoulder and said, "Tommy's mother. A picture taken on the day of his graduation from High School."

"She looks proud."

"She was. Her son was the school captain. A widow who ran a coffee-shop; in Sintra, I believe. It was probably the first day off she'd had in thirty years."

"She looks extremely well dressed," Carter remarked.

"Yes she does, doesn't she. But when Tommy told me that she

150

was too busy to attend his graduation, I knew it was because she simply didn't have clothes suitable for the occasion. It took all my tact and persuasion to persuade him to accept the $1,000 that I pressed on him to enable her to buy some. He was curiously reluctant to accept money as such. One evening I made the mistake of putting $30 in his pocket without his knowledge: he turned up the next evening with a present for me—a flowering orchid that had cost him $35. I've still got it; one of those white ones hanging under the porch as you come in."

"But the roses were from Tommy Loi?" Carter still had his finger on the photograph.

Cresswell peered at it again and replied, "They were; and the little gold chain with the cross. He saved up for months to buy that."

"Presumably this photograph was taken in 1938?"

"To be quite specific it was taken on the 27th day of the 7th Moon 1938."

Carter suddenly became aware of the low hum of the air-conditioner, a sound he had not noticed before.

"Do you always go by the Chinese calendar?" Carter asked with a slight grin, hoping that his voice was not overcasual.

"No, but before he left for the U.K., Tommy made me promise that on the anniversary of his graduation day I would send his mother a bunch of roses on his behalf. He impressed upon me that I was to send them on the 27th day of the 7th Moon, and not to send them on the anniversary as shown by the Western calendar, otherwise they would not arrive on the same day each year—the same day that is, according to the Chinese Lunar calendar."

"I see," Carter remarked thoughtfully, "it would be rather like Easter in the Western calendar, in that it would be variable, falling on different dates each year."

"Exactly," Cresswell replied, "but owing to the war, of course, it was a promise I was able to keep only once. And since my return, I have not felt in a position to honour it."

The 27th day of the 7th Moon.

Carter wanted to leave as soon as possible; there was something he had to check on right away. He refused another drink and stood up, began the usual civilities. . . .

151

"Have I contributed anything towards your store of knowledge about this $450,000 worth of Communist terrorist?"

"I think you have, actually sir," Carter replied, giving Cresswell a frank look, "but it remains to be seen."

Cresswell looked thoughtful and even uneasy for a long moment, then he said, "Before you go, Carter, may I point out to you that the information which I have given you was given in the belief and on the understanding that you would seek to capture Tommy alive. I trust that you will honour that understanding." Cresswell's gaze was level, his voice sincere.

"I will try sir," Carter paused and added, "I promise you that."

"One final thing Carter. I appreciate the difficulties . . . It may not be possible. Especially with Tommy's strength of character. And particularly as he's embraced the Communist cause. . . . You'll find him a formidable opponent, you know. But, should anything happen . . . I would appreciate it if you would let me know."

"This also I promise."

Nothing more was said until they walked down the stone steps towards the car in which the chauffeur still sat waiting. Cresswell's Malay was fluent, Carter noticed, when he said, "A thousand apologies 'Dullah. I completely forgot about you."

Abdullah's teeth flashed as he said, "Think nothing of it Tuan."

"Take Mr. Carter to the Ritz, 'Dullah."

They shook hands. Cresswell said, "I've forgotten your cheque for the carpet."

"Send it to me sir. C/O Police H.Q., Sintra."

When Cresswell's car dropped him at the Ritz, Carter thanked Abdullah, ran up the steps and walked across the foyer to the receptionist's office; as the receptionist handed him his key he looked at the calendar on the wall behind her. In Singapore, calendars give two sets of figures, one in English, the other in Chinese.

The 27th day of the 7th Moon was ten days away.

13

Eight p.m. As Ah Ling carried his bags into his bungalow Carter picked up the 'phone and dialled a number. His heart leaped when he heard her voice say, "Hello."

"It's me darling."

"Oh, Ralph!"

"Shall I send the car?"

"No. I'll take a taxi. It's quicker."

She rang off.

Carter walked down the road that led to the main gates of the Mess compound and stood waiting beneath one of the floodlights until a sentry called, "Do not stand in the light, Tuan." Carter apologised and stepped back into the darkness. That had been a very stupid thing to do. His leave had made him careless.

After what seemed an eternity the taxi arrived. They embraced in the darkness, then walked slowly arm in arm to his bungalow.

An hour later, or two or three, she ran her lips over his chest and then looking up into his eyes said, "You've been faithful, honey."

"No I haven't," he replied primly.

"Oh yes you have," she purred.

"I tell you I haven't!"

"Four times?"

He put his hands under her arms and pulled her up to him so that he could kiss her lips as she lay on top of him. "You haven't gone yet, darling. And I'm superstitious about even numbers. Anyway, it's all your fault; all I wanted to do was lie here reading the bible in an orderly manner, but you keep distracting me."

She nibbled at the lobe of his left ear.

"See what I mean?" he said.

But the sex act was an expression of their love, not its object. Carter suddenly realised that it had become unthinkable for him to

153

commit it with anyone other than Nancy. His previous experiences were a pale shadow: animal, mindless, committed with faceless creatures whose names he had long forgotten or had never known.

To Nancy he was Her Man.

"A police officer telephoned me the day after you'd gone," she purred in his ear.

"What?" Carter tried to sit up but she was on top of him. "What did he want?" he asked indignantly.

"He wanted me to go out with him," she smirked. She put her hands on his chest and looked down at him. "You're angry," she said gleefully.

"Of course I'm angry. What the hell did he think he was up to anyway?"

"Darling, you're jealous!" she cried triumphantly.

"Of course I'm jealous. Why shouldn't I be?"

She put her hands behind his head and pulled it towards her, squeezing his face against her breasts, then letting his head fall back upon the pillow she leant forward and rolled her forehead backwards and forwards along his. Lifting her head slightly she looked into his eyes and spoke into his lips, "I love you, Ralph. And I shall go on loving you." She had never thought it possible to feel so deeply, so intensely, about another person. It was a glory and an ache.

"Sleep here tonight, darling," Carter whispered.

"Oh honey, I can't. You know Matron's rules."

In the morning, Ah Ling arrived with two cups of coffee instead of just one, as if he had been doing it for years. "He must be psychic," Carter thought. He had given both Ah Ling and Chan On Yan the night off. "Perhaps he'd had a chat with one of the sentries," he concluded.

When Carter walked into the office, Halroyd stood up, extended a hand and said, "Am I glad to see you!"

They shook hands and sat down, "How come?"

"Well, trying to run the Projects Section in addition to all this bloody lot," Halroyd gestured towards the files heaped in his trays, "is just not on. There's so much happening."

"Good or bad?"

"Well, good mostly. Sometimes even very good. In the first

place, surrenders have increased rapidly since you left; we had no less than twenty-seven last month alone. Some of them real hard core boys from No. 2 Company, and even a couple from one of the killer-squads."

"Really!"

"Yes. And that reminds me, the Projects Section's lost one of its lesser targets. Lim Tsing Wa."

"No!"

"But yes. It appears that he had some "traitor" or other tied to a palm tree one night, and was giving him the treatment with a pair of scissors, when the traitor's wife stepped out of the darkness and belted him round the neck with a parang."

"Killed him?"

"Almost certainly yes. At least, the two surrenders from one of his killer-squads say so."

"They were present when he died?" Carter asked with a shrewd look.

"No. But they were certain he had died. A blow on the neck from a parang is not the sort of thing one survives. It requires hospitalisation and surgery at the very least. You of course, Ralph, would want his skull so that you could get his dentist to identify his teeth, but all the evidence points to his death. So much so, that our 'Wanted' posters now display his photograph with the familiar diagonal red cross over them. Deceased. Certainly Lim Tsing Wa hasn't been heard of for over three months."

"And the woman who did it? What does she have to say?" Carter put in.

"You've been away too long, Ralph," Halroyd said with commiseration. "The woman who did it is in no condition to say anything. You know that particular kind of bamboo that grows so fast?"

"Yes."

"Well they tied her face downwards. . . ."

"Never mind sir. What else has been happening?"

"There's been a sharp decrease in incidents. And another thing, the Communists have suffered severe losses in the course of their attacks. You see Ralph," Halroyd grinned, "the 'X' squad located two more dumps. Rifles blow up in their faces, hand-grenades go off in their hands before they can throw them: that sort of thing. Their

155

morale had suffered badly, particularly because there is so much sickness among them. Stomach trouble," he added placidly.

"Have any of those who've surrendered got stomach trouble?" Carter asked.

"About fifty per cent I suppose, possibly more. Why?"

"Well is it curable?" Carter asked with a note of remonstration.

"No it's not. At least Dr. Kowalski says it's not."

"Have you told him what causes this stomach trouble, sir?"

Halroyd sighed wearily and said, "I have told him what I *suspect* causes the stomach trouble Ralph, but there's a whole stack of files in your 'in' tray that'll put you in the picture. Diaries mostly. They'll tell you all about the misfortunes that have befallen the comrades: they even had one of their camps burn down when a pressure lamp exploded and set fire to the roof." Halroyd gave Carter a quizzical look as he added, "And Ralph, one of our surrenders is blind and badly burned as the result of a similar explosion elsewhere."

Halroyd paused to let it sink in.

"Oh, and by the way Ralph, Chief Inspector Lau's squatter woman is well pregnant: so that particular little project might well pay off."

"And Daniel?"

"Daniel has received his seventh or eighth payment of a thousand dollars—I can't remember which—and hasn't so much as bought himself a new tie."

"Blast!" Carter said with feeling.

"But young Inspector Chivapathy was in here some weeks ago, and he was telling me that Daniel visited this mistress of his, what's her name . . . ?"

"Khatijah."

"Yes, in Kampong Glam, one night every week without fail. Every Friday, to be more precise."

Halroyd looked at Carter speculatively for a moment, then smiled in agreement as Carter said, *"Every* Friday?"

"Exactly. And Chivapathy's a married man too. I asked him if he thought that Khatijah was never indisposed. Anyway, a closer watch was kept on her house after that, and it transpired that there is a door in Khatijah's bedroom giving direct access to a room in the

156

house next door—the house next door being on a corner. The rest was easy. On alternate Fridays Daniel goes from Khatijah's bedroom into the house next door, then out from there and straight into a van outside the door—the van being owned by some Indian cloth-merchant. Well, we've checked on the road blocks and the records show that half an hour after curfew, the van arrives at the police road block at the 21st mile Ventnor Road, with one passenger in it, but it arrives at the road block at the 25th mile with just the driver in it."

"So Daniel's gone visiting one of the labour lines on Dartford Estate."

"Precisely, but which one? There must be 10,000 Indian tappers on that Estate, employed on ten Divisions."

They sat looking at each other for a few moments. They both knew that if Daniel went to the trouble of getting into the van only by way of Khatijah's bedroom, he had good reason for doing so; and that good reason might well be that he was visiting his brother Emmanuel.

"Well I've played it gently," Halroyd continued, "I thought I'd better wait for your return as I didn't want to botch the whole thing up by having some over-zealous detective making indiscreet enquiries. So now you know as much as I do." Halroyd took out a cigarette, offered one to Carter and asked, "Have a good leave?"

"Nothing exciting. I made the enquiries that were necessary, though."

"Any leads?"

"Yes, a rather good one. In about another week's time, Tommy Loi is going to come out of the jungle, go to the Keng Wah Nurseries just outside Kampong Lallang Pendek, and select a bunch of roses to be sent to his mother on the occasion of the anniversary of his graduation from High School."

"The Keng Wah Nurseries?"

"They're the only ones in Tommy Loi's operational area, sir. There are no other nurseries within thirty miles."

"He may send someone else . . ."

"No he won't." Carter replied emphatically.

"Why so sure?"

"Because he's queer, sir."

"And that makes a difference?"

"It makes all the difference. He'll select those roses himself. He'll be like a woman buying a new hat, he certainly won't send anyone else to do it. And he'll go either the day before or on the day of his anniversary so that the roses will be nice and fresh when his mother gets them."

"He might go there a week in advance, Ralph; point to a rose bush and say, 'In a week's time, send that one, that one and that one' . . ."

"No he won't. He will have to hold the whole goddam bunch in his hands; all wrapped up in tin foil just as his mother's going to receive it." Halroyd blew out his cheeks and drummed on the table with his fingers. "That is what he is going to do, sir," Carter insisted. "Before I left the U.K., I must have read damn nearly every book on the subject, and I was even able to discuss it with a police consultant psychiatrist."

"And?" Halroyd prompted.

"Queers almost invariably display a depth of feeling and sensitivity to a marked degree; quote."

"So what?" Halroyd looked blank, "I don't see that it necessarily follows that Tommy Loi will therefore have to go and purchase his roses personally."

"May I submit, sir," Carter said with heavy patience, "that a person who possesses 'depth of feeling to a marked degree,' will, when he is sending roses to someone he loves and whom he has not seen for years, be under a bloody compulsion to go and purchase them himself."

Halroyd took the cigarette from his mouth, grinned and said, "All right, so the penny's dropped; but it doesn't by any means follow that he's absolutely bound to turn up. He might be sitting in his camp nursing a nasty flesh wound, he might be having a spot of stomach trouble for that matter, or he might be away attending a State Committee meeting somewhere."

"Yes, but you do agree that if he *can* select his roses himself, he will?"

"I agree that no harm would be done by acting on that assumption; but fill me in with the info you picked up on him in the U.K."

Carter told him the story in detail, omitting nothing. When he

158

had finished, Halroyd said with a slight note of reproof, "You're at it again Ralph."

Carter looked blank. "At what?"

"At getting emotionally involved, Ralph," Halroyd said evenly. "You're sorry for the bastard."

"Well so I am," Carter replied defensively. "At the age of seventeen he's dazzled and corrupted by some wealthy queer who sends him to the U.K., where, as it turns out, he becomes a sitting duck for the Party."

"I doubt, Ralph, if you can corrupt anyone who would not in any case have become corrupt; as Cresswell said, he recognised him for what he was, that's all. But be that as it may, the only thing that need concern you regarding Khan Hock Loi is that he's an important Communist leader who's got to be eliminated."

"I can eliminate him and still feel sorry for him."

"You can, Ralph," Halroyd agreed in level tones, "but it's dangerous to have any feelings at all towards those you have to kill, because feelings affect one's judgement. All feelings! Except perhaps hate—and even that can affect one's judgement adversely on occasion. One should feel nothing. Nothing at all. In this job there's no room for emotion, Ralph, there is room only for dispassionate calculation. You cannot *afford* to let yourself become emotionally involved. It's as simple as that. But if you must think about Khan Hock Loi as a person, then think of him as a person who kills British soldiers: but don't have an 'he never had a chance' attitude towards 'Tommy Loi'—as you call him—because that's bloody dangerous."

Carter looked at him curiously; his tone had been conversational throughout, but it had held overtones—overtones which conveyed concern, and something in the nature of the message, "It baffles me that it should be necessary for me to keep on having to explain this. It's so basic: it's basic to every Intelligence organisation anywhere."

Halroyd, Carter thought, has a "thing" about emotional involvement.

A week later, Carter was sitting in the Khan Hock Lum coffee-shop near Police H.Q. having breakfast. Stacked in front of him

159

on the marble table were half a dozen flat circular bamboo boxes of "sui maai," the Chinese breakfast dish of which he was so fond. He did not think that visiting the coffee-shop had been a particular dangerous thing to do; he had only just returned from leave, and the killer-squads had had little time to direct their attention towards him, furthermore, he'd never been there before and had no intention of coming again. If it were thought he might return, there were those who might take it in turns waiting—for weeks, maybe even months.

The other customers—clerks mostly—looked at him with curiosity. Europeans never visited the coffee-shop; certainly not for breakfast, nor were they likely to have ordered it in Chinese even if they had. Tommy Loi's mother served him herself. A big woman for a Cantonese, heavily built without being fat. A formidable woman: one of strong character. She had been running this coffee-shop since the death of her husband twenty-five years before, and had built it up by sheer hard work. She wore her black hair straight back and tied in a bun. Carter recognised "the little gold chain with the cross" which hung from her neck, recalled that before he had left for England, Tommy Loi had been educated only at Christian schools. As she put down the last of the bamboo boxes in front of him, she stood, arms akimbo, looking at him as if she wanted to speak.

Carter peered into one of the bamboo boxes to see which particular delicacy it contained, then looking up said, "Yes old woman?"

"I have heard of only one Tuan in Sintra who speaks Cantonese," she said quietly and slowly, "it is said of this Tuan that even the walls crumble because of him; his presence could bring much trouble to one who seeks only to earn an honest living and be left in peace."

"Have no fear, old woman," Carter replied softly. "I am sure the Tuan of whom you speak would not wish to burden you with his presence. Were he to come here it would be but once—and then only to savour the excellence of your sui maai."

"I can think of many reasons why such a Tuan should honour my humble shop with his presence," she replied darkly, adding as she turned away, "but none of them is such as to set the mind of an old woman at ease."

160

The same afternoon, Carter stood on the rostrum in a lecture room in Police H.Q. addressing his Field staff who sat at tables in front of him. "State Committee Member Khan Hock Loi, the Commander of the 3rd Company of the Kepayan Regiment—the word regiment being in this case typical Communist propaganda jargon for battalion—is going to walk into the Keng Wah Nurseries some time tomorrow, or possibly the morning of the following day, and select roses to be sent to his mother. That, at any rate, is what I think he will do if he can. Now you've all had plenty of time to study the 'Special Person' files that have been so laboriously prepared and built up on him. You have, I hope, committed to memory the various photographs prepared by the photographic branch: you know what he would look like if he wore a flat cap, long hair, dark glasses, a moustache and a beard. You know what he would look like with just a beard, with dark glasses and a moustache, with ordinary glasses and a hat. In fact you should be able to recognise him instantly, whatever he wears and whatever he does not wear, and I sincerely hope you can."

Carter paused and looked from face to face. "Sergeant Rahman, does he smoke?"

"Yes, sir."

"How much?"

"Fifteen to twenty cigarettes a day, sir."

"What brand?"

"Players Medium, sir."

"Good." The answers had been pat, and with no hesitation. "What does he keep his cigarettes in, Sergeant Lo?"

"A leather case, sir. With his initials on the outside. A European called Brown gave it to him sir, in England."

"Inspector Chivapathy, what languages does he speak?"

"English, Malay, Cantonese and Mandarin, sir."

"Put them in the order in which he speaks them most fluently Chiv."

"Cantonese, English, Mandarin and Malay, sir."

"Sergeant Major Lim, what weapons does he normally carry?"

"On operations, sir, a sten-gun, a Browning automatic pistol and two Japanese grenades. In camp, just the pistol."

There was not much, now, that was not known about Tommy

Loi: information having been derived from every conceivable source, but particularly from the statements of surrendered terrorists.

"Now I want you all to look at some photographs which were taken yesterday by an R.A.F. helicopter," Carter went on. "Put the light out somebody and let's have a look at them."

Carter stepped down from the rostrum as Chief Inspector Lau switched on the projector and the pictures appeared on the screen. They watched in silence for a minute or two, then Carter said, "Now this is the Keng Wah Nursery." A minute or two later Carter called, "Hold that one, C.I. Back a bit. Yes, that one!"

Carter waited while they studied it, then said, "Now look at it. From our point of view it's a piece of cake. A triangle. On one side, the trunk road, beyond the road, rubber, rising quite steeply up a slope. On the northern side, more rubber, and—this is very important—on the remaining side of the Keng Wah Nurseries, a river; swollen by the recent heavy rains and travelling, so I'm told, at about five knots. South of the point of the triangle, the road goes over the river by the bridge and then through Kampong Lallang Pendek—one of the many villages, you will note, that the Government has still not yet got around to fencing in. The hedge surrounding the nurseries is hibiscus, four foot high and well kept, and there is only one entrance—through the double wooden gates. So if he does go in there, our friend Tommy Loi has had it: there is no nearby jungle or swamp that he can make a dash for, and the flower beds, bushes and few wooden buildings will offer him scant protection. Remember that he cannot swim and will dive into that river only as a very last resort. Let's see the rest of the film, C.I."

When the film was over Carter went through the plan again: "The telephone in the Keng Wah Nursery"—Carter glanced at his watch—"has already been switched off. As quite a lot of their business is done by telephone, they are not likely to waste much time in complaining about it, if, indeed, they have not already done so, and they will send someone to Kampong Lallang Pendek to ring up from there and complain. Well there's a curfew on, so nothing much can be done tonight about it, but at seven a.m. tomorrow morning Team 'A' will arrive in our Posts and Telegraph's van and commence repairing the 'phone. The van will be parked outside the shed which passes for an office, and Sergeant Rahman will remain hidden in it—one never knows, the gardeners there must be assumed to be pro-Communist and it's always a good thing to keep a little surprise in reserve. Team 'A' will, of course, find that the telephone wires are shot to hell and need complete replacements—a long job. Take it in turns to have coffee and lunch, but never less than two people in the nursery at one time. Now Team 'B' with its load of vegetables will come chugging down the road at 7:15 a.m., the engine of the lorry will be giving off steam and the lorry will come to a grinding halt just opposite the main gates of the Keng Wah Nursery and on the other side of the road. Now don't overdo the steam business, we don't want to have to buy yet another new engine. C.I. Lau will go into the Keng Wah and ask about the nearest garage: the nearest garage is of course, in Kampong Lallang Pendek and C.I. Lau will walk the couple of hundred yards into Kampong Lallang Pendek and no doubt return with a mechanic from the garage, a mechanic who will no doubt discover that the lorry's water pump is defective. This will mean that Lau will have to ring up Sintra for a replacement, a replacement which might well take two days to arrive. Now the net result of all this is that in a predominantly pro-Communist area, you will have a perfectly natural explanation for your presence. Only use the radios in the van and the lorry to establish contact with Sergeants Morgan and Hardcliffe in the first instance, and make sure that nobody can hear you while you're doing it."

Sergeant Major Lim raised his hand, "What about me, sir! I only got back this morning and I missed the other briefings."

"You, sergeant major, have a job after your own heart. You're a fisherman, so sit on the bank on the other side of the river from the Keng Wah and fish away to your heart's content. But make sure your fishing tackle includes a carbine, the river's about thirty yards wide at that point."

There were no answers to Carter's "Any questions?" So he went on, "Sergeant Morgan will be on listening watch at mile 24, he can arrive by road with his jungle squad in from two to three minutes. Sergeant Hardcliffe will be upstream with his squad in four outboard motors; he also will be able to arrive at the Keng Wah within about three minutes. So on receipt of the code word 'Mango,' they will descend on the Keng Wah. Remember, let Tommy Loi get in, but when and if he is in, just keep him there. Make him keep his head down until the place is completely surrounded and his chances of

163

escape impossible. One final word: try and take him alive if you can. But don't hesitate to kill him if he might otherwise escape. Dead, he's just another corpse; alive, he becomes a useful weapon."

There were two of them walking along the jungle path wearing the uniform of the Communist Liberation Army. The taller and younger of the two walked in front, in his right hand he held a sten-gun, on his back he carried a pack. He wore no badges of rank. The other wore the insignia of a Member of a State Committee, he also carried a sten-gun, and in addition, a Browning 9mm automatic pistol in a holster at his waist: over his right shoulder he carried a side pack.

Their step was almost jaunty, this was an outing for them. Cooped up in a jungle camp in constant fear of surprise attack, emerging only to make forays fraught with danger and attended with discomfort, they could look forward to the infrequent visits they made to civilisation: twice a year perhaps. Even such civilisation as was offered by the squalid little township of Kampong Lallang Pendek, was a joy to them. They could go shopping, buy cigarettes and razor blades, soap and toothpaste, sweets and chocolate; many things. They could sit on real chairs at real tables, holding in their left hands a bowl of rice, while with deft chopsticks they could choose from among the many dishes set in front of them—a slice of beef cooked in oyster sauce, a prawn fried in batter, a piece of roasted pigeon. Many things. And they could order drinks which would actually be served cold: so cold that moisture would condense on the outside of the glasses. And they could wear civilian clothes!

They walked for three hours; only the monkeys acknowledging their existence, shrieking at them from the safety of the tree-tops far above. Once, the younger man stopped and held up a warning hand. The other came up behind him and looked over his shoulder at the green and yellow banded snake which swayed in front of them barring their path; "It must be a female, Ah Bpo," he remarked, "the male gets out of the way."

Ah Bpo laughed, said, "Pity it's not a python."

They rarely had fresh meat to eat in the camp: an occasional deer, sometimes a wild pig. A python was a rare luxury. Arrived at a small clearing in the jungle fringed by a rubber estate, they

164

changed into their civilian clothes, Ah Bpo packing their uniforms and caps in his haversack and stowing it under a bush together with their sten-guns.

"How do I look, Ah Loi?" Ah Bpo asked as he pirouetted in front of him.

"Like an unemployed clerk," Khan Hock Loi replied, "your shirt is creased and your trousers need pressing."

Ah Bpo shook his head with mock sadness, "I knew there was something I'd forgotten. I could so easily have sent them to the dry-cleaners."

They dropped their gaiety as they came out of the jungle and into the rubber. They had been safe in the jungle, they would be reasonably safe when they reached Kampong Lallang Pendek; but right now, they looked exactly what they were—Communist terrorists in civilian clothes coming out of the jungle. The side packs they carried bulged heavily and would excite suspicion; Khan Hock Loi's under the weight of two Japanese hand-grenades and an automatic pistol, Ah Bpo's under the weight of a Smith and Wesson point 38 revolver and twenty or thirty spare rounds. But as well as their appearance, their very presence would incite suspicion. What reason could two such men possibly have for walking through a rubber estate at two o'clock in the afternoon, when most of the rubber-tappers were in bed? But luck was with them; they came out of the rubber without seeing anyone, and where they had planned—by the small Chinese primary school near the main road. They stood at the bus stop in front of the school, listening to the school children chanting. Schoolteachers perhaps? With books in the packs under their arms? They waited only ten minutes before a bus arrived and as they climbed aboard and sat down Ah Loi was saying, "He runs the school as well as can be expected. But he has too many pupils; he's over-worked, that's all."

"It's always the same," Ah Bpo replied, "too few schools, too few teachers, and not enough money. Not enough for schools at any rate; but enough for guns and troops and planes."

Ah Bpo, Ah Loi thought, couldn't resist saying just that little bit too much. He must speak with him later.

In another half hour they sat in a coffee-shop in Kampong Lallang Pendek, drinking cold beer. Khan Hock Loi put down his empty glass and said, "I'm going to the Nurseries now. Stay here until I get back, I'll only be a few minutes. Then we can do our shopping, have an enormous lunch, and be on our way."

He stood up and picked up his side pack from the back of his chair.

"Can't I come with you?" Ah Bpo asked, his voice almost plaintive.

Khan Hock Loi hesitated, "Better not. I'll only be gone a few minutes anyway."

From his table in the coffee-shop, Ah Bpo watched him walk the hundred yards to the bridge at the end of the shops on the other side of the road. He walked unhurriedly, casually, among the people on the five-foot way outside the shops. An inconspicuous figure with nothing about him likely to arouse even the slightest suspicion in these surroundings.

Ah Bpo watched him cross the bridge and pass out of sight. All at once he felt uneasy. Tommy Loi had hardly been out of his sight for over three years. He decided to follow him, paid his bill and walked out of the shop and along the road to the bridge. He stood behind one of the iron girders watching Tommy Loi walking along the road beside the grass verge on the other side of the bridge a hundred yards away. He wanted to follow him, but once past the bridge, Tommy would see him if he happened to look back, and Ah Bpo did not want him to know he had disobeyed him. As Tommy Loi turned in at the gate of the Keng Wah Nurseries and out of his sight, Ah Bpo came out from behind the iron girder, walked slowly over the bridge, and stood indecisively. Then, hearing shots coming from the direction of the nursery, he ran up the slope to the right of the road and into the rubber. Frantically, he ran between two rows of rubber trees that ran parallel with the road. Estimating that he was opposite the nursery gates he stopped and tried to peer into the nursery through the foliage of the rubber trees on the slopes.

Below him, twenty yards away, a deserted lorry loaded with vegetables stood at the side of the road, its open bonnet proclaiming the reason for its presence. As the shots from the nursery continued, he moved away from the lorry until he could see into the nursery through a gap in the trees. He stood horrified.

Four men, three of them wearing the uniform of the Posts and Telegraph's Department, and one in civilian clothes, were firing at

166

Tommy as he dodged about among the bushes and the flower beds. The four men signalled to each other; three of them would fire simultaneously at Tommy while the fourth ran right or left, trying to get behind Tommy and cut him off from the river. With feverish hands Ah Bpo undid the straps of his side pack and took out his revolver: for a short moment he stood considering his next move— the best way of drawing the fire from Tommy. From the corner of his eye he sensed a movement; instinctively he flung himself forward and down the slope as a sub-machine gun from the lorry sputtered the earth behind him. He fired one shot at the lorry before running behind the row of trees at the side of the road, and one more shot before he dashed across the road and into the rubber trees on the other side. He was near the river now, and behind the men who were firing at Tommy. Bent double, he zigzagged through the trees until he was near the hedge around the nursery. Forty yards away, inside the nursery, a man crouching behind a wheelbarrow fired at Tommy. Taking careful aim Ah Bpo fired, saw a piece of wood fly off the handle of the wheelbarrow and the man fling himself sideways. A very near miss. Ah Bpo fired at one of the other men, but two others were firing at him now. Good! But why didn't Tommy make for the river? It was his only chance of escape.

From his left now, someone else was firing at Ah Bpo. The one from the lorry. Ah Bpo stood behind a rubber tree and fired two quick shots at him, then felt suddenly naked as a bullet from behind him buried itself in the tree near his face and a Police lorry screamed to a halt not fifty yards away. Men in jungle green poured from it and ran towards him, fanning out in all directions.

Panic-stricken now, Ah Bpo fled in the only direction possible— to the river; ignoring the man who stood on the other bank taking such careful aim he flung himself into it, amazed that he had been able to reach it at all and wondering where he'd been hit. As he surfaced for air the water spurted in front of his face. He dived and swam under water. The river swept him along. He stayed with it for about two hundred yards before dragging himself out at a muddy bank and stumbling into the bushes, where he lay panting and listening to the shots, in the distance.

He started as he saw a movement on a mudbank down stream, but it was only a white bird settling on a log. Slowly the log opened its mouth and let the bird pick at the meat between its teeth. Ah Bpo shuddered: at least he had been spared that. Perhaps it was fear of crocodiles that had kept Tommy from the river. A new sound, coming swiftly nearer. He crawled under a bush and peered out cautiously as an outboard motor, full of armed men swept by.

A trap! It must have been a trap. But how could it have been? It was only yesterday that Tommy had told him they would be visiting Kampong Lallang Pendek today. Nobody else in the camp had known where they were going. It couldn't have been a trap. But it was. It must have been. But how? How? Oh the might and the cunning of the Imperialists! Poor Tommy.

He thought he heard the outboard motor returning. He had dropped his revolver when it had run out of bullets, and he had abandoned his side pack in the river; there was nothing further he could do—except make sure he wasn't caught. He crept through the bushes and came out into a rubber estate. Keeping well away from the river he ran in the direction of Kampong Lallang Pendek: there were many there who would help him. After a few minutes he could make out the backs of the row of shops through the rubber trees; cautiously, continually looking around to see if he were observed, he made his way out of the rubber and into the vegetable garden behind one of the shops—the third shop from the end of the row. Leaving the garden, he walked through the deserted rooms behind the shop and into the shop itself.

The old woman with her back towards him stood in the doorway of the shop, watching the people streaming excitedly towards the bridge.

"A gunfight on the other side of the bridge."

"I need dry clothes, Mother. And I need them quickly." Ah Bpo spoke softly, urgently.

The old woman turned slowly and looked him up and down impassively. "An old woman cannot stop a young man taking whatever he needs." But her eyes twinkled their sympathy and understanding.

"I will pay, Mother."

"If you do not get out of those clothes quickly, my son, you might pay with your life."

She moved swiftly towards a heap of clothing on a table and

168

rummaged through it; selecting a pair of trousers she held them out to him, "These will fit you well enough."

As he changed his trousers she took a red shirt from the pile. "That is too bright, Mother."

"It is different from what you have on. Wear it. They are not searching now for a young man with a red shirt. And this cap also, your head would draw the attention of the blind."

Ah Bpo had a crew cut.

"And these also," she said, as she handed him a pair of sunglasses.

As he left the shop Ah Bpo said, "There is money, Mother, in my wet trousers."

"I will keep it for you, my son," she replied levelly, nodding her head.

Ah Bpo made his way to the crowd at the bridge. On the other side of the bridge he could see a crowd of perhaps a hundred persons watching what was happening in the Keng Wah Nursery, from behind the safety of the rubber trees on the right of the road. But the policeman on the bridge would let no more across now. Ah Bpo pushed himself to the front of the crowd and spoke to one of the policemen standing on the bridge—a corporal. "My father works in the nurseries. I am worried for him. Please let me through."

The Malay looked at him, said, "All right. You and you only, but no more. And stay well behind the trees," he warned, as he let Ah Bpo pass, "they fire real bullets."

Ah Bpo joined the crowd clustered behind the rubber trees overlooking the Keng Wah Nursery; seeking the best view he went to the front, but a policeman ordered him back with an angry gesture. Ah Bpo moved away a short distance and found a spot.

The shooting had stopped now, but the place was thick with armed men in jungle green uniform. They were everywhere. From the positions of these men, and the way they were facing, Ah Bpo knew instantly where Tommy was. He was holed up in a wooden storehouse at the end of a short dirt road that led to its doors—completely surrounded. There were even men on the other side of the river.

There was a European in charge, a short thick-set man who wore three white stripes on his arm and who spoke into a radio he held to his ear. Behind his arms his uniform showed large wet patches.

"How ugly they are," Ah Bpo thought, "faces and necks the colour of turkey wattles." Ah Bpo almost sniffed to see if he could smell him.

To Ah Bpo, it seemed as if the police had an air of expectancy, were waiting for something. They were in no hurry to take Tommy. Then Ah Bpo looked to his right where a civilian car hurtled down the road and skidded to a stop by the side of the police lorries. A tall European carrying a sub-machine gun got out of the car. A European with fair hair. The one called Blondie. The People's Enemy No. 1. Ah Bpo knew him at once from what he had heard; knew instinctively that this was the one who had set the trap. He took careful note of the car, noted the unusual fact that the driver was Chinese; he ignored the number plates, knowing that the number plates on the cars of such police officers were changed frequently. He watched every move as Blondie spoke to the European Sergeant and to a slightly built Indian who wore the uniform of the Posts and Tele-graph's Department. They were obviously explaining the position, several times Blondie nodded. Then the three of them walked to where a police armoured car was parked on the dirt track that led to the wooden storehouse.

The back of the armoured car was open and Blondie spoke for several minutes to someone inside. Then a loudspeaker on the armoured car sounded, "Khan Hock Loi, surrender now! You have two minutes in which to surrender. Two minutes before we burn your hut down with phosphorus grenades. Come out now with your hands up, or stay where you are and burn to death. Two minutes! From now!"

Silence for one minute and thirty-five seconds.

Then. "Don't shoot. I'm coming out."

Ah Bpo was stunned: he could hear Tommy's voice even from where he was standing, seventy-five yards away. He gazed in horror as one of the two wooden doors of the storehouse swung open to reveal Tommy Loi. A Tommy Loi who stood with his hands up level with his ears; a Tommy Loi who leant forward with his shoulders hunched as if in fear of a sudden blow from behind. A Tommy Loi who walked slowly forward pleading, "Don't shoot. Don't shoot."

170

From flower beds and ditches, from behind sheds barrows and dung hills, the men in jungle green stood up to see the man whom the Government had priced at $450,000—dead or alive.

Suddenly Blondie stepped out from behind the armoured car, twenty yards from Tommy and facing him along the track, his sub-machine gun in his hands.

"Tommy Loi, stay where you are! Stand still!" he ordered.

Tommy looked at him uncomprehendingly and continued to walk slowly forward.

Blondie raised his sub-machine gun, roared, "Stand still! Blast you stand still!"

As Tommy Loi started to run towards him, Blondie fired a short burst. Tommy pitched forward on to his knees, his head went back and he seemed to fling his arms up in a gesture of supplication before he fell forwards and sideways on the track. Ah Bpo actually *saw* one of the hand-grenades that fell from his armpits. Saw Blondie fling himself to the ground, heard him shout, "Down! For Christ's sake down! Down!" Just a moment or two before one of the grenades exploded.

"Look at them fall!" The cry was drawn from Ah Bpo's lips. A cry of exaltation, of triumph and awe. . . . And of relief. There had been those awful moments when he had thought that Tommy would actually let them take him alive.

From where he was lying on the dirt track, Carter saw Sergeant Jimmy Rahman walk round from the back of the armoured car just a fraction of a second before the grenade exploded—even as Carter opened his mouth to scream at him to get down. He watched in mute horror as Jimmy's hands went to his chest, saw the expression of stupefaction on his face as his knees crumpled under him and he slid to the ground and sat propped up by a wheel of the armoured car.

Even now some of the Malay police were still on their feet. Carter screamed at them to get down—but this time he spoke in Malay. He had not done this the first time; and not all of them had seen the grenades fall. They had stood in bewilderment, knowing neither what he was saying nor the reason for it.

They lay now, waiting for the second grenade to explode. But not all of them lay face downwards, and one didn't lie at all, but

171

knelt holding his stomach, his mouth working to make sounds which would not come.

After another twenty seconds or so, Carter stood up and climbed into the armoured car: a moment later the loudspeaker ordered, "The men between here and the river are to move to the right or left keeping well down."

After his order had been obeyed, Carter climbed down from the armoured car and walked to where the second grenade lay by the edge of the track, picking it up as slowly and gently as he could, he turned and walked carefully towards the river, holding the grenade just above the ground. At the river bank he tossed it into the river, stood looking at the water for a moment before taking out a handkerchief and wiping his face and neck. Then he turned and ran back to where Sergeant Rahman sat propped against the wheel of the armoured car. Going down on one knee beside him Carter turned his body gently, supporting his shoulders with his left arm. Jimmy Rahman slowly opened his eyes and looked up at Carter's face, weakly he tried to smile as he whispered, "Mati-lah saya, Tuan."

"No, Jimmy, you are not. And you must not think you are," Carter said softly. Then as Jimmy closed his eyes he said urgently, "You are going to live, Jimmy. And you must keep telling yourself you are going to live; because you are going to live. Do you understand, Jimmy?"

Again the weak smile, then a whisper, "Selamat tinggal,* Tuan." Then he died.

"Selamat jalan,† Jimmy," Carter whispered.

Carter looked up as a shadow fell across them. Sergeant Morgan. "What's the score?" Carter asked fearfully, his voice almost inaudible.

"Well if I heard what I thought I heard just now," he indicated Jimmy Rahman's body with a nod of his head, "it's five dead and eight injured, sir."

"So many?" Carter replied, shocked.

"Afraid so, sir. Bit sudden like, wasn't it? New one on me."

Carter looked down at the face below him, but he didn't see it:

---

* Goodbye. Literally, "safe stay." Said by one going on a journey to those who remain.
† Selamat jalan. The reply. Literally, "safe journey."

he could see only an elderly little fat man in shirt sleeves and braces standing in the doorway of a council flat, nodding sagely as he said, "Yes, I can believe that. He'd be good at whatever he turned his hand to, would young Tommy."

14

It was half past five but the heavy black clouds would bring darkness early. Carter stood at his office window looking down at the police courtyard. The lorry bearing Khan Hock Loi's body turned in at the gates. Already, an eager crowd peered through the railings.

The procedure was routine. Whenever a ranking Communist terrorist had been eliminated, and before his body arrived at Police H.Q., detectives would spread the word that an important Communist had been killed. A crowd would then collect outside the railings at Police H.Q. to witness the arrival. In the courtyard, the body would be transferred from the police lorry to the van which would take it to the morgue, and although the body wouldn't exactly be on view, the crowd would have every opportunity of viewing it.

Carter approved of the procedure; it gave the lie to Communist claims that particular Communist leaders were still alive, for there would always be those in the crowd who would recognise the corpse—either from "Wanted" posters or from personal acquaintance.

Carter watched as Khan Hock Loi's body was taken from the lorry and placed on a stretcher on the ground, pending the arrival of the van. The van driver always took just two minutes to arrive.

But something seemed to have drawn the attention of the crowd. Many of them were turning round, attracted by something in the road behind them. Khan Hock Loi's mother. Screaming. Her face bloody, where she had torn at it with her own hands, her hair streaming out behind her, she ran down the road. Blindly, her hands outstretched in front of her, her breasts heaving with exertion, she ran between the sentries at the gate and flung herself on her knees beside the stretcher.

Overawed, the sentries made no move to restrain her; nor did anyone approach her as she mourned over the body, kissing and caressing the face of her dead son.

For a long moment she crouched over the body, motionless and silent. Then she knelt upright and moved the head and shoulders of the body until its head rested in her lap; for a moment she knelt unseeingly, clasping the head to herself with both hands, until with a sudden jerk she flung her head back and howled like a dog.

Carter turned as his office door opened behind him.

Halroyd. His face black with anger, his voice thick with rage as he hissed, "Five men died today, and more may yet die, because you were so fucking keen to keep a killer alive! Your own staff could have got him in the first minute! But you told them you wanted him alive. So five men died! *Now! Now* can you understand that you *must* learn to control your fucking stupid feelings!"

Shocked, Carter stood motionless, gazed at the open doorway, scarcely hearing the echo of Halroyd's slow footsteps along the empty corridor. Then from among the turmoil of his thoughts in the minutes which followed, one thought emerged with frightening clarity. *It was true.* He had done just that! Gambled with lives that were not his to lose. Gambled and lost! And for what? For what? He stood motionless for several minutes, then turned towards the window and numbly noted the fact that it was raining.

Twenty miles away, in a small clearing just inside the jungle from a rubber estate, Ah Bpo half sat, half lay on the ground, staring vacantly at the stream of water which fell from the tree above.

He would never see Tommy Loi again. Never, ever, ever. No one would ever see him again. He was gone. Nothing would ever know him again.

Never again would his shadow lie long upon the parade ground as he led them in song at morning parade. Never again would the quiet words of caution, "Steady, comrades," fall from his lips as the Imperialist truck rounded the curve on the road below.

Never again the cool reprimand, the curt command, the word of praise, the words of love. . . .

No one would ever hear his voice again. Ever!

For perhaps a year or two, his aged mother would tend his grave, till she too would join him.

175

Then no one would mourn him. His name would never be mentioned: he was gone, gone as if he had never been.

Gone and forgotten!

Suddenly Ah Bpo sat up. Perhaps even he, Ah Bpo, would forget him. There would be nothing to remember him by. Memories fade. And do not pleasant memories fade fastest?

With quick determination Ah Bpo stood up, walked to the bush where he had earlier stowed the haversack and their sten-guns, picked up one of the guns and cocked it: holding it firmly under his right arm, he placed the lower joint of the middle finger of his left hand over the mouth of the barrel, then closing his eyes, he pulled the trigger. Teeth clenched, he stood before the stream of water a long time: his right hand holding his left wrist, the water falling directly on the stump of the finger. Then deciding that water alone would not stop the blood from flowing, he finally staunched it with the aid of the lace from one of Tommy's jungle boots, using his right hand and his teeth to make a tight knot.

No. Ah Bpo would not forget Khan Hock Loi.

Nancy looked down at the head in her lap, caressed the fair hair fondly, "Why so depressed, honey?"

"Funerals depress everybody," Carter replied, "and I spent most of the afternoon in the Muslim cemetery."

She raised his head and kissed his forehead, "Poor darling," she murmured.

"It's not just the funeral either," Carter went on, "it's my job." He lay quiet for a few minutes, occasionally flicking the ash from his cigarette into the ashtray on the floor beside the bed. "I work out a plan and try to foresee every single possibility; the plan is successful, but the price of success always seems to be more than I ought to have had to pay." He lapsed into silence again, then after a minute or two, went on, "Five men died yesterday because I tried to keep one man alive. And because it took me several seconds to realise that a man whom deep down I knew would never surrender, and who would never cringe the way he was cringing, could only be doing so for a reason. He walked a long way in those few seconds: right into the middle of a whole jungle platoon. And another thing, I shouted out a warning in English instead of Malay, a mistake which made it a bloody sight worse."

176

"But we all make mistakes, darling, and nobody can foresee everything."

"It's not so much a question of not having foreseen what ought to have been foreseen, so much as a question of the occurrence of the totally unforeseeable. Like that lorry driver who killed all those people when he was himself dead."

"But that wasn't your fault, honey," she protested, "someone tried to kill you. . . ."

"I know, but none of it would have happened but for me. I'm rather like the monkey's paw in a story by Jacobs, I grant every wish, but in such a way that the result is disaster, and a fervent regret that the wish was ever made."

"Poor darling, you *are* miserable," she said stroking his chest.

"I know," he replied, looking up at her, "and I've only been back eleven days."

She bent down and whispered, "And eleven glorious nights."

But he ignored her and went on, "My cardinal error was in caring whether the bloody man lived or died at all."

"But you don't want to kill anybody really, do you, darling? Not unless you have to."

"I know I don't *want* to, baby, but the point is I shouldn't care whether I have to or not. It's the *caring* which is the mistake, because it puts you at an immediate disadvantage; it ties your hands and restricts your methods."

He raised his eyelids, read the blank look on her face and said, "Look, honey, why do you think a surgeon is forbidden to operate on his wife and children?"

"Well, I suppose it's because his love for them might, well, er, distract him . . ."

"Exactly! He's emotionally involved, isn't he? So instead of displaying total dispassion, and concentrating on what he's doing, he's terrified he's going to make a mistake and his hands are trembling so much he daren't make an incision."

"Yes, darling, but that's got nothing to do with you in your job, has it?"

"I've learned it's got plenty. From here on, I display surgical dispassion: and if my scalpel slips occasionally, I shall say, 'tch tch tch. Next.'"

She looked down at him, but he wasn't looking up at her, and he didn't seem to be joking. There were times when she simply didn't understand him at all, so she said, "I don't know what you're talking about, honey."

"Dispassion, darling: singleness of purpose. Killing as many Communists as possible as cheaply as possible."

She daren't tell him so, but she didn't like it when he talked like this. He oversimplified things. Some of her school friends were in the jungle. Misguided perhaps, and certainly misled, but nevertheless fighting for something in which they believed. They were not just criminals and murderers; not all of them, anyway. But she banished these thoughts, lifted his head, and twisted her body round until she lay facing him.

Since Carter's return from leave, Halroyd had ordered him to travel to and from the office only in an armoured car. But after the first week Carter had wrung from him the concession that he could make one third of these journeys in the car of a fellow officer provided he never travelled more than once in the same car each week.

This particular morning he was travelling to the office in Harry Vardon's car. A year or two older than Carter, Vardon had much the same background, a keener intelligence, an analytical approach to the many problems that confronted him as O.C., C.I.D., an abrupt manner, and a tongue as sharp as a razor. He was respected rather than popular—too many people had cut themselves—but above all, he was efficient. Although—at least in Carter's opinion—he paid overmuch attention to the letter, rather than the spirit of the law.

As Vardon drove out of the gates of the Mess compound with Carter sitting beside him, Carter said, "Go by the Christian cemetery road, Harry."

"What the bloody hell for?"

"I'm interested in a funeral that took place there a week or so ago. In fact, with the aid of telescopic lenses, I had it filmed. There were only a handful of mourners, but there was one mourner missing."

"So?"

"So I've had the place watched since then. All day and all

178

night. But I couldn't keep it up indefinitely, so I called the watch off yesterday. Now I think I'd just like to visit the grave myself."

"Morbid bastard," Vardon commented, but he took the cemetery road.

The Christian cemetery was not a big place, perhaps some four hundred yards square surrounded by a seven-foot high brick wall and with an imposing entrance of large wrought iron gates. Behind the gates a wide gravel road divided it neatly into two halves; only that part of the cemetery to the right of this road was "occupied," the other half being simply a small field.

Carter got out as the car stopped outside the gates and said, "I won't be long, Harry."

"Better not be, I've got a High Court case in half an hour," Vardon replied sourly.

Inside the gates Carter crunched down the gravel road for fifty yards then turned on to the grass between the graves. He knew the way from the film of Khan Hock Loi's funeral. Arriving at the grave he looked at it for just a fraction of a second before flinging himself flat beside it. He was probably in mid-air when the shot was fired. Beside the grave, he rolled over on his back and drew his Colt, then knelt facing the direction from which the shot had come. He thought he detected a movement behind a gravestone some twelve yards away, but wasn't sure. Realising that his adversary had the advantage of knowing where he was, he scrambled and zigzagged through the gravestones for a distance of about five yards, bent double, and away from the direction of the shot.

He peered cautiously round a gravestone but could see no one. He heard the iron gates clang heavily, and then, from nearby, two quick shots. He looked over the gravestone and caught a glimpse of a close-cropped head beside a stone monument eight or nine yards away, but even as he looked a bullet zinged off the stone by his head.

Carter ducked. By God the man was quick!

A single shot from the direction of the gates. Vardon. Crewcut was somewhere between them, but it was difficult to know just where. Instinctively, Carter and Vardon positioned themselves so that Crew-cut could retreat only towards the wall: they would get him at the wall. But it was very dangerous indeed to make any movement that was not completely shielded by gravestones.

Carter was a good shot with a pistol—he used the "pointing-finger" grip, his index finger lying along the barrel and squeezing the trigger with his middle and third fingers—but Crew-cut was in a class of his own. He made every shot count. And not only was he accurate, but he was so quick. Twice as Carter dodged from one gravestone to another bullets missed him only by inches. To Carter it seemed that Crew-cut fired much more frequently at him than at Vardon. But however good he was, Crew-cut had only one pistol and one pair of eyes. Vardon and Carter were some forty yards apart, and they had now positioned themselves where they could see each other along the neat rows of gravestones that ran parallel with the wall; they exchanged signals and gave each other covering fire as they ducked forward in brief dashes from one gravestone to the next.

Crew-cut was steadily being forced back towards the wall. Forty yards from the wall he did what he could postpone no longer; he sprinted to the wall, zigzagging between the gravestones. Carter and Vardon kept pace with him, watching expectantly for the moment when he would turn and fire—when Crew-cut fired it was wise to be behind cover.

Carter knew what Crew-cut was going to do. He was going to fire half a dozen quick shots at Vardon and Carter, leap on to a gravestone, and from there to the top of the wall.

Crew-cut did just that. While he was doing it, Carter concentrated on the wall behind him, waiting for the moment when Crew-cut would have to be on top of it. In the brief moment when Crew-cut leapt from the gravestone to the wall, Carter stood up and began taking aim: allowing for the Colt's tendency to kick up and to the right, he aimed at a point six inches below and to the left of the small of Crew-cut's back. In the fraction of a second in which Crew-cut checked his balance on top of the wall Carter squeezed the trigger, knowing he couldn't miss. The hammer of the Colt clicked forward on to an empty chamber. Carter was left with the indelible memory of a left hand fully extended and with a bandage over the stump of a middle finger as Crew-cut disappeared over the wall.

While Carter was still mouthing oaths, Vardon came up panting, wiping blood from his face. "Christ! Did he get you?" Carter asked in alarm.

180

"Bloody nearly. He chipped off a bit of gravestone no more than two inches from my face. Can that bastard shoot!"

"You can say that again." Carter agreed. "I'm not absolutely certain, because I never got a proper look at his face, I was too busy keeping my head down. But I'd swear it was the missing mourner—a character called Ah Bpo. But nobody ever told me that he could shoot like that."

"We'd better not stand here," Vardon remarked, glancing along the top of the wall.

"I wonder how he lost that finger," Carter mused, adding, "come and have a look at this."

He led Vardon to Khan Hock Loi's grave. On it was a bunch of roses, a large wreath of lilies, and a framed photograph of Khan Hock Loi. In front of the photograph, upright in the earth, was a burning joss-stick.

Pointing at the joss-stick with the toe of a shoe, Carter said, "I hit the deck because of that. The bloody thing hasn't been lit for more than four minutes." Glancing at Vardon he explained, "Khan Hock Loi's mother is a Christian, and in any case, she isn't here, is she?"

Vardon gave him a long hard look, said slowly, "By God, Ralph; your uncanny bloody prescience will lead you back here one day—feet first. And that's for sure."

But Carter was only half-listening; he was reading the card attached to the large wreath:—

To Tommy.
On the last anniversary of his graduation.
In grief.
With guilt.
David.

Carter recalled his words to Cresswell. "If you met me you wouldn't know me either."

That also, was for sure.

It had been Elizabeth who had made the call to Singapore; Carter couldn't bring himself to do it personally.

Inspector Chivapathy's teeth shone whitely against his face as he sat in the chair on the other side of Carter's desk. At twenty-three he looked about eighteen, had an infectious grin and entered into everything he did with joyful enthusiasm.

"He's ordered a car, sir. And he's taking driving lessons."

Carter sat back and put both hands behind his head as he said, "Well, well, well."

"Yes sir. And he says he will pay cash down. A Morris Minor sir. $5,000. That means insurance, Road Traffic tax, petrol and servicing. It's all money, sir," Chivapathy said happily. "And he's also bought a Rolex, sir. With a gold strap. $875!"

"Thank you, Chiv. Keep me informed."

When the door closed Carter found himself thinking, "The fool! The bloody fool!" But it occurred to Carter that though he had always felt that Project Chameleon would be successful, he had never quite known why. Yet it was beautiful in its simplicity. Those who feel themselves inferior are under a compulsion to impress. It was as simple as that.

In the course of the next six weeks, Daniel Nathan moved into a large house in a better neighbourhood: he furnished it with new furniture, and had a garage built for the car. An Indian maid appeared at the door the day he moved in and was promptly given the job she sought.

The rent of the house was $75 per month; the maid's wages were $45.

Daniel's salary was $175 per month.

Daniel did not get his eleventh payment. He got a telephone call instead. An Indian voice telling him to ring Sintra 4792. "Between six and seven o'clock. Any night. Sintra 4792."

An additional telephone in Carter's lounge.

The same evening, as its light flickered on and off, Carter picked up the receiver and said, "Yes, Daniel?"

There was a long pause; then an angry and frightened voice saying, "Who are you, and what do you want with me!"

"I want your co-operation, Daniel."

"Who are you? And why should I co-operate with you?"

"You have good reason for co-operating with me, Daniel. In fact you have a thousand good reasons. You've been getting them every month, haven't you?"

182

A long pause; heavy breathing. "Who *are* you? What *do* you want with me?"

"Well this evening, Daniel," Carter's voice was bland, almost casual, "I want you to go to the Rex cinema. The nine o'clock show. Come out through the door on Cross Street and you will be met by a fat Indian who will greet you as an old friend. Go with him."

"Go? Go where?"

"To meet me, of course."

Carter put the 'phone down.

Assistant Superintendent Anthony Cherian would meet Daniel. He was "on loan" for that specific reason. Fat, jovial, balding. Everybody liked him. In his mid-fifties, he would be retiring soon. Just the man to put Daniel at ease.

At midnight Carter was sitting in a flat on the top floor of the Taai Lung Bank building. A flat used by those who wanted to speak to Special Branch officers, but who didn't want to be seen doing it: a flat normally used by a Chinese prostitute. Because the Special Branch paid her rent, she let S.B. officers use it when required.

The telephone.

"Mr. Cherian's met him, sir. They're just getting into his car." Sergeant Major Lim's voice.

"Thank you, S.M. How does he look?"

"Not happy, sir. Frightened."

"Thank you, S.M. Goodnight."

The 'phone again, seven minutes later.

"They're getting out of the car now, sir; they'll be with you in two minutes."

"Thank you, Lo."

Carter did not say "goodnight," because Sergeant Lo would be ringing him again to tell him where Daniel had gone after he'd left the flat. Sergeant Lo was ringing from a call box opposite the bank, his motor-cycle nearby.

Now that the screws were on, Daniel's every move was closely watched.

The doorbell.

Carter got up, walked along the short passage and opened the door.

183

Assistant Superintendent Cherian and Daniel Nathan.

"Thank you, Tony; there's no need for you to wait."

"Goodnight, Ralph."

"Goodnight. Come on in, Daniel." Carter's voice was genial; he spoke as if Daniel were an old friend.

Daniel followed him into the lounge and stood behind an armchair while Carter busied himself with drinks at the sideboard.

"What do you want with me, white man?" But there was more spirit in the words than in the tone in which they had been uttered. The tone was one of fearful apprehension.

"Sit down, Daniel. You drink Guinness I believe." Carter poured out a glass of Guinness from a bottle, placed it on the table in front of the armchair behind which Daniel was standing, and sat down facing him.

Daniel was everything Carter had been led to expect. Short, slight, shifty. Carter hazarded the guess that Daniel's normal attitude was one of challenge: he was the sort of person who anticipated hostility, and, because he anticipated it, he provoked it.

"Do sit down, Daniel," Carter said with weary patience.

Reluctantly, looking at Carter nervously, Daniel sat down.

"Cigarette?" Carter asked, proffering a packet.

"No."

"Well help yourself to your drink. I bought it specially for you. Never drink it myself, but I believe it's very nourishing."

Daniel picked up the glass, then put it down again without raising it to his lips. "Look, what *do* you want with me?"

"Mr. Cherian told you you would be meeting a Special Branch officer, didn't he?"

Daniel nodded.

"Well, Daniel, the Special Branch is part of the police; and it's the duty of all good citizens to co-operate with the police, isn't it?"

Carter drank some brandy soda before continuing. "So, Daniel, we want you to co-operate with us in arranging the surrender of your younger brother."

Daniel stood up quickly, "My own brother! Help you get him to surrender! You must be mad! In any case, I couldn't help you even if I wanted to. I haven't seen him for years."

"Pity about that," Carter remarked blandly, "there's $450,000

184

reward for Emmanuel. You would of course, have got it, if you'd been able to arrange his surrender or capture."

Daniel glared down at him, "Shit on you!" He spat, before turning and walking out.

Daniel didn't get his twelfth payment either. On the seventh of the month Carter sent for Chief Inspector Lau.

"You know the proprietor of the Man Woo Loong provision store, C.I.?"

"A fellow clansman, sir. I know him well." Lau replied woodenly.

Carter wondered if Lau simply meant that the proprietor was a fellow-Hakka, or if he meant that he was a member of the Waa Kee Secret Society. Probably both, Carter concluded.

"Daniel Nathan's wife buys all her provisions there. She will not yet have paid her bill for last month. Will your fellow clansman stop her further credit until her last month's bill is paid—if you ask him?"

"I'm sure he will, sir."

"The same applies to the petrol pump near the Basle Mission Primary school. Can you do that too?"

"The owner, sir. A distant relative."

"I would like it to be done today if possible, C.I."

"Sir."

Carter sent for Inspector Chivapathy.

"That agent of yours. The one you planted on Daniel's wife."

"Yes, sir."

"She hasn't been paid her first month's salary yet, has she?"

"No, sir. But I told her not to make a fuss about it."

"Well tell her to make one hell of a fuss now. She gives three days' notice today, and says that if she doesn't get paid by the end of the three days, she's going to the Labour and Social Welfare Department to make a formal complaint against her employer."

"Yes, sir."

"Oh, and Chiv, has he any outstanding bills concerning the car?"

"He hasn't paid for his first servicing yet, sir."

"The manager would press for payment if you asked him?"

"Oh yes, sir. Of course."

185

"Ask him to press for payment by 'phone tomorrow, using the school 'phone. Daniel has a coffee break at ten-fifteen; you know the number of the teachers' Common Room."

"Yes, sir."

Carter called in Sergeant Major Lim.

"You remember getting the details of Daniel Nathan's new house, rent and so on?"

"Yes, sir."

"He hasn't paid last month's rent yet, has he?"

"No, sir."

"The owner would press for early payment if you asked him?"

"Of course, sir. Everyone likes to oblige the police in small matters."

"Well ask him to insist on payment tomorrow. Using the school 'phone between ten-fifteen and ten-thirty."

"Yes, sir."

In Halroyd's office Carter said, "Would you mind getting on to the Head of the Public Works Department, sir? I don't know him, and if Daniel hasn't paid last month's water and electricity bills, it would be excellent timing if he could be served with formal notice that his electricity and water was going to be turned off if he doesn't pay within three days."

"Certainly, Ralph. When would you like it done?"

"Tomorrow, sir."

The following evening, the new 'phone in Carter's lounge started flashing at precisely six o'clock. Carter looked at his watch and waited until the second hand had completed one and a half revolutions before picking up the receiver and saying, "Yes, Daniel?"

"I want to talk to you." Daniel's voice was an urgent whisper. "Drive your car to the petrol kiosk in Cross Street at ten p.m. A youngish Indian will climb into the front seat beside you while you're filling up with petrol. . . ."

"I can't!" The whisper was even more urgent now.

"Can't? Can't what?"

"Can't drive my car anywhere." Daniel paused. "I haven't got enough petrol."

"You'd better take a bus then. Anyway, be at that petrol kiosk at ten and a car will collect you."

At ten p.m. Carter sat in room 22 of the Oriental Hotel waiting for Inspector Chivapathy and Daniel Nathan. The room had been booked for one evening only; it was one of the few rooms in the hotel with a bathroom which had a door giving access to the garage.

At ten-fifteen, Carter answered the rap on the bathroom door, bade goodnight to Chivapathy, and led Daniel through the bedroom to the lounge.

As Carter poured out a Guinness, he took stock of Nathan who was pacing restlessly about the room.

My God; the change in the man, Carter thought. Nathan had wilted visibly since Carter had last seen him some five weeks before. He had aged. And gone was the spirit that he had shown on that occasion. He was beaten, and he knew it. He had a hunted look.

Carter put Daniel's drink on the table in front of an empty armchair, and sat down in another. He watched Daniel pacing up and down for a minute or so and then said softly, "Well, Daniel?"

Daniel shook his head two or three times and said, "My brother will never surrender. Why, if I mentioned it he would probably hit me." His voice was wan, dejected.

Carter accepted Daniel's admission that he still met his elder brother Emmanuel with an understanding nod and said, "Well, we'll just have to capture him then, won't we."

Daniel continued his pacing about the room as he replied, "But you'll never capture him! He knows that if you captured him you'd only hang him. He'd fight to the death!"

"If we captured him, Daniel, we wouldn't hang him. I suppose that's the irony of it. We don't hang captured Communist terrorists in this State; we would simply say he'd surrendered. The thought that he'd surrendered would worry the Communists no end, Daniel. You see, they wouldn't know whether he was talking or not, would they?"

Daniel paused in his pacings and with his hands on the back of a chair addressed Carter directly for the first time since his arrival, "Is that true?" he asked eagerly.

"Of course it's true. Go to the public library if you like, and go through all the old newspapers. No Communist terrorist captured in Kepayan has ever been hanged."

"So if you captured him, he would not be hanged? You promise me that?"

187

Carter's voice held sincerity as he said slowly, "I promise you, Daniel, that if we in the Special Branch capture your brother alive, we will treat him as if he had surrendered voluntarily. This means that we would bring no charges of any kind against him. He would simply be detained." Carter paused. "Now, Daniel, you can tell me how we're going to capture him alive."

For two very long minutes, Daniel resumed his pacing, then putting his hands on the back of a chair, he whispered, "I meet him once a month," looking appalled at the sound of his own voice.

"On Dartford Estate, Daniel?" Carter risked prompting.

Daniel looked, if anything, even more appalled as he said, still in a whisper, "Yes, that's right. On Dartford Estate. But how . . ."

"Never mind, carry on."

"Well, once a month I meet him on Dartford Estate."

"Where, on Dartford Estate?"

"At the house of Mandore Raja Gopal."

"Which Division?"

"The fifth."

"You say you meet him once a month, Daniel. But I happen to know you visit Dartford Estate *twice* a month!"

Bloodless now, his face almost grey, Daniel whispered, "Yes, I do, but Manny only comes once a month. I go on alternate Fridays, but he can't always get there, and I don't know whether or not he'll be there, unless . . ." Daniel stopped.

"Unless what?"

"Unless he's missed two appointments in a row; then he's sure to be there, he's never missed three in a row."

"When did you last see him?"

"About seven weeks ago."

"So he's missed the last two appointments, Daniel?"

"Yes."

"When are you seeing him again?"

Carter had to strain his ears to hear the scarcely audible reply. "Next Friday."

15

In Halroyd's office Carter was outlining the plan. "We have these photographs of Raja Gopal's house, sir," Carter remarked handing them across the desk, "it stands in the rubber on a slight rise about a hundred yards from the labour lines on the fifth Division— the labour lines of which Raja Gopal is, of course, the Mandore in charge. As you can see, it's the usual top-heavy wooden house, with part of the upper floor supported on concrete pillars: three rooms upstairs, and two on the ground floor. The verandah which runs right round the house on the upper floor, being directly accessible from the wooden staircase at the right, which you can see in the third picture. That staircase does, of course, act as the main entrance, although there is another staircase inside. Daniel always takes a bottle of Scotch with him; Emmanuel and Raja Gopal drink it and Daniel sticks to his Guinness. They usually sit up talking all night; Emmanuel leaving at about four, just before roll-call for the tappers. The bottle of Scotch I shall give Daniel has been doped, Emmanuel and Raja Gopal will pass out, Daniel will signal to us from the verandah with a torch, and that's it! We simply nip in and collect Emmanuel."

"What about the dog?" Halroyd asked.

"Well apparently it's been trained not to bark when Daniel or Emmanuel arrive, but as it hasn't been trained not to bark at us when we arrive, I shall provide Daniel with a hunk of doped meat which he can toss to it as he goes into the house. That should do the trick I imagine."

"What arms does Emmanuel carry?" Halroyd enquired thoughtfully.

"In the house, apparently none at all, sir. At least, so Daniel tells me. As you know, he favours the rifle, but according to Daniel Raja Gopal asked him not to bring arms into the house as it frightened his wife. Daniel says he never sees him armed."

189

"And Raja Gopal's wife?"

"After the usual civilities, she leaves the men to it and goes to bed."

"You propose taking *all* your Field staff, I suppose?"

"I think so, sir. I have not, of course, told Daniel that I personally propose being there at all, but I did intimate to him that I would arrange that there would be sufficient people there to deal with the removal of Daniel in a discreet and efficient manner. Daniel simply hides in another room until Emmanuel has been collected, and then at the first opportunity creeps out and trots off to school as usual, as indeed, he always has done in the past."

Halroyd looked thoughtful; "It sounds too bloody easy to me, Ralph." His voice was emphatic.

"There's no reason why it shouldn't be easy, sir."

"Well, have Sergeant Morgan with his jungle squad at instant readiness at the police post at the twenty-first mile, and take a walkie-talkie set with you so that you can get in touch with him if necessary. *And,* Ralph, act entirely on the assumption that Daniel is leading you into a trap."

Carter looked surprised, so Halroyd explained, "The loss of the whole of my Projects Section, in one fell swoop so to speak, would be difficult to explain away, Ralph; even for me."

"One other thing, sir," Carter remarked uncertainly, "what do I do about Raja Gopal?"

Halroyd smiled sweetly, said, "If you're concerned about his personal safety, then, Ralph, you've got problems."

"Mandore Raja Gopal, sir, has a wife and a small child," Carter pointed out tartly.

They sat looking at each other. They both knew what they were talking about. If Raja Gopal were arrested and Daniel wasn't, he would put two and two together and make four out of it. Even in prison, he could pass the word. Daniel and his family would not live long.

On the other hand, if Raja Gopal were not arrested, the Communists would automatically assume that he had informed on Emmanuel Nathan; any doubts they might have on this score would not deter them from using Raja Gopal as an example for what they do to "traitors."

Carter broke the silence, "As I see it, sir, the snag is that once

190

the Opposition gets its hands on Raja Gopal, he's bound to talk, bound to put the finger on Daniel; it's his only hope."

"I don't altogether agree with you there, Ralph. I don't think they'll give Raja Gopal a chance to talk; and even if they did they wouldn't believe him. Who would know exactly—apart from Raja Gopal, his wife, and Emmanuel himself—that Daniel was in the house on the night of Emmanuel's arrest? I very much doubt if anyone else *would* know; it's hardly a thing that any of them would risk talking about. And another thing, the Comrades would need to be pretty sure of themselves before they knocked off the brother of a State Committee Member." As Carter didn't reply, Halroyd went on, "This is one of those situations in which, if someone's *got* to die, the only thing you can do is make sure that it's not *your* agent."

"So?" Carter enquired quietly.

"So don't arrest Mandore Raja Gopal. By protecting him from his one-time pals, we are at the same time endangering the security of our own agent—Daniel."

They were all in jungle green and they were armed with automatic weapons. They sat or squatted around a rubber tree some fifty yards from Mandore Raja Gopal's house. The seven of them; Carter, and the six members of his Field staff. The moon was bright, but beneath the rubber trees it pierced the blackness only in isolated patches. The laterite road leading to Raja Gopal's house showed clearly. The corrugated iron roof of the house glistened; the house was a black shadow in the brightness of the garden.

They had been there an hour, suffering torment from the mosquitoes and saying nothing. Sergeant Major Lim nudged Carter's elbow. But Carter had seen it too, a shadow near the road. A shadow which moved swiftly.

Two minutes later a light showed for a moment as a door in the house opened and closed.

An hour or so later the same door opened and stayed open, as someone on the verandah signalled in their direction with a flashlight.

This was it. They would separate now and come into the house from three different directions; Chief Inspector Lau and two others from the left, Sergeant Major Lim and Sergeant Lo from the right, Carter and Inspector Chivapathy from the front. They melted into the darkness keeping away from the patches of moonlight. Carter and Chivapathy walked slowly: the others had farther to go.

A naked island in the rubber, the area round Mandore Raja Gopal's house and garden showed bright as day. From the darkness of the rubber Carter dashed through the brightness to the shadow of a durian tree: Inspector Chivapathy following him a moment later. To his left, and diagonally from him Carter caught a glimpse of someone running towards the rear of the house. Carter lifted up one of the five strands of barbed-wire which formed the fence around the garden, and stepped through. He held it up for Chivapathy, holding a lower strand down with a jungle boot as he did so, then they made the short dash through the garden and stood in the darkness under the verandah. Chief Inspector Lau was already there, and others quickly joined them.

From the rubber forty yards away came the sudden staccato burst of a sten, followed almost immediately by the heavier thump of a Thompson. Then all at once the sounds of a variety of weapons. As they stood stunned a figure burst from the darkness of the rubber, tore across the moonlit space outside the fence, jack-knifed over the fence and did a neck roll in a patch of vegetables, before leaping to its feet and joining them, panting desperately.

Sergeant Lo.

Carter grasped him by the shoulder, "Where's Sergeant Major Lim?"

"Out there, sir." Lo gasped.

"How many are there?" Carter demanded.

"I don't know, sir. Many! I think many!"

Carter said in an urgent whisper, "Take up defensive positions around the house. Don't shoot unless you think you might hit some bastard, but when you do shoot, change your position to give the impression there are more of us than there are. Where's the walkie-talkie?"

But even as he asked the question Carter knew the answer; it was with Sergeant Major Lim.

For several minutes they lay in the darkness under the verandah peering out from behind the concrete pillars at the darkness under the rubber trees. An uncanny silence; then sudden pandemonium as they were fired on from two sides. Then after a minute or so a whistle blew and the firing stopped.

192

Carter stood up and walked across to where Chief Inspector Lau lay behind a corner pillar. Going down on one knee beside him he whispered, "I'm going to see if the 'phone's still working, and," he added evenly, "if Daniel Nathan's here, I'm going to kill him."

In the darkness below the verandah Carter found a door. He tried the handle but it was locked from the inside. Stepping back, he fired a short burst from his Reising sub-machine gun and the door crashed open. He knelt beside the doorway and peered into the room.

In the light from a small oil lamp an Indian woman with a child in her arms huddled in a corner of the bed by the wall. Carter stepped swiftly through the doorway and stood to one side. The woman looked at him in mute terror, then turned as if to shield her child from him with her body.

He moved across the room to the other door and carefully tried the handle. As he flung the door open, he stepped aside expecting a shot. The door led to the bottom of a staircase. He climbed it tensely, silently, keeping well to one side, transferring his weight gently from one step to the next, until he could see the glimmer of light which showed from under a door to the right of the short passage at the head of the stairs. Crawling quietly along the passage he arrived at a door, reached up and turned the handle slowly; carefully holding the door closed, he sat down facing it and kicked it open.

There were three men in the room. One sat slumped at the table, his head on his arms. Emmanuel Nathan, a half-empty bottle of whisky in front of him. A second lay on his back on the floor; presumably Raja Gopal. The third, cowering under the sink in abject terror, Daniel Nathan. The floor a pool beneath him.

Catching sight of the telephone, Carter scrambled to his feet, stepped into the room and closed the door behind him. Ignoring Daniel, he made for the 'phone. He blinked his eyes with relief when he found it was still working. But the operator took a long long time, before she said, "Number please."

Carter gave her the number, listened through an eternity of clicks, heard the other 'phone ring three times, then a voice say "Sergeant Morgan here."

"We're in trouble. Surrounded. Get here quick."

193

"Right!" The 'phone slammed down.

Happier now, Carter put the 'phone down, turned to Daniel and said, "I told you to hide in another room, you nit! I don't want anyone to see you."

Without a word, Daniel scuttled through the door. Carter stood listening to him as he opened and closed the door on the other side of the passage. Then he went to the table, lifted Emmanuel Nathan's head by his hair, examined his face carefully, pulled one of his eyelids back and let the head fall. Beyond a doubt, Emmanuel Nathan. All $450,000 worth. Out cold.

Dragging him from his chair, Carter laid him out on the floor. It would be ironic, he thought, if Emmanuel were killed by a stray bullet.

Carter found himself looking at the problematical Raja Gopal —a man destined to die very soon. A man who might—if given the chance—talk! He walked to where he could put his hands under Raja Gopal's armpits and lifted him into a sitting position. Then he dragged him to the wooden partition, and left him propped against it still in a sitting position, his head hanging forward on his chest. Carefully Carter counted the number of floorboards from Raja Gopal's crotch to the corner of the door some five feet away— the door which gave on to the verandah outside. Twelve floorboards.

Carter turned out the light and opened the door of the verandah. He stood for a moment letting his eyes get accustomed to the darkness. He was in dark shadow although the reflected light of the moon did give some light.

He went down on his knees and counted the floorboards, feeling the cracks between them with his fingers until he got to number twelve. Raja Gopal was on the other side of the half-inch boarding with his back against it.

Carter followed floorboard number twelve to the verandah rail: holding his sub-machine gun with the butt just through the railings, and pointing in the direction of the edge of the rubber, he raised the muzzle until it pointed to a spot two foot six inches above the point where floorboard number twelve disappeared under the partition and into the room.

He squeezed the trigger ever so slightly so that it only fired one round. He went back into the room, closed the door and switched on the light. He walked over to Raja Gopal, bent him forward,

194

saw that from between his shoulders the blood flowed freely from a mess of flesh and wooden splinters, and propped him back. He switched off the light, opened the door and stepped out on to the verandah; pausing again to let his eyes get accustomed to the light, before making a complete circuit of the verandah, and carefully watching the edge of the rubber around the house for any sign of movement.

There were enough of them—judging by their fire power, the whole of Nathan's independent platoon, some thirty or forty men—that if they were prepared to lose eight or nine men they could take the place by storm. Morgan would not be there for another ten or fifteen minutes.

But eight or nine men was a lot of men to lose, Carter told himself as he walked down the stairs that led from the verandah. Nevertheless, one never knew.

At the bottom of the stairs he started, as a voice behind him and a few inches from his ear said, "Tuan?"

Chief Inspector Lau, taking no chances. There had, after all, been a shot upstairs.

"Yes. I got through. Pass the word that Morgan's on his way and should be here in about ten minutes. We've also got Emmanuel. Tell Inspector Chivapathy to go and handcuff his hands round a pipe or something."

"And the shot, Tuan?"

"A stray bullet. It killed Mandore Raja Gopal."

"An easier death, Tuan, than the one which awaited him."

Lau returned to Carter's side a few moments later. "They have been silent for too long, Tuan; they are up to something."

As if in answer to Lau's whisper, a voice from the rubber called, "You there. We've got something you want, you've got something we want. We will exchange?"

The voice spoke in Hakka, so Lau whispered, "You understand, Tuan?"

"Yes. They want an exchange of prisoners."

"As always, Tuan, they lie. Lim is already dead."

"Get Lo to reply that our man is already dead, and we do not exchange the living for the dead. And tell him to speak in Mandarin. Don't you do it. They might recognise your voice."

"They know who we are, Tuan. . . ."

195

"No, they don't! And they mustn't find out either. If they do, they'll be prepared to pay a high price to knock us off."

As Lau left Carter's side to find Sergeant Lo, Carter said to a figure lying nearby, "Warn those at the back. This might be just a diversion."

A moment later Lo's voice rang out in Mandarin.

Three minutes later, some thirty-five yards away and just inside the rubber, a flashlight shone on a chubby body, held up against a tree, its arms pinioned behind it. The left leg of his jungle green trousers showing wet and scarlet, his head hanging forward: Sergeant Major Lim.

The voice called, "See! Your man!"

Carter recognised the words as Mandarin and whispered to Sergeant Lo, "Tell him he speaks Mandarin like a Malay whore and we can see that our man is already dead."

As Lo cried out the reply Carter took careful aim. He watched as a hand holding a knife came out from behind the tree before which Lim was held upright and with bent head. The point of the knife found Lim's chin; slowly, unwillingly, Lim raised his head.

Carter fired a long burst and Lim's body crumpled at the knees. The man holding Lim's arms from behind the tree now let them go and Lim fell forward on his face.

Then the flashlight was extinguished.

In his grief and rage Carter ignored his own instructions and fired till his magazine was empty.

Much anger now.

The Communists raked the darkness under the house with every weapon they had while hand-grenades exploded harmlessly in the soft earth of the garden around the house.

After two minutes or so the whistle blew again, and then silence. But not for long.

Carter's men took it in turn to hurl insults. Carter couldn't stop them. Didn't want to. Couldn't in any case understand all that was said.

"Didn't expect that did you? Spoilt your fun, didn't it? Sons of whores fathered by pigs!" Sergeant Lo's voice.

Someone else: "Shame on your ancestors! Barbaric dupes! Half men with pawned minds!"

And much else besides.

Goaded, the Communists started firing again, but not as fiercely as before.

An explosion among the rubber trees was accompanied by a shrill scream. Presumably a "doctored" grenade detonator.

Under the house they roared with laughter.

Sergeant Lo cried, "Chairman Mao made that one himself, comrades."

Lights in the distance; Sergeant Morgan's armoured personnel carriers. They could hear them now; coming in dangerously fast for the Estate's laterite roads.

"Bye bye, comrades. You'd better crawl back to your storm drain now. Mustn't fight equal numbers."

"Will you know your way without your Commissar, comrades?"

"Hear me! The 'People's Enemy' Lau Yui Ming! There are five of us. Do you understand? Only five! And we've got your man! Do you understand? We've got your man!"

Chief Inspector Lau actually followed this with a laugh. The first that any of them had ever heard from him.

Carter and Halroyd sat in the flat in the Taai Lung Bank building sipping drinks and waiting for Daniel Nathan. Before them on the table, an immense pile of ten-dollar notes. In bundles of one hundred. $450,000.

In reply to Daniel's query as to how he would be paid the reward money, Carter had said, "We will pay you in any currency you care to name, even in roubles if you like. You can have it in gold nuggets, diamonds, or even buildings."

But the door of Emmanuel Nathan's cell had scarcely closed behind him when Daniel rang up to say that he wanted it in ten-dollar notes.

"In ten-dollar notes?" Carter had replied. "What's wrong with hundreds and thousands?"

"You said I can have it how I liked."

"And so you can, Daniel," Carter had said, "but do you realise what that amount of money is going to look like in tens?"

"I want it in tens."

A long pause, then, "All right, Daniel, you shall have it in tens. But go and buy two of the largest suitcases you can find and bring them with you."

197

That had been in the morning.

"I suppose he's earned his money in a way, Ralph. Finding himself in the middle of a fire-fight must almost have killed him with fright."

"It bloody well nearly killed me with fright, too."

"Still, Daniel couldn't have known that Emmanuel always kept his boys within hailing distance," Halroyd observed.

"I think there was more to it than that. I noticed that Emmanuel was carrying a pocket flashlight—one of those things not much bigger than a pen. I suspect that every now and then he used to go out on the verandah and signal his boys that everything was all right. When they didn't get the signal they moved in to find out why. They chose the moment we chose."

Halroyd glanced round the room. "We must get shot of this place, we've been using it a bit too much lately."

Carter got up as the doorbell rang. He disappeared along the passage and returned a moment later carrying a huge suitcase. Daniel followed, carrying its twin.

Carter said, "Daniel Nathan, sir." And to Daniel, "The head of the Kepayan Special Branch, Mr. Halroyd."

But Daniel didn't hear him: he stood looking at the pile of notes in awe.

Carter opened one of the suitcases, touched Daniel's shoulder to bring him out of his trance and said, "You'd better count them as you pack them."

But Daniel didn't bother. Working feverishly he transferred the notes from the table to the suitcases on the floor. When both suitcases were completely full there were still four bundles left over: he stuffed two of these into his trousers pockets then, on an impulse, placed the remaining two bundles separately on the table in front of Carter and Halroyd. "For you," he whispered.

Halroyd picked them up and said, "Stuff them in the front of your shirt, Daniel." And producing a piece of paper, "Sign here." Daniel signed.

Carter helped him with one of the two suitcases to the car outside. It was very heavy. It didn't occur to Carter until later, that Daniel had uttered only two words from the time he came to the time he left.

"For you."

16

Carter flicked the switch on his desk in answer to Halroyd's buzz. "Sir."

"Pop in a minute, Ralph, would you."

Carter was surprised to see Harry Vardon in Halroyd's office. The O.C., C.I.D. rarely had official business with S.B., his business being criminal, not political, offences.

As Carter sat down, Halroyd said, "Tell Ralph what's on your mind, Harry."

Vardon turned towards Carter and said, "I want Emmanuel Nathan's fingerprints."

Vardon's manner was always abrupt but Carter felt that this time he was also spoiling for a fight.

"Then, Harry, if you want them, you shall have them," Carter replied evenly.

"Today?"

"As soon as I can get them taken, Harry, but," Carter added with just a trace of sarcasm, "is one permitted to ask the reasons for your interest in this particular political prisoner?"

"Yes," Vardon replied stiffly. "I understand from Mr. Halroyd that Emmanuel Nathan was captured in the house of one, Mandore Raja Gopal, on Dartford Estate three nights ago."

Carter nodded before remarking, "But I'm afraid neither Raja Gopal nor his house exist any more. As soon as Sergeant Morgan's jungle squad left the area, the Communists returned and burnt his house down. With, so I am told, Mandore Raja Gopal, his wife, and their small child still in it."

"Be that as it may, Ralph," Vardon said tersely, "the same morning, a rubber-tapper found a Lee Enfield rifle leaning against a tree near the smouldering ruins of Raja Gopal's house. Ballistics tests have proven it to be the rifle used to kill Wainwright, Lieutenant Hamilton, and a Gurkha soldier. If the prints on the rifle match

199

Nathan's, we have a case against him for murder, and a further case against him for possession of arms."

"When those shots were fired, Harry," Carter pointed out, "it doesn't by any means follow that Emmanuel Nathan was holding the rifle."

"That will be for the Court to decide," Vardon snapped. "But if the fingerprints on that rifle turn out to be Emmanuel Nathan's, then I'm bringing a charge of murder against him under the Penal Code, and a further charge of "possession of arms" under the Emergency Regulations. They both carry the death sentence."

Halroyd said, "What you are proposing, Harry, is that he be tried in accordance with the provisions of the Criminal Procedure Code, and then be found guilty and sentenced to death under the Emergency Regulations."

"You may look at it that way if you wish, sir," Vardon remarked, "though there would be nothing illegal about it. But the Penal Code offence may well stand on its own."

Halroyd leant forward across his desk as he began, "Now look, Harry, we've got some bloody good reasons for not wanting him charged at all. . . ."

Vardon stood up, "I do not doubt that you have, sir, but they are not reasons that C.I.D. can take into account in a case of murder."

"While you're in your charging mood, Harry," Carter remarked icily as Vardon walked to the door, "you might consider a charge against me, for the murder of Khan Hock Loi. It would make just as much sense."

"What now, sir?" Carter asked after Vardon had gone.

"Give him the prints. They'll match all right."

"But we've got to stop him bringing the charges, sir."

They sat in deep thought. They both knew that once charges had been brought against Emmanuel Nathan, the machinery of the law took over; everyone would do what the law required him to do. The case against Nathan would go forward inexorably. Only the Attorney General would have the power to withdraw the charge, but once the fact that Nathan had been captured and had been charged became public knowledge, then it was doubtful if the Attorney General would or could use his powers. Even if he felt there was good reason for their use—which in any case he might not so feel.

Halroyd broke a long silence, saying, "You know, Ralph, the fact that he killed Wainwright is the biggest bugbear. It lets emotion into it. Everybody knew Wainwright, and that Nathan should be reprieved for any reason whatsoever will strike a great number of people as a flagrant miscarriage of justice. But I'm flying to Federal H.Q., tomorrow, and I'll have words with all the right people. A thing like this could affect our surrender figures no end. The Communists are bound to claim that Nathan surrendered. Pity about that bloody rifle though."

After dinner that night Carter and Vardon found themselves alone in the Mess lounge, sitting together at the bar.

Carter toyed with a glass of brandy, "So the fingerprints on Nathan's form matched those on the rifle, Harry."

"Surprisingly enough, Ralph. They did." Vardon replied.

"What's surprising about it? It was bloody obvious that they would."

"It was bloody obvious that they should," Vardon corrected, "but if they hadn't there would have been no case, would there? And I shouldn't think that S.B. are above making a little error, like taking half a dozen people's prints together and getting the wrong names on a couple of the fingerprint forms, for example."

Carter looked at Vardon quizzically, "Did you really seriously think that I might do a thing like that, Harry?"

Vardon returned Carter's gaze as he replied, "Frankly, Ralph, yes."

"That, Harry, is precisely the reason why I didn't do it."

For a moment their eyes held.

"Frankly, Ralph," Vardon said wearily, "I just do not even begin to understand your attitude towards this case, nor, for that matter, your attitude towards Nathan. I happened to pass the S.B. cells this afternoon, and in one of them I happened to notice *you* —having a jolly little chat with Nathan, with, of course, coffee provided."

"My attitude, Harry, springs from the knowledge that had I been born Emmanuel Nathan instead of Ralph Carter, I'd almost certainly have done the same as he did."

201

"And ended up in that cell?"

"Probably not. I'm not as trusting as he is. But for your information, Harry, it was a most useful little chat. He told me that I used to meet a little Malay waitress at one o'clock in the morning at the junction of Claremont and Davis Streets, and that if I had met her just one more time it would have been my lot, as a killer-squad was waiting for their Uncle Ralph."

"Jesus! Did he actually tell you *that?*"

"He most certainly did, Harry," Carter assured him in level tones. "One of the members of the killer-squad asked my driver for a light, so that he could look into the back of my car to see if I was stretched out asleep on the back seat."

"Well why didn't they kill your driver?"

"Because I might have shown up the following week of course. And in any case, it wasn't him they were after. Incidentally, although he didn't know it, when this character was asking Chan for a light, Chan was pointing a gun at him through the door of the car. That's why I had the lining removed—so as not to have any bullets hitting the window or door levers on their way out."

Carter held up his glass to the light, examined its contents critically, said, "Foresight, Harry, is to be strongly recommended," and drained it.

"Smug bastard," Vardon commented sourly.

"I remember Chan telling me about that night," Carter went on, "he told me he'd smelt danger. I shall pay more attention to his sense of smell in future, at the time, I thought he was just being melodramatic."

"Brother, are you living on borrowed time," Vardon commented, shaking his head.

Ignoring the remark, Carter continued, "And another thing. I've got a nickname. 'Blondie.' Nathan's quite proud of it; he was telling me that he had asked one Lim Tsing Wa by name, when he was going to get Blondie. At a State Committee Meeting no less. But, Harry, before that he had said—and I quote—'I said to the man that's going to kill you,'—unquote. And later he didn't deny that he had said it to Lim Tsing Wa. Now the point is, Harry, that Lim Tsing Wa is supposed to be dead. So much so, that our 'Wanted' posters depict him with the red diagonal cross over his face; but Nathan spoke of the man that *is* going to kill me. So I suspect that in the case of Lim Tsing Wa, our red diagonal crosses are a bit premature. I reckon he is still alive because one doesn't talk about what the dead are *going* to do, does one? So you see, Harry, my 'little chats'—as you call them—are not simply part of a 'be nice to Emmanuel Nathan campaign'; their purpose is the acquisition of info. In point of fact today's was the first of what I trust will be many. Nathan's deliberately been left alone since his arrest; nothing to read and no one to talk to, except me, that is, whenever I feel like it. He doesn't appear frightened, but he's certainly very bored and lonely. . . ."

"Life will get more interesting for him when he stands in the dock in the High Court and hears the evidence against him for murder," Vardon interjected.

"You're a victim of 'the Law's been broken and someone's got to pay the price,' mentality, Harry. The sanctity of the Law and of people paying their debts to society. All that cock!"

"It's not cock to me, Ralph," Vardon replied with asperity, "I happen to believe in the sanctity of the Law."

"Oh for Christ's sake, Harry. How the hell can you? It was an offence to attempt to commit suicide yesterday, but it's okay today. Two men can't rodger each other today, but it'll be all right tomorrow. All sorts of crimes are 'abominable,' except murder, of course, which is simply 'wilful.' The Law's loaded with such screaming absurdities—dating from the time when it sentenced starving kids to death for stealing apples. I know you have to apply the Law, Harry, but you don't have to light candles in front of it for Christ's sake."

"It'll make no difference to Nathan whether he's charged with 'wilful' or 'abominable' murder, Ralph. And your verbal diarrhoea will alter neither my attitude nor that of the Commissioner."

"Does he know about this Nathan deal?" Carter asked, suddenly concerned.

"He does indeed. And he agrees with me. And you will no doubt be among those present to hear him say so, at a meeting in his office tomorrow morning."

"Oh, Harry. You do not know what dogs you are letting loose. You just do not know!"

Vardon looked at him curiously: Carter had spoken in something like a horrified whisper.

Later, in his bungalow while he waited for Nancy, Carter lay on his bed thinking of his interview with Emmanuel Nathan that afternoon. He pictured the scene in Nathan's cell as the door closed behind him. Nathan sat at the table smoking a cigarette and looked up with interest at his first visitor: beside him on the table, a cigarette tin that served as an ashtray, half full now with short butts. Carter's instructions had been quite specific. He had said, "Nathan is to be kept under a twenty-four hour watch. And that includes when he's in the toilet. When he's taken into the exercise yard there shall be no other prisoners in it; nor shall he even see, let alone meet, other prisoners. No one is to talk to him at all, not even to reply if he says, Good morning, or asks what day it is. And no books, no writing material, nothing that will serve to occupy his mind. But should he ask for anything, I want to be told immediately. The first time he asks for anything, the answer is to be, 'I will pass your request to the Inspector,' after that, the answer is a nod."

Carter was playing the mind game. Nathan had gone for a drinking session in Raja Gopal's house and had woken up in a police cell. All that Nathan really knew of his whereabouts was that he was still in the Tropics. If Carter had had the proper facilities Nathan wouldn't have known even that. In an air-conditioned building with glazed windows, and seeing only European guards he could have been anywhere, anywhere at all. He could have been led to believe that he had lain in a coma for eighteen months: the scars on his head and the occasional calendar bearing witness to the truth of this. "Psychiatrists" could have ministered to him and in their efforts to nurse him back to mental health could have relieved him of every single scrap of information he had ever acquired as a State Committee Member—positions of Communist camps and dumps, the names of agents, sources of arms and ammunition, the lot. The information thus acquired would bring the end of the Emergency that much nearer, much wealth and many lives would be saved. But Carter would have to make do with the limited facilities available.

Nathan was gregarious; very much the social animal. He liked people, and he liked to be liked. Liked also, to be the center of attraction. The treatment he was getting would go harder with him than with most—and it went very hard with most. The first forty-eight to seventy-two hours are the worst; after that, a defence mechanism comes into play to preserve sanity. That was why Carter was where he was on the third day after Nathan's arrest. In Nathan's cell.

Carter could remember the conversation almost word for word: every nuance of tone, every glance.

"My name's Carter. I'm an Assistant Superintendent of Police."

Nathan's eyes were cautious, yet displayed keen interest. He said, "I'm Emmanuel Nathan. Comrade State Committee Member of the Kepayan Regiment of the Communist Liberation Army."

Carter grinned, "I know."

"I know you too. You're the one we call Blondie." As Carter didn't answer Nathan went on, "As a matter of fact it was me that gave you the name. I said to the man that's going to kill you, 'Never mind all the shit about the small-fry, when are you going to get Blondie?'" He added proudly, "We've called you 'Blondie' ever since."

As Carter had expected it would be, it was a relief to Nathan to talk.

"And just exactly how did Lim Tsing Wa answer your question?" Carter asked, his voice casual.

Momentarily Nathan's eyes widened before he replied, "Who said anything about Lim Tsing Wa?"

Carter was surprised to meet a senior Communist who couldn't play poker, but then he remembered that Nathan was only on the State Committee to lend it a multi-racial character. This, he told himself, is going to be interesting. One could read Nathan like a book.

"I was there when you said it," Carter replied to Nathan's question, "it was at a State Committee Meeting."

Nathan didn't even attempt to hide his surprise, "Man, if we'd known you were there you could've taken the chair."

Inwardly, Carter marvelled at Nathan's naïvety. *Never mind all that shit about the small-fry, when are you going to get Blondie?* It could hardly have been said to any one other than the boss of the killer-squads, either Lim Tsing Wa or his successor—but Nathan's eyes had told him that it had been said to Lim Tsing Wa. And although State Committee Members kept in regular touch with each other they very rarely actually met except at Committee Meetings—twice a year.

Catching the scent Carter pursued it. "But Lim Tsing Wa

hasn't been in a killing mood for some time. He got in the way of a parang I believe."

Nathan's eyes registered his acknowledgement of his mistake before he said, somewhat uneasily, "Anyway, it saved you $450,000."

Too late had Nathan remembered the red crosses on the "Wanted" posters of Lim Tsing Wa. He had even lied unconvincingly.

"Mind if I sit down?" Carter asked.

"No, why should I? It's your house, not mine."

Carter sat down and they examined each other's faces across the narrow table; then Nathan held out a packet of cigarettes, "Smoke?"

Carter took one and lit it. He said, "Thanks, but they're mine anyway. I supply them."

Nathan grinned, "Good for you." Then in a tone of genuine curiosity, "How'd you manage to get me, Mister?"

Carter puffed smoke at the ceiling. "Next question."

"Someone ratted on me. I'm certain of it."

"Of course," Carter agreed equably, "$450,000 is a lot of loot. And you got careless; regular visits to Mandore Raja Gopal's house. Most unwise. Someone noticed."

"Balls! The drink was doped. I'm sure of it."

"Well it didn't need to be, you had enough of it. One whole bottle of Scotch between just two of you in about an hour."

Nathan's eyes widened again and he said, "Who else was arrested with me?"

"Nobody." Carter replied with apparent slight surprise.

Carter read the bewilderment.

They sat looking at each other, Nathan with both elbows on the table, Carter with his right elbow on the table, head leaning against the hand at his ear, their faces close.

Carter said slowly, "Your comrades have killed one of the two men who were drinking with you that night."

Nathan's face suddenly wore an expression of shock, his voice was a hoarse whisper, "Which one?"

"Does it matter?" Carter replied indifferently.

Nathan swallowed hard. "Yes, it does."

"Really," Carter's voice expressed mild surprise. "Then if you tell me their names, I'll tell you which one got himself killed."

Nathan brought his hands up to his head and rested his forehead against the heels of his palms. Carter couldn't see whether his eyes were open or closed. He watched him shaking his head slightly behind his palms.

Slowly Nathan lowered his hands to the table. "You know Mister, I can't tell you that."

His voice implied that Carter should never have asked. Carter was thinking, Of course you can't. Surprised you had to think about it at all. It would have created difficulties if you had.

Aloud Carter said, "Pity," and flicked the ash from his cigarette into the tin on the table.

Carter's eyes went back from the ashtray to Nathan's face and as if something he saw there prompted him, he said in a tone of surprise, "Christ. It really does matter to you, doesn't it?"

Nathan gulped and nodded.

"It was Raja Gopal who died." Carter read the relief as he continued, "Your boys came back later in the morning and burned the house down. With him, his wife, and the kid still in it."

"The stupid bastards!" Nathan's voice was savage.

Carter broke a long silence when he said evenly, "Answer me one question Nathan. The man that got away; the man that ran out of the house when the dog barked as my boys closed in: was he in any way a man it would have paid me to kill?"

Nathan seemed amused at the question; he grinned and said, "No, Mister, he wasn't."

The look on Carter's face was one of doubt, but he said seriously, "Actually, at the time, we thought it was you."

"You were there?"

"Of course."

"You said my boys 'came back.' "

"That's right." Carter agreed.

"So you ran into them eh?"

"That's right."

"You're still here man."

"My sergeant major isn't."

"I reckon I'm worth a police sergeant major."

"Not that one you weren't."

Their conversation had gone on for a long time after that. Nathan had talked about everything—from how welcome the prison food was—"Man, I was sick and tired of that Chinese food in the jungle"—to Carter's narrow escapes from assassination—"You just can't imagine how lucky you've been."

Carter had given him plenty of bait, but he hadn't always risen to it. But he had risen once though; beautifully.

Carter had said, "I could never understand why you didn't get shot for losing your whole company. People have been shot for much less than that. And you'd got no right to leave your operational area without orders."

"I was ordered to leave it, that's why. And I had a written order to prove it."

"From Lo Heng?"

"Who else gives orders to Company Commanders?"

"But Lo Heng denied having written it, didn't he?"

The widened eyes: the unspoken question, "Now how do you know that?"

But Carter hadn't answered the question; it was always a good ploy to tell a prisoner things he thought you couldn't possibly have known, it made it easier for him to tell you other things—that you might not know.

Looking back on their conversation Carter wondered if Nathan had fallen for the story of Daniel running out of the house when the dog barked. Curious how two brothers could be so totally different. Daniel was not one hundredth part of the man that Emmanuel was. It crossed Carter's mind that he liked Emmanuel but he banished the thought immediately. He was not going to make *that* mistake again.

Lying on his bed Carter considered his talk with Emmanuel Nathan from every conceivable angle. Clearly Emmanuel was not a dedicated Communist—he hadn't even known his Communist catechism. Having argued that if a man had more intelligence than his fellows then his intelligence should be used for the benefit of the community, and not simply for his own benefit, Emmanuel had been at a complete loss to answer Carter's query as to what was to be done with someone who was intelligent but so lazy that he just didn't want to use his intelligence. "Wouldn't he have to be given some material incentive?" Carter had asked. It was unlikely, Carter thought, but given time it was not impossible that Emmanuel Nathan might actually get around to co-operating. Carter had promised to let him have some books, but these would all be books by disillusioned Communists: *The Light That Failed, I Believe,* etc., etc. Later Carter would let members of the "X" squad visit him so that they could flaunt their freedom at him.

It would be worth trying. And it might, it just might, come off. But if Emmanuel Nathan were charged with murder that would be the end of it.

No one could be expected to co-operate with his executioners.

Commissioner Davidson sent for them at half past eight the following morning. Halroyd, Carter and Vardon. He looked angry as they filed into his office. After they had sat down he said, "I heard something yesterday which I find it difficult to believe, but before expressing my opinions, I'd like first of all to verify the facts. Now I am, of course, aware that Nathan—more usually referred to both in the press and elsewhere as 'Killer' Nathan—was captured by you, Carter, some nights ago, but I'd like you to fill me in with some of the details; how exactly, was this capture effected?"

"We had acquired the services of an agent, sir," Carter replied in a candid tone, "an agent who used to join with Nathan occasionally in all-night drinking parties in the house of a Mandore Raja Gopal on Dartford Estate. Having been advised as to when one of these parties was to take place, an S.B. team simply waited in the rubber near the house until the agent signalled that Nathan had passed out."

"And you were in charge of that team?" Davidson put in.

"Yes sir. After the agent had signalled we split up and converged on the house from different directions. Unfortunately Sergeant Major Lim and Sergeant Lo ran into a group of terrorists apparently waiting for Nathan in the rubber at the back of the house. Sergeant Lo made it to the house. Sergeant Major Lim didn't."

"Couldn't Sergeant Lo have stopped to assist Sergeant Major Lim?" Davidson asked.

"Under the circumstances sir, no. They were heavily outnumbered. I think they probably ran into the whole of Nathan's independent platoon. Sergeant Major Lim's body was found later, badly mutilated."

Davidson looked concerned, "Did they capture him alive?"

"He was certainly not alive when they mutilated his body, sir; he'd had half his chest shot away."

"Well thank God for that at any rate," Davidson put in, relieved.

"I thought at first that our agent had led us into a trap, sir," Carter continued, "but when I went into the house, Emmanuel Nathan was slumped at a table with an empty bottle of Scotch in front of him. Fortunately the 'phone still worked, and I put in a call to Sergeant Morgan, who relieved us after a short while."

"It seems to me you were in a pretty tight spot there, Carter," Davidson observed, "facing a whole platoon, just a few of you."

"We were reasonably safe under the house sir, and the opposition had to cross quite a wide space, lit by brilliant moonlight, to really get at us."

"And so after Sergeant Morgan arrived, you simply collected Nathan, brought him back and locked him up?"

"Yes, sir, apart from the fact that before locking him up I had him medically examined; the doctor certified he was drunk."

"I see," Davidson said, and turning to Vardon, "And the following day you came into possession of a rifle."

"Quite so, sir. I received a call from one of the Assistant Managers on Dartford Estate to the effect that one of his tappers had discovered a rifle propped up against a tree, not far from the still smouldering remains of Raja Gopal's house. The Assistant Manager in question, sir, was Mr. Lloyd. You might know him."

Davidson nodded, "Yes I think I do. Rather a nice looking chap. Clean cut. Rather unwisely rides a motor-bike, I've seen him in the Club fairly often."

"Yes that's him sir," Vardon continued, "well he had sufficient sense not to touch the rifle, and to instruct that no one else touched it either."

"Yes, he looks an intelligent chap."

"Well sir, the rifle was duly collected, and given the usual treatment. It proves to have been the weapon which killed Wainwright, Hamilton, and a Gurkha soldier."

"And the most recent fingerprints on it were Nathan's," Davidson supplied.

"The only fingerprints on it were Nathan's," Vardon corrected.

"So you have two charges against Nathan," Davidson observed weightily, "one for the possession of arms, and the other for the

210

wilful murder of Wainwright. A murder actually witnessed by the Manager of Ayer Biru Estate, if I remember correctly."

"Exactly, sir." Vardon agreed.

"And now Charles," Davidson said, speaking to Halroyd for the first time since he'd entered the office, "am I correct in believing that you told O.C., C.I. yesterday, that you'd got 'Bloody good reasons for not wanting these charges brought at all'?"

"You are indeed, sir," Halroyd agreed equably. "Nathan is of far more use to us alive than dead. . . ."

"It's not a question of his *use*, Charles," Davidson cut in, "it's a question of Law. It is no function of ours to pick and choose as to whom we will bring charges against."

"We have never yet brought charges against a captured terrorist, sir," Halroyd reasoned, "we have treated them all as surrenders, a policy which has paid dividends, as you know. . . ."

"But capital charges didn't lie against them Charles," Davidson snapped, beginning to have difficulty in containing his temper.

"All of our Captures, sir," Halroyd pointed out, "have been liable for capital charges; either for possession of arms or uniform or b . . ."

"But dammit man! This Nathan fellow killed one of your own officers! To say nothing of Lieutenant Hamilton and others." Davidson exploded.

"Hanging Nathan, sir, will not bring Wainwright back to life." Halroyd's voice was icy, his face white with anger.

In contrast, Davidson's face was purple. They watched him as he took a cigarette from a silver cigarette-box on his desk; noticed the slight tremble of the flame as he lit it with his lighter. But his voice was controlled as he said, "I trust, Halroyd, that you are not suggesting that my wish that charges be proffered against Nathan derives from any desire for revenge; because I do assure you, that my whole motivation derives not only from a desire that justice be done and be seen to have been done, but also from a sense of duty— which you, Halroyd, seem to lack. You appear to have forgotten that the Police Force Ordinance enjoins all Police Officers to take cognizance of all those offences of which they happen to be aware. There is no proviso! It does not say, 'providing the Special Branch do not find it inexpedient!'"

211

Halroyd returned Davidson's angry look but elected to remain silent.

Addressing Vardon, Davidson went on in emphatic tones, "When you leave this office you will cause this Nathan fellow to be charged with murder and possession of arms, and with no further delay. And you, Halroyd, will render O.C., C.I. every assistance. Have I made myself clear, gentlemen?"

Halroyd leant forward, "I am flying to Federal Police H.Q., this afternoon, sir. May I request that the charges be deferred, so that the matter can be discussed at a higher l . . ."

"No you may not!" Davidson barked. "I'm in charge in this State. The murder took place in this State! And we can prove who committed it! And that, Halroyd, is what we're going to do!"

As they walked away from the Commissioner's office, Carter murmured to Halroyd, "The Court case, sir, is going to get a little tricky."

When Carter walked into his office, Elizabeth said, "Chief Inspector Lau wants to see you, sir."

"Send him in, Elizabeth."

A moment later Lau looked across Carter's desk, "The woman's time has come, sir."

"So has Nathan's, C.I."

"They are to charge him, sir?"

Carter looked at Lau impassively, thinking, Now how in the name of God can he possibly know about the controversy over Nathan? No doubt voices raised in anger incite keen interest, but rarely do they travel with such speed. Carter had come straight from the Commissioner's office.

"They are, C.I." Carter replied wearily.

"It is a mistake, sir."

"I know it. But what do you have in mind for State Committee Member Betty Wong?"

"The child, sir, is due within the next few days. The woman Wong has promised to deliver it. Tonight I will take Sergeant Lo and we will wait for her, sir, on the storage platform below the attap roof of the hut. The husband will lead us."

"And that is your plan?" Carter asked sharply.

"Yes, sir."

212

"Well it's a bloody bad plan! And you will not do it, C.I. I'm not losing any more men, and certainly not you. You will select two men from the 'X' squad to lie on the platform under the roof; the husband can guide them, instead of you. You can help yourself to the rest of the 'X' squad, and stick around in the jungle nearby. Give the two men a Verey pistol, and watch for their signal when they've got Betty Wong. And that's it. You're not putting your life in the hands of the husband, C.I., however well you think you may know him."

Betty Wong was dead within seventy-two hours. So was the woman whose child she had just delivered, and the child, together with four other Communist terrorists, and the two men from the "X" squad.

No one will ever know precisely what happened that dawn in the squatter-area. Presumably, from above her head on the wooden platform that ran a third of the length of the roof, the two men from the "X" squad had watched Betty Wong until after she had delivered the child; they had then called on her to surrender. She had tried to run and they had shot her. Or maybe they had just shot her. They had then fired the Verey pistol. Chief Inspector Lau's party arrived to see four uniformed terrorists carrying away Betty Wong's body. They had killed them all. Inside the hut, the woman and child were dead, and blood dripped through holes in the wooden platform where it had been raked by bullets.

The husband had vanished. But he re-appeared with Chief Inspector Lau one night in the flat above the Taai Lung Bank building, where he was given a credit slip for the $450,000 already paid into his account with a bank in Bangkok.

Idly, Carter wondered how much Chief Inspector Lau had received from that little deal.

17

Carter read only the headlines of the newspapers stacked on his desk, before tossing them aside. The Psychological-Warfare merchants were having a field day.

"Kepayan State Committee Member to face Capital Charge."
"Caught at last! Terrorist Leader to answer Death Charges."
"Sharp-Shooter Nathan for High Court Trial."

Now, thought Carter, for the long slow curve.

In point of fact, the curve though long was not slow. It began in Switzerland a week later in one of those Communist weekly magazines from which the Faithful learn the current focus of attention. In Basle.

Quoting an article supposedly from a correspondent in Delhi it read:

Show Trial For Malayan Liberation Army Leader

Leaders of all parties here are outraged at the latest attempt by the Imperialists in Malaya to cloak their war of aggression against Malayan workers in an aura of legality by the Show Trial of a Malayan Liberation Army Leader.

Thirty-year-old Emmanuel Nathan—a popular hero among the much-exploited Indian rubber-tappers—faces charges which carry the Death Penalty.

Whilst the Capitalist Press has hailed Nathan's capture as a great victory it remains understandably silent as to the circumstances under which it was carried out. But it is widely believed here that Nathan was trapped while paying a midnight visit to his ailing father—who ekes out a precarious living as a rubber-tapper on one of Malaya's many British and American owned rubber Estates.

214

A photograph showed a twenty-year-old Emmanuel Nathan smiling happily.

A lot can happen in a month. And a lot can happen at the same time.

In Delhi an Indian Member of Parliament demanded to know why, when the British were persecuting their compatriots in Malaya, the Indian Government nevertheless permitted more Britishers to live and work in India than there had ever been—even before India had thrown off the Colonial yoke.

In Bombay the leaders of certain stevedore unions discussed the possibility of a boycott of British shipping during the period of the "Show Trial."

In Paris Vietnamese students went on a hunger strike outside the British Embassy.

In Cairo British leaders were burned in effigy outside the British Embassy in "A popular demonstration of Afro-Asian Solidarity in the face of Anglo-American Imperialist aggression against Coloured Workers."

In Djakarta the British Ambassador's car was wrecked.

In Tokyo 25,000 students, in blocks of 1,000, shuffled along the Ginza in a minor—for Tokyo—"Anti-Imperialist Demo."

At a conference of newly-emergent nations an African delegate unsuccessfully sought to include Nathan's trial as an item for discussion on the agenda.

In London the committee of the Colonial Freedom Alliance listened attentively as a well-known Member of Parliament gave them a careful briefing on the requirements of British Law regarding demonstrations and the raising of funds for the defence of Emmanuel Nathan.

In London's Middle Temple someone met Mr. Northcourt, K.C., and enquired, "Can you accept the brief, comrade?"

Northcourt replied, "I can comrade, indeed I can."

At Scotland Yard the Commissioner reluctantly agreed that students from the London School of Economics could raise funds for the defence of Emmanuel Nathan, by street-collection, between the hours of ten a.m. and five p.m. only.

In the House of Commons a Conservative M.P. questioned the

215

"Wisdom and Justice of bringing charges against persons for acts of war. Even for acts of civil war. For after all, that is what the Emergency in Malaya is. Civil war."

At the T.V. studios the leader of a television team answered the telephone to hear a voice say, "Full coverage to that Colonial Freedom Alliance meeting in Trafalgar Square tomorrow, Arthur, it's very topical."

And much more besides. In many places.

Nancy had the paper spread out over Carter's naked body. She was kneeling by the bed and reading the caption under a photograph taken at London Airport which depicted Mr. Northcourt, K.C. accepting a tiny bunch of flowers from a little Indian girl. In the background, students packed the viewing gallery and a banner in front of them wished success to Northcourt on his "Mission for Justice."

Northcourt had obtained permission to defend Emmanuel Nathan against charges carrying the penalty of death, his expenses being paid from funds collected by sympathisers.

"I don't understand it, darling," Nancy remarked, "you say that Northcourt is a Communist, yet the Communist Party's banned in Malaya, so how can he come here?"

"Well it's not banned in the U.K., and in any case, proving that someone is a member of a Communist Party can get a bit difficult."

"He looks handsome," Nancy remarked, still looking at the photograph of Northcourt, "tall, thin and dignified. . . ."

"And with a carefully cultured Gor'blimey accent," Carter put in.

"What's a Gor'blimey accent, honey?"

"It's an accent which proves you're a member of the proletariat, darling."

"But how can you be a member of the proletariat if you're a K.C.?"

"You can't, darling. You can only pretend you are. There's a big problem there."

"Anyway, I think he's nice."

"I'm sure he is, darling. I just can't wait to meet him."

216

Carter was sitting in Halroyd's office talking about the forthcoming court case. "This Northcourt bastard is a very very clever man, Ralph, and he's more than a match for you. So don't you go taking him on. None of your witty rejoinders, you've got a difficult enough task as it is. What sort of briefing have you given Chivapathy?"

"I've told him to act dumb; if necessary, to pretend his English or hearing, or both, are defective, and to know nothing about Sergeant Major Lim's death or Daniel's presence on the night in question. He's good at acting dumb, you should have seen his reaction to my questions as to what he was doing at a 'blue film' show when O.C., Anti-vice, raided it."

"Yes, Ralph," Halroyd said heavily, "that's just the sort of crack that Northcourt will make you wish you'd never uttered."

Carter didn't reply to this. Instead he commented, "Northcourt has been spending an awful lot of time with Emmanuel Nathan."

"He's entitled to, he's Nathan's lawyer."

"Yes sir, but I can't imagine what the hell they can be talking about. Certainly Nathan can't tell him much about the circumstances under which he was arrested, he was out like a light at the time."

"What particularly galls me, Ralph, is our Commissioner's insistence that Nathan be interviewed by Northcourt in a vacant office. He actually said he wouldn't like Northcourt to think S.B. was recording their conversations."

Carter laughed, then remarked wonderingly, "Did he really say that? But surely, sir, these Communist machinations all over the world must have given even him doubts as to his wisdom in bringing the charges. . . ."

Halroyd almost spat. "Doubts? Davidson? If Nathan was the only person in the whole world who knew the code to the mechanism of a hydrogen bomb due to explode next month, he'd still want him hanged. Justice would have to be seen to have been done even if there was no bastard left to see it!" Halroyd paused and sighed heavily before going on in a milder tone, "But in all fairness to Davidson, he's simply out of his depth; his generation never had to contend with an efficient international organisation which uses democratic processes for the sole purpose of undermining democratic institutions. And he couldn't possibly have foreseen Nathan's value as a propaganda weapon; to be perfectly candid, I didn't completely foresee it myself. But of course Nathan's the only non-Chinese of

State Committee rank in the Communist Liberation Army. He's Indian! By the time the Communists have squeezed the last drop of propaganda juice out of Nathan's court case, whenever anyone mentions the Liberation Army in Malaya it'll conjure up thoughts of a multi-racial guerrilla army, representative of all the Peoples of Malaya, and certainly not one which is ninety-five per cent Chinese. The court case against Nathan played right into their hands, and it's not over yet, not by a long chalk, and I'm very worried about it. I'm also, Ralph, worried about you, not only what you're likely to say in court, but also your personal safety." Halroyd's voice was in deadly earnest and his face showed concern as he went on, "The whole country knows that you are to be present as a witness in the High Court of Kuala Lumpur at ten o'clock next Monday morning. The Communists know it better than anyone else; so you will take no risk of any kind whatsoever. You will arrive at and leave the High Court in one of the bullet-proof cars they're so proud of there; and your personal safety in K.L. will be the responsibility of a Sergeant Hatton, and you will obey him in all matters relating to that safety. Have I made it clear enough for you?"

In the back of the car, Carter peered through the thick green glass at the Greek columns that enclosed the courtyard behind the High Court.

Sergeant Hatton had said, "Don't get out, sir, until I tell you."

Carter followed Hatton's eyes. A Chinese standing beside one of the columns and holding a brief case gave a slight nod. Hatton turned to the other side of the courtyard, where a Malay window-cleaner looked in their direction: momentarily he raised his right thumb.

"You can get out now, sir."

Carter turned to Inspector Chivapathy sitting beside him, "O.K. Chiv. This is it."

As they got out of the car Sergeant Hatton said, "Just follow me, sir. I'm afraid the only way to the witness room is through the Central Lobby; but it's crawling with reporters, I'm afraid."

Coming through a side door, they were half way across the lobby before the reporters cottoned on. "That must be Carter, prosecution's chief witness."

In the witness room a few minutes later Carter thought glumly

218

that if the Communists had ever had any doubts as to what he looked like tomorrow morning's papers would certainly dispel them.

There were not many witnesses for the prosecution. Much of the evidence was incontrovertible, relating to the finding of the rifle, the fingerprints on it, the ballistics tests, etc. The only witnesses likely to give Northcourt scope for his well known histrionics were Carter, Chivapathy and the Estate manager who had witnessed Nathan shoot Wainwright. Carter was to be the first witness.

There were no defence witnesses in the case "Rex versus Nathan." As the other witnesses chatted among themselves, Carter considered the case against Nathan. It was, he felt, open and closed—at least, on the possession of arms charge. The charge of murder would rest on the strength of the evidence of the Estate manager; but a jury which is convinced of the guilt of the accused on one capital charge can find him guilty on another with an easy conscience, even where they are not wholly satisfied with the evidence on the second charge—a fact of which Vardon was well aware.

Carter felt that he could afford now to admit to himself that he actually liked Emmanuel Nathan; certainly nothing that Carter could do, or refrain from doing, would affect Nathan's fate. During their numerous chats in Nathan's cell a curious relationship had developed between them—a relationship compounded of understanding and respect. Once Nathan had said, "You know something, Mister, you talk to me as if I was white. No other European I met ever did that, they talked to me as if I was a piece of furniture, or else as if I was an imbecile child. But you, you don't do that."

And once Nathan had asked, "It was Danny who ratted on me, wasn't it?"

"Danny? Who's Danny?" Carter had replied.

"My elder brother, Daniel."

"I don't know him Emmie. Why should you think it was him?"

"It could have been. And he hasn't come to see me."

"What's his job, anyway?"

"He's a schoolteacher in the Basle Mission in Sintra."

"Well maybe with a job like that it's a bit difficult for him to admit his brother's a leading Communist."

"Yeah, of course. I hadn't thought of that." Nathan had sounded relieved.

A voice echoed, "Call Assistant Superintendent of Police, Mr. Carter."

Carter stood up as the door opened and an usher said, "Mr. Carter."

Carter walked into the court, bowed to the judge, and stepped into the witness box.

"I swear by Almighty God. The truth. The whole truth. Nothing but the truth."

The courtroom was packed. Admission by ticket only, security reasons. Reporters mostly; from East and West and Left and Right and Center. A few V.I.P.s' wives, displaying their importance by their presence, and a score or so of left-wing students who had come to see how their champion Northcourt defended the rights of the underdog.

Carter looked across at Nathan in the dock some yards away; Nathan grinned and raised a thumb. The judge noticed this and looked questioningly from Nathan to Carter before saying, "You know the accused, Mr. Carter?"

"I do, my Lord. I arrested him."

"He doesn't seem to hold it against you."

"He's an intelligent man my Lord."

The judge smiled faintly but Carter noticed that Northcourt was not amused.

Crown Counsel led Carter through much of his evidence.

Acting on information received on such and such a date at such and such a time, he had lead a party of Special Branch officers to the house of one Mandore Raja Gopal on the fifth Division of Dartford Estate. They had waited for a while in the rubber and had then split up into small groups before converging on the house. During the course of this manoeuvre an unknown number of terrorists had fired on two of his men, killing one of them, a Sergeant Major Lim. A fire-fight then developed between the Special Branch officers under the house and the terrorists in the rubber around it.

"Yes." Carter had entered the house and discovered the accused in a drunken stupor slumped across a table.

"Yes." The man in the dock was the man he had discovered.

"Yes." He had ensured that the accused be given a full

medical examination as soon as possible after his arrest. Etc., etc., etc.

As Northcourt stood up to begin his cross-examination Carter knew a moment of pure revelation: but of course, of course! In addition to what he had gleaned from Nathan, Northcourt had received information from the other side! Almost as well as Carter, he knew what had happened that night among the rubber trees.

Northcourt took up his position in the center of the court and looked steadily at Carter. Outwardly calm, Carter awaited the question tensely. They would not have liked each other as persons, even had they not each represented what the other most despised and detested. As it was. . . .

"Does the oath you took before you gave your evidence, *mean* anything to you, Mr. Carter?"

"It means no less to me, sir, than it would mean to you. . . ."

"Never mind what it would mean to me. You're the witness. I'm not."

Carter wanted to scream at him that the oath didn't mean a fucking thing to him. That the truth didn't mean a fucking thing to him either. That even if it did he couldn't tell it. Otherwise Daniel, brother of the accused, would be dead within twelve hours after the morning papers hit the streets. While he, Carter, would be pleading guilty to a couple of murder charges.

Instead he replied, "It means something to me."

Northcourt snapped, "But not much!"

Carter didn't answer. In any case, Northcourt wasn't asking a question.

"In your evidence, Mr. Carter, you stated that the accused and Mandore Raja Gopal were alone in the room when you entered it?"

"I did."

"No one else was there?"

"No."

"I put it to you that your spy was there." Northcourt's voice was raised slightly.

"I don't know who you mean," Carter replied.

"I mean the spy who gave you the information on which you acted."

"Oh I see," Carter replied, "you mean the citizen who fulfilled his lawful duty by assisting the police. No. There was no need for him to be there. He told me when and where to go, and I went."

"You gave him his thirty pieces later," Northcourt sneered.

Northcourt was permitted to get away with many such asides. Both Crown Counsel and the judge seeming rather to stand in awe of him. Unaccustomed to a barrister of international repute who yet paid scant attention to the conventional rules of court conduct, they seemed unwilling or incapable of checking him at all.

"You stated, Mr. Carter, that when you went into the room the accused was in a drunken stupor?"

"I did, yes."

"He hadn't been drugged by your spy?"

"He had an empty bottle of Scotch in front of him sir," Carter replied patiently, "and he was subsequently certified by a doctor as being drunk."

"But it was over two hours later when the doctor saw him, wasn't it Mr. Carter? And during those two hours the accused was completely in your power, wasn't he Mr. Carter? With the accused in a drugged state, you had plenty of time to pour alcohol into him, hadn't you Mr. Carter?"

Carter told himself that however much Northcourt needled him, he must on no account let him succeed in his efforts to make him lose his temper.

"I do assure you sir," Carter replied evenly, "that the only thing I had time for was trying to ensure that we were not overrun by the terrorists who surrounded the house."

Northcourt's next question, Carter thought, was overcasual.

"You say that your sergeant major was killed whilst you and your men were 'converging on the house,' was the way you put it if I remember correctly."

"That is so."

Northcourt raised his hand, pointed at Carter, and in a voice filled with sincere anger roared, "I put it to you that it is not true that your sergeant major was killed in the manner you suggest! I put it to you that for reasons known only to yourself, you yourself shot him, Mr. Carter, and that you yourself shot him deliberately! And in cold blood!" Northcourt let the last four words drop like strokes from a hammer.

222

Looking astonished at the absurdity of the allegation, Carter cast an appealing look at the judge.

After a long pause the judge said mildly, "A reply is called for, Mr. Carter."

"I'm sorry my Lord," Carter replied in a tone of slight remonstrance, "but I was somewhat taken aback. The truth is, of course, that rather than shoot one of my *own* men I would shoot any number of K.C.s."

Northcourt's face went purple but when the laughter subsided he barked, "You will not slide out of it quite so easily, Mr. Carter. I again put it to you that it was you, you, Mr. Carter, and not men from the Liberation Army, that shot your sergeant major that night."

Carter closed his eyes for just a fraction of a second; long enough to see a picture of a chubby body pinioned against a tree in the light of a torch.

"Men from the Liberation Army."

Facing Northcourt, his left hand on the rail round the witness box, Carter leant as far forward as the rail permitted, then raising his right hand he pointed his forefinger at Northcourt as he hissed, "Yes, Mr. Northcourt. I shot my sergeant major that night. And after I'd shot him I mutilated his body, Mr. Northcourt. I cut off his penis Mr. Northcourt. And I put it in his mouth! And, Mr. Northcourt K.C., I have photographs to prove it! Mr. Northcourt. Kremlin Callboy!"

In the shocked silence which followed Carter slowly lowered his hand to the rail in front of him.

It was not so much what he had said, as the sheer venom of the tones with which he had said it; and the look of naked, undisguised, undisguisable hatred with which he had addressed Northcourt, which shocked the court.

Even Northcourt looked shocked. Was shocked.

After many long moments, the judge tapped on his table with the end of a pencil; three times, very slowly. In the tense silence of the crowded courtroom the taps rang loudly.

"I can quite understand, Mr. Carter," he began, "that the tragic loss of your sergeant major is a matter about which you justifiably feel very deeply. And I can very well appreciate your feelings over the deplorable act of mutilation to which you have referred,"

223

he paused, then in tones of heavy reproof went on, "but this is a court of law. And I expect a police officer, and particularly an officer of your rank, to comport himself accordingly. I shall deem it my duty to refer your conduct here today to your superiors, but I shall treat any such further outburst, Mr. Carter, as a contempt of this court, and shall act accordingly."

"I understand, my Lord."

The judge looked at Carter as if considering some additional reproof, but instead he cast an enquiring look at Northcourt and said, "Mr. Northcourt?"

"No further questions," Northcourt replied gruffly.

The judge looked at Counsel for the Crown, who shook his head. "Then you may stand down, Mr. Carter."

Face tight, Carter bowed and walked out; every eye following him. Inwardly he was elated. He was off the hook!

The case was routine and even boring thereafter, but it had its moments: once when Northcourt said to Chivapathy, "So it doesn't bother you, being a traitor?" And Chivapathy answered, "Oh no sir. It doesn't bother you, does it?"

And again, when the European manager who had been standing with Wainwright at the moment when he had been shot, was being cross-examined by Northcourt; the manager being unshakable in his conviction that Nathan had been the man who had waved the rifle after the shot was fired. Nathan, he said, had worked for two years as a dresser in the Estate hospital. He knew him well. He was bigger and taller than the average Indian and in any case he knew him personally. No, Indians did not all look alike to him; he employed five thousand of them, and they all looked different.

Emmanuel Nathan was found guilty on both charges, and sentenced to death.

Carter visited Nathan in his cell the following day. As they shook hands Nathan said, "You were great, Blondie, great! I thought you were going to climb out of that witness box and tear Northcourt to bits."

"He was supposed to have been on your side, Emmie."

"My side, my arse! I didn't have any side. I was just the ball in a game. And Northcourt wasn't there to see I got a fair deal, he

224

was there to make propaganda for the Party. But," Nathan's voice changed, became curious as he said, "you know something? He told me that you really had shot your sergeant major. He had a visitor at his hotel one night—one of my boys I guess—anyway, it was someone who gave him all the dirt."

Carter explained what had happened.

Nathan nodded, "I could never stop them mutilating bodies. It's in them to do it, and that's it."

"Incidentally, Emmie, my sergeant major was the younger brother of the wounded Communist courier you nursed that night when Camp 4 went up."

Nathan leant back, looked at Carter, his eyes wide but said nothing.

After a long moment Carter said, "I'm sorry. I had no right to tell you that."

They sat in silence for a minute or two, then Nathan asked, "What now?"

"What do you mean, 'What now?'"

"Well what happens before I get strung up? That's what."

"The Court of Appeal will review your case and uphold the verdict."

"Then?"

"The case will come before the High Commissioner and his cabinet, who will consider whether or not to make a recommendation for mercy." Carter paused and puffed at his cigarette.

"But they won't make a recommendation for mercy, will they?"

Carter shook his head sadly, "No Emmie, they won't; not now they won't."

"What do you mean by the 'Not now'?"

Carter stirred uncomfortably before replying, "Well, if your international comrades hadn't made such a bloody big hoo ha, the Cabinet might well have found it expedient to be magnanimous. But they can't now, as they'll be frightened of magnanimity being interpreted as weakness. It would look as if they were bowing before the weight of Communist propaganda."

"So they show they don't give a fuck for Communist propaganda by recommending I be strung up?"

"Something like that."

"Who do they make their recommendation to?"

"The king. He signs the death warrant."

"Do you mean to say he actually signs it himself?" Nathan asked incredulously.

"I do believe he does, Emmie. It's a big parchment thing with black ribbons on it."

Nathan looked thrilled to bits, "Well what d'yer know! I actually take up some of the bugger's time!" He sat grinning for a few minutes drinking it in, then said, "What then?"

"Then you get strung up, I'm afraid."

"Yeah. But just exactly how do they do that, Blondie?"

"You have your hands tied behind your back, they stand you on a trapdoor, with a noose round your neck; someone pulls a lever, the trapdoor opens and you break your neck. It doesn't take long."

"What happens if I scream and fight?"

"What do *you* think?"

Nathan nodded, "Yeah. Who's there for all this?"

"The Press. The magistrate who heard the preliminary enquiry, the Prison Superintendent, a doctor. . . ."

"What's he there for?"

"To certify death."

"Good. Good for him. What's the magistrate there for?"

"It's a requirement of the law."

"What about the judge? Doesn't he have to be there? I liked him. When he sentenced me to death I thought he was going to cry."

"No the judge doesn't have to be there."

"Nor the police officer who arrested me?"

"No. Thank Christ!"

"How long do you reckon I've got?"

"Six to eight weeks."

"Can't they do it any quicker?"

"Not really."

Nathan broke a silence after this, when he said in a bright voice, "You know something Blondie? I don't care. I really don't care! At first, I was worried I might start sniveling or something; but now I know I don't care. I really don't!" But his voice lost its brightness, and became dispirited, "I've had time to think about it . . ." He lit a cigarette. "I don't like the idea of being hanged . . .

226

It doesn't give you a chance to show much dignity somehow. There's contempt in it. I'd prefer a firing squad. . . . But I'd rather be *tortured* to death than spend the rest of my life in a cage."

Not quite two months later Carter was sitting in the Mess lounge one evening playing Russian poker with three colleagues. Beside their elbows on the table—and despite Davidson's strictures—were piles of notes. In Russian poker there are four players; each has thirteen cards which he arranges in three hands—two of five cards and one of three. These hands are each arranged in poker fashion and in ascending order of strength, beginning with the hand of three cards. Three players play against the fourth—the banker—and the bank changes after every fourth deal.

A few yards away from the card table half a dozen other police officers were sitting or standing at the bar. One of these turned up the volume of the radio as the nine o'clock news came on. Nobody paid much attention to it until the announcer said, "Emmanuel Nathan, a Member of the Kepayan Communist State Committee, who was recently found guilty of the murder of a police officer and sentenced to death, was hanged today in . . ." The rest of the sentence was lost in ironic cheers.

Sitting opposite Carter at the card table, John Craven, a burly fifty-year-old in charge of police stores, commented, "Served the bastard right."

Someone switched the radio off.

Half an hour later the 'phone in the hall rang.

Mark Dawson, a dark twenty-five-year-old sitting on Carter's right said, "A thousand pounds to a pinch of shit it's for me." As the Officer Commanding the Central Sintra Police District this was a fairly safe bet: most calls—at night anyway—*were* for him.

A Malay steward appeared in the doorway, "Tuan Dawson ada telephone."

Dawson stood up and said, "Sod it," and went to answer the 'phone. A moment later he stuck his head round the door and called to one of the people at the bar, "Stand in for me Sandy. There's a hoo ha in the Oriental Hotel and I've got to dash."

Arthur Collings took his place at the card table and they continued playing.

Dawson returned about an hour and a half later. For a moment he stood in the doorway looking across at the group playing cards.

Someone called, "What was the hoo ha, Mark?"

As he walked across to the card table Dawson replied, "Very peculiar indeed. Most peculiar."

He stood behind and to Carter's right as he continued, "A very messy hoo ha, I might add. An Indian gentleman strung himself up with piano wire behind a door in the Oriental Hotel; I really don't know whether he chocked or bled to death. But the most peculiar thing was that the room was ankle deep in ten-dollar notes. Three hundred and ninety-eight thousand, seven hundred and sixty."

"Three hundred and ninety-eight thou! Jesus!" someone exclaimed.

Sensing something in Dawson's manner, the officers at the bar drifted across and formed a group at the table. This was interesting. Carter was banker and was dealing the cards.

Dawson stood looking down at him. When he had finished dealing Carter picked up his cards, glanced up at Dawson and said, "It wasn't in room twenty-two, by any chance?"

"Indeed it was, Ralph. Indeed it was." Dawson replied. "And perhaps you might be able to tell me who he was?"

"Didn't he sign the hotel register?" Carter asked drily.

"Yes, he did. He signed it in the name, 'Mahab Harata.' Which sounds more like Japanese than Indian to me. But he was wearing a heavy gold ring with the letters 'D.N.' engraved on it."

Carter sorted his cards as he commented, "It was one Daniel Nathan. A schoolteacher from the Basle Mission, and the brother of the Emmanuel Nathan who was hanged today." Carter looked up at Dawson as he added, "S.B. only makes a small charge, Mark, when it gives the Uniform Branch the benefit of its infallible guidance."

"But I think I would have guessed, Ralph, that the gentleman had some connection with S.B.," Dawson replied, "because the most peculiar of all the peculiar things about this particular hoo ha was that the deceased had an envelope sticking out of his jacket." Dawson produced an envelope and held it towards Carter, saying, "This envelope, and it's addressed to Assistant Superintendent of Police, Ralph Carter. Special Branch. Police H.Q. Sintra."

Since Carter made no move to take it he placed it on the table at Carter's elbow. The envelope was heavily stained with blood.

228

They all looked at Carter as he finished sorting his cards and placed them face downwards in three neat piles in front of him. Someone asked, "Aren't you going to read your mail, Ralph?"

Carter picked up the envelope, opened it, took out the single sheet of paper it contained, read it, folded it and placed it on the table beside him. Then looking around at the three others seated at the table said, "Okay?" Meaning "are you ready to play?"

But they just sat looking at him.

Someone said, "Let's hear the message from the dead, Ralph."

"Morbid bastards," Carter said irritably as he picked up the sheet of paper and opened it. In a bored voice he said, "It has a printed heading, 'The Oriental Hotel Sintra.' Beneath that, in a clear schoolmasterly hand it reads, 'Lo I hate wealth and ease thus sadly won. What rich spoils could profit, what span of life itself seem sweet bought with such blood? But you didn't keep your promise Mr. Carter. You didn't keep your promise.'" Carter tossed the paper on to the table beside him, saying, "That's all it says. He didn't sign it. Now let's get on with the game."

They all watched him as he turned his cards over and said, "Beat this. Three fours in the first hand; a full house in the second, and four eights in the last."

For the first time since he'd read the letter Carter looked at the faces around him; faces which displayed anger, scorn, disgust and contempt. He sensed that John Craven spoke for them all as he said in a voice heavy with disgust, "By god! You're a callous bastard!"

Carter's face went white. He asked icily, "What would you have me do John? Beat my breast and cry 'Mea culpa'?"

"No. But you might at least show some sort of feeling for the poor bastard. After all, he is dead. And it's bloody obvious why."

Carter replied with barely controlled savagery, "Look, you deal in stores. You don't tear your guts out when you're a few pairs of jungle boots short! Well I deal in lives. And I don't tear my guts out either, when one or two happen to get themselves filched. Because there's fuck-all I can do about it!"

Nothing further was said. So they carried on with the game and the others drifted back to the bar.

18

Naked to the waist, barefoot, and wearing sarongs, the two Malays sat in Carter's office. Mat and Salleh. About the same age, twenty-two or three, they were a tough-looking pair. Stocky and handsome and with nothing subservient about them.

Mat was the spokesman. "We have walked these many days to see the Tuan, and the first Tuan was the one they call the C.I.D. Tuan and he sent us to you."

Carter nodded. Harry Vardon had rung just a few minutes before.

"Where have you come from, Mat?"

"From Kampong Tanah Puteh."

"I'm sorry. I don't know where that is," Carter replied.

"It is near the Chinese squatter-area which is called Kong Lee."

"Really," Carter said in surprise, "and you *walked* from there?"

"We had no money for the bus, Tuan."

"But one has to eat and drink and find somewhere to sleep, Mat."

"We are Malays, Tuan."

"Of course," Carter replied. One tended to forget Muslim hospitality. Indeed it is not easy for the European to understand a custom which prescribes that a stranger shall be well received, well fed and sheltered, and sent on his way with gifts. "And what brings you to me?" Carter asked.

"It is this, Tuan," Mat said, standing up and unrolling the paper he had been holding in his hand. It was a "Wanted" poster, showing the members of the Kepayan State Committee with diagonal red crosses over the faces of Lim Tsing Wa, Khan Hock Loi, Betty Wong and Emmanuel Nathan. Placing it across Carter's desk Mat pointed to the picture of Lee Chin, one-time lawyer, and said,

230

"This man, Tuan. We know where he is. It is true that if we kill him we will get a reward of $450,000?"

"It is," Carter replied, "but I would prefer he were captured alive."

"If we capture him alive, will we get more than $450,000?"

"The poster says 'Dead or Alive,' Mat."

"It will be easier to capture him dead, Tuan."

"Tell me about it."

"We were hunting deer, Tuan, in the Chinese squatter-area that is called Kong Lee, and Salleh heard a groan; nearby was a small hut, and we looked in. This man"—pointing to Lee Chin's photograph—"lay on a bed. On the table were many books and papers."

"He didn't see you?"

"No Tuan, his eyes were closed as he groaned."

"You are sure it is this man?" Carter asked, his finger on Lee Chin's photograph.

"It is the same man, Tuan. When we went into the village to sell a deer for cloth, Salleh saw this poster. We do not read but someone read it for us."

"Well, all that needs to be done, Mat, is for you to lead a small party of police into the squatter-area and they will capture him. Is that not so?"

"But then, Tuan, the reward money would be shared among many, instead of but two."

"Not at all, Mat. If you and Salleh lead a small group of policemen into the squatter-area, and they capture this man, then you will each get $225,000. Policemen are not eligible for rewards."

"It is not possible, Tuan, for Salleh and I to take others. The Chinese squatters know us; they know we hunt for deer, but if there were others with us, the sick man would quickly be moved."

Carter could understand this. The Kong Lee squatter-area was big. Secondary jungle with many squatter huts and cultivated patches of land. But the patches were only patches; Lee Chin would need to be moved only a matter of twenty yards and a thousand men wouldn't find him. Carter pictured the sequence of events. Mat and Salleh with half a dozen policemen would enter the squatter-area; some aged crone would see them and would hang out a sheet to dry on the roof of her hut, or she would light a fire. A mile away in the squatter-area a squatter would get the message—and carry Lee Chin just twenty yards.

Carter said, "Well why not go at night, Mat?"

They laughed. Mat said, "At night, Tuan, no one moves. There are many swamps. Even Salleh and I would not go at night. There is talk also of a tiger, but of this we are not sure."

Carter stood up and said, "Come now with me."

He took them down to what was called the Police Museum. It was a large hall with a central corridor to the left and right of which were numerous cubicles. Each cubicle was devoted to a particular aspect of police work—gaming instruments, narcotics paraphernalia, counterfeit notes and the equipment with which they were made etc. One cubicle was devoted to pictures of motor vehicles; a witness might not be able to say, "It was a Morris Minor that knocked the man down," but he could point to a picture of a Morris Minor and say, "It was one of those."

Carter led them to a cubicle in which there was Communist clothing and equipment; they were hardly inside before Salleh walked over to a tunic hanging on the wall with several others, "on the table in the hut Tuan, was one of these."

The tunic he had selected bore the insignia of a Member of a State Committee.

Carter left them wandering around the cubicles and stood looking out of the window at the end of the corridor. It could only be Lee Chin. He was bound to be sick if he was using "doctored" insulin. But supposing it wasn't. To what extent were civilians at liberty to kill Communist terrorists? Every extent presumably. "Dead or alive." But supposing they killed him and it wasn't Lee Chin? Wasn't a Communist terrorist at all. Wasn't a Communist tunic, or wasn't his tunic? What then? Manslaughter? Mistaken identity. Sorry about that, but we all make mistakes, don't we?

"Tuan." Carter turned and Mat beckoned him. As he walked towards him Carter noticed that he was standing in the doorway of the Narcotics cubicle. Mat took his sleeve and led him in, pointed to a hypodermic needle and said, "On the table in the hut, Tuan, was one of those."

Back in his office Carter said to them, "You may kill the sick man. But only if the sick man is this man." Carter pointed to

232

Lee Chin's photograph and added, "If it is not this man, there could be much trouble."

"It is this man, Tuan. Of this we are sure."

After they had gone Carter looked at Lee Chin's file. A man with a Cause. A man with considerable ability and talent. That was the trouble.

Both Halroyd and Carter had regretted their decision about the insulin. However sick Lee Chin might be, he was still churning out skilful Communist propaganda.

Quite simply, he wasn't sick enough.

They returned ten days later with Mat carrying a gunny sack. Grinning, he held it by its corners above Carter's desk and a human head fell on Carter's blotting pad. Salleh produced a pair of spectacles and adjusted them over the ears.

"See, Tuan, it is the same man."

"And here," Mat said, rummaging inside the sack, "is his uniform."

Carter took it; it bore the insignia of a Member of a State Committee. From a pocket he took out an envelope addressed to "Comrade State Committee Member, Lee Chin."

"Put the head back, Mat, in case my secretary comes in. It is the man. For this you get $450,000."

It had been, Carter thought afterwards, the only successful project which had cost only money.

In this he was wrong, for within two weeks both Mat and Salleh were dead. Contrary to Carter's advice they had made ostentatious display of their new-found wealth and had boasted of the manner in which it had been acquired—thus attracting the attention of a Communist killer-squad. They had died painfully. Incensed, their fellow-Malays rose up in anger; armed with shotguns and parangs, they swept through the squatter-area that was called Kong Lee, sparing neither man, woman nor child: unsophisticated peoples see things in simple terms. Mat and Salleh had been killed by Communists. The Communists who had killed them had all been Chinese. Did it not then follow, that all Chinese were Communists?

Chan On Yan drove fast. Too fast for Carter, who was sitting beside him. Carter said, "Slow it down a bit, On Yan, it's tough

233

enough on the suspension as it is." Carter was referring to the weight of the steel plates behind the seats.

Carter was in a cheerful mood. It was Christmas, and he was to spend three days with the Erringtons in Chadwick Estate. Three days in which to relax, to get away from it all. Three days in which the words "Communist terrorists" would probably never be uttered; while the word "Project"—if it were ever used at all—would conjure up visions of replanting rubber, or building a bridge.

Carter recalled his discussion with Halroyd the previous day. Halroyd had said, "You will travel in an armoured car or not at all." "But there hasn't been an ambush on that road for six months," Carter had expostulated, "and armoured cars are hot and uncomfortable and Chadwick Estate's a long way."

Halroyd had relented slightly, "All right, you can go there in your own car, but you'll come back in an armoured car. And that's it!"

Carter grinned at the memory: Halroyd never let up.

Chan On Yan slowed to take a corner. It was the last thing he ever did, for the bullets that suddenly shattered the windscreen took half his face away.

Carter leant over and grabbed for the steering wheel to find that it was no longer a wheel but a couple of jagged spokes. He tore gashes in his hands as he tried to turn the spokes to keep the car on the road amidst the hail of bullets. Without On Yan's foot on the accelerator the car was slowing rapidly. Carter very nearly succeeded in getting the car off the grass verge and back on to the road, but a two-foot high ant hill thwarted him; the car glanced off it, and toppled slowly into a deep gully.

For a fraction of a second Carter lay stunned, then frantically he wriggled out through the open roof of the car and tore down the gully away from the ambush, drawing his pistol as he ran. The shooting had stopped now. In the gully he was out of their sight. He ran fifty or sixty yards before the gully became a concrete wall with a circular hole in it. As he ran up the side of the gully he was again visible and bullets spattered the ground about him. He zigzagged through the rubber trees towards the jungle two hundred yards away. If he could only get there, he'd be safe; they'd never find him. Figures from his right converged to cut him off; figures

234

with caps that bore a red star. Someone was overtaking him from behind, the shots were becoming closer, louder; the man behind him didn't have to zigzag. Abruptly Carter stopped behind a rubber tree, turned and fired rapidly at the pursuer behind him; taken unawares, the man seemed almost to run eagerly at the bullets that tore into him. Carter went down on his left knee as a bullet found his left thigh, then got up and dashed for the jungle now thirty yards away. He was amazed that he could still run at all.

As the jungle closed around him he could have cheered. They would never find him here. He would go in another fifty yards. With difficulty he crashed his way through the thick undergrowth. Suddenly he stopped, horrified; he was in the rubber again. It was only a jutting outcrop of jungle and he'd run right through it.

A man stepped out from behind the nearest rubber tree, not ten feet away; a man who held a sten-gun pointed at Carter's chest. Carter stood, holding his pistol at his side, unable to move, staring at the sten-gun and the hand with one finger missing which supported the barrel: held by a man who had run round the jutting outcrop, listened to Carter's noisy progress, gauged where he would emerge, and waited.

The man spoke; his face composed, his tone mild, almost conversational as he said in English, "I want you to know pain," and pointed the sten-gun from Carter's chest to his crotch.

Many things happen more swiftly than it takes to tell of them. Carter did three things at once; screamed, "Not there," sank forward on to his knees and raised his pistol. Then as the man squeezed the trigger a piece of the sten-gun tore itself away and carved across the side of his face.

A doctored bullet.

Carter fired at the falling body, leapt up and ran along the edge of the jungle. Then he turned and dived into the jungle as if it were a lake. Inside, bent double, he zigzagged for twenty yards before going down on one knee beside a huge tree trunk. Gasping, trembling in every limb, he took stock of himself. He could have screamed with the pain in his hands and in his thigh. His left trouser leg felt sodden. He told himself that all he had to do was to stay alive for ten minutes. They couldn't stay much longer; the ambush must have been heard, a jungle squad must soon be on its way.

He heard voices behind him, heard someone say in Cantonese, "He's just got Ah Bpo." A voice with rage in it.

He decided to reload his pistol. Slowly, very slowly, he moved a trembling hand towards the spare magazine at his side. It wasn't there.

In shrill panic he made the mistake of making swift movements: movements to ascertain that the magazine that was always clipped to his belt was not there now.

A few inches from his face a hand-grenade dropped on to the tree trunk in front of him; he stared at it numbly as it hesitated uncertainly for a moment before rolling over the other side. Its explosion drew a short sharp scream from him, then in the smoke and dirt he dived over the tree trunk and snaked through the thick undergrowth. Behind him a voice called, "I've got him, I've got him."

Slowly now, Carter wormed his way away from the voices. He came to an open patch of lallang, thick and coarse grass some three feet high. It offered the protection of invisibility, but they might think that he would not be so foolish as to try to hide in it, it was so small; not even half the size of a cricket pitch. He wormed his way into it. Slowly, very slowly. He watched the leeches on the stems of the lallang tracking their way from stem to stem towards him; there were so many of them that he thought their collective movement might well give him away. He felt one on an eyelid and slowly plucked it off; aware that in doing so he was breaking it, leaving its head inside to form the inevitable ulcer. But it was on an eyelid. Arrived at what he judged was the center of the patch of lallang, he turned over on his back and lay with his right hand holding the pistol at his chest. He was immune to the bites of the red ants; the pain in his hands and thigh covered all. He tried to bite at a leech on his upper lip, then clamped his mouth tight shut, not so much against the leech but rather to control the movements of his jaw-bones and the panting of his breath. He cursed the thumping of his heart for fear they might hear it as he lay motionless, every faculty alert to screaming point.

He had a sudden thought: if someone followed his blood trail, they might see his feet before he saw them. Slowly again, very slowly, he turned on his right side and made a "U" turn in the lallang, closing in on the track he must have made coming in. Through the stems of the lallang he saw the track, knew it from the clusters of leeches that clung to the blood on the coarse grass. His blood. He lay on his right side, his right hand holding his pistol by his head.

The voices were all around him now, urgent but not close. Time was against them.

He fought off drowsiness as the moments dragged by. He became conscious of a movement near his head; heard the faintest of rustles. A snake? He told himself he must not move even if it crawled over his face. The rustle was nearer now. Then between the stems of grass six inches in front of his face, he saw a hand. A left hand. He watched it in terror. Its fingernails were long and dirty, and it had a wart between the tendons which join thumb and forefinger. The hand became a wrist with a watch on it. The watch mesmerised him; it became important to try to read it, but its face was upside down. He watched in sick fascination as with torturing slowness the wrist became a khaki sleeve, then an elbow, then all at once a shoulder and the back of a head—a head which wore a khaki cap. They were lying head to head in the lallang, both facing the same way—but the other man had his back to him.

Trying not to make any sound at all, Carter slowly brought his right hand behind the head, his pistol almost touching it. But he must have made some sound because the head slowly turned, became a Chinese face with a red star on its forehead. As the mouth opened he pulled the trigger and the head dropped.

They must have heard the shot and they must see the smoke from it. He had an overwhelming compulsion to leap up and run. But part of his mind told him he mustn't, and every part of his body told him he couldn't.

He lay asking himself what had led this man to come worming his way into the lallang. He had found the blood trail, so why not call his pals? No. He had wanted to be the clever boy who got Blondie. He'd have been singled out for special praise at the next prayer-meeting of the comrades.

A new sound. A distant roar becoming louder as it gathered momentum. A wind sprang up as the first heavy drops fell. Rain! As it poured down on him Carter wept with relief. Tropical rain! Now nothing would be heard at all in its tumult, not even pistol-shots.

He reached over and took the cap with the red star off the head in front of him, then put it on his own head. If he ran into one of the comrades it might give him just that fraction of a second advantage. . . .

He lay in the rain waiting for time to pass. He must have dozed, for he suddenly realised that not only was it no longer raining, but that he could not even hear the rain in the distance. But he could hear distant shots.

He rose to his feet, staggered slightly, then weaved out of the jungle and into the rubber, and sat propped up against a rubber tree. He desperately wanted to sleep but knew he mustn't. Then he heard voices a hundred yards away, and in particular a European voice shouting orders in execrable Malay.

Sergeant Morgan's voice.

They were only fifty yards away now. Painfully he climbed to his feet and leant against the tree; he could see them now, coming through the rubber in line abreast, Sergeant Morgan in the center. He wanted to call "Morgan," but the words wouldn't come, it was too much of an effort. Then he stood for a moment in frozen horror as several of them fired at him, before he flung himself to the ground behind the tree.

"Get behind him! Cut him off!" Sergeant Morgan's voice.

Carter screamed, "It's me, you daft bastard! Carter!"

Carter heard Morgan telling his men to stop firing, then call, "Who is it?"

"Me. Carter."

"Well stand up then."

With an immense effort Carter dragged himself slowly to his feet and leant his head on his arms against the tree.

Sergeant Morgan came running up and Carter turned his face towards him wearily. In reply to Carter's look of hurt protest, he said, "It's your hat sir. It's not exactly 'Gazetted officers for the use of,' now is it?"

With an angry gesture, Carter tore it off and flung it from him. Then he fainted.

In the hospital, two hours later, Nancy stood by the lift gates on the third floor. The lift was in use and coming up. As it passed her she caught a glimpse of Dr. Kowalski bending over the patient on a trolley; saw the white face, the fair hair. . . .

She stood for a moment while it registered, then turned and ran up the stairs screaming. "No, no, no."

Round and round up eight flights; passing shocked faces, brushing aside the arms that sought to restrain her. On the seventh floor, still screaming, she ran along the corridor towards the group with the trolley on its way to the Operating Theatre. Dr. Kowalski turned and came to her, caught her by the shoulders, shook her, then slapped her face.

She calmed down immediately, and in a tiny voice asked, "Is he badly hurt, doctor?"

"No," Dr. Kowalski boomed in assurance, "he will be all right. He has lost some blood, but it is nothing serious. Go and have a cup of tea now, and try not to worry."

She turned and walked back along the corridor.

A few nights later, as she turned on the light in her room, a hand clamped over her mouth and strong arms held her tightly from behind, then lifted her and swung her round so that she faced the curtains as a man stepped out from behind them. The man whose death she had greeted with tears of relief. Lim Tsing Wa. But he was not the Lim Tsing Wa she had known. He held his head hunched towards his right shoulder, and though she knew he was only four years older that she was, his hair was grey. All of it.

He stood looking at her, his eyes glittering their amusement. When he spoke his voice was no more than a croak. "Good evening, comrade."

Above the hand over her mouth, her eyes looked at him in horror.

To the man holding her he rasped, "Release her." The hand was taken away from her mouth but she didn't turn round, instead she stood transfixed, looking at Lim Tsing Wa.

"Surprised to see me, comrade?" Still with his head hunched towards his right shoulder, he grinned. It gave his mouth a twisted look. "Death, comrade," he went on, "is the safest of all disguises."

She found her voice, felt an upsurge of defiance and said, "What do you want from me?"

Across the room, Lim gave her a long look of contempt before rasping, "You have failed me before, comrade. Now I have come

239

to tell you that you will not fail me again. Not that is," he added with his twisted grin, "if you wish your father to live."

"My father?" she whispered.

"Your father, comrade. The little fat bourgeois is in my hands."

"I don't believe you."

Lim indicated the telephone on the bedside table, "We can wait, comrade, while you telephone your mother. We are not in any hurry," he said, sitting down on the edge of the armchair.

For the first time Nancy looked at the man behind her: a stocky Chinese peasant of about her own age, indistinguishable from millions like him. She looked from one to the other unbelievingly, then went to the telephone and placed a long distance call.

No one spoke as they waited for the call. Lim's companion wore a look that was totally devoid of expression, Lim an expression of boredom. Nancy sat with shoulders hunched, her hands on the bed on either side of her.

The 'phone rang and she grabbed it. "Is that you? Yes, it's Nancy. . . . Yes of course I'm all right. . . . A car accident, Mummy?" She thought quickly, "Perhaps someone with the same name, Mummy. Some other Nancy. . . . Two men came with a car to take Daddy to the hospital? Are you sure, Mummy? No I haven't seen him, Mummy; perhaps he's found out there's been a mistake. . . ." She couldn't go on, and put the 'phone down.

Her father. The little bald chemist who told the same jokes over and over again. In a state of shock she gazed unseeingly at the carpet.

Lim stood up: "Do you believe me now, comrade?"

She threw herself on her knees before him, her arms clinging to his legs, "Please, oh please let him go. He never did anybody any harm, oh please, please let him go. . . ."

Lim bent down, put his fingers under her chin and lifted her head so that he could see her face. He examined it carefully. His plan was going to work. She was his, now. She would do precisely what he wanted her to do. But how could he have made the error of recruiting her? With her, her family would always have come first. And Carter, how strong were her feelings for him? It would not be enough now, just to kill Carter. For a moment or two he moved his fingers slightly, causing her head to make slight nodding movements.

240

It would be necessary to impress upon her the logic of mathematics; that it was not only her father's life which was at stake, but the lives of every member of her family—theirs, or Carter's. In order to ensure her obedience he must also terrify her.

He flicked his fingers up forcing her head back, "Listen carefully, comrade," he rasped. "You are no longer a person. You must not even think you are a person. You must not even think at all. Because you are now a machine, and machines do not think. When I switch you on, you will do as I wish: when I switch you off, you will do nothing that I do not want done. If you do not do as I wish then your father will die. Your mother also, will die. And your aunt, your mother's sister, of whom I believe you are particularly fond. They will all die, comrade; and they will all die very slowly. If it becomes necessary, then I shall arrange for them to watch each other die." Lim paused, thought for a moment, "I shall have to give some consideration as to whether the eldest should watch the youngest die, or vice versa. Do you understand, comrade?"

Nancy nodded numbly, but this didn't satisfy him, for he leant down and shook her roughly by the hair. "Tell me comrade, what you understand."

"If . . . if I don't do what you say, then we . . . all my family . . . we will all die." She spoke in an awed whisper, as if she did not fully understand the words she spoke.

He looked down at her, bowed before him, and again put his fingers under her chin, raising her head until he could look at her face. "You remember your Shakespeare, comrade? Of course you do. I taught it to you, didn't I? Your Richard the Third? Well for you . . . even the dogs in the street will bark at your shadow. Your white-monkey lover will vomit when he sees you. You understand, comrade?" he choked.

Flicking his fingers up and her head further back, Lim turned and sat on the edge of the armchair, facing her.

She remained kneeling, looking up at him, her mouth slightly open. It occurred to him that there was a further possibility to guard against: "Your suicide, comrade, would not save your father's life, would it? Nor would a letter to your white-monkey save the other members of your family, even if your white-monkey was sufficiently interested to try to give them protection; and with you dead, why should he? He doesn't know them, does he? No, comrade, your

241

suicide would achieve nothing, for you would hear your family's cries even in hell, and it would not satisfy me until I was sure you could hear them, and hear them clearly."

He looked at her with satisfaction, noting her dazed expression, her trembling chin. Yes, she would now do precisely what she was told. He leant towards her, one hand on his knee, "Listen carefully, comrade, to what you will do. You will get from your white-monkey all the information that you possibly can. Everything. Plans, movements, everything. And, comrade," his voice becoming slower, "you will arrange for your white-monkey to be captured. Captured, not killed. Captured. And by me. . . ."

"But he is in hospital," she said tonelessly, "he is dangerously ill with pneumonia. He may die. . . ."

"Better for you that he lives, for until I have these fingers," he spread the fingers of both hands in front of her face, "on your white-monkey's throat, your father will remain under my protection, and until that moment, you will tell me everything you learn. Everything!" Lim fumbled in a pocket, took out a piece of paper and handed it to her, "These are the code words you will use when you are telephoning Dr. Lum. I have also added his number, in case you have forgotten it."

She accepted it automatically.

Lim stood up, glanced at his colleague and nodded towards the light switch. The light went out. In the darkness she heard him say, "Goodnight, comrade."

Then she was alone.

She remained kneeling for some time, then got up stiffly and groped for the switch. In the sudden light she blinked at the paper in her hand, slowly opened it and began to read, "Arms and ammunition—furniture, pistols—books, hand-grenades—oranges, armoured cars—timber lorries, etc., etc." She recognised the handwriting. She had seen it many times. At school. At night, after school. No, it had not been a nightmare. She wanted to weep, but tears wouldn't come. She began to fear for her sanity. What could she do? She was a machine, the man had said so. Poor Daddy! What could she do? Except what the man told her to do. But Ralph? How could she? Oh, Ralph. . . . Daddy. . . .

She walked to the 'phone and dialled a number. A woman's voice answered.

242

"How is the patient in room 16?" Nancy asked.

"Oh Nancy, it's after two in the morning. He's much better, and his temperature's nearly back to normal."

The voice was sympathetic, understanding.

"Thank you," Nancy said, replacing the 'phone. What could she do? What could she do? Except what she was told to do.

19

Carter was sitting in the lounge of his bungalow, a brandy soda on the side-table at his elbow. It was midnight. He had been out of hospital for about a month. He'd been given a month's convalescent leave, but he hadn't gone anywhere; didn't want to go anywhere without Nancy. After ten days moping about the Mess, he'd gone back to the office.

Nancy had tried to get leave but Matron wouldn't hear of it, "You know we're understaffed, Nancy, how can you even ask?" Matron, Carter decided, had been born out of her time: she should have been wrestling instructress to some Amazonian queen, or a chariot driver under Boadicea.

He was worried about Nancy. It seemed to him that she had not recovered from the shock of seeing him in the lift on the way to the Operating Theatre. There had been that awful business of her running screaming through the hospital. It seemed to have taken something out of her; she seemed curiously listless, tired, vague, her mind always on other things. And she cried so easily. Only that same evening, making love to him with an intensity surprising even for her, she had burst into tears after the climax. Hugging and kissing him as if it were the last time before they parted forever.

It had been two weeks since he had said to her, "Darling, what *is* troubling you? What's on your mind?" He had felt her stiffen beside him in the darkness. She had said, "Nothing, Ralph, really, nothing." But there had been something akin to panic in her voice and he had switched on the bedside lamp and looked at her. "Are you sure?" Then because she hadn't answered, "Look darling, are you pregnant?" And she had laughed and cried at the same time.

He still wondered sometimes if she were pregnant. Women could act strangely when they were pregnant.

Certainly there was something wrong; and she needed her leave more than he did. Now would be a good time for him to go on leave. He smiled to himself. The Projects Section had eliminated its chosen targets; all of them. The only persons on the Kepayan State Committee worthy of respect for their courage or efficiency had bought it. Coming to think of it, he had very nearly bought it himself. He shuddered at the thought of the sten-gun in Ah Bpo's hands; Christ! the casual way he had said, "I want you to know pain," as if he was making an idle remark about the weather.

There were nights now when Carter found himself waking up in a cold sweat; the memory of a grenade hovering uncertainly on the top of a tree trunk, a wrist-watch seen through a few stems of lallang, vivid in his mind. Even Dr. Kowalski's sleeping pills didn't seem to help much.

He looked up as a tap came at the door and Ah Ling's face appeared behind the glass. He beckoned him in with surprise. Ah Ling had taken Nancy home only half an hour before; there was no need for him to return at this hour.

"Yes? Ah Ling," Carter asked as Ah Ling closed the door behind him and stood uncertainly in front of it.

"It is the Tuan's woman, Tuan."

Carter sat up, asked anxiously, "Is she all right, Ah Ling?"

"There is nothing wrong with her Tuan, but tonight when this 'phone rang," he nodded towards the 'phone on the sideboard, "and the Tuan went into the bedroom to take the call on the extension, she listened on this 'phone. Before the Tuan returned she replaced the receiver." Ah Ling looked ashamed as he added after a short pause, "I was watching, Tuan, through the window."

"I see."

"And then, Tuan, she asked me not to take her to the Nurses' Hostel but to drop her at the fire station."

He stopped, so Carter prompted, "Go on."

"Well Tuan, I dropped her at the fire station and drove off, but I did not go far, I went back and followed her on foot."

This, Carter thought to himself, is all very odd. "And, Ah Ling?"

"Tuan, she went into the Saam Loong Coffee-Shop and used the 'phone."

"Really, Ah Ling?" Carter remarked. The Saam Loong Coffee-

Shop was not the sort of place a woman of Nancy's class would normally enter. It was little better than a shack.

"Yes Tuan; it is a wooden building on a corner. And while she was using the 'phone, I listened by the window. I did not hear all she said, but I heard the words, 'Chadwick Estate,' and 'Tomorrow morning.'" Ah Ling shifted uncomfortably for a moment and said, "That is all, Tuan."

"Thank you, Ah Ling, goodnight."

"Goodnight, Tuan."

Carter sat immobile listening to Ah Ling's receding footsteps. Ah Ling's words ringing in his ears like an echo in a canyon. That is all, Tuan. That is all, Tuan. That is all, Tuan. It is said that in the moments which precede an earthquake, there is a silence. Birds stop singing, dogs do not bark, frogs do not croak; throughout the animal world there is a silence. If one were aware of it one might run out of the house before it collapsed and thus save one's life.

It was as if he had heard this silence: Carter felt an overwhelming need to dash out into the darkness; so strong was this need that he resisted it only by an effort of will. He told himself that he must sit quietly and think.

If someone were with him in the lounge, and the 'phone rang, he answered it on the extension in the bedroom. If someone were with him in the bedroom, he answered it on the extension in the lounge. Whoever it was who was with him. It was instinctive with him: the result of training and experience rather than a measure of distrust. If someone overheard something on the 'phone he might, in all innocence, repeat it. And repeat it to the wrong person. What exactly *had* Sergeant Morgan said on the telephone that night? Carter had sent him a coded signal telling him to report to his office at ten o'clock today. Morgan was to confirm receipt, which he could do either by telephone, or, if the 'phone were not working, by signal.

But what exactly had he said?

Had he said, "Sergeant Morgan here, sir, I shall comply with signal number 12345,"—as he should have done,—or had he said something like, "Signal 12345 sir, I'll be in at ten tomorrow as arranged." Or even, "I'll be in tomorrow morning as arranged." It's very easily done.

But Sergeant Morgan had no need to mention the words "Chad-

246

wick Estate." Nancy knew that Sergeant Morgan was stationed on Chadwick Estate. It was absurd, he told himself. There must be a perfectly simple and entirely innocent explanation. There must be. There had to be.

Perhaps Ah Ling had made it all up; he didn't like Nancy anyway. But the words, "Chadwick Estate." Carter hadn't used them, and even if he had, Ah Ling couldn't have heard him use them in the bedroom.

No. It was true!

All right! So it was true. But what was the explanation? Chadwick Estate. Where he was to have spent Christmas with the Erringtons. But he hadn't quite made it, had he. Every detail of the ambush flooded through his mind, from the moment when the windscreen had shattered until the moment when Sergeant Morgan's face had started spinning round him.

There had not been an ambush on that road for seven months. There had not been one since.

"I don't think Matron likes me. I'm on duty again this Christmas darling."

"I won't be here anyway, Nancy, I shall be spending Christmas with the Erringtons."

It had been in this chair that he had said it. It had been about nine o'clock at night and about three weeks before Christmas. She had not long come off duty and was wearing her black cheong saam and the Mikimotu brooch he had given her for her birthday.

It had been Chadwick Estate then. Would it be Chadwick Estate again today?

Number three Company's operational area; once commanded by Khan Hock Loi. Aided by the man who wanted him to know pain, Ah Bpo. Carter shuddered. God, how close can one get! But was it possible?

The hysterics and "No no no's," he'd been told about—could they be an act? But tonight. Why didn't she use the 'phone in the hospital, the one by her bedside? Was it because outgoing calls could be overheard by the operator in the hospital exchange? And the 'phone in the Saam Loong Coffee-Shop? Coming to think of it the Saam Loong Coffee-Shop would offer the nearest available 'phone to the hospital, at night anyway.

"Chadwick Estate," she had said. Or had she? Maybe Ah

Ling had misunderstood her. But they were both Cantonese, why should he have misunderstood her? and he had been sure enough of the facts to report them, however reluctantly. But why had he been watching? Or had he simply been waiting around for the buzzer to summon him to take her back to the hostel, and had just happened to glance in when she was doing her listening-on-the-extension act?

"Chadwick Estate." Surely to God she couldn't have been responsible for his ambush. But she *had* known that he was going to Chadwick Estate for Christmas. Only one or two other people had known where he was going until after he had gone. But if she *were* working for the Opposition, she had had plenty of other opportunities to arrange for him to have a pistol shoved into his back. They had not made a great number of visits, and certainly not regular visits, to town; but they had gone often enough—to the cinema, or dinner, or both. And when he had felt like taking her out he had usually said, "Glad rags tomorrow, honey; dinner." Sometimes he hadn't even said this, as he had asked her to keep clothes in his bungalow in case they felt like going out on the spur of the moment. He had never told her where he would be taking her to dinner—but only because it wasn't important, there were plenty of places to go to; it was simply a question of saying, "Now where shall we go for dinner?" Now. Not tomorrow. Which left her no opportunity of telling anybody where they were going, if she had wanted to tell anybody, that is. But he had often asked her where she wanted to go. Against this, she had never known when he was going to ask her. And again, there was the quite obvious fact that she wouldn't want him to get knocked off while she was with him; she might get knocked off as well. Always provided, of course, that that was what she did want. Now that he had come to think about it seriously, his trip to Chadwick Estate at Christmas had been the only time when she had known where he was going when she would not be with him.

But surely this was all absurd. Could she really have tipped them off? Could it really be true that she had been the instrument that had caused him to go through *all that?*

Could it?

And all that that implied. The tears. "You must go, Ralph." "I love you Ralph. And I shall go on loving you."

All pretence? All an act?

Supposing she had been a Communist agent all the time, and had fallen in love with him. That sort of thing happened. That's why women made such unreliable agents. No, this would mean that she had fallen out of love with him just before Christmas.

For another hour he gnawed at the problem: examining it from every conceivable angle. Suddenly he stood up and with all his strength hurled his glass at the wall. As it shattered to pieces, he said, "The bitch! The bitch! The scheming double-faced bitch!"

He had arrived at the only possible explanation of her conduct. Picking up the 'phone he spoke to the Signals Duty Officer, "Send me a despatch rider, I have a message for you to encode. Immediate and Operational."

Going to his desk he took out a signal pad and wrote a message. A message to the effect that Sergeant Morgan was to anticipate an ambush on his way to Sintra. He was not to travel in his own armoured personnel carrier, but in Sergeant Lloyd's. Morgan's armoured personnel carrier was to contain only the driver; Lloyd's, with both Morgan and Lloyd in it, was to contain a minimum of one section of Morgan's platoon.

The despatch driver arrived.

The 'phone rang half an hour later. His signal had been acknowledged.

He looked at the brandy bottle beside him. He had drunk three-quarters of the bottle; by rights he should have been rotten drunk. But he wasn't. He was stone cold sober.

This had happened once before, when he had been stung by a jelly-fish at Malacca; one of those huge Portuguese man-o-war things that can literally paralyse a man. A doctor had blandly suggested that if he wanted to sleep he had better get drunk. But however hard he had tried, he had not been able to get drunk.

He looked at his watch. It was five-thirty. He would ring Chief Inspector Lau; Lau was not a man who needed much sleep anyway.

And he had to know. Had to find out for sure. Somehow.

He was not to know that just before Christmas, Mrs. Errington had told one of her servants, "Mr. Carter will be staying with us for Christmas, make sure the sheets in the spare bedroom are aired."

And that within twenty-four hours, Ah Bpo was saying emphatically, "I would recognise his car if it were a mile away, comrades."

Even less was he to know that for the last three weeks Nancy had been telling herself, "I must tell them something. I must!" In a hopeless situation, she feebly played for time; but took the irrevocable step that could only make the situation worse.

It was nine-twenty-five a.m. Carter stood on the verandah of the Operations Room looking at the Table, waiting for a square to light up as the Voice said, "Two police armoured personnel carriers under attack at mile such and such Ventnor Road." He knew that a square *would* light up and that the Voice would say just that. The photograph he had been given by Chief Inspector Lau was still damp in his pocket.

Nine-thirty-eight. The light and the Voice, as expected.

Nine-thirty-nine. The Voice, but this time the voice of the Duty Officer sitting in front of him, directing a police jungle squad to the scene of the ambush.

The Duty Officer concluded his instructions and then looked round and up at Carter curiously; he was on the point of saying, "You must be psychic," but he thought better of it when he caught sight of the expression on Carter's face, an expression of pain as Carter gazed unseeingly at the Table, lost in his thoughts. A strange fellow, Carter, he thought; and his manner and attitude had been one of suppressed rage from the moment he had arrived some two hours before, and said, "Put the jungle squad at mile 22 Ventnor Road on immediate alert."

Nine-forty-three. The light going out as the Voice begins, "At 09:25 hours, the first of two police armoured personnel carriers travelling 100 yards apart, was blown up by a mine at the 24th mile Ventnor Road. Hearing the explosion, the driver of the second vehicle switched off his engine and coasted down the road; rounding the corner where the explosion had taken place, they surprised a group of a dozen Communist terrorists gathered around the other armoured personnel carrier, which was lying on its side. In the short fire-fight which followed, three Communist terrorists were killed and blood trails indicate that at least two others were wounded before the Communists withdrew. The driver of the first of the armoured

250

personnel carriers was killed when the mine exploded. A Police jungle squad with tracking dogs is now pursuing the terrorists."

Carter turned and walked out.

For how many other deaths had darling Nancy also been responsible? Small wonder she was beginning to look haggard; the strain of Mata-hari-ing was sure to tell eventually.

Halroyd looked up at Carter in surprise as Carter came in and stood in front of his desk. He had never seen him looking like this before; never seen him in such cold fury.

"Sit down, Ralph. What's wrong?"

Carter sat down, but didn't answer immediately. Just sat there. He has something of Chief Inspector Lau about him now, Halroyd thought wonderingly, icy. A calm violence.

Finally, in a voice thick with rage, Carter said, "The nurse Nancy Chong is a Communist agent."

Halroyd sat back in his chair, looked at Carter for a long moment with wide eyes, then said, "Are you sure about this?"

"Yes I am," Carter snarled, eyes flashing.

"Jesus Christ!"

Carter explained about the telephone call and the resultant ambush before going on, "Early this morning, I told Chief Inspector Lau to give her room a going over. He showed up in Public Works Department uniform with an electrician friend just after she'd gone on duty, and went through the motions of checking for a fault in the wiring. In a drawer in her room he found a list, which he photographed." Carter took an envelope from a pocket and handed it across the desk.

Halroyd opened the envelope and looked at the photograph therein: it began, "Arms and ammunition—furniture." At the bottom was a telephone number, "Sintra 72109."

"The telephone number?" Halroyd asked.

"A coffee-shop in town," Carter explained, adding, "you remember that Communist courier who got himself shot by Gurkhas about ten months ago?"

Halroyd nodded.

"You remember he had a telephone number among his papers?"

"Yes, it was something of a dead loss," Halroyd observed, "belonged to an Indian clerk in the Agriculture Department who proved to have no Communist connections whatsoever."

"Well the number of that clerk's 'phone was 61098, sir."

"So?"

"Add one to each figure and you get 72109."

"I see."

"And the writing, sir, so Chief Inspector Ramanath assures me, is that of Lim Tsing Wa."

They looked at each other steadily for a long moment, then Halroyd said, "So it might be, but he might have written it two years ago."

Halroyd had never accepted Carter's story about Nathan's slip of the tongue regarding Lim Tsing Wa.

"Chief Inspector Lau swears that the list has a newish look about it, sir. But in any case I've told him to return tomorrow and borrow it for half an hour. Ramanath will tell us how old it is within two minutes."

"Anything else?" Halroyd asked.

"No. Only that I've sent Sergeant Lo to check up on her background. School, badminton clubs, cultural organisations etc. Something I should have done about two years ago, if I'd had any sense. It would have saved me a very unpleasant little experience."

"How come?"

"I told her I'd be spending Christmas on Chadwick Estate."

"Christ!" Halroyd exclaimed in exasperation.

"I know. I didn't think of it until last night, when the possibility of her being a Communist agent crossed my mind for the first time. It was about three weeks before Christmas, she'd been bleating about having to work over the holiday and I said not to worry, I wouldn't be around anyway, I was spending the Christmas on Chadwick Estate. It came out like a reflex." Carter still spoke with repressed anger.

"What now?" Halroyd asked, after the long silence.

"Use her!" Carter replied savagely.

Halroyd was taken aback by the venom in Carter's voice; it occurred to him that he would have to keep careful tabs on all Carter's plans and actions now. Hate also is an emotion. But this was not the time to point it out. He said placidly, "How, Ralph?"

"She listens to 'phone calls. Give her something to listen to."

252

"Go on."

"Well the first item on that list, sir," Carter said, pointing to the photograph in front of Halroyd, "refers to arms and ammunition; I suggest someone rings me up and talks about a consignment for somewhere."

"She'd never fall for that. That's the last thing that a police officer would talk about over the 'phone."

"The caller could sound drunk."

Halroyd nodded slowly, "Yes he could, couldn't he? I could do that myself, couldn't I? You've put a tap on the 'phone in the coffee-shop?"

"Of course. A twenty-four hour watch."

"So we would know whether or not she *has* fallen for it, wouldn't we?"

"We would," Carter agreed.

"Then what?"

"Well, instead of an armoured personnel carrier loaded with arms and ammunition, we will give them something interesting to attack. An armoured personnel carrier with half a dozen British soldiers in it holding flame-throwers, for example."

Halroyd stood up and said thoughtfully, "I like it. If, if she falls for it, we can fix it so that the route for the arms and ammo is along the Ventnor Road; from the seventy-third to the eighty-ninth miles is a Prohibited Area, isn't it?"

"So?" Carter asked.

"So we can bomb it and shell it! We could make quite a thing out of it, couldn't we? Good propaganda. A spectacular Combined Operation! That Prohibited Area is even well within range of the sea. We could include one of those Naval frigates that are always on patrol, and the brigadier's dying to use a battery of mortars he hasn't found any use for yet. Work out a project, Ralph, with all that in mind, and I'll discuss it with the Brig, as soon as it's ready."

It is difficult to make love to someone you hate; especially when it is someone you once loved. The ashes of a dead love provide no tinder for fires of passion, are rarely warm enough to foment lust. But, Carter told himself, he would prove himself as good an actor as she had proved herself an actress. He also would act—and well.

His sex life had now become inextricably involved with his job, a facet—a very important facet—of a project.

She had done it well enough. Was still doing it. She hated him. Had tried, and very nearly succeeded, in getting him killed. Yet she could still hug him to her and caress him as if he were as dear to her as life itself.

It is easier for a woman to pretend to a passion that she does not feel than it is for a man. Hate kills lust as well as love. In order to enable him to complete the act, the physical and yet theatrical act, he had to have his lust kindled; she had to do now what she had once so impulsively done when he had lain in a hospital bed. Every time. It was the only way he could complete the act and carry on with the play.

The last five nights had proved him a successful actor.

He lay on top of her breathing heavily in her ear.

She grasped his hips. "You're hurting me, darling."

For one shrill moment he almost hissed, I want you to know pain. God, she had caused *him* enough! Instead he whispered, "Sorry, darling."

God! This was murder. How *had* she been able to do it? And for so long! . . .

Sergeant Lo in his office that morning; grinning like a Cheshire cat. Pleased with himself. "She joined the Party very young, sir. In high school sir. Nearly six years ago now. Two of the members of her cell identified her photograph, sir. Separately and immediately. Surrenders, sir. One of them surrenderd six months ago, and the other over a year ago. And, sir, it was their form master who recruited them into the Party, Lim Tsing Wa, sir."

The duplicity of the bitch. "I love you, Ralph. And I shall go on loving you." God all bloody mighty! Had she ever played *him* for a sucker.

He glanced at his watch; nine-twenty. They must bathe, get dressed and go into the lounge. Halroyd was to 'phone at two minutes to ten.

When the 'phone rang Carter said, "Excuse me, darling," and went into the bedroom, closed the door behind him noisily, and picked up the 'phone.

"Halroyd here, Ralph." His voice was slurred.

"Sir?"

254

"That truckload of arms and ammo for the new police station at Ventnor Estate. We're short of vehicles, do you think we could send it on its own?"

"Don't see why not, sir. It's a fair risk. Road ambushes are few and far between these days."

"I think sho too. I'll send them sometime the week after next; the new station will be ready then, all we need do is to have a few guards on the bridges on the day in question. Mussen get our truck blown up eh? Come on over an' have a drink."

"I'd rather not."

"Come on."

"Thank you, but no, sir. Goodnight."

"Night, Ralph."

Carter put down the 'phone, thinking, it could never happen. He looked angry when he walked back into the lounge. He noticed Nancy's face was pale. "What's wrong Ralph?" she asked nervously.

"My boss. Stinking drunk. But that's no excuse for careless talk."

Later he kissed her goodnight, then hugged her. Over her shoulder, he raised his eyebrows questioningly at Ah Ling, standing in the doorway.

Ah Ling gave a slight nod.

She'd listened.

After they had gone Carter grinned to himself in wry amusement at the recollection of Ah Ling's explanation as to why he had been looking through the window. "Watching over you, Tuan." Watching over him, for Christ's sake! A European magistrate would send him down for six months as a Peeping Tom, without a thought. Yet it was true. In his curious way Ah Ling had been seeking an opportunity to enhance his value in Carter's eyes, and, with this in view, had been "watching over" him.

Bloody good job he had. And Carter had had to tell him to carry on watching over him, thereby setting the seal of approval on it. But when all this little lot was over, Carter decided firmly, Ah Ling could cease his "watching over" act, forthwith.

An hour later Chief Inspector Lau arrived with a tape recorder and they sat and listened to the recording of Nancy's recent telephone call to Sintra 72109. Heard the telephone ring twice, then a man's voice rasp, "Hallo," in Mandarin.

"May I speak to Dr. Lum please?" Nancy's voice; breathless Cantonese.

"Speaking," the voice croaked in Cantonese.

"It's me Doctor. I'm sending some furniture to the new house on Ventnor Estate, which will be completed the week after next, and as you're always interested in furniture, I thought you might like to go and see it."

"Good girl. Good girl." Dr. Lum croaked. "But what day the week after next?"

"Er, er, it will be the day when the children are playing on the bridges."

Carter shot Lau a glance which read, Couldn't she think of anything better than that?

"I see." The croak again. "Will the furniture be in one or two lorries?"

"Only one, Doctor."

"I understand, but when is your fiancé going to have a chat with me? I've asked you so many times to arrange a meeting."

"Er, well he's asked me to go on leave with him to Penang, but Matron won't let me have my leave. She just won't." Nancy's voice was frightened. Terrified of being overheard, Carter assumed.

"Penang," the voice of Dr. Lum went on, "that's interesting. I could meet him in Penang. You must try to get your leave. You really must. Goodbye."

The receiver was put down abruptly, and Lau switched the recorder off.

"I'm not surprised that the good Dr. Lum brought that conversation to a halt. It would arouse anyone's suspicions. 'Children playing on bridges!'"

Lau looked impassively at Carter as he commented, "You would do well, Tuan, to kill that man. Before he kills you."

"Surely to God, Lau, we can identify a man with a voice like that!" Carter said. "Get her voice taken out and play the recording to members of the 'X' squad, or some of our more co-operative recent surrenders."

"It is not necessary, Tuan," Lau replied blandly.

Carter looked at him in surprise, "Why not?"

256

"A man who has been hit in the neck with a parang might talk like that; he might be able to recover his life, but he's unlikely to recover his natural voice, Tuan."

There were times, Carter thought, when Lau was way ahead of him. But he wished Lau would sometimes speak in a tone which betrayed interest; whatever he said, was said with toneless dispassion.

After Lau had gone, Carter considered the situation created by Nancy's telephone call. The Communists were desperately short of arms and ammunition. The temptation to attack a lone truck carrying arms and ammunition would be well nigh irresistible, and they would need to make sure the attack was completely successful; they would also need quite a lot of men to carry away the loot, so they would need to attack with at least two platoons, and possibly a whole company. Their ambush positions would therefore need to be fairly extensive.

Now that the Communists had got the message certain plans would be put into effect. The Public Works Department had already been told to clear the bushes and tall grass at all likely ambush points along the Ventnor Road except where it ran through the sixteen miles of jungle and Prohibited Area. An army of labourers had been working on this for several days, but their numbers would now be rapidly increased. The presence of the labourers working on the roadside, and the fact of the roadsides having been cleared of cover at likely ambush points, would force the Communists to dig their ambush positions somewhere along the sixteen miles which had not been cleared—in the Prohibited Area. An area in which unauthorised persons were liable to be shot on sight; the road itself being restricted for the use of military and police vehicles, and only such civilian vehicles as were specially authorised—the latter being expressly forbidden to stop whilst in the Prohibited Area.

The truck would roll in eight days, giving the Communists time to prepare their ambush positions—within the Prohibited Area.

Carter recalled the discussion in Halroyd's office the previous day concerning the coffee-shop with the back room which housed telephone number 72109. A coffee-shop which was situated on a main road in one of the most thickly populated parts of Sintra—a jumble of shops, garages and tenements. An impossible area to cordon off and comb. A swift attack on the coffee-shop might lead to the discovery of a heavy door which could cost precious seconds to demolish; behind it, an empty room with a trapdoor which led to a maze of cellars, or a sewer, and that's all. Or else there would be a gunfight in which civilians were liable to get themselves shot. In any case, it would lead to the loss of a valuable source of information. No, telephone number 72109 must be heard but not touched. Already it looked as if it might lead to a singularly unsuccessful Communist ambush. Carter grinned. The blame for it would fall squarely on Comrade Nancy's shoulders. She would come in for a severe reprimand. The Communists do not forgive failure; after heresy, it is the sin which cries most loudly for vengeance.

But Carter was thinking about Penang.

Just after his release from hospital he had asked her to go with him to Penang for a week's leave. And Comrade Lim Tsing Wa had said he could meet her fiancé there.

Maybe he could.

A project began to form itself in Carter's mind. Maybe the meeting could be arranged. As boss of the killer-squads, Lim Tsing Wa was unlikely to be mixed up in the ambush, and in Sintra he would be difficult to trap. But in Penang, at, say, an isolated seaside bungalow . . .

He sent Sergeant Lo to Penang the following day.

Halroyd and Carter sat together in the semi-darkness of the verandah watching the progress of a police armoured personnel carrier as it made its way across the surface of the Table. Code-named Hazel, it contained eight British soldiers who sat stripped to the waist, and who held the nozzles of flame-throwers behind the narrow slits which provided the only ventilation. Volunteers, they knew what to expect.

The Voice droned out Hazel's position every quarter of a mile, as it wound its way at twenty mph along the Ventnor Road. Presumably the radio-operator was simply reading the milestones.

"It must be stifling in that bloody thing," Carter whispered.

"It'll get hotter outside, I hope," Halroyd replied.

So far, so good. Hazel still had ten miles to go before it reached the beginning of the sixteen-mile stretch of road that ran through the Prohibited Area. One mile behind Hazel, a convoy of army

258

trucks carried a company of British soldiers: code name, "Abel." Similarly, at mile eighty-nine, another company: code name, "Baker."

Behind the ridge of hills that ran more or less parallel with the road an R.A.F. helicopter circled patiently. Helicopter Charlie. If and when Hazel was ambushed, Charlie would direct the mortar fire from the battery of mortars on Ventnor Estate, and the guns on the Naval frigate in the bay. It had been calculated that it would take Charlie no more than fifty-eight seconds to reach any ambush position on the sixteen-mile stretch.

Police sentries were guarding the six bridges; had been guarding them since dawn. By now, Carter hoped, the comrades knew this and were waiting tensely in ambush. He speculated idly as to how they might have got the message. A man at the top of a tree, a man with field glasses? A dog with a message attached to its collar, seeking out its master? A fire in a squatter-area? But it didn't matter how they got it as long as they got it.

"Hazel reports mile seventy-one."

Two miles to go.

In the Duty Officer's chair the brigadier bent forward to his microphone 'phone and the Voice said, "R.A.F. to scramble now. Naval and Military guns, stand by three."

Carter felt a sudden pang of rage. The center of the Table became Nancy's tearful face. It was she, Nancy, who had let loose these dogs.

"Hazel reports mile seventy-three."

"Action all stations."

Hazel was now within the Prohibited Area.

Halroyd and Carter listened with increasing unease as Hazel continued to report its position every quarter of a mile; when it reported mile eighty-five they glanced at each other in alarm. Surely all this effort and organisation was not simply going to prove a waste of time?

Carter was wiping his forehead when the Voice said, "Hazel reports tree down on road and exploding mine between miles eighty-five and three-quarters and eighty-six. Under heavy small arms fire from North only. Flame-throwers in action."

"Red Wing to attack north of flame-throwers."

"Red Wing leader has Hazel visual. Going in."

"Charlie has Hazel visual."

"Charlie to assume fire control."

"Hazel to withdraw on completion flame-throwers."

"Red Wing two has Hazel visual. Going in."

"Abel at mile eighty-five."

"Hazel unable to withdraw due fallen trees on road, before and behind, but no longer under fire."

"Baker at mile eighty-eight and a half."

"Red Wing has Hazel visual. Going in."

"Blue Wing standing by."

They could not hear helicopter Charlie directing the guns, but they knew his instructions: deliberately wide at first, he would direct the guns as close to Hazel as he dared. But they heard him clearly enough when he said, "Charlie reports civilian car at mile eighty-six and a quarter."

Halroyd and Carter looked at each other in amazement. Civilian traffic was banned that day. It had been banned on alternate days for the last week. Surely it was not part of the ambush?

But the brigadier paused only for a moment before leaning forward to his microphone, "Blue Wing to destroy road 100 yards west of Hazel."

"Abel at mile eighty-five and a half."

"Blue Wing Leader has Hazel visual. Going in."

"Baker at mile eighty-eight."

"Blue Wing Leader reports road destroyed as instructed."

"Baker to be advised of destruction of road at mile eighty-six. Civilian car to be detained."

"Cease fire. R.A.F. to return to base."

Carter slumped back in his chair exhausted.

Three minutes can be a long time."

Halroyd said, "O.K. Let's go."

They accompanied the brigadier to a helicopter on the roof of Police H.Q. Its rotors were already turning. It dropped them in a dry paddy field at mile ninety-one, where a scout car was waiting to take them to the scene of the ambush.

At the scene, Carter gaped in amazement. To the north of Hazel, and for a distance of about four hundred yards, the jungle no longer existed. Huge trees that had stood for decades had been tossed aside, or snapped like matchsticks, or else stood leaning against the trees which marked the periphery of the red-brown field with its vista of craters. For a moment, Carter experienced a pang of sadness, as if the jungle were some huge helpless animal upon which some needless suffering had been inflicted. But mainly his feelings were of awe. That it was possible for this to be done at all.

In three minutes.

Nearer Hazel, along the roadside, the trees still stood with smoke rising from their blackened trunks, and from the skeletons of bushes. Overall hung the smell of burnt flesh. A unique smell; cloying, sickly-sweet. Along the other side of the road fourteen bodies lay in a neat row, each covered with a blanket.

As they got out of the scout car Halroyd and Carter exchanged glances. Only fourteen.

Hazel had been very lucky indeed. It had been ambushed as it rounded a sharp corner. Just in front of its front wheels, was an oil slick created by the emptying of a barrel fitted on bamboo supports in a bush at the side of the road. A rope had been used to tilt the barrel. The oil slick extended for twenty yards, at the end of which was a fallen tree lying across the road. In front of the tree was a shallow crater where a mine had exploded. Once on the oil slick Hazel would have run into the tree, and stopped above, or very near, the mine. Another tree lay across the road behind, and only six feet from Hazel.

From the jungle nearby came a thin high-pitched scream.

As if in answer to the question, a major stepped forward to the brigadier, saluted and said, "We just can't find him, sir. When we get near him, he stops."

From the attitude of the men standing around, Carter sensed there was something wrong. He was soon to know what it was. They were shown the ambush positions; there were two of them, both well dug. One was on the North side of the road, opposite Hazel, the other, on the South side, was opposite the mine crater and the oil slick. The first contained room for about fifteen or twenty men, the other for about sixty. Hazel had been fired on only from the North, and the whole of the counterfire had been concentrated there; the men in the second ambush position hadn't fired at all. With Hazel in the position it was in, they would have been firing in the direction of their own men in the first ambush position. It was a very badly sited ambush position altogether.

The men in the second, larger, ambush position, had escaped completely. All sixty of them.

They stood looking at the second ambush position, the brigadier, Carter, and Halroyd, when a voice behind them roared, "Come on down outer there, you bastard!"

They turned to see an army corporal pointing his carbine into the foliage of a tree whose huge branches stretched across the road. They discerned a movement in the tree and watched as a slight figure in khaki, wearing a hat with a red star, climbed down. He stood with his hands up in a state of sheer terror as the belt of grenades at his waist was removed and while he was searched. They all stood looking at him. Saw him shaking in every limb; noticed that he couldn't control the movements of his jaw.

"All right, you can put your hands down now, Bonzo," the corporal said to him. But Bonzo didn't understand, so the corporal moved forward to pull his hands down for him. But Bonzo cowered away from him, his hands half protecting his head, expecting to be struck. The corporal looked affronted, then turned to some soldiers nearby and said, "Whose got a drink for Bonzo? I think he's had a bit of a fright like."

A young soldier stepped forward unscrewing a water-bottle. He held it out to Bonzo, but Bonzo looked at it uncomprehendingly, so the soldier took a swig from it to show him what to do. Bonzo took the water-bottle gingerly, looking fearfully at the faces around him, read only sympathy, put it to his lips. When he had finished drinking, the corporal offered him a cigarette. "It's duty-free, Bonzo, otherwise I couldn't afford it."

Again Bonzo didn't seem to understand, so the corporal took a cigarette from the packet and stuck it between Bonzo's lips. As the corporal lit it for him he said, "Keep your jaw still, Bonzo, otherwise I'll burn my fingers."

Bonzo took two or three puffs and looked in utter bewilderment at the faces around him. Then he sank into a squatting position and sobbed.

Not an unreasonable thing for a boy of fifteen to do under the circumstances.

As they walked back to the scout car Halroyd commented to Carter, "Bloody good thing he didn't start slinging those grenades around, otherwise he might have evened up the score. We walked under that tree! You know, Ralph," he added thoughtfully, "shells and bombs don't win this kind of war. This kind of war is won with bamboo hairs."

They had forgotten to ask about the civilian car. It belonged to a Malay who had a fruit stall in Sintra market. The Prohibited Area was rich in jungle fruits because no one was allowed to collect them, and he had taken advantage of this fact; that was all. But it was not an advantage that he would take again. He had seen what could happen in a Probibited Area. A Naval bombardment for stealing fruit! No charge was brought against him.

20

When Carter went to Penang to inspect the two bungalows that Sergeant Lo had selected he took Sergeant Morgan with him. After they had inspected the bungalows Carter explained his plan, but Morgan was unenthusiastic. "I get it, sir. Whilst Lau, Chiv, Lo and me are sitting around in the dark in one bungalow, you'll be champering away at your oats in the other."

The two bungalows were exactly the same; they stood on a small cliff overlooking the beach and were about a hundred yards apart. A tall bamboo hedge marked the grounds between them and they were approached by separate roads which led through a dilapidated rubber estate from the main road four hundred yards away. Each bungalow had a telephone.

When the police carpenter arrived Carter explained to him what he wanted done. He wanted a small platform built in the kitchen of one of the bungalows, four feet below the apex of the sloping roof, and large enough for a man to lie on. Thinking of the fate of the members of the "X" squad who had killed Betty Wong, Carter said, "I want the platform to be made from the wood of the iron-wood tree."

The Chinese carpenter laughed. "It would be too heavy, Tuan. The wood of the iron-wood tree is as heavy as . . . well, iron, and it is very expensive."

"I couldn't care less about that," Carter replied, adding emphatically, "I want it made from the wood of the iron-wood tree. You can nail it above that cross-beam."

"You can't drive nails into the wood of the iron-wood tree, Tuan," the carpenter remarked pityingly.

"I don't care how you put the platform there," Carter insisted, "but I very much care that it be made of the wood of the iron-wood tree."

"As you wish, Tuan," the carpenter said, resignedly, thinking,

264

It will need special machinery to cut it; it will need strong supports; it will be difficult to do and will cost much. But don't take any notice of me, I'm only twice your age and I've been a carpenter all my life.

It was late afternoon and Nancy was coming off duty. As she walked across the main lobby of the hospital, a girl in the office by the main door called, "Nancy, I've got a parcel for you."

Nancy turned and walked to the counter, where the girl had placed a brown paper parcel about the size of a large dictionary. "You'll have to sign for it, Nancy; it's registered and express delivery."

As Nancy signed, the girl continued, "It's very heavy." She laughed, "Maybe it's a large diamond from the boyfriend."

Nancy forced a smile and glanced at the name and address of the sender, but neither conveyed anything to her, although the parcel had been mailed in Sintra. She picked up the parcel, tucked it under her arm and walked to her room. Placing it on her dressing table she searched for the scissors. She eventually found them in the bathroom and told herself she must try to remember to put them in the medicine cabinet whenever she used them in future. Then she began to open the parcel. It was very carefully made. Layer after layer of heavy brown paper. Six layers. After removing the sixth she discovered a biscuit tin, its lid sealed with cellotape. It felt very cold to the touch. She lifted the lid and saw an envelope lying on a piece of cardboard. She opened it and read in a familiar hand, "It was a very bad consignment of furniture, Nancy. You really must arrange that appointment. You really must."

She removed the piece of cardboard and found a block of ice. Embedded in it, and clearly visible, was a human ear. She screamed, turned, tore at the handles of the french windows and ran into the garden.

"Matron says I must go on leave," Nancy said dully.

Carter had been expecting this; Halroyd had had a quiet word with Matron. "Darling, that's wonderful," he replied excitedly, "but when?"

"Any time I like. Tomorrow, if I want."

Carter hugged her to him, then held her at arms' length, one hand on each shoulder. "But darling, why so unhappy about it? It's great! We can leave for Penang the day after tomorrow. I'll ring up tonight and book a quiet bungalow by the sea. There are dozens of holiday bungalows in Penang, we'll have no trouble in getting one at all."

"You haven't forgotten that we can't make love for several days?"

"Come off it, darling. Being with you is what matters. Surely you must know that?"

"Are you sure you can get away, Ralph?" she asked unhappily.

"'Course I'm sure. I'm owed lots of convalescent leave, remember?"

"Will you know the address of the bungalow before we leave?" she asked, her voice little more than a whisper. "I'd like to have my mail forwarded."

"Afraid not, honey. Won't know till we're there. A friend of mine will fix something for us; he'll choose a decent place, I'm sure. Then all we need do is swim and lie around in the sun. It'll be great! We both need a rest. And really, honey, you're beginning to look ill. Are you sure you're all right?"

She put her head against his chest and said, "Yes, of course I am," her voice scarcely audible, but it had urgency in it as she added, "Do you think we really ought to go, Ralph?"

"Of course I do, darling," he replied. "Now no more about it. It's as good as fixed!"

After she had gone he found himself wondering whether, now that the final crunch was clearly on its way, she was beginning to have second thoughts. She really did look desperately unhappy. Perhaps she did have a twinge of affection for him after all. Well it was too late now. The only thing that mattered was to get Lim Tsing Wa.

Later again, after listening to the recording of her telephone conversation with Dr. Lum made shortly after she had left his bungalow, he changed his mind. She was just a brilliant actress, that was all. "You haven't forgotten we can't make love for several days?" "Do you think we really ought to go, Ralph?" As if she were genuinely reluctant, while all the time she was trying to get him knocked off.

But he wished Dr. Lum wasn't so abrupt on the 'phone. After

saying, "Remember to ring 892311 as soon as possible after you arrive in Penang. Have you written that down? That's right," he had hung up. Leaving Carter with the impression that she had wanted to say something more, to ask something. But no doubt Dr. Lum's abruptness was due to his fear of what Nancy might say. Her use of code words was surprisingly naïve. "Children playing on the bridges." But why did she always take such a long time before replacing the receiver? She sometimes held it for over a minute after the good Dr. Lum had rung off.

But what the hell! The important thing was to get Lim Tsing Wa. That would bring his score to five out of seven. He was way ahead of the field; in the other States, nobody had got more than two; some hadn't even got any!

Carter had told Nancy that they would go to Penang by train. Ah Ling would pick her up at nine-thirty, bring her to his bungalow, and they would catch the ten-five train. But after she arrived at his bungalow he gleefully announced that he'd been lucky enough to secure tickets on the eleven-fifteen 'plane.

"We'll be there hours earlier, honey," he said delightedly.

Halroyd had said, "That Lim Tsing Wa bastard must know where you are *only* when *you* want him to know where you are. Otherwise you might find yourself getting knocked off at the railway station, or even on the train."

At the airport in Penang they were met by the "estate agent," who had secured for their use a Morris Minor. He took them in it to the bungalow. He showed them around the bungalow and said, "You'll enjoy your stay; it's wonderfully peaceful here." Later, while Nancy was admiring the view from the cliff and he was alone with Carter, he said quietly, "The others are all fixed up in the other bungalow, sir."

"No snags?"

"None, sir."

Carter nodded, "Good. You'd better go now. I'm due back on stage for the 'crunch' scene."

They shook hands.

As Inspector Thiam Pak Yin walked to the main road he idly wondered what Carter had meant by his last remark.

Carter picked up their luggage and carried it into the bungalow through a door which led along a short passage to the kitchen. As he passed through the kitchen he glanced up at the platform below the ceiling. He did not like its position; it gave an unobstructed view of the windows and of the door to the lounge, but it gave no view at all of the doorway through which he had just come. But the kitchen was built in such a way that it was the only place in which the platform could effectively be put.

In the late afternoon they went swimming. Then they drove into town, had dinner, and went to the cinema. There was little danger in this. Lim Tsing Wa didn't know where they were staying. For this information he would have to await Nancy's telephone call—a call which she had not yet been given a chance to make.

Carter was glad that the whole charade was drawing to its conclusion. The act had become a strain. The need to plant kisses on a neck which he would far rather have squeezed with both hands had become an intolerable burden. He found himself wondering what he could ever have seen in her. She looked almost haggard. Her face was drawn and there were bags under her eyes. She was dull, dispirited and boring to be with. Her former gaiety had vanished. She said little, never even smiled, and carried with her a curious fearful listlessness which Carter found particularly irritating. She had shown better ability as an actress in the past, Carter thought, and the act wasn't over yet; she ought to have been able to carry on to the final curtain. And another thing, there wouldn't be any point in her kindling his lust for him. Or would there? Why not? This was probably going to be the last night. Let it end as it had started!

In the bedroom, before they got undressed, he carefully adjusted the curtains. There were at least two of his men patrolling the grounds outside, and he'd no intention of providing them with any entertainment. He'd noticed she'd taken a couple of sleeping tablets, so he hadn't got all that much time to waste. After they'd got undressed he whispered, "Come here."

In the morning, after a late breakfast, Carter said, "I'm going into town, honey; I've got to buy drinks and things. Care to come along?"

"No, I'll stay here, Ralph," she said wanly. "I've got housework to do, the bed to make, and," indicating the dishes on the table, "the washing-up to do."

"Okay, honey. Is there anything you want?"

He hadn't thought she'd go. She had a call to make.

"Yes, darling, we haven't got enough sugar."

"Anything else?"

"No, darling."

He drove into town, made his purchases and had a couple of beers. He'd give her plenty of time. Then he drove back past the entrance that led to his own bungalow and parked the car near the entrance to the next. Looking cautiously around him and hoping Nancy hadn't gone for a walk, he walked through the rubber trees towards the other bungalow.

Chief Inspector Lau opened the door for him and he walked through into the semi-gloom of the curtained lounge. Through the open bedroom doorway he saw Sergeant Morgan asleep on the bed. Sergeant Lo sat wearing a pair of earphones, the tape-recorder in front of him.

"Inspector Chivapathy's outside, sir," Lau explained, "keeping an eye on her. She hasn't left the house this morning."

"Well I hope he doesn't let her eye fall on him," Carter remarked.

"He won't, sir," Lau assured him as he switched on the tape-recorder, "but hear this. Five minutes after you'd gone."

Carter listened to someone dialling a telephone, heard it ringing, then a man's voice saying "Hello" in Cantonese.

"Is that 892311?" Nancy's voice.

"That's right."

"Can I speak to Dr. Lum?"

"Dr Lum? Hang on . . ."

The 'phone was in the inevitable coffee-shop.

A delay of two minutes, then. "Dr. Lum speaking." A familiar croak.

"We are at the forty-third and a quarter-mile. A white bungalow called 'White Orchid.' It's at the end of a dirt road on the right." Nancy's voice was a taut whisper.

"That's good. That's very good. Has he brought any books with him?"

"No."

"You're sure?"

"Yes. I searched his things. He hasn't."

A long pause. Then, "Well, go on." An impatient croak.

"When he's asleep I'll leave the kitchen door slightly ajar, and the light on."

"And all the other lights off?"

"Yes, I suppose so."

"But what if he wakes up?"

"He won't. I have something from the hospital to put in his drink."

"Good. Good." Dr. Lum's voice oozed its satisfaction. "What time do you think we should pay our visit?"

"Ten or eleven . . . When the lights are out. . . . Except the one in the kitchen, I mean. How many of you will there be?"

"As usual, two."

"Do tell me about . . ."

"Not now, not now. Tonight. Don't worry."

The 'phone was put down and Lau switched the recorder off, remarking, "She doesn't sound very happy, sir."

"Well I shouldn't think that she ever wanted to be so closely involved. Telling them where I'm going so that they can knock me off is one thing. But being present when it's done is a different thing altogether."

"You know, sir," Lau said thoughtfully, "that's the first time he's ever given her a chance to ask a question. 'How many of you will there be?' And that other thing she wanted to ask, 'Do tell me about . . .' There is something here, sir, that we do not know."

"We know all we need to know, C.I. Have you gone through her kit?"

"Yes, sir. While you were swimming last night. We found a small bottle of white crystals, like salt." Lau handed an envelope to Carter and said, "This stuff. I suppose it's the something from the hospital she talked about; anyway, we replaced it with real salt."

Carter took the envelope and said, "I take it she hasn't got any books either?"

"No, she hasn't, sir."

"Not even a little .22 in her handbag?"

"No. We searched everything and everywhere."

270

"My Reising is on the platform?"

"Not yet, sir. I did not think it wise to put it there while you were away. I suggest you go somewhere this afternoon. I'll put it there then."

"You know, C.I.," Carter said thoughtfully, "if she's going to leave the kitchen light on, anyone looking through the kitchen window would see me climbing up on to the platform."

"The kitchen has plastic curtains, sir."

"Exactly. Plastic curtains which show shadows! Can you rig up an extension so that I can switch the kitchen light on when I'm on the platform?"

"Of course. But give me plenty of time, sir."

"I will."

"Will you be going out again, sir? After you come back this afternoon, I mean."

"No, once we're back we're back. It would be tempting fate to leave the place after dark, now. There's lots of food, so we won't have to go out for dinner."

They went over the plan in the next few minutes. It was quite simple: Lim Tsing Wa and his henchman would get into the kitchen, but no further—and not out.

Nine o'clock. Nancy and Carter sat in the darkness of the small patio outside the french windows of the lounge. Before and below them was the sea; an endless grey phosphorescence flickering in the light of a dying moon. The waves on the shore providing a rhythmic background to their stilted conversation. Behind them the lounge was lit by a solitary table lamp on the sideboard.

Carter had insisted that they sit in the darkness of the patio. "After that long drive today, Nancy, I'm tired. Let's just sit and watch the moon slide into the sea."

He was not so much tired as concerned about his silhouette.

"Another drink, honey?" Nancy asked, her voice holding a tremor.

Carter noticed the tremor. Keyed up, he noticed everything. This is it, he thought, but said, "Please, darling, but not too much brandy." As she stood up from her armchair Carter stood up from his and said, "And now I'll pee, in the China Sea."

He took a couple of paces towards the darkness beyond the

patio, turned towards Nancy as she walked into the lounge, and said, "That rhymes, darling." Humming to himself he walked across the patio, round a corner of the house and stood looking into the lounge through a chink in the curtains.

He watched as Nancy took a small bottle from her handbag, opened it, poured its contents into his glass, then filled it up with soda water. Looking frightened, she held it up to the light and shook it slightly.

Beside him in the darkness a voice said, "It's only salt, sir." Inspector Chivapathy.

"I hope there wasn't more than one bottle," Carter remarked.

"There wasn't, sir."

Carter went back to the patio still humming. Nancy joined him and put his glass on the side table next to him. Carter picked it up and said, "Cheers, darling," and put it to his lips. Brandy and soda and salt. He grimaced, then standing up said, "You forgot the ice, darling."

"I'll get it, Ralph."

"No don't bother. But where's your drink?"

"I don't think I want one, darling." Such a small voice.

"Have a ginger ale. I don't like drinking alone; in any case, we promised ourselves an early night, remember?"

"All right, Ralph, just a small one."

At the sideboard, he took his time. She couldn't see him from where she was sitting, and he had his back towards her. He emptied his salted brandy soda into the ice-bucket and poured himself a saltless one; then poured the contents of the envelope that Lau had given him that morning into a glass and filled it with ginger ale.

Returning to the patio, he handed Nancy her drink and sat down. In the semi-darkness he watched her carefully as she put her drink to her lips and swallowed a mouthful. For a moment she was still. Then she seemed to half rise, her mouth working as if unable to speak, and fell back in her chair and remained motionless.

"Jesus Christ," Carter thought, "that could have been me." He decided he must get the stuff analysed, it might come in useful sometime. He pulled back one of her eyelids. She was out. He picked her up, carried her into the bedroom and laid her on the bed.

It was much better this way. On an impulse he stepped on to the bed so that he could see the top of the wardrobe. The bottle of chloroform was there, together with the pad of cotton-wool. Chief Inspector Lau was completely reliable. But Carter was glad he hadn't had to use the chloroform. It had such an unpleasant smell.

He looked at his watch. Nine-forty. He switched off the bedroom light, opened the door and crossed the room to the french windows, closing them noisily. This was the signal that Nancy had been satisfactorily dealt with.

He drew the curtains behind the windows carefully, switched off the table lamp and went into the blackness of the kitchen, closing the door behind him. Feeling his way in the darkness he walked along the short passage and opened the outside door, leaving it slightly ajar. Then, taking the cover of a matchbox from his pocket, he placed it on the cement floor behind the door, some six inches from the hinged side. Still in darkness, he went back into the kitchen and clambered up on to the platform. He found the electric wire and ran his fingers along it until he felt the switch. He turned on the light.

It worked. Bless that man Lau, Carter thought. It was a powerful light. One hundred and fifty watts. Far too strong for a small kitchen. Nancy had complained about it the previous evening. But the metal light shade was below the level of the platform, and although he wasn't in complete darkness on the platform, anyone looking up at it would be blinded by the light. Apart from this it was not a bad thing that two men who would come from the darkness should suddenly move into a strong light. Eyes need a few moments to adjust.

Crouched on the platform he picked up his sub-machine gun and checked it. The Reising was on fully automatic and was cocked. There was also a cushion for his knees. Bless that man Lau.

He knelt with the Reising across his knees. He hoped they wouldn't be long; it was an uncomfortable position. He looked at his watch; three minutes past ten. He had that feeling in the pit of his stomach, and his pulse was racing. He heard the very faintest of sounds and tensed further. He almost laughed as a rat appeared by the sink, looked furtively around and began gnawing at a bar of soap. He was glad the rat had shown up. It gave him something to look at. And it was company.

It was hot on the platform. The perspiration ran from his hair and down his face and neck. At eleven minutes past ten the rat scurried away. Thanks for the tip-off, Carter said to himself as he lifted the Reising from across his knees.

A slight sound. The sort of sound a matchbox cover makes when it moves a few inches across a cement floor. He found himself looking down on the heads of two men who made swiftly and silently for the lounge door. The first man was a slight figure who held his grey head tilted towards his right shoulder and carried a pistol in his right hand. The second man was bigger, younger; he held a sten.

As greyhead tried the handle of the lounge door, Carter said, "Move! Die!"

They froze. Carter was on the point of saying, "Drop those guns," when there was a deafening blast as bullets pounded at the underside of the platform and ricochetted off.

There were three of them. One he could not see.

The moment the firing started, Carter squeezed his trigger. He had a fleeting vision of movement, the younger man with his mouth open sinking to the floor, the older turning beside the door, as the room plunged into darkness. The one hundred and fifty watt bulb had been shattered by a bullet.

Carter's head reeled. His ears ached with the noise. In the small kitchen the noise had a physical effect. One could feel it. It stunned.

Below him in the darkness were three men. One almost certainly dead, another perhaps dying—and a third very much alive.

How long had it all taken? Three seconds? Four? Carter could not control the trembling of his limbs. He kept his mouth open so that his quick breath would not be heard. He sensed movement below him, but if there were sounds to hear he could not hear them for the buzzing in his ears.

He almost screamed as something hard and heavy brushed his thigh then fell beside him on the platform. Frantically he scooped it off with his arm and crouched down sideways.

A flash of light and an explosion of indescribable violence as

274

the grenade burst below him. Surely to God the third man had collected some of that!

A plop, a vivid light, and a scream, simultaneously. A man spun into view below Carter screaming and clawing at the Verey cartridge burning at the back of his neck. Carter silenced him and was able to fire two careful bursts at the motionless bodies of the other two men before the thick white smoke from the cartridge hid everything.

The smell of burning flesh sickened him; his eyes streamed from the smoke.

"Are you all right in there?"

Morgan's voice came to him as if from a great distance. He could scarcely hear his own voice as he bawled, "Yes," in reply, and clambered down from the platform. In the dense smoke Carter screamed, "For Christ's sake drag him out!" The glowing center of the smoke moved out along the passage to the accompaniment of heavy coughs.

Carter had opened all the windows by the time Morgan, Chivapathy and Lau had returned.

"What a turn up for the book," Morgan said delightedly, placing a lighted flashlight upright on the table. "I only fired the bloody thing to put a bit of light on the subject. Couldn't see a bleeding thing. Right in the back of the neck, eh? Didn't half take the sloppy bleedin' grin off his face, didn't it?"

Chief Inspector Lau was examining the two corpses on the floor with the aid of his flashlight. He looked up at Carter and said, "This one is Lim Tsing Wa, sir."

"It can't be," Carter replied, "Lim's about my age. That's a man of fifty."

Lau tore open Lim's shirt, pointed to the knotted scar at the base of Lim's neck and said, "A parang bites deep." Lau stood up and moved away from the body, but he kept his flashlight on it.

They stood for a moment just looking at the body, then Lau said, "The woman, Tuan?"

"Yeah, let's go and have a look at her."

They followed him into the bedroom and switched on the light. She lay as he had left her, but something about her caused Lau to pick one of her arms up by the wrist. He was still holding it as he said, "She is dead, Tuan."

"Dead? She can't be . . ."

"See for yourself, Tuan." Lau held out Nancy's hand palm downwards towards Carter. "Look at her nails. Poison. No?"

Carter looked and nodded his agreement.

Lau shook his head as he remarked, "I shall never understand women. Never, ever, ever. The powder she got from the hospital to put in your drink was lethal. She was prepared to kill you herself rather than let you be tortured."

He tossed Nancy's arm across her body as he went on—"The silly bitch. As if Lim Tsing Wa would have forgiven her for that!"

In Halroyd's office Carter asked, "How did the meeting go, sir?"

"Quicker than usual. Davidson's on tour. Incidentally, the Brig sends his congratulations on the elimination of Lim Tsing Wa. But fill me in with all the details."

Carter told him the story.

"Dicey, eh Ralph? The third man nearly put paid to the whole deal."

"Two would have been company, sir. Three made it an awful crowd."

"Incidentally, Ralph, we had a bit of luck while you were away. The 'X' squad turned up another dump."

Picking up some photographs from his desk he tossed them over to Carter. Carter went through them carefully and suddenly grinned. "Yes, I thought you'd find the two crates of Benedictine amusing, Ralph."

Carter handed the photographs back. "What now?"

"That was what I was going to ask you."

"Well sir. I would suggest a white hot knitting needle and a few drops of potassium cyanide. Potassium cyanide's rather fashionable just now."

"But I seem to remember you saying that as Lo Heng was such a bloody bad Regimental commander, we should let him live."

"That was true at the time, sir. But times have changed. He's important now because he's bloody nearly the only State Committee Member left. We must eliminate him to demonstrate that he *can* be eliminated: make the mortality rate of State Committee Members so high that noboby wants to be promoted."

276

"Yes. Let's promote William Lai. He won't be any good as a Regimental commander either."

"Another thing, sir. They're desperately short of ammunition. I think we should doctor three-quarters of it now."

"Can do. Anything else?"

"Yes. We must advise the brigadier that the Communists are leaving bottles of poisoned liquor lying around. Otherwise we'll have British Tommies guzzling it if they find it."

"That is a point. A very good point."

21

The minute on the file was typed in red—His Excellency's minutes were always typed in red—it was as follows:—

> "Inspector-General of Police.
> Folio one.
> 2. From time to time—inevitably—allegations are made in the House of Commons and elsewhere of brutality on the part of members of the Security Forces in their dealings with the civilian population and captured terrorists: few of these allegations, however, have been found to have any basis in fact. So much has this been the case, that I have had occasion to intimate to the S of S that he would be better advised to dismiss them with a cutting remark, rather than to cause us to engage in pointless enquiries. But Northcourt's allegation is unique: he accuses an Assistant Superintendent of Police of (1) of murdering his own sergeant major, and (2) of committing perjury in the High Court.
> 3. Northcourt's political sympathies are, of course, well known, but the nature of his charges is so unusual that he has had little difficulty in arousing the interest of a formidable 'group of left-wing M.P.'s'—he is, after all, a man of considerable intelligence and ability.
> 4. Cause this matter to be investigated."

As it happened Carter was in Halroyd's office when Davidson walked in.

"No, don't go Carter. This involves you in particular." They sat down and Davidson went on, "This Northcourt fellow's been stirring it up in London—probably smarting under his defeat in the High Court, I shouldn't wonder—anyway, he's alleged that he's 'reliably informed' I think were the words used, that you did in fact shoot your sergeant major, Carter, on the night of Nathan's arrest. Personally, I can't imagine why they don't tell him to go and jump in the nearest pond. He's clearly a Communist. But the Secretariat wallahs seem to want to placate him, and Superintendent Jenkins has arrived with a court order to exhume Sergeant Major Lim's body. He's already asked me to hand over your Reising for ballistic tests, Carter. These H.Q. people seem to think we've got nothing better to do than jump to their attention. . . ."

"It will not be necessary, sir, to hand Superintendent Jenkins my s.m.g. I did shoot Sergeant Major Lim that night. The Communists had him wounded but alive; they offered him for barter. I had to shoot him." Carter's face was white.

For perhaps half a minute Davidson looked at Carter. Then incredulity giving place to anger, he turned to Halroyd and snapped, "Were you aware of this, Halroyd?"

"No, sir." It was Carter who had replied. But he had spoken too quickly, too anxiously.

Davidson knew he lied. They both knew Davidson knew.

Davidson's manner changed and he seemed almost to be talking to himself, "This is very serious, you know. It means a Court of Enquiry at the very least."

As soon as Davidson had gone Halroyd said, "You bloody fool!"

"Oh?" Carter replied angrily.

Halroyd stood up, paced up and down as he said, "We could have moved the bloody gravestones on Lim's grave, so that they could have dug up some other bastard. We could have issued you with another bloody gun. We could have got Stan Kowalski to let us have any bullets he found in the body. And for all we know, there aren't any bloody bullets in the body. . . ."

"There are. I shot him at forty to fifty yards. . . ."

"Well we're fucked now. . . ."

"*I* am fucked," Carter corrected gently.

"Sorry, Ralph. Thanks for that anyway."

"Do you know Superintendent Jenkins, sir?"

"I've heard of him, but I've never met him."

"Well you might have heard that he's efficient. He was able to tell Hanson that I had a Reising s.m.g. So he's already collared armoury records. He knows the number of that Reising, and how long I've had it. He's got one of his satellites standing on Lim's grave as of right now. And he'll be present when the body is examined for bullets. After that, it's simple."

Halroyd looked at him, knowing he was right. Then he said, "Christ all fucking mighty! It's almost as if we were all working for that bastard Northcourt!"

Superintendent Jenkins was an officer of the highest integrity and reliability; given a job to do he did it, come what may. He had arrived in Sintra with a Court Order authorising the exhumation of the body of Sergeant Major Lim Thau On, and with instructions to ascertain if any of the bullets found therein had been fired from the sub-machine gun on charge to Assistant Superintendent Mr. R. Carter. It did not occur to him that Carter's admission that he had shot Sergeant Major Lim obviated the need for the exhumation. Jenkins had his instructions. He was present when Lim's remains were disinterred, he followed the van to the hospital, he was present when the X-rays were taken, when the negatives were examined on the screen, when Doctor Kowalski removed a metal object from the remains and when he signed the certificate. As Carter had observed, Jenkins was efficient. He was also an armaments expert, and was able to explain that the reason why Lim's remains contained no more than the buckle of a belt was that bullets fired at close range can go right through a man, and that even at longer range, bullets are likely to go right through a man held in a rigid position—with his back to a tree for example—because his body wouldn't "give" with the impact of the bullets.

His Excellency read only the "findings" and "recommendations."

"The Court finds:—
(a) That Assistant Superintendent of Police, R. Carter, C.P.M., shot and killed Sergeant Major Lim Thau On.
(b) That having done so, he failed to report the matter to his superior officers.
(c) That he committed perjury in the High Court in the case 'Rex versus Emmanuel Nathan.'

The Court is agreed that:—
(a) Carter's action in shooting Sergeant Major Lim was justified.

(b) That his perjury in the High Court was inescapable.

(c) That his perjury did not contribute to the verdict of the High Court.

(d) That his failure to report the manner of Sergeant Major Lim's death was a gross neglect of duty.

Recommendations

The Court is divided as to its recommendations.

Mr. D. Howard, D.F.C., M.C.S., holds most strongly to the view that 'under the circumstances' Mr. Carter's failure to notify his superior officers of the manner of Sergeant Major Lim's death was 'both understandable and excusable. He wishes to be recorded as holding the view that, 'There are times when common sense itself dictates a neglect of duty.' He attaches great weight to the evidence of Mr. Halroyd and Dr. Kowalski, and points out that the repeated attempts on Carter's life, 'must have placed him under a constant and severe mental strain.' He is of the opinion that Carter's neglect of duty, 'Should be seen in the light of the mental strain which that duty itself imposed upon him.'

His recommendation is that Mr. Carter be reprimanded and transferred to another Colony.

This is not a recommendation with which the other members of the Court (Mr. Justice Brown and Mr. R. D. Henderson, M.C.S.) can associate themselves. Their view is that Mr. Carter's failure to report the manner of Sergeant Major Lim's death to his superior officers, was totally inexcusable.

Their recommendation is that Mr. Carter be summarily dismissed from the service."

Folio 19 was a letter from the Inspector General of Police forwarding two documents. The first read as follows:—

"I hereby certify that an X-ray examination carried out by me at the Sintra General Hospital on the body of Police Sergeant Major Lim Thau On, failed to reveal the presence of any bullets."

Signed

S. Kowalski,

Medical Officer in Charge,

Sintra General Hospital.

The second was a letter of resignation from Assistant Superintendent Mr. R. Carter.

His Excellency was not given to superfluous comment; his letter to London was of the "attached please find documents which are self explanatory" variety.

The Minister read his letter carefully; he never signed "blind," even when signing letters he had himself dictated. It read:—

"Dear Northcourt,

I have now received a reply concerning your allegations against Assistant Superintendent of Police Mr. R. Carter, C.P.M.

Somewhat to my surprise the authorities in Malaya acceded to your request that the body of Sergeant Major Lim Thau On be disinterred, and at Appendix 'A' hereto —in the form of a certificate signed by a Doctor Kowalski— you will find the results of the post-mortem examination; results which must be regarded as exonerating Carter completely.

I must advise you that as a result of your allegations— or perhaps more accurately, as a result of the fact that your allegations were considered to merit investigation— Carter has tendered his resignation. The position therefore, is that your allegations have occasioned a great deal of unnecessary inconvenience to the authorities in Malaya, the service of a gallant and efficient officer have been lost to the service, and your allegations remain unsubstantiated.

You will appreciate that I shall bear this case very firmly in mind should similar allegations be made in the future."

There was a postscript:—

"I shall of course be discussing this matter personally with those members of the House who approached me on your behalf."

The Minister appended his signature, tossed the letter into his "Out" tray, considered for a moment whether the members of the Court of Enquiry ought to be reminded of the provisions of the Official Secrets Act, decided against it and reached for his telephone.